ELEMENT 42 is a work of fiction. All persons, places, things, characters and incidents are the product of the author's imagination or are used fictitiously. Any resemblance to real people, living or dead, or events or places, is purely coincidental—the author is simply not that smart.

Published by
Machined Media
12402 N 68th St
Scottsdale, AZ 85254

If you would like to use material from the book in any way, shape, or form, you must first obtain written permission. Send inquiries to: seeley@seeleyjames.com

Print ISBN: 978-0-9886996-5-6
Digital ISBN: 978-0-9886996-4-9

Sabel Security Thriller #3 version 5.3
Pia Sabel/Jacob Stearne Thrillers #3 version 5.3
ELEMENT 42 released April, 2015
Formatting: Andrew Montooth
Cover Design: Andrew Montooth

ACKNOWLEDGMENTS

My heartfelt thanks to the beta readers and supporters who made this book the best book possible. Alphabetically: Carol Coetzee, Philip Henry, Richard Houston, Court Kronk, Ell Meadow, Steve Manke, Pam Safinuk, Rosemary Valdez, and Chris York.

- Extraordinary Editor: Lance Charnes, author of the highly acclaimed *Doha 12* and *SOUTH* and *FAKE* (coming soon). http://wombatgroup.com

- Medical Advisor: Louis Kirby, famed neurologist and author of *Shadow of Eden*. http://louiskirby.com

- Problem Solving Editor: Jane Turley, humorist, columnist, and author of *A Modern Life* and *The Changing Room*. http://janeturley.net

A special thanks to my wife whose support has been above and beyond the call of duty. Last but not least, my children, Nicole, Amelia, and Christopher, ranging from age fifteen to forty-two, who have kept my imagination fresh and full of ideas.

for Father
1920-2014

Chapter 1

The voice in my head returned when I stopped taking my meds. My caseworker said the voice was part of my condition—PTSD-induced schizophrenia—but I call him Mercury, the winged messenger of the gods, and a damn good friend. For years, he was my biggest ally in combat and helped me predict the future. I'm not talking about very far into the future. Sometimes minutes, sometimes seconds, and sometimes just enough to see it coming. Mercury would draw my attention to small changes in air density, the faint sounds of rustling cloth, or the weak electrical charge of someone lurking nearby.

He saved my ass more than once and, as is always the case with gods, there were those who believed and those who didn't. Believers fought and lived and died beside me without ever disrespecting Mercury. Non believers sent me in for evaluations. My docs didn't believe in gods, they believed in meds. They told me they were smarter than my abandoned deity, so I took their advice until one day everything went wrong and good people died.

I was resting in a dark jungle when I reaffirmed my faith in that ancient divinity. Prama, the hotel owner, was drawing lazy circles on my chest with her finger when Mercury spoke to me in a voice loud and clear and slightly panicked.

Mercury said, Dude, you better think about your future real fast cuz it's coming. Can you hear it?

I raised my ear off the sweaty pillow and listened to the noises coming from a ways down the road. Tin doors squeaked open, truck springs creaked, boots hit the ground, voices issued commands. It wasn't hard to predict the future. Sixty seconds from now at the hotel up the lane, soldiers would throw doors open, drag sleepy eco-tourists from warm beds, shove them against the wall, push a photo in front of them, and bark in whatever tribal dialect they speak in that corner of Borneo, "Have you seen this American?"

They were searching for the perpetrator of something.

I hadn't perpetrated anything, but I was pretty sure I knew who had.

Prama was about to speak when someone pounded on my door. Four thumps, all rapid and demanding. The way MP's bang on doors. My heart stopped until I heard Agent Tania whisper-shout, "Jacob. Damn it. Wake up!"

That clinched it. I knew who the perpetrators were.

My eyes rolled to the ceiling and I thought about life and death and love. I'd thought I was dead twenty-three times and didn't care much for the experience. I'd never been afraid of it. I'd killed all the people who tried to kill me. Plus a bunch more who were thinking about it. I didn't want to check out on account of some hajji with an AK-47. But I thought I'd left all that behind.

My job at Sabel Security had become a matter of careening from one ill-conceived, spur-of-the-moment crusade to the next. Death had been more remote when I walked point in Kandahar. If all I cared about was life and death, the choice was obvious: re-enlist.

But then there was the love part.

"You gone answer door?" Prama said.

It was the love part that kept me on the job. I was in love with my boss, Pia Sabel. Tall and strong and built like a tiger. She was the kind of woman a man like me would die for.

Well. Theoretically.

Romance with her was so remote I may as well crush on a movie star. To her I was just one of the staff.

Tania pounded on the door again.

I extricated myself from under Prama's naked body and savored the scent of the jungle motel's ancient battle with mildew. A glance at the clock didn't tell me much. 3? 4? I snapped on the light and blinked at the mirror until my reflection came into focus. I looked like hell.

I yanked the door open and Agent Tania, sleek and exotic, glared at me, her nostrils flaring.

She was the real love in my life. I'd fallen in love with her when I'd pulled her from a burning Humvee in Nuristan Province. She refused to date me until after we'd both left the Army. It lasted fourteen glorious months. Then I blew it.

"I hope you're not paying for that." Tania pointed her nose past my shoulder.

"HEY!" Prama said.

"Wait, the hotel lady?" Tania half-asked. "Really. Never mind. Just MOVE."

"Yeah, I heard them down—"

Tania was already sprinting away. "Get the translator, we leave thirty seconds ago."

I kicked my t-shirt in the air, pulled my boxers up, and slipped into my shirt on its way down. Five seconds later, I had my trousers on and scooped a handful of ammo into my cargo pocket. I zipped my travel bag closed and kissed Prama on the lips while I pulled my Glock from under the pillow.

I said, "Happy birthday."

"Best birthday yet," Prama said. "Jacob Stearne come back next year?"

"Wouldn't miss it," I lied and bolted.

Tania tossed our duffels from the second-floor walkway into the alley below. Ms. Sabel, an Olympic athlete, caught them with ease and stuffed them into the back of our rented SUV.

Bujang, our translator—a pocket-sized Borneo local who was attending Georgetown when we hired him—looked a little stunned and sleepy when I dragged him out. He scratched his head and watched the women as if it were a tennis game. I picked him up and tossed him to Ms. Sabel. She broke his fall, landed him on his feet, and spun back so fast her ponytail hit him in the face.

The bang of an explosion echoed in the street, far side of the building. Tania and I vaulted the railing together. Ms. Sabel slipped into the driver's seat and racked the seat back. Tania lunged across Bujang. I took shotgun. Slinging our SUV through the mud, Ms. Sabel navigated the alley by moonlight before turning onto a jungle trail. Surrounded by dark green leaves and darker green shadows, the jungle was so thick that anything could lurk an arm's length from our shoulders.

We thudded through ruts and potholes, across a muddy rice paddy, and onto a cart path while tree branches slapped the truck like a drum roll. Finally she found an actual road, a single lane of soft mud. The back end slid wide when she made the turn and I shot Ms. Sabel a *slow down* glance that she ignored.

"This road goes to Bandar Udara Yuvai Semaring," Bujang said.

"Do they have an airport?" Ms. Sabel shouted over her shoulder.

"It's in Indonesia," he said.

"Shit." She slammed on the brakes, revved the engine, slipped the clutch, broke the back tires loose, and spun the truck around in the lane. Mud and bugs splattered in our open windows, bringing the smell of shredded leaves with them.

"What happened?" I said. "I thought we were here to donate a school."

"Later," Ms. Sabel and Tania said in unison.

I shot a glance at Bujang. He shrugged.

Apparently, whatever happened since Prama poured me that first drink involved Ms. Sabel pissing off two of the three countries claiming parts of Borneo. Maybe she'd offended all three, but I wasn't going to ask about Brunei.

"Where does this road go?" Ms. Sabel asked.

"Gunung," Bujang said. "It's a national park."

"Where'd we leave my jet?" she asked.

"Marudi, on the other side of the park."

"How far?"

"Four hours."

"It's only a hundred freaking miles to the coast," she said.

Bujang waved his hands at the dark, twisting road before us. "Four hours."

She took his estimate as a challenge and pushed the pedal down. I checked my seatbelt and gripped the A-pillar's grab handle. We slipped around corners, climbed up mountains, flew down slopes, bounced our butts through dips and bumps for over an hour before a hint of light began to creep through the murky, overcast sky.

"Bad news," Ms. Sabel said with her eyes on the mirror. "Lights."

I craned around to peer between the stacked duffels and caught a glimpse of cone-shaped lights moving through the trees in the dark valley below. Three vehicles by my count. They could carry four to six guys each, meaning twelve to eighteen hostiles.

Odds like those represented a serious tactical problem.

I signed onto this mission because it was supposed to be a Sabel Charities trip. A simple fly-in-fly-out deal where my only mission was to keep Ms. Sabel safe from over-enthusiastic admirers and the occasional kidnapper dumb enough to try something with the young billionaire. But once again, I'd underestimated how much trouble she could find in the middle of nowhere.

I glanced at her to gauge how deep a hole we were in. Her solid biceps, visible through her skintight Under Armour, flexed and strained through every shift. Her legs tensed and contracted as she worked the brakes and clutch. Her eyes, intent and determined, never lost their laser-focus on the curves ahead.

Mercury said, I don't know what she did in the Kayan village last night, bro, but these guys want your heads.

Chapter 2

The faint light of sunrise began to color the east, turning shadows into recognizable bits of jungle. Ms. Sabel slowed, her gaze fixed on a figure on the edge of the road. Ahead of us on the right, a girl carried a small body. Feet dangled on her left, a head and arms dangled on her right, everything unnaturally limp.

Ms. Sabel slammed on the brakes. We slid twenty yards past the girl and came to a stop. Before I could figure out what was going on, Ms. Sabel was out of the truck, running toward the girl.

She was losing focus on our hastily revised mission to get out of the country alive.

I said, "We don't have time for this."

"Don't I know it." Tania hopped out. "But it's quicker to help than argue."

With no other choice, I followed them. Bujang pressed his face to the glass.

The girl kept staggering toward us. In her arms was a string bean of a boy with long, scrawny arms and legs. His eyes were crusted shut and his mouth hung open. The girl kept walking, her face streaked with tears, and her eyes fixed on the distance ahead.

Ms. Sabel stepped into her path and held her arms out, a passive offer to help, but the girl didn't slow or change direction.

"What's wrong?" Ms. Sabel asked as she walked sideways with the girl.

Over six feet with sandy hair, Ms. Sabel was an unusual sight in Southeast Asia. The girl gawked as if a mythical giant had spoken.

I waved Bujang over. At the same time, I caught a whiff of an odd scent. I sniffed again and traced it to the boy. He had a strange acidic smell, like burnt vinegar.

"He's sick." Ms. Sabel said. "I can help."

Bujang spoke in Malayo, his gaze darting to the road behind us. When the girl realized we were trying to help, her eyes fluttered and closed. Relieved and exhausted, her knees buckled. Tania steadied her and Ms. Sabel slipped the boy from her arms.

"He's hot," she said, looking at me. "Really hot."

Not my area of expertise. I knew nothing about kids and less about sick ones. I shrugged.

Tania huffed and ran to the SUV to rummage through the back.

The girl spewed her language in a frantic voice with pleading eyes. Her voice broke up and she blubbered through a phrase that she kept repeating. Ms. Sabel and I shared a glance. We didn't need Bujang to tell us the boy was dying.

"Uh, her name's Kaya," Bujang said, trying to keep up with the girl's words. "Lost her grandmother two days ago. Grandfather too. Mother went for help yesterday but never came back. Her brother came down with it this morning."

"Came down with what?" Ms. Sabel asked.

"I don't know. She's Melanau, a small tribe, hard to understand."

Tania returned with a couple of wet bandanas. They wiped the boy's skin.

"Where was she taking him?" Ms. Sabel asked.

"A clinic over the ridge."

"Let's go."

"Wait a minute." I held up my hands. "We have a ten-minute lead on—"

"Let's go." Ms. Sabel's gray-green eyes stabbed through me, leaving no doubt who was in charge.

I drove while the women sat in back with the boy stretched across their knees.

Ms. Sabel and Tania made soothing sounds and reassured the kids, but I could sense the boy shiver and shake and gasp.

I stepped on the gas and charged up the hill. Bujang pointed to a break in the sinister depths of the jungle where two tire tracks disappeared into the bush. The trail was so tight that bugs jumped in our windows.

When we had a straight stretch, I took a look in the back. Ms. Sabel stroked the boy's forehead with the wet cloth and dragged her hand down his brown face. The burnt vinegar smell grew stronger. She wiped the gunk out of his eyes, tugged at the crusty bits, and dabbed at the corners. His eyelids fluttered, then opened.

They were blue.

Not the iris but the sclera. The part of his eye that should be white was robin's-egg blue.

I turned back to the road and blinked.

In another two hundred yards, the track opened into a clearing where two small trucks and a shiny minivan were parked on the left. A giant awning covered half an acre of folding cots.

Two musclemen in black, semi-official looking uniforms, with holstered guns on their hips, watched us from under the awning. They weren't Americans or Europeans, but they weren't Malaysian either. More men in black hovered behind trees in the jungle, just shadows in the dismal tangle of leaves. Off to one side stood several expedition tents. A short man in a lab coat poked his head out, then stumbled forward with a woman and another man in black right behind him.

The woman, a dumpy, home-dyed blonde in white shorts and a Lakers t-shirt, ran toward us waving her arms. "Go away. Go away. Quarantine. You have to leave."

Ms. Sabel, out of the car with the boy, headed straight for the woman. "He's sick. We need a doctor."

A man in black shoved the lab-coat guy. Lab-coat said, "I'm Doctor Chapman, what can I—"

"We don't know what's going on," the Lakers lady said. "There's been some kind of outbreak around here. You have to leave."

Ms. Sabel marched between them, headed for the cots. Chapman and the Lakers lady glanced at each other. Tania and I started to follow Ms. Sabel when Lakers lady pulled my shirtsleeve. I gave her my soldier look—*let go or die*. Her lips flopped as if she were going to say something but changed her mind. Her eyes dropped and so did her hand. One of the men in black tried to bump shoulders to slow me down. The guy smelled like a wet dog. With a quick twist, I avoided him and pushed on.

We reached the awning with the doc and his lovely assistant in hot pursuit. The place smelled of mud and jungle when we got out of the car, but under the awning it was all burnt vinegar. More than thirty cots were neatly arrayed in rows. Most had old people in them, but only a few were young like the boy. A growing sense of horror gripped me. I'd been in a few triage clinics on battlefields, but nothing like this. Judging by the stiff and uncomfortable postures, half the patients were dead and the other half were dying.

Mercury said, Ebola. Let's go.

I said, It's not Ebola.

Mercury said, What, so you're a doctor now?

No puking or diarrhea.

Mercury said, Could be Ebola.

Something tugged at the back of my brain, a subliminal observation not yet fully formed. I looked and listened. Green canvas flapped above us in a slow breeze, bugs and birds chirped and droned in the jungle, and some lone animal gave a dismal cry that echoed through the trees. None of the men in black were talking.

The cots had letters and numbers on them, lettered columns and numbered rows like a spreadsheet. At various intervals there were low tables with racks of vials and syringes and other doctor-looking things on them. Beyond the awning, a path ran into the jungle.

"These are very serious cases," Dr. Chapman said.

Ms. Sabel pushed the boy's limp body into Chapman's chest. "Do they all have blue eyes?"

Chapman squinted up at Ms. Sabel. He hesitated, took another look at her, then examined the boy. Ms. Sabel shifted the boy's weight and pulled his eyelids open with her free hand.

Dr. Chapman gasped.

"Put him down, um…" Chapman looked around for an empty cot, eyed one, and pointed. "Over here. Put him here."

They huddled around the cot and I backed away. Next to me, an old man's hand flopped out from under a sheet and made a weak grab at my leg. His eyes were blue and lined with crusty gunk. The skin around his mouth and nose was gray and dirty under four-day stubble. He shivered as if suddenly freezing and opened his mouth. He mumbled words. Bujang stood behind me, stunned and scared.

"What did he say?" I asked.

"Bad cloth." Bujang shrugged. His eyes darted around the area, doing his best to avoid eye contact with the men in black.

Mercury said, Yo homie! Do you feel the tension in the air? Do you feel the bullets in your future? Seven minutes until you become Jacob 'Swiss Cheese' Stearne.

Tania tugged my shirt. "We've got to get out of here. Those guys were right behind us. You need to get Pia moving."

"Me?" I asked but she didn't answer. "Going to tell me who we're running from?"

"Local militia. We need to move."

"You notice anything wrong with this place?"

"Yeah, we're in it. We should be on the road to Marudi."

"No. I mean, something's off." I scanned the area again and crossed to one of the cots with equipment on it. There was a rack filled with vials of what I guessed was blood.

A few yards away, Ms. Sabel raised her voice. "Then what the hell is it, Ebola?"

Chapman said, "No. I don't think so. I mean, no, it couldn't be."

"Then what?"

"I'm not sure. I need time to … um."

"Where are your diagnostics?" She scanned the cots.

I picked up a vial of blood for a closer look. Next to them was a paper pad with numbers all over it that matched the cot numbers.

"Don't be touching that stuff, moron," Tania said. "Don't you know what contagious means? Get Pia, we need to go."

Without looking, I could sense Bujang vigorously nodding his agreement. I grabbed a dirty gray cloth, wrapped up three vials, and stuffed them in my cargo pocket. I planned to confront our reluctant Doc Chapman with them. As I passed the old man again, I stopped. I'd seen enough dead men to know one at a glance.

Gruff, guttural noises drew my attention back to Ms. Sabel and Chapman. Two of the men in black were pointing guns at Ms. Sabel. Tania and I drew our weapons and fanned out. Tania had the guy on the left while I took the guy on the right, but an unknown number of men still lurked in the shadows. At the current rate of escalation, our chances for leaving alive were rapidly diving to zero. I gave Ms. Sabel the universal signal for retreat: wide eyes and a nod toward the truck.

Chapman turned to the guy I pegged as the leader and put his hands out, a feeble gesture to stand down.

The guy in black pushed him aside and spoke in a language I didn't understand. Then he pushed Ms. Sabel.

Chapman stepped between them. "It's OK. Everything's OK now."

"I asked what's going on here." Ms. Sabel's voice echoed in the clearing. "And I'm not leaving until—"

"You better leave," Lakers lady said. "These guys don't value life like we do."

Ms. Sabel turned away, leaving Chapman, Kaya, and her brother behind.

The two men followed close behind Ms. Sabel, their pistols locked on her. One guy sent a warning shot into the dirt near Tania's feet and she replied with a dart that grazed his ear. He lifted his weapon and put his hands up with a mocking grin. Three more men stepped out of the shadows, ready to kill.

Mercury said, Dude, what did you notice about that guy?

I checked out the leader. I said, He has a scar where his eyebrow should be.

Mercury said, He's seen some shit, you feel me?

Ms. Sabel brushed past me, making a beeline for the truck. Tania and Bujang ran ahead and jumped in. I held the gunmen at bay while walking backward.

My boss opened the driver's door, put one foot in, and glared back over the hood at Chapman. "I'll be back with the authorities, Chapman."

I still had one foot on the ground when she floored it. Mud spewed on my arm and leg before I could get all the way in.

Chapter 3

Ms. Sabel spun the SUV around the clearing before flying down the muddy lane behind the awning. When the men in black saw we were heading away from the main road, they shouted and ran after us. We slid our way through dark jungle until we came to another clearing. This one had a pit, freshly dug. She slammed to a stop.

"Take a picture of that," Ms. Sabel said.

I leaned out and snapped a few photos on my phone. It was a trench eight feet wide, four deep, and twelve long with burlap sacks covered in white powder at the bottom.

Mercury said, Your seven minutes are up, dawg.

It's bad enough when your parents try to be cool, but when a 2,500-year-old tries it's awkward as hell.

You get used to it though.

Tania screamed. "Drive!"

Gunfire echoed through the jungle. Ms. Sabel put her foot down. We bumped and slid through the brush only slightly faster than the men in black could run. She pulled away from them on the twisting path before they could take too many shots at us.

"Did I ever tell you why I left the Army?" I asked Ms. Sabel.

She gave me a corner-of-the-eye glance.

"Because I was tired of getting shot at all the time," I said. "I wanted to become a professional chef and kill trout instead of Taliban. Then the Major called me with a job offer, and here I am, in the middle of nowhere, bodyguard to a woman who turned building a school into a war. Want to tell me why people are trying to put a bullet through my brain?"

"You just took a picture of a mass grave and all you can worry about is who's shooting at you?" Ms. Sabel said. She changed gears, splashed through a bumper-deep streambed, ground her way up the bank, but said nothing more.

I ignored her sneer. "If they kill us, we'll never find out what's going on back there."

No one spoke.

"Is this clinic the reason people were trying to kill us?"

"No," Ms. Sabel said. "The other guys were local police. Or something."

I thought about the clinic's men in black. They had the Eurasian look of Central Asia, an area as big as North America that reaches from the Caspian Sea to Mongolia. Definitely not natives of Borneo. I never saw our predawn pursuers but her answer addressed that. "OK, where do you want to start? Want to tell me about why the local police want us dead?"

No one spoke.

I said, "I took the night off because of the jet lag—"

"Yeah," Tania said, "we know all about your *jet lag*."

"—while you guys went to the village to talk about the school. So what happened?"

"Forget the school," Ms. Sabel said. "Focus on the death camp. Can we free those people?"

What did I do in my past life that had me ducking so many bullets in this one? I sighed. Somewhere in the world there had to be a saucepan with my name on it.

"Not without a firefight involving roughly twenty casualties, mostly civilians," I said. "They have superior numbers, knowledge of the terrain, unknown firepower, vehicles. And we have—nothing."

"You're angry," Ms. Sabel said.

"Explain it to her, Tania," I said.

"Only thing Jacob cares about is getting laid," Tania said. "Warlords don't bother him, death camps don't bother him; all he wants to do is stick his dick in—"

My fist clenched. "No! We beat the mercenaries in Algeria because we did our homework. Tell her about how you execute successful missions, Tania. How plans are made, recon is analyzed, resources are allocated, assignments—"

"He's in a mood because he wants to sleep with you but all he can get are hotel maids."

Ms. Sabel shot a glance my way before I could hide my beet-red face.

"Just so there are no misunderstandings," Ms. Sabel said, "I never date employees, past, present or—"

"You've mentioned that before."

I caught her suppressing a smile. Needless to say, the conversation was dead for the next mile.

"Then we need to form a plan," she said. "We need to allocate resources, make assignments—"

"Really? The clinic?" I said. "How many men do they have? How many weapons?"

"I left Kaya back there. We can't just let those people die."

"Maybe their healthcare system sucks. You can't save the whole world, you know."

"Why was I given all this wealth if *not* to save the world?" she said. "At least the parts I run across. I want to go back."

Ms. Sabel earned her billion the old-fashioned way—her dad gave it to her. My dad did a coin toss: Sis won the family farm. I joined the 75th Rangers, *Sua Sponte*. But I enjoyed Ms. Sabel's naïveté for a moment before continuing the argument. "We have the local militia out to kill us and you want to go back? How's that going to work?"

"We can get to Marudi," she said. "Alert the authorities, maybe get some help."

"The authorities? Isn't that who's chasing us?"

"We need to press the opportunity immediately," she said.

Ms. Sabel lived by the phrase *press the opportunity immediately*. It was a leftover from her days playing international soccer and she drilled it into Sabel employees in every email she sent. An easy expression when you're running around a stadium full of shrieking fans. Not so much in Borneo's darkest jungle.

She focused on another mud bath in the road. We sank to the axles, the tires spun, caught, and spun again. Twisting the steering wheel back and forth, she found firmer spots until we pulled up the opposite bank. From there, the road led up and over a ridge where she stopped to check the map. We looked across a deep and misty valley lined by razor-sharp mountains.

We checked behind us. We couldn't see the road beyond the last turn.

Then a truck rounded the corner. Two men leaned out of the side windows. Ms. Sabel put our SUV in gear and dropped the clutch. Bullets ripped through the leaves on my right, shredding them into green confetti. She flew into the first set of switchbacks with the back end sliding through the turns. Mud clods flew off our tires, sailed over the cliff, and disappeared into the abyss.

I stretched out the window and pointed my Glock at the enemy when she came close to rolling us on the turn. I couldn't see them, so I dropped back in my seat.

"You think of a plan then," Ms. Sabel said. "That's what I pay you for, isn't it?"

"Dead guys don't cash paychecks."

"Are you afraid?"

"I buried a lot of good friends between Baghdad and Kabul. You've only buried your parents. You should—"

I shut up and squeezed my eyes closed. You never know how stupid and thoughtless you can be until you do it. My eyes re-opened and stared at the winding road ahead.

I said, "Look, I'm sorry…"

She wiped her nose on her shoulder without taking her hand off the wheel. "Come up with a plan to save those people."

Tania moved her mouth close to my ear. "Nice one, asshole." She leaned between the front seats. "Dumb as he is, Pia, Jacob's right. I counted seven guys—that I could see—and there were at least twelve following us. The authorities in Marudi aren't going to listen. We

26

need to get out of Malaysia and call Kuala Lumpur, let them handle it. We could've taken down either one of those groups—not both."

Tania's mysterious beauty and flowing black, curly hair masked the battle-hardened veteran inside. Women weren't assigned to combat duty when she joined, but her exceptional sniper skills brought her to the action anyway. Before she went back to West Point, she'd seen more action in two tours than most men in twice that.

She rummaged around in the back for a moment, then handed me two bricks wrapped in black plastic. She might hate me, but she understood when I was uptight and needed to express my feelings with some C4.

"Stop after the next turn," I said.

Before we came to a complete stop, I was out and running to the nearest tree. I planted our remotely detonated explosives at knee height, facing the road. The charge was made to blow doors, but I figured it would drop the tree into the road.

Mercury said, Hey homie, would a Centurion be so timid? If one brick is enough, why not double up?

I added a second brick in the dirt under a root and jumped back in the truck. Ms. Sabel had us rolling instantly.

We stopped at the next turn, and waited for our pursuers. As soon as they rounded the corner, I flipped the switch. The whole tree flew five feet in the air, separating into four pieces, all of which landed in the road. The first truck ran smack into a chunk of tree, flipped onto its side, and blocked the road.

~~~

A few hours later, we arrived in Marudi, where Ms. Sabel's Gulfstream waited. After we scrubbed like surgeons in the washrooms, we wandered around the terminal while the boss exhausted her efforts to get the locals interested in her conspiracy theories. After nearly an hour, Ms. Sabel stormed out of the administrator's office and headed for the jet.

"Idiots don't believe me," she said as she strode past us. "Or they don't care. You were right, Tania, we'll call the capitol."

We swung in behind as she marched across the tarmac and climbed aboard Air Sabel, where she sat at the polished executive table.

"What's that clinking noise?" the boss asked when I walked past her.

I reached into my cargo pocket and pulled out the three vials of blood wrapped in the dirty cloth.

"I forgot about these. I meant to ask Dr. Chapman about them."

We each took a tube and examined it. They were made of glass and had wax stoppers. That was the extent of our collective expertise.

"Fingerprints," Tania said. Ms. Sabel and I had been holding them like toys, while Tania held hers delicately by the ends.

We adjusted our grip but we'd already wrecked most of the surface.

Tania picked up the cloth. "Stinks like chemicals."

Ms. Sabel wrapped the vials back up and set them aside.

Sabel Security headquarters in Washington, DC, was ten thousand miles away. We were scheduled to refuel in Kobe, Japan, and I was short the sleep I'd missed when I celebrated Prama's birthday.

(Actually, Prama was less than half her name. I couldn't pronounce the whole thing. She had one of those Asian names with seven syllables, and I grew up in Iowa where the toughest phrase was *crop rotation*.)

I stretched out on one of the sofas in the back and closed my eyes. Just as I drifted off, my dreamscape filled with the image of Ms. Sabel dressed like a Valkyrie. She charged at me, hair flowing behind her, swinging an axe and yelling, "Think it's funny to watch a man strangle your mother? I was four, goddamn it! Four! I couldn't stop him!"

I jerked awake at the nightmare. Embarrassed, I peered around to see if anyone noticed my jolt. We were just taxiing onto the runway for takeoff.

I settled back and closed my eyes again. This time, I stood alone at the base of the mountains of Tora Bora. I wore combat boots and boxers that flapped in the icy wind. My fingers clutched a child's plastic knife. A thousand Taliban poured over the ridge, screaming *Allahu Akbar* and firing AK-47s. I slept like a baby.

Chapter 4

On the fortieth floor of a gleaming office tower looming over Guangzhou, China, Violet Windsor flipped her hair over her shoulder before checking the final slide of her presentation. She faced the group seated at the teak table under halogen lights, tugged her pinstripe jacket down her trim frame, smoothed her pants, and concluded her speech. "Thus proving Windsor Pharmaceuticals can counter an engineered virus should anyone attempt such a heinous attack on China."

The group applauded. She motioned to her assistant, who raised the boardroom's halogen lights, sparkling the jade inlay on the teak table.

A shooting pain rose from the socket of her prosthetic leg. Dressing in a hurry was always a mistake with the new maid. The girl never got her stump sock smoothed out. She silently cursed the stupid peasant and pushed past the pain.

"Are there any questions?" she asked.

Her gaze fell on Chen Zhipeng. The thin man smoothed his few strands of gray hair without showing a hint of any emotion, good or bad.

"There was collateral damage or side effect?" Anatoly Mokin asked in his thick Russian accent. The short, square-jawed former commando leaned back in his seat with a smug look.

Violet fought the urge to say, *Fuck you*. Instead, she took a deep breath and glanced at the handsome American, Ed Cummings.

"As a matter of fact," she said, "there were a few unfortunate terminations. As I am sure you are aware, in a dress rehearsal for biological warfare, danger is the point, and side effects are unavoidable. However, I assure you, the local Kayan tribal elders have already accepted our generous restitution for their regrettable losses. In addition, they have signed confidentiality agreements. Nothing will point back to Windsor—" she looked at Chen "—or our investors."

Violet's phone buzzed on the table where she'd left it. The noise caught the group's attention for a split second as everyone's gaze fell to the incoming text lighting her screen. A second later, a buzz from Marco Verratti's phone, then Ed Cummings's, distracted the group.

Chen Zhipeng gave them each a contemptuous glance before addressing Violet in his clipped Chinese accent. "There were no intrusion by outsider or detection by authority?"

Chen's inability to enunciate plurals grated on her nerves. "I understand one of our board members paid an unscheduled visit this morning."

Chen counted heads around the table. She waited until he figured it out for himself. His gaze came back to her. "Wu Fang?"

"I'm afraid so," she said.

"I will speak to him."

Verratti, the portly Italian, held up a hand briefly. "This is a tremendous success, *Signorina* Windsor. I admit that I hesitated to invest the Collettivo's resources in a woman so young, leading a company so new, but you've exceeded my expectations. *Brava*, young lady, *bravissima!*"

He rose to his feet and applauded. After a moment's hesitation, the others stood and joined in. Last to rise was Chen, who applauded faintly as he cast a suspicious eye on Verratti.

Violet took a bow with a beaming smile. As the congratulations died down, the attendees—mostly Windsor's senior staff plus Chen and his entourage—picked up their pads and tablets to leave.

She accepted congratulations at the door, shaking hands and thanking each person for his or her contribution.

When his turn came, Chen Zhipeng bowed slightly. "Very good, as your friend said, Ms. Windsor. Such excellent result impress me very much. In fact, I want to know all detail. Prepare a full report, including the 'regrettable loss', at your earliest convenience. Be in my Beijing office tomorrow at three."

Chen strode out the door. His assistants nodded curtly and scurried after their boss.

Last to leave were Verratti and Cummings. They stood at the far end of the room, bent forward with their hands on the chrome railing, looking at the cityscape below. She picked up her Hermes purse and walked toward them, ignoring her stump-pain with every step.

She edged herself in between them, putting an arm around each. "Gentlemen, we're about to make a whole lot of money."

The two men straightened up and turned to form a triangle, their stern faces hardened.

"Element 42 is even better than expected," she said. "It's especially effective for people over sixty. The older they are, the faster it acts. As well as people with immune deficiencies or other pre-existing conditions."

She studied their grave faces. The younger, leaner Cummings glanced sideways at Verratti. Neither man spoke.

"Why so glum, boys?"

"You haven't read Teresa's text," Cummings said. "Take a look."

Before she could read it, Verratti said, "Pia Sabel visited the test site a few hours ago."

Violet staggered back, her face pale.

"I thought you gave Mukhtar strict orders to eliminate anyone who stumbled on them," Cummings said. "I don't know what went wrong, or why he didn't—"

"Because he recognized her," Verratti said.

"Why? Who is she?"

"Washington's darling," Violet said. "Everybody pities her because her parents were murdered, yet she went on to win a gold medal. Like she was some kind of inspiration. Big deal. They forget she was adopted by a billionaire."

"Do you mean Alan Sabel? Sabel Capital, Technologies, Satellite, all those companies? So what? Why didn't Mukhtar take care of it?"

Violet gave Cummings a disdainful look. "The search party would bring a tsunami of investigators."

"Well, that's the least of our worries," Cummings said. "What the hell was Chen doing here? Who let him in?"

"I did," Violet said. "He put more money into this venture than you ever dreamed of—and he might run China someday. He goes to any meeting he wants."

"That's the last thing we need right now." Cummings clenched his teeth and scanned the room. "You've got to get rid of him."

"I know. I know. But he wants me in Beijing tomorrow to deliver a full report."

"Why? Do you think he knows?"

"You mean about Sabel or Philadelphia?"

"Either."

"He has spies everywhere. He knows something. Don't worry, I'll handle it." Violet paused and caught the gaze of each man. "I always do."

"What about Wu Fang?" Verratti asked. "Why was he on Borneo?"

"I don't know. I made damn sure he knew nothing about the field trial."

"Looks like he found out. Did Sabel have anything to do with it?"

"She showed up hours after he left."

"What about Mukhtar? Will he keep quiet?"

Violet texted Mokin's lead security man. "There, I just promised him a big bonus to keep his mouth shut, but he works for Anatoly. So, your guess is as good as mine."

"We should hold up the operation," Verratti said.

"Absolutely not," Cummings said. "We'll deal with this, but we have to keep it moving forward."

Violet's phone buzzed with another text. A second later, Verratti and Cummings received the same text.

"Holy shit," Violet said.

"What's the big deal?" Cummings asked. "So what if we're missing three vials? That's nothing."

"It could prove Element 42 existed before Philadelphia," Verratti said. "They would figure out it's not a natural occurrence."

"Fucking Sabel," Violet said. "Goddamn do-gooder's probably taking them to the CDC or NIH to find a cure. She won't let anything stand in her path to sainthood."

"You know her?" Cummings asked.

"I know people who know her."

"We need to get those back right away," Verratti said.

"What should I do, call her up and say, 'Hey Pia, did you run off with three vials of blood from a super-secret clinic where a whole bunch of people died?'"

Verratti ran his fingers through his thick black hair. Cummings glanced away and straightened his Harvard tie.

"I'm open to ideas, gentlemen." No one spoke. "I don't need to remind you, if anything leaks before Philly, we have to halt the operation. If we stop the operation, Windsor's stock won't soar, and if Windsor's stock won't soar, we won't see the returns we need."

"The Collettivo expects big returns. Very big." Verratti scowled at her. "I have some friends in the US. I'll have them take care of the vials."

"Be careful, she's dangerous. Her daddy gave her Sabel Security for a birthday present."

"Here comes more trouble." Cummings nodded toward the front of the boardroom.

Anatoly Mokin's voice boomed across the space. "Ah, you have board meeting without me? You not have quorum."

"We were just chatting," Violet said. "Join us."

Anatoly approached them with a swagger. "Were you chatting about bribing Mukhtar?"

Violet inhaled. Verratti and Cummings tensed.

"Whatever do you mean?" Violet smiled.

"Mukhtar is loyal. When someone tries to bribe my people, they call me. You should not do this. Very bad. By the way, Pia Sabel is *pizda*. Whore. You told Chen about her?"

"Not yet."

"If you want good advice, hold nothing back from Chen." Anatoly turned and walked away. Over his shoulder he said, "No bribing my people. You pay Mukhtar big bonus anyway."

The three didn't breathe until he left the room.

"I hate that guy," Violet said.

"Hire someone else for security," Cummings said.

"Find me an alternative. Who can poison aborigines in some godforsaken jungle without asking questions?"

Cummings watched Verratti.

"Not the Mafia," Verratti said, spreading his hands wide. "I can get the vials back, not … the other thing."

"I know some people," Cummings said.

"Edwin Harold Cummings, IV—you 'know people'?" Violet laughed. "Has the hedge fund business turned so rough that you need to 'know people'?"

"CIA contractors. I got them capital after the fiasco in Iraq. They run top-secret, black-budget operations for the intelligence community." He paused. "Their work comes with a certain amount of immunity from prosecution."

Chapter 5

Tania kicked me awake. "Just cause you smoked Mokin in Algeria doesn't mean you can coast forever. You're on duty, asshole. Act like it."

Why I was still in love with the woman was beyond me, but I let it pass and analyzed my surroundings. The engines were stopped and the airstair had been lowered. The cockpit door stood open and the seats were empty. I smacked my lips and swept the inside of my mouth with a dry tongue. Swinging myself upright, I put my boots on the floor, took a deep wake-up breath, and looked around. Tania stood over me, arms crossed and a scowl so tight it could lead to premature wrinkles.

Bujang the translator sat across from me, reading a book. Ms. Sabel was not in the cabin. Voices came from outside.

Following the sound, I peeked around the bulkhead to see Ms. Sabel standing at the bottom of the airstair talking to two men in suits and one uniformed Japanese policeman. Several options ran through my head about what to say next.

Their voices raised in volume as they tried to talk over each other.

"No, you listen to me," Ms. Sabel said. "You did *not* revoke my passport. I left Borneo four hours ago. There's no way you got a court order in—"

"It's not a revocation, it's a restriction—"

"Then show me the court order."

The two men in suits—who I judged to be Americans by the rolls of fat hanging over their belts—glanced at each other. The fatter one turned back to Ms. Sabel. "We have it, just not—"

"Do you have anything to back up your bullshit?"

The thinner guy opened a leather binder and pulled out a waxy curled sheet. He extended it to Ms. Sabel as if it were a bloody dagger with her fingerprints. I descended the airstair and peeked over her shoulder.

"Nice of you to join us, Mr. Stearne." Her tone shrank me half an inch.

The paper was an old-fashioned fax. I remembered them from my childhood. This one was written in Japanese. Or Chinese for all I knew. I glanced at Ms. Sabel and found her staring at me.

Mercury said, Caller ID, dawg.

"Want me to get the translator?" I asked.

"This means nothing." She shoved it back at the thin man.

"It details your violent assault on the Malaysian official in question," the thinner man said.

Mercury said, Hello? Anybody home? Caller ID.

He clasped his hands over the binder, leaned back slightly, and tucked in his chin as if he'd just proven her guilty of stealing the Mona Lisa. He slowly unfolded his arm to retrieve the fax. I was fighting the urge to punch him when something on the paper caught my eye.

"Gimme that." I snatched it from him. "This is an official complaint from Malaysia?"

"Indeed," the thin man said. "Straight from the Commissioner of Sarawak, Borneo."

I pointed at the top line with the originating phone number. "Then why did he fax it from China? The prefix 86-20 is Chinese, isn't it?"

I snapped a pic of the header before the Japanese officer grabbed the fax from me. He stared at it for three seconds, then glared at the men in suits. They backed up a step. He began shouting in Japanese and waving his arms. The men in suits tried to speak, but he cut them off with more shouting. The men in suits turned and walked away.

The Japanese officer faced us and bowed several times, repeating a phrase with each dip that I took as an apology. "*Moushiwake arimasen deshita.*"

"*Arigatau gozaimasu.*" Ms. Sabel bowed. *Thank you very much.*

The officer backed up, continually repeating his phrase.

She climbed the airstair ahead of me. "Good thinking back there. I'm un-firing you for sleeping on the job."

"What did those guys want?"

"Embassy guys. They said the Pak Uban filed an assault complaint. They wanted me to turn the jet around and return to Borneo."

She took her seat and stared out the window.

I took the seat facing her, the one Tania usually snapped up, and tapped my finger on the table. "The villagers you pissed off back there—how did they get the State Department to fall for a faked fax? Who are they connected to in Guangzhou?"

She shrugged without looking at me.

"You know," I said, "your father might have been right when he told you not to pick a fight with President Hunter. I'll bet she's behind this."

"She's looking for an excuse to take me down, but it's 2:00 AM in Washington. It's unlikely she would've heard about Borneo."

"Who did you piss off in China then?" I asked.

Her gaze snapped to me and drilled a hole clean through. "How would anyone in China know about some jungle warlord's problems?"

"What happened back there?"

"Doesn't matter." She turned back to the window.

Tania stepped out of the cockpit and stood in the aisle with her arms crossed. She stared at me as if I were in her seat. Then she turned to Ms. Sabel. "Pilot says wheels up in twenty. There's a sushi bar in the executive terminal. Want me to grab some fish?"

Ms. Sabel smiled at her, then turned to me. "Grab your things. You're going back to Borneo."

"What, to get killed?"

"You weren't with us—the Pak Uban wouldn't know you from any other tourist. Head to the commercial terminal and grab a flight to Sarawak. Take Bujang with you. I want to know if the Pak Uban filed charges, has any connections in China, all that kind of thing. Oh, and while you're at it, see if the government did anything about that death camp."

"Want me to bring about world peace too?" I said. She gave me a dirty look. I darted to the luggage compartment to grab my stuff.

Tania escorted me into the Executive Terminal, where we stopped at the sushi bar and placed orders to go. Bujang stayed a step behind us.

"Who's this Pack Urban?" I asked him.

"Pak Uban," he said quietly. "It means 'white haired uncle.' It's an unofficial title of respect for regional and tribal leaders. Like a mayor, police chief, and judge rolled into one. There are several of them."

I turned back to Tania. "What happened back at the village?"

"We learned that the local boss raped women on a regular basis. Pia messed up the guy and two of his henchmen."

"You couldn't stop her?"

Tania glanced at me as if I were spoiled milk. "Stop her? Men always think like that. I helped her."

Ms. Sabel had taken up boxing in high school and Tania spent several years as an Army MP. The women had themselves a feminist's dream day. Good for them.

Our orders piled up. Plenty of yellowtail and spicy tuna with avocado and mango were stacked in boxes on the counter.

"So you beat them up and they decided to kill you?" I asked Tania while I watched the chef slice through the fish with surgical precision.

"One of them had a knife and Pia took it away from him. She heard how you cut Kasey Earl's ear off when he raped that girl back in Kandahar."

"She cut his ear off?"

"Unoriginal," Tania said.

I studied Bujang for a clue. He kept his head down. I said, "By any chance, is the Pak Uban related to the guy who's now missing body parts?"

Bujang said, "First-born son."

Tania grabbed her order, lifted her nose at me instead of saying goodbye, kicked out a hip, and swiveled her way down the terminal.

Bujang observed every swivel until I snapped my fingers in front of him.

"We're going to see the Pak Uban?" he asked with a lump in his throat.

"You don't think he's going to be happy to see us?"

"He knows you were with them."

I picked up our food and marched down the terminal, heading for the commercial airlines.

Of course the local warlord would know everyone who comes to his fiefdom. His jungle drums have been beating a BOLO for me since dawn and, no doubt, he'd know the minute I set foot on Malaysian soil again.

Some days, I just can't wait to go to work.

Chapter 6

Borneo's jungle had grown three shades darker since I left. Prama beamed a smile from under the ice pack she held to her right eye. "You gone get these guys, Jacob?"

"Consider them dead."

"They pay for damage lobby first. Then you make dead."

I glanced across the small room at a workman who swept sawdust and shards into a trash bin. "No problem."

She held out the keys to her aging Nissan pickup.

Bujang followed me outside and we waved off the chopper pilot. The Nissan creaked and clanked nicely over the rough roads while Bujang navigated.

Long after dark, we parked the truck and walked to a clearing overlooking the Pak Uban's village. The huts were larger than I expected—two or three rooms each, some with porches. All of them were made of unpainted boards with enough gaps between them to see clear through. I scanned the village for a long time, then handed the binoculars to Bujang and showed him how to switch from thermal to night vision.

"How many people live there?" I asked. "I counted six."

"Many more than that. Maybe fifty or sixty."

"Are they hiding?"

He shrugged and handed back the binoculars. On my second sweep, I saw a hut with a large open doorway and three armed men inside. Two men in black, who looked like the death camp crew, got off a motorcycle and went in. The black uniformed guys were taller, stockier, and had lighter complexions. One of them had a scarred eyebrow. I handed the binoculars back to my companion and pointed them out.

While he watched, I assembled my favorite assault rifle's infrared laser scope and silencer. When I finished, I noticed Bujang's open-mouth stare. I held up one of the Sabel Darts and pointed to the paper-cone tip. "A needle filled with concentrate of Inland Taipan snake venom, followed by a dose of a powerful sleeping medication. The venom causes instant flaccid paralysis lasting long enough for the sleep medication to take effect. The target sleeps for three to four hours. Don't worry, I'm not going to kill anyone."

His eyes searched mine. I didn't blink until he believed me.

Sabel Darts were the subject of endless debates among the thousands of vets in the company. There were people like Tania, who would do whatever the boss told her, even if she insisted we all wear pink tutus. On the other side were people like me. I'd once surprised a Taliban platoon and sprayed lead until my mag emptied. They didn't die. They shot back because, little known fact, most hajjis smoke crack or crystal meth to keep their courage up, just like the Nazis before them. Darts would've made them laugh.

But I'm not paid to make policy decisions, so I use the tools I'm given.

Mercury said, Bro, tell me you were man enough to sneak a couple mags of real bullets.

I said, It was just a charity trip. To build a school.

Mercury said, I'm so ashamed for you right now.

"There are two men from the death camp," he said. "Eight of the Pak Uban's men, and the Pak Uban himself."

"What are they doing?"

"Discussing something."

"Where are the other villagers?"

"Next village, maybe." He pointed to a ridge beyond. "A feast, I don't know."

I checked it out with my thermal scope and saw a residual glow of light beyond the ridge. A bigger village with twice the population.

"OK," I said, "you go back to the truck. If anything bad happens, get the hell out of here."

He watched me as I slipped from tree to tree, working my way closer to the hostiles.

A hundred yards out, I dropped three men as they patrolled the empty village. Another was taking a leak when he fell. The fifth heard noises and came out to investigate. He saw me. We stared at each other for a second. He ran back to the hut's open door.

I fired.

He fell facedown in the hut's doorway.

Mercury said, You love stirring up trouble, don't you, bro? Get ready, danger-junkie, cuz here come the pros. Watch for the pigs in the pen, they squeal when anyone comes near them.

Two men ran out into the dark. They separated and began a systematic search. I dropped behind a stack of wood. They had the advantage of knowing the terrain. I had the advantage of being smarter and better trained. A theoretical standoff.

Each time I found one of them in my scope, he disappeared before I could drop him. I listened for their footsteps but all I heard were the jungle's night creatures singing and chirping to each other. Then I saw one and lit him up with an infrared laser beam, visible only in my scope, but he disappeared behind a hut before I could fire.

The two men in black left the main hut and ran across my line, distracting me. Their footsteps were easier to track. They swung behind a hut to my left and kept going. They were leaving. I liked that just fine. When I heard a motorcycle fire up and buzz away, I relaxed a little and went back to searching for the local boys.

Mercury said, Yo, am I talking to myself? Did I say watch the pigs? Can't you feel the gravity over there?

Pigs squealed ten yards to my left but I heard a voice twenty yards to my right. I concentrated on the pigs and kept my ear open in the other direction. A heat signature came into my scope. A man crouched behind a waist-high wall. Aiming for the exposed area, I took a shot. The shape fell with a thud and the pigs grunted.

The voice on my right whispered again. An untrained soldier, fearing the worst, calling to his wingman. A dead giveaway. Duck-walking toward him, I tossed a dirt clod to my left. He stepped into view, making an easy target.

Mercury said, Friendly fire? You? Tell me you recognize that fool.

Something about the heat signature looked familiar. I listened again and heard him whisper. "Jacob?"

The damned translator. Bujang was just another special-ops-wannabe.

I had half a mind to drop the guy right there when I caught a glimpse of the other hostile aiming at my man. Quickly shifting my aim, I dropped the bad guy before he pulled his trigger.

I ran to Bujang and slapped a hand over his mouth with the meanest glare I could muster. He froze, eyes wide, and began to tremble. When he calmed a little, I let go, strode through the hut's open door, and dropped the last guard.

The Pak Uban stood in the back of the room, staring into the barrel of my weapon. He raised his hands. I slapped plasticuffs on his wrists and pointed to a chair at the small table. Then I relaxed a little and checked for weapons, hidden doors, threats of any kind. The room was clean, had a wooden floor, a fire pit in the corner, and two beds along one wall. The second room had beds, all neatly made with heaps of clothes between them. On one mat lay a man with a bandaged groin. I winced.

I called for Bujang to join me.

On the table were stacks of 100 ringgit bills. Malaysian currency worth about thirty cents on the dollar. A quick count of one stack and an estimation of the rest gave me roughly forty thousand ringgits. Twelve thousand dollars. I scooped it into a t-shirt and slapped it into Bujang's hands.

"Tell him it's for Prama, um, the hotel lady," I said.

He peered at me with confusion twisting his face. "Do you mean Pramashworisasmita?"

The hotel owner's moniker fell from his tongue like water over Niagara.

46

"Yeah, her. And tell him I'll put bullet holes in him if he doesn't tell me what I want to know."

Mercury said, Chop off his fingers, one knuckle at a time, bro. He'll talk fast.

I said, No way.

Mercury said, Word, dawg. Worked every time for Marcus Crassus.

Who?

Mercury said, The general who squashed Spartacus like a bug. Now there was a Roman who knew how to get things—

We're not going there.

My translator and the Pak Uban began a discussion that started out rough and quickly escalated. The Pak Uban tried to rip my head off with his eyes then turned back to Bujang and hissed at him. The two of them bickered for several more rounds, Bujang's hands gesturing wildly. They stopped arguing for a moment and looked at me over their shoulders. I gave them my soldier stare: *Do what I say or die.* They went back to arguing vehemently in their language. Finally, they agreed to disagree. The Pak Uban didn't look cowed, but willing to negotiate. I could live with that.

Bujang reported. "The men in black were looking for us. They paid him to find us."

"How was he planning to do that?"

"They did not know we left Borneo."

"So then, he wouldn't have filed any complaints with the authorities in Sarawak or Guangzhou." I thought for a moment. "Has he seen anyone with the blue eye disease?"

Bujang discussed things with the Pak Uban for a moment. "No. He thinks I'm crazy. There's no such disease here."

"Bullshit. Half a village was laid up in that clinic."

Bujang shrugged.

"What was he supposed to do when he found us?"

"The men will come back here and double the cash if he has our heads."

"Does he know those guys?"

"He's never seen them before. But he liked them."

The smug bastard was pissing me off. "Yeah, they gave him money and didn't cut his son's balls off."

"Ms. Sabel didn't cut the man's balls off, sir."

I raised an eyebrow.

"She cut off his dick." He sighed. "She said it was justice for the victims."

My knees clamped together and I winced. I work for one twisted woman.

The Pak Uban said something and Bujang waved it off.

"Earn your keep, Bujang. What'd he say?"

"He said, you will be back—then you will be his bitch."

Chapter 7

When I returned to Washington, the Major summoned me to Sabel Gardens, Alan Sabel's sprawling estate in Potomac, Maryland. It was a big house built by a big man who had done big things. His biggest thing was adopting four-year-old Pia after her parents were murdered. It was a noble thing to do, but he'd built the palace to distance himself from his little girl's many unanswered questions. Decorated in mahogany, marble, and furniture culled from the finest English manor houses, his overcompensation came through loud and clear.

I'd been there for the company's annual party and pulled the coveted guard duty a couple times, but I'd never had the full tour. Agent Marty, the man in charge of estate security, took me around the grounds. He did his best to put me at ease. I'd been on a couple missions with him but this was the first time I'd seen him with a cane. His limp was noticeable. I didn't ask and he didn't mention it.

As we hiked the impressive grounds, and the grandeur's intended effect of minimizing my self-worth took hold, I felt underdressed in my jeans with only a leather jacket to cover my t-shirt's slogan: *If you can't dazzle 'em with brilliance / riddle 'em with bullets.*

The Major, known as Jonelle Jackson outside the Sabel empire, approached us as we rounded one of the outbuildings. In the Army, she'd saved me from charges for assaulting an officer because she agreed he'd deserved it. Later, I'd left the Army in a storm of accusations. She found me and gave me a job that paid better than frying fish and slinging fries.

I delivered my verbal report when she joined us.

"The authorities in Sarawak refused to investigate?" The Major asked. She seemed taller than the last time I saw her. Forty-year-old women don't grow much, so I chalked it up to her feeling more confident in her role running the company.

"They didn't refuse," I said, "but they didn't look motivated. I can't blame them. Some American comes in and says there's a mass grave in the jungle and all he has is a before and after picture of a hole in the ground."

"Any trace on the cars?"

"My picture was unreadable on one, the other old car was unregistered, and the newer one was rented to Dr. Chapman. He turned it in and left the country for Hong Kong."

"And the death camp was evacuated?"

"Cleaned out. We landed the bird where the awning had been in the morning. Tire tracks all around, the hole filled in, but not a scrap of paper or trash left behind."

Agent Marty led us across the outdoor workout area. A mountain of straw bales stood on one side of an obstacle course with tires and logs and ropes. Half a dozen young women were moving the straw bales from one mound to another in the crisp autumn air. I knew from personal experience, moving bales could be hard work or great exercise depending on your attitude.

"The Pak Uban didn't know anybody in China?" The Major asked.

"Not that he would admit to. He didn't even have phone service, so I tend to believe him."

Marty led us to the soccer fields where more young women worked on soccer drills as the rising sun stabbed between the trees, turning the morning's frost into steam that rose gently into the air.

A reporter with a video camera, logo emblazoned on the side, recorded the girls. I recognized him: Otis Blackwell, the Channel 4 reporter who saved my ass with a live broadcast not too long ago. Were it not for him, President Hunter's jack-booted thugs would've dumped my body in the Chesapeake.

"Who are these people?" I asked. "I thought Ms. Sabel decided not to play on the National Team this year."

"Meet our newest security challenge," Marty said. "St. Muriel's High School soccer team, Pia's alma mater. As of this morning, fifteen teenage girls and five coaches will practice at Sabel Gardens."

"How did that happen?"

"They tracked her down on her morning run and begged her to help them prepare for the season. So, she put them to work."

"Met her on her run? Bro, she runs at four in the morning."

"That's why she agreed to help them. She said any teenagers willing to get up at that hour deserved all the help in the world. From the looks on their faces, I don't think they were planning to start today." Marty laughed. "Be careful what you ask for."

"Where was Ms. Sabel running? Who was on guard duty?"

Marty grinned and slapped me on the back. "We always let her run alone because she's up earlier than the bad guys and runs faster anyway. But the girls were waiting for her on the C & O Canal. That proves we can't ignore the security gap any longer. And that's why you're here today, Jacob. You're the only agent who can run a 10K in under forty minutes."

"I haven't run a 10K in six months."

"Grab some steroids and hit the treadmill then, 'cause she does a 10K in thirty five on a bad day." Marty turned on his cane and headed for the car barns.

My bonus from the last mission was big enough to land me a house, a car, and a dog. Some crazy idea had come over me that I was old enough to stay home on my off-hours and trim the hedge, keep up with my cooking, maybe make furniture. Somewhere in the back of my mind was the idea of getting married and having some kids. Instead, I would be spending my off-hours nursing shin splints and a sore Achilles, the things that kept me off the track team in my one and only college year.

"Pia requested you for this detail," the Major said. "You impressed her on your last mission."

Hell, I'd impressed myself. It was the first mission with Ms. Sabel where I'd walked away without a bullet wound.

Marty led us down the brick apron between the car barns. "Cousin Elmer handles everything with wheels. He's an old-fashioned chauffer, the CEO of Sabel Automotive, and these barns are his kingdom. All the exotic two-seaters are in this one, and the sedans and limos are in the other. Only the Bentley and Mercedes limos are bulletproof. When she takes a friend in a two-seater, you take a matching car."

"Is she a good driver?"

"Jacob, you *know* she doesn't do anything halfway."

As if on cue, Ms. Sabel rounded the far end of the barn looking like a Wall Street banker in a blue suit—with an eye-catching short skirt. The designer probably meant for it to reach nearer to the knee but tall women have fashion challenges. I had no complaints watching her long legs flash in the morning sun.

Cousin Elmer backed a burnt-orange McLaren 12C Spider out of a stall, steam rising from its center-mounted tailpipes.

She waved and called out. "Perfect timing, Jacob. Hop in."

I glanced at the Major, who motioned for me to go. I started for the car.

"Did you fill him in?" Ms. Sabel said to the Major.

"Haven't had a chance to cover everything yet," Marty said.

Five steps away, I spun back to the Major and Marty. "What?"

Marty said, "I'm leaving the post here. I'm moving to the marketing department."

"Why? You've been in charge of Ms. Sabel's personal security since forever."

"Last time I caught a bullet," he lifted his cane, "it lodged too close to my spine."

Pia Sabel, most dangerous woman on Earth—to those who stand next to her. He'd caught that bullet trying to rescue her from Syrian kidnappers.

"Who's taking your place?" I said.

He smiled. The Major waved me toward the McLaren. I took that to mean my worst possible job scenario was about to happen: Tania Cooper would take Marty's job. I would end up working for a woman who hated me but for whom I still had some serious passion. That marriage fantasy I mentioned earlier? It starred Tania.

Ms. Sabel was buckling into the driver's seat when I approached. Cousin Elmer held the passenger door open for me.

Before I clicked my seatbelt, Ms. Sabel lit up the back tires and took it to the 8500 rpm limit in first gear. We shot through the front gates before they had fully parted and were on River Road before I dared steal a glance at her legs.

Mercury said, You just got done thinking about marrying Tania and here you are, creeping on your boss. What's up with that, homie? Are you a professional or just another dawg?

I kicked myself and said, I'm human. But you're right. Remind me to never sneak a peek at the boss, it's a bad career move.

She slowed it down on the public road, flew through town, and slid into St. Muriel's parking lot before explaining our trip.

"I'm going to tell the headmaster about taking over the soccer team. It'll only take a minute. Then we'll take the blood vials you found to the labs at NIH and see what's in them." She handed me two vials and climbed from the car. "Wait here."

I tried to tuck the vials into the envelope-sized glove box. Not happening. So I pushed them under the seat and hopped out. "There're only two vials here."

She glanced back over her shoulder without breaking stride and pressed a finger to her lips, *shh*, with a mischievous smile.

I watched her walk. And it had only been two minutes since I swore not to check out the boss. I took a deep breath and tore my eyes away. I was on duty and acting like I was at the beach. Then I remembered—I was on duty.

"Wait." I bounded up the stone steps. "You can't go in a building before I've cleared—"

A security man put his hand out when I opened the giant door. I scrutinized the hallway. She was gone. I recognized the security man as a Sabel agent and nodded at him. He nodded back. Sabel Security was everywhere. The place was secure. So I hadn't actually blown it.

Mercury said, Dawg, tell me you're paying attention to your surroundings. Trouble's coming. Can you feel it?

I stepped back outside to admire her street-legal race car when I saw a Cadillac cruise by. It rolled too slowly even for a school zone. Two beefy guys inside it stared at me like I was a hot babe. That raised my suspicions. Any hetero American male would be staring at the McLaren. Not that I mind getting checked out by gay guys now and then—it's flattering, but you don't expect them to be cruising a girl's school. So I ruled out gay guys and proceeded down a few steps.

The Caddy's passenger looked at something in his hand, then back at me, then his hand, then me. He spoke to the driver. They stopped in the middle of the street and got out and left the car doors open. They were big guys, steroid-gulping gym rats.

I stopped halfway down the steps.

The beefy guys had their eyes on me as they crossed the parking lot. I returned the favor. Their suits flapped as they walked, exposing shoulder holsters.

"Private property, gentlemen." I held up a hand. "State your business."

They kept coming. The gray-haired guy with the craggy face spoke. "You're Jacob, right? You got something that belongs to me."

"Stop right there."

They didn't stop. They crossed onto the sidewalk, five yards away.

"Give me the test tubes you stole and we won't hurt you."

"Hurt me? A couple of goons from Pittsburgh?"

They stopped and glanced at each other, trying to figure out how I knew they were from Pittsburgh. Simple—his accent.

"We're just asking nicely," he said. "So give them up and nobody gets hurt."

"I never take things from stupid people. Ain't fair." I dropped down the last few steps, adrenaline coursing through my veins like ice water. "Even if I had stolen something, you're the last goons on earth

I'd trust to return it. So let's make a deal: you tell me who sent you and I won't rip your arms off."

Taunting the lesser primates always gets me in trouble. The younger guy's face scrunched up with anger. He lunged for me. Time slowed down and training kicked in. I waited until his outstretched fingers were within a millimeter of grabbing my shirt. I stepped aside like a matador and let him charge through. I remembered a video of Ms. Sabel in a soccer game. She'd flown past an opponent who stomped on Ms. Sabel's metatarsals, breaking her stride, and sending her to the ground.

I tried it.

Worked like a charm.

The guy did a face-plant on the steps. His teeth and cheekbones crunched as he collided with the stone.

Without looking, I instinctively took a step back as Gray-hair's fist swept past my nose. The momentum of his roundhouse carried him past his balance point. I twisted, smashing my elbow in his lower back, and sent him forward into the hedge.

The first guy stood up, blood pouring from his face, and pulled his gun.

Pulling a gun on a veteran is a bad idea on a monumental scale. It really pisses us off and brings out all that pent-up anger we harness to win wars. I dove to the ground, rolled, and came up three yards from where he was busy unloading half his magazine. My dart hit him in the neck.

Gray-hair thrashed his way out of the bushes and ran behind the stone balustrade along the school's front steps. My first dart hit the wall behind him, my second hit the banister.

Gray-hair managed to squeeze off three rounds that shattered two glass windows before I put him down with a dart in his arm.

Chapter 8

Violet Windsor's heels clicked on the marble as she strode through Windsor Pharmaceutical's executive reception area with a coffee in one hand and her Chanel purse in the other. The red handbag matched the red and black enamel of her corporate décor perfectly.

Ignoring a frightened look from her secretary in the outer office, she hummed a tune, entered her office, and crossed to her desk.

A shadow by the window startled her. Standing in the unlit room, Chen Zhipeng stared out at the view, hands clasped behind his narrow back. From her office's perch high above the city, she could see clouds of pollution rolling in from the industrial sector, across the urban landscape, and south to Macau.

"Such a sunny day," he said quietly. "A little rain would solve so many problem. It would wash the pollutant out to sea; refill the aquifer; clear the air; sustain our way of life."

"Oh yes, climate change is a terrible problem. Rising sea levels, typhoons, that kind of thing are dreadful."

"Climate change, yes; but typhoon, no. Everyone talk about monster storm. They make a good story because you see it on TV. No one think sunny sky is a problem. But sunshine is biggest problem for the future."

Violet stood still. "That's not why you came."

Chen faced her and examined her head to toe. "You disappoint me."

Violet dropped her purse and phone on her desk. She motioned to a meeting table and crossed to it. On the table lay the report she'd given Chen in Beijing two days earlier.

"I don't understand, *Shifu*," *great teacher.* "What have I done?"

"Your report omit several important fact." Chen stayed at the window, his short, thin frame a silhouette in the morning light behind him.

"It covered everything of significance."

"You cover science only," Chen said. "Equally important, Pia Sabel visit site. Also, eight kilo of Element 42 is missing. Also, entire production run of Levoxavir, missing."

"I understood the drugs were to be destroyed by Anatoly's people. You insisted we leave no physical evidence. If Mukhtar didn't get the job done, I'll speak to Anatoly. What about Wu Fang? Perhaps he took some of—"

"Wu Fang learned about Borneo from Dr. Chapman. He is in reeducation camp now."

"I will look into this matter right away," Violet said.

"You were young in 2008 and your mistake easy to forgive. You are old enough to bear responsibility now."

"You spared me and I am grateful." She bowed her head. "I learned my lesson, *Shifu*. You have always been the most honorable teacher."

"Element 42 is very dangerous program. You promised top security and assured me, no discovery. Yet, I learn of these many problem from other people." Chen moved to her. "Violet, let me be clear—it is important that you fix these problem." He chopped the air with his hand. "No connection to China. No connection to Wu Fang. No connection to Windsor Pharmaceutical. You understand, your company is expendable, the Party and China are not."

Violet watched him stroll out as if he owned the place. A few seconds after he left, she took a deep breath and closed the door. She staggered, steadied herself with a hand on her desk, rounded it to her chair, and fell in. She pulled off her designer prosthesis and massaged her stump. It always throbbed when she lost her temper. She straightened the sock and slipped it back on. Her Marni pump fell off. She cursed the stupid maid and grabbed another double sticky tape. She shoved it in her shoe and pressed it on the leg.

She leaned forward and pressed the intercom. "Get Verratti and Cummings on a conference call right now."

Violet planted her face in her hands until the call came through.

"It's one in the morning in Milan," Verratti said.

"Chen knows Element 42 is missing." She waited as the men gasped. "He said Wu Fang is being reeducated."

"That's not good," Cummings said. "Are they going to kill him?"

"No. Chen's rivals would find out and hang him."

"That's a relief. At least we don't have to make excuses about losing a board member."

"That's not all," she said. "He knows about Pia Sabel."

"Does he know about the vials?"

"He didn't mention them, but if he knows about Sabel, we have to assume he knows."

"I've engaged Velox Deployment Services, the black-budget contractor I told you about. Should I send them after Chen?"

Verratti scoffed. "He's the equivalent of the Treasury Secretary in the US."

"Then we have to speed up deployment," Cummings said. "The sooner Philadelphia happens, the sooner he'll know who did it, and we'll be safe."

"For god's sake, Ed," Violet said. "The man just threatened me. We won't end up in a reeducation camp. If he figures out what we're doing, he'll just kill us."

"No," Verratti said. "Ed's right. We go ahead with the plan, we'll make tons of money, and Chen can't touch us."

Cummings chimed in. "If he did, he'd have to acknowledge how he knew. As long as Chen and China are kept out of it, he won't care. We can still make billions."

Violet's fingers ran over the small jade statue of Wu Zetian, China's only female ruler.

"Risky," Violet said. "But then we definitely need those vials. Where are we on that, Marco?"

"I'm waiting for my American friends to report. They should be done soon."

"What about Velox?" Violet said. "Can we count on them as backup?"

"They're Sabel Security's biggest competitor," Cummings said. "Their man chomped at the bit when I told him who's involved."

"OK, then we need to move fast. We should deploy more cities than Philadelphia. We'll need more drones and people to work them."

"And more Element 42 and more Levoxavir," Cummings said. "We can use Velox to supplement Verratti's men on deployment."

"Then we know our assignments," she said. "I'll set a follow-up call for tomorrow."

When they clicked off, Violet stared out the window for several minutes.

She picked up her phone and dialed. She ended up in voicemail, so she left a message. "Prince, if I recall correctly, you're friends with the Sabels. Give me a call some time. It's been too long."

Chapter 9

No one had knocked on my door since my Mormon neighbor brought over a plate full of cookies on moving day. She was young and pretty and newly wed and gave me the feeling she wanted to roll back her church's century-old ban on plural marriage, only with a whole new gender bias. My newfound longing for marital bliss hadn't reached that level of desperation, but I didn't mind investigating any experiments she might have in mind.

When I opened the door, it wasn't my Mormon neighbor. The disappointment rolled out in my tone of voice. "Emily. What brings the *Post's* ace travel writer to Bethesda? Won't they spring for Paris?"

"I'm not on the travel desk anymore," she said.

"Let me guess. They assigned you to Sabel Security after you smeared Louisa."

She smiled wide and tossed her arms in the air as if she'd jumped naked from a cake. To accentuate her enthusiasm, she twirled around, letting the centrifugal force lift her skirt. But she turned too quickly for her stiletto heels and toppled over. I caught her in a dip that left us nose to nose. She giggled. I glanced around the yard to make sure my Mormon hadn't seen us.

"May I come in?"

"As a reporter?" I asked.

"If you'd like. But I'd rather do the dominatrix thing like your boss."

I dropped her on her butt in the doorway. "Don't talk like that about Ms. Sabel."

She scrambled to her feet and pushed the door open before I could slam it behind me. I made my way to the kitchen, where I'd been experimenting on a new recipe for bacon-wrapped lamb stuffed with feta and sun-dried tomatoes. I glanced over my shoulder. Emily and my puppy were trotting behind me, parallel to each other. The two of them stopped in the doorway and cocked their heads in unison. Then she checked out the dog.

"What's his name?" she asked.

"Anoshni."

She scrunched up her nose. "What?"

"It means something in Navajo. Miguel gave him to me."

"Who?"

"My buddy from the wars."

"What kind of dog is he?"

"He's an American. Like the rest of us, a mix of everything. What do you want?"

"Big gunfight at the school this morning. Who were they?"

"Collection agency wanted to repo my TV."

"You don't have a TV. You're a reader." She regarded my cramped kitchen. "At least you used to be."

I turned the bacon. Slow cooked, cracked pepper, aromatic, and crispy.

She slinked over to me and stroked my arm. "Are you mad at me?"

I slammed the pan on the burner and leaned in close enough to make her step back. "You don't think an African-American woman has it hard enough in business? Louisa didn't deserve that."

Louisa, a kidnapping victim, had been grateful when I'd rescued her. We'd dated until Emily and the *Post* ran a tabloid-style article about us.

I turned to the counter, grabbed the salt grinder, and put a light dusting on the lamb.

"I report the truth, Jacob. You rescued her, she slept with you."

"Sabel Security's Extra Services—a lurid headline if there ever was one, Emily. I don't mind you going after me. But the picture of Louisa answering the door was low. Really low."

"We weren't planning on a picture until we saw what she was wearing. Who could take her seriously?"

"We were serious. You made her sound like a—"

"And we weren't serious?" She stomped. "You stood me up, Jacob. Left me at a coffeehouse waiting for my big romantic weekend."

I didn't have a comeback for that one. I'd done my usual screw-up with Emily. A random woman told me her divorce-is-lonely story and I did what I always do—I fell for it. Maybe I didn't deserve a real marriage. I'd just get shot in the back by a jealous lover anyway.

I ground some pepper on the lamb, then realized I'd forgotten the olive oil. Getting into tense conversations with formers will always ruin your cooking.

"I apologized for that once." I drizzled the olive oil lighter than I'd have liked but I didn't want to wash off the seasonings. "If that doesn't work for you, deal with it somewhere else."

"What about the shooting?" she asked.

I turned to her. "Honestly, Emily, I have no idea. Couple goons from Pittsburgh mistook me for someone else."

"Did it have anything to do with this?"

Emily tossed her tablet on the counter next to the lamb. A full-color picture of the trench on Borneo filled her screen. Unlike the last time I'd seen it, it was open, dirt piled to one side. Three men in real Malaysian police uniforms stood with shovels on the right. Second body from the left was Kaya, the girl with the sick brother. Dirt covered part of her dead face. Her corpse wasn't alone; the pit was full.

I gagged and staggered back a step. "Where did you get this?"

"It's all over the newswires in Malaysia."

"How did you—"

"I have alerts set to ping when your name comes up. And your name came up as the man who reported this mass grave to authorities in Sarawak."

I inhaled deeply through my nose and tried to get my churning stomach under control. I'd seen a lot of ugly deaths in war zones, but these were innocent civilians. When I joined the Army all those years ago, it was to protect innocent civilians. "How many?"

"Seventeen in one pit; twelve in another."

"What happened?"

"You tell me."

I sketched enough of a story for her to think I was opening up but not enough for her to write a column. "I'm not sure what's going on there, but keep this off the record for now."

She leaned back, crossed her arms. "You're headlining a mass grave story that's all over Kuala Lumpur and you think the *Post* is going to suppress it?"

"I'm not *headlining*. We stumbled on suspicious guys and reported them to the authorities. That's all."

"And then two men shoot up a private school in Potomac." She leaned out of the kitchen to glance around the living room. "Over a TV you don't own?"

The trouble with being attracted to smart women is that they're hard to manipulate. So I opted for the direct approach. Clicking through a few options on her tablet, I emailed the picture to myself. When she figured out what I was doing, she turned red and her neck strained as if she would bite me any second.

Smoke poured from the bacon. I turned off the burner, pushed the skillet away, put my hands on either side of the stove, and fought my urge to pick up the smoking pan and throw it.

"Anoshni!" Miguel stood with one hand on my doorknob. His hair brushed the top of the frame and his shoulders filled the width. The puppy tackled him. He scooped up the dog and strode straight to us.

Emily and I kept up our glaring contest.

Miguel said, "Hey, you a friend of X-ray?"

Emily squinted at him. "Who?"

"Second battle of Fallujah," Miguel said, "Jacob grabbed the squad's machine gun and fired two hundred rounds into the wall of a house we were about to search. When we went inside, we found six dead hajjis who'd been planning to ambush us. So, we call him X-Ray."

Mercury said, And still no credit for my hard work? Why do I bother with you, fool?

They did one of those long looks into each other's eyes.

I took the opportunity to leave. "Emily, Miguel; Miguel, Emily. Lamb is ready for the stuffing, recipe's on the counter. I gotta go."

Tossing my apron at Miguel, I was out the door and driving before either of them could register a protest. It would probably work out for the best. I could get clear of Emily and Miguel could have a girlfriend. She'd go for him. He was bigger, better looking, more charming, and had that Native-American-mystical-earth-spirit-thing going for him.

My phone rang halfway up River Road. It was FBI Special Agent Verges. "I've been permanently assigned to you, Jacob. What did you do to piss off LaRocca?"

"Who?"

"The guys who shot up St. Muriel's? They're made men in the LaRocca crime family."

"What?"

"Jacob, don't play dumb with me. We have to work together whether you like it or not. So tell me, how did you get mixed up with the Pittsburgh mob?"

"Back up, what do you mean 'assigned'?"

"The Director and Alan Sabel are old pals, but his little girl pissed off the president. So, President Hunter tells the Director: no more special treatment for Sabel Security. But Directors don't turn away old friends, so he assigned me as the special liaison."

Nice. They assigned a guy who graduated Quantico last summer as my guardian angel.

"Meet me at Sabel Gardens," I said. "I'll bring you up to speed."

He choked. "You mean, um, the place where, like, the Sabels live? Like, the mansion?"

"What's the matter, Verges? Billionaires make you nervous? Bring your balls."

I hung up, but he called back.

"Bro, what's the dress code out there?" he asked.

"What's the LaRocca crime family?"

"Pittsburgh Mafia, dating back to Prohibition. They own western Pennsylvania but they've never made a move east of Harrisburg before."

"Good to know. Thanks." I clicked off.

He called back.

"I'm serious, Jacob. Help me out here. Casual or what? I can't make the Bureau look bad my first time out."

Tempting as it was to remind him about his balls, I took pity on him. "Nine times out of ten, she's wearing Lululemon. Her household staff dresses casual but pricey stuff like Hugo Boss, Kate Spade, that kind of thing. Alan sleeps in ten-thousand-dollar PJs."

"What are you wearing?"

"Jeans and a t-shirt." I hung up and put him on ignore.

I glanced at my wardrobe. The jeans looked expensive because I'd had them for a decade; the faded and shredded parts were real. The t-shirt had an American flag circled by the words, *Back-to-Back World War Champs.* Not the best attire for the occasion. I glanced around the car for some options. A t-shirt covered the back seat, left over from when I took the pup to the vet. It read, *US ARMY / UNDEFEATED FOR 238 YEARS.* Below that in small print: *Fuck Vietnam.*

I stuck with what I had on.

My brain spent the rest of the drive spinning through different ways to break the news about Kaya and the pit to Ms. Sabel.

My other old Army buddy, Agent Carmen, greeted me in the entry hall and walked me down a highway of marble. She'd been in motor maintenance but joined in every house-to-house mission she could sneak into. No braver woman ever served her country.

She opened the door to a room lined with books floor to ceiling, a couple fireplaces, overstuffed leather chairs grouped in nooks, reading tables with lamps, and a globe the size of a car. "Don't touch anything, Jacob. We count spoons, you know."

My mood wasn't in sync with her humor. She gave me a shrug and left.

Tania walked in as if she owned the place. "What you got that's so damned important?"

I showed her the picture on my phone.

Tania fell into a wingback chair, tried to speak but only mouthed random words.

Chapter 10

Ms. Sabel came in a second later wearing a dripping-wet one-piece swimsuit. She toweled her hair while looking at us curiously. Everything I'd planned to say evaporated.

She said, "What's wrong?"

I held the picture out and let it speak.

Ms. Sabel inhaled her sobs, trying to keep her composure. We were silent for a long time.

"What ties them together?" Ms. Sabel said after we regained our collective senses. "China, Borneo, Pittsburgh?"

"What were they doing?" Tania said. "Science experiments? Chemical spill?"

I closed the laptop on the desk. "Only thing I can find are a bunch of tattoo-nuts who dye their sclera blue."

Both women curled a lip at that idea.

Carmen stuck her face around the door. "FBI guy is here. He asked for Jacob."

"Put him in the library," Ms. Sabel said.

"Verges had something on the guys from Pittsburgh," I said.

"You talk to him." She tapped my phone's screen. "But first, where did you get this picture?"

"Emily from the *Post*. She's been assigned as the Sabel Security reporter."

"You're OK with Emily?" Ms. Sabel eyeballed me.

"It was just a revenge article," I said. "I'm over it."

"Got what you deserved," Tania said.

Ms. Sabel scowled at Tania then faced me. "And Louisa?"

"She said the black community will accept a black man dating a white woman but not the other way around."

"Sounds like an excuse."

"Real," Tania said. "Except if it's the right guy, we don't give a shit."

Ms. Sabel looked to me. I shrugged. Even though she was only a quarter African American, Tania was right—Louisa had grown tired of me anyway.

"If you can deal with her," Ms. Sabel said, "bring Emily in on this. She knows more than we do."

Ms. Sabel gave me directions to the library, and after a long stroll, I found Verges.

"Nice suit," I said. He looked younger than the last time I saw him, if that was possible.

"Thought you were setting me up." He studied me and frowned. "You really are dressed like a farmer."

"You don't worry about the dress code when you've killed people to save your boss's life. But don't worry, someday you'll stop peeing your pants at the first sign of danger and you'll have a chance to be a hero too."

I let him search for that snappy comeback he would find a day too late while I slipped behind the bar. The shelves were empty. "Tell me about the LaRocca family and the guys I subdued."

"Zebo Amato and Sonny Pecora are suspects in several killings." Verges pointed at a hidden mini-fridge. "The Pittsburgh office has them under surveillance."

"And your guys let them come after me?" I opened the mini-fridge and found pints of Murphy's Stout in cans.

"We didn't know they left Pittsburgh." Verges licked his lips.

"Verges, if I ever get in trouble with the FBI, can I get the same surveillance team?"

"We need to know what you were discussing before the shooting. We couldn't hear anything on the school's security video."

I handed him a Murphy's and recounted the conversation as best I remembered.

Verges sucked down half the can in a single go. "What did you steal from them?"

"I've never even been to Pittsburgh."

"Could it be related to this?" Verges brought out a big phone and spun it on the bar with a flourish.

"Old news, Verges. The body on the left is a girl named Kaya." I recounted the highlights of Borneo except for stealing the vials. "Now tell me how the Pittsburgh mob is connected to Borneo."

He shook his head and emptied his Murphy's. "The only ties we know about are the Sinaloa Cartel and a financial crime syndicate out of Italy. Borneo's a new one. Say, that was good beer. Could you toss me another?"

"Aren't you on duty?"

"I left the office at six." He licked his lips like a salivating dog staring at a bone.

I handed him a fresh one. "I want to chat with Amato and Pecora. Can you get me in?"

"These guys are lifelong mobsters. You'll never get anything out of them."

"Is that your way of saying they're not in FBI custody?"

"Montgomery County, but made men won't talk to you."

"I got an Al Qaeda operative talking." I'd accidentally blown the poor hajji's toe off while mishandling my side arm. The guy thought I was interrogating the hard way and started talking. I was smart enough to listen. But there was no need to explain all that to the FBI's greenest kid.

"I can't do anything to help you."

"Liaison, huh? That means you keep your ear open to what Sabel Security's doing and give us nothing."

"Something like that."

Carmen stepped in, followed by Tania and Ms. Sabel, who'd found a cover up that didn't cover up much. Carmen did a quick room check and left.

Ms. Sabel strode up to Verges with Tania a step behind her and introduced herself. "How can you help us?"

71

He opened his mouth and I cut him off. "President Hunter won't let him help us. But he's off duty, so he's offered to call the Montgomery County Sheriff to get us an interview with the bad guys." Verges started to shake his head, punting the idea. "Because he lives in mortal fear of pissing off Alan Sabel and having Alan call Director Shikowitz."

Ms. Sabel extended a hand. "Thank you so much, Agent Verges. It was a pleasure to meet you. Now if you'll excuse us."

Agent Verges took a moment before he got the hint. He left his empty can on the bar.

Then there were three of us. Ms. Sabel positioned herself in front of Tania and me.

"The shock of the picture pushed some unfinished business to the side. But I have to address it tonight. Both of you, have a seat." Ms. Sabel paced with an uncharacteristic nervousness while Tania and I sat on the edge of a nearby love seat.

Ms. Sabel said, "You know Marty's moving to marketing. And that means I'll need someone to manage security for Dad and me— Sabel Gardens, the jets, the special missions, charity events, the staff, that kind of thing. The Major drew up a list of candidates but I picked you two instead. I know co-captains are rarely a good idea, but Lewis and Clark pulled it off, so I'm sure you can work out your differences."

She turned and walked out of the room while Tania and I took a moment to recover from the shock.

"What did she mean, 'picked you two instead?'" I said.

"What did you do?" Tania smacked my shoulder. "I had this thing wrapped up and you go sticking your goddamn nose in it. This is my career, dickhead. You go after her and tell her you refuse."

"Me?"

"Yes, you. If you screw me out of this job, I'll never speak to you again."

"You aren't speaking to me now. Tormenting maybe, but not speaking."

She slapped me faster than a frog catches a fly and waited for my reaction, hand poised for a second strike.

I flashed back to a better time. Tania and I woke up late. We took the Metro to the Tidal Basin and strolled through the cherry blossoms hand-in-hand. One of the best days of my life. It was a happier thought than a slap and I decided to hold on to it. I got up and walked out.

Ten steps down the hallway, I stopped and looked around. Artwork covered the walls. There were doors and intersecting hallways as far as the eye could see. I had no idea where I was in the sprawling mansion.

And I was in charge of security.

Chapter 11

Carmen came around a corner with Tania behind her and waved to me. "There you are. Everyone's waiting for you in the dining room."

We followed in line, Tania a step behind me. The crowd milling about the mahogany paneled room didn't notice us at first, but Alan Sabel's vigilant eye found us through the sea of people. He clinked his cocktail glass with a fountain pen.

"Hey everyone, I want you to meet Tania and Jacob." His voice boomed through the room with contagious enthusiasm. "Jacob's the hero who saved Pia's life last summer and Tania is the heroine who saved Pia's life in May. They've just agreed to take over the Special Missions Group of Sabel Security."

The crowd broke into cheers and applause. Politicians, generals, businessmen, and minor celebrities surrounded us and started pumping our hands and pounding our backs. Several faces were familiar from the news. The adoration lasted a minute, then everyone turned back to their conversations.

Mercury said, Oh dawg, these are my peeps. You get me in with these psychopaths and we can find a demi-god role with your name on it.

I said, We're not going to social-climb this crowd. I don't care about being a demi-anything. And show some respect, they're governors and CEOs.

Mercury said, Like I said, psychopaths. Don't knock the social climbing thing. All you need are fingernails.

A gong rang and a serious voice announced dinner. Like a school of fish in slow motion, the crowd swiveled, walked through an arch, and took their seats at a table so big you could park a bus on it. Tania and I glanced at each other and turned for the exit, assuming our services were no longer needed among the rich and powerful.

"Over here," Ms. Sabel waved to us from the head of the table. Somewhere she'd found a simple cocktail dress in black with sparkly things sewn into it forming an abstract river that swirled from shoulder to thigh. Her father sat at the other end, surrounded by all the faces I'd seen on TV.

Tania snatched the chair on Ms. Sabel's right before I even saw it. I took the chair opposite.

Before I could take a stab at dinner conversation, MsTania gazed up at the last man to arrive. Judging by the way she swooned, he must've been a perfect ten. The leather on his shoes glowed as if they had been polished for a hundred years. His sport coat flowed like water. His smile twinkled in the candlelight as he charmed the ladies with his greetings. He even had a cravat.

Who wears a cravat?

"Jaz Jenkins," he said.

Jaz-and-his-cravat extended a hand across the table to me.

We could only manage a weak finger-shake across the expanse of oak between us, but it was enough to dislike him instantly. Maybe it was the way Tania kept staring at him with big upturned eyes while he and I sized each other up in the male custom. One thing I could tell at first glance: whatever Ivy League had given him a head-start on Wall Street hadn't taught him how to kill people.

We took our seats and a man flapped a napkin in my lap.

"Jaz is the son of Bobby Jenkins, Jenkins Pharmaceuticals," Ms. Sabel said. "He just started working for his dad this morning."

I smiled and tried to think of something witty but all that came to mind was, *I say old sport, thank god for nepotism, eh?* But I said nothing and ended up looking like a grinning fool. I turned to Ms. Sabel. "I'm sorry, I didn't know there was a formal dinner or I would've dressed—"

"Don't worry about the glitz. Dad has a business dinner every night. I usually eat in the kitchen with Cousin Elmer. I just dreamed this up a few minutes ago when I heard Jaz was back in town."

"Back?" I turned to Jaz. "You've been away?"

"I was five when Mom got divorced and left Maryland, so you can't say I'm back, really. But I've visited Dad a few times over the years and I just adore Angel." He smiled at Ms. Sabel.

I wanted to knock his perfectly polished teeth into Tania's lap for using such a disrespectful familiarity.

He shared a glance with Tania that raised my territorial instincts to DEFCON 1. "Where do you live?"

"I'm from Omaha," he said as if it were a good thing.

He grew up two hundred miles west of my family farm, so we talked about corn country. Normally farming conversations bore women to death, but Tania was just as doe-eyed at the end as at the outset.

Jaz turned to Ms. Sabel. "Say, Angel, how would you like to join me for a football game on Sunday?"

She winced when he said 'Angel'.

"DC United's away this weekend." She frowned. "Oh, do you mean that game where the center grabs the ball with his *hands* and hikes it into the *hands* of the quarterback who either *hands* it off to the running back or throws it with his *hands* into the *hands* of the wide receiver?" She paused. "Why do they call that *foot*ball?"

Tania stared at Ms. Sabel with big, wide eyes.

Jaz drooped.

As a member of the brotherhood of men, I felt sorry for him. And his cravat.

Ms. Sabel's voice dropped a notch. "I'm. Sorry. I get carried away. Sometimes. You know 96 out of 100 people around the world think of football as, uh. Oh boy. Sure. I'd love to see the game. That would be nice."

My phone buzzed in the awkward silence that followed. I glanced at it.

"Verges came through," I said. "They're expecting us in twenty minutes."

"You mean the LaRocca guys?" Ms. Sabel asked. "What's your plan?"

"Wish we had more time to prepare." I thought up a quick one. "I'll need to borrow a lawyer for an hour. Sorry, I—"

"Kevin," Ms. Sabel called to someone halfway down the table.

A well-dressed, middle-aged man looked up. She nodded at the exit. He excused himself from the table.

A servant put a bowl of soup in front of me. It was an exquisite bowl of soup. I'd cooked up the same dish just before we left for Borneo. Butternut squash with pears and pecans, an award-winning recipe that was all the rage in cooking circles. I savored the scent of simmered onions with delicate hints of ginger and nutmeg as Ms. Sabel and Tania left the room. With deep regret, I pushed out of my chair, shrugged at Jaz-and-his-cravat, and chased after them.

They slowed in a gleaming, bustling kitchen where Ms. Sabel pulled a black duster over her dress and tossed back her ponytail.

Carmen came around a corner and stopped me. "Are you leaving? My shift just ended. Let's find Miguel and get a drink."

I didn't have time to explain our urgency. "Miguel's at my place with Emily. I whipped up a dinner but had to run."

"Emily's at your place?" She noticed my irritation. "OK with you if I join them?"

"Wine's in the cabinet." I gave her a smile and punched her shoulder.

I caught up with the women and the attorney Kevin halfway to the car barns. A door rose, spilling a square of light on the brick plaza. A Maserati Quattroporte GTS backed out, stopped, and Cousin Elmer hopped out. He held the driver's door for Ms. Sabel. Tania took shotgun with the same combative glare she'd used at dinner. Kevin and I struggled for legroom in the back.

At the front gate, a young guy and one of our agents argued. Otis Blackwell, Emily's archrival from the TV side of the news, faced us. Rumor was he'd taken Ms. Sabel to the prom in high school.

Ms. Sabel rolled her window down. "What brings you out tonight, Otis?"

The reporter leaned to the window. "Mass graves on Borneo, shootings at St. Muriel's, that kind of thing."

"How did your documentary turn out? Asian rivers, wasn't it?"

"Thanks for remembering," Otis said. "You're close. It was water conservation in China. We're having distribution issues at the moment. But thank you for funding the project. What happened on Borneo?"

"No comment," Ms. Sabel said. "But I owe you one. I'll call you."

Otis frowned and put his hands on her window. "Why didn't you call the Malaysian authorities?"

"I did, they … No comment."

"Right now, the news feeds make it sound like you were involved somehow. You should tell your side of the story before it gets out of hand. What did you find? How much did you see? Who did you tell?"

"We found a … No comment."

Kevin leaned across her. "I'm her attorney. She said she will call you. Back away—NOW."

Otis stepped back and put his hands up.

Ms. Sabel rolled forward before putting the hammer down on the accelerator.

Driving and talking, Ms. Sabel had me go over the plan several times. When we arrived at the Montgomery County Detention Center, Kevin and Ms. Sabel went into the administrator's office to finalize visitation arrangements.

Tania and I waited in a room with neatly grouped chairs sitting on the only scrap of carpet in the otherwise concrete building. Fluorescent lighting buzzed over our heads while an officer filled in paperwork at a big desk.

Tania leaned over and scowled at me. "You mess this up for me and I'll mess you up."

"Mess up what?"

I smelled burnt vinegar, same as the death camp. I sniffed the air. I wasn't sure if it was coming from Tania, or a memory of the smell.

"This job," she said. "I don't know how you wormed your way into this deal but I'll wreck you if you think you can cut me out."

Not wanting a confrontation, I stood and examined a plaque on the wall. Detention officers-of-the-month going back five years, minus the last six months, were listed on little brass tags.

Tania came up behind me. "You turned down Officer Candidate School in the Army because you didn't want your psych evaluations coming up. You know they'll check. Why did you go for this one?"

I looked over my shoulder at her. "I didn't put in for it. I didn't know Marty was leaving until this morning."

She grabbed my arm with a hot hand. "Don't mess with me, Jacob. I deserve this promotion."

"Tania, we talked her out of preventing a mass murder."

"We could've been killed. Or worse."

"She doesn't care about dying. She has some weird philosophy about death." I pulled her hand off me. Her whole arm was hot.

"Yeah, she told me that. If she dies, she joins her parents and if not, she has to fix the broken world we live in. Noble theory. But I know the real Pia, and she wants to live. No way she was going to flame out on Borneo."

"She thinks we should've tried harder." I bit the inside of my lip. "After I saw that picture of Kaya, I agree with her. We could have pulled it off." I reached for her forehead to check her temperature but she batted my hand away.

"Could have? We were outgunned big time. Gimme some of what you're smoking."

"Think about it. We park off the road. The Pak Uban flies by. You and I circle around and sneak through the bushes, pick them off, one at a time."

"You listening to those voices in your head again? More likely, the Pak Uban backtracks to the clinic and we face thirty hostiles with only three weapons and a translator."

"Might have worked." I shrugged. "Ms. Sabel thinks we should've tried."

"What's all that got to do with the promotion?" she asked.

"Tania." I gently squeezed her feverish arm. "It's not a promotion."

80

Chapter 12

Blue glass from Violet Windsor's ultra-modern condo reflected the dawn's rays down to the streets of Guangzhou like solar reflectors. People below held newspapers over their heads as much to block the rays as to fend off the industrial silt eternally suspended in the air.

"What do you mean 'arrested,' Marco?"

Violet took an orange from the bowl and stepped onto her balcony, where a strong breeze fluttered through her hair. She pulled her Dolce & Gabbana bathrobe tighter and retied the belt. Five hundred feet below, the city bustled with morning traffic as fourteen million people began their working day.

Marco Verratti made excuses on the phone while she checked the air quality index on her tablet. 154, the unhealthy zone, but that was at ground level.

"Your friends in Washington failed?" Violet interrupted him. "You're telling me that in a matter of days, your people managed to get arrested without destroying the vials? Can these men be traced back to you?"

"Violet, these situations are difficult—"

"I warned you she was dangerous," Violet said. She squeezed the orange so hard it split open. "How could you be so stupid?"

"I sent an attorney to—"

"Oh, god no. They'll follow the money back to you."

"You don't leave men incarcerated or they'll eventually rat you out. No, I take care of my people."

"Take care of your people? Are you crazy?" Violet said. "Pia Sabel will take care of your people. She'll have them turned against you in a day. Don't underestimate her. You have to do something. I don't care what it is. Blow up her house or—"

"Those are not options. She's stepped up security at Sabel Gardens, she has bulletproof autos, agents—"

"Thanks to you and your bumbling idiots!" Violet hurled the orange into the wide-open space before her. She looked at the juice dripping from her hand. "You thought you could beat Pia Sabel with street thugs? I should revoke your shares in the company and throw you off the board!"

"You can't do that."

"This is China. I can do anything Chen lets me."

"Don't threaten me," he shouted. "I have the package and my people are standing by with drones to deploy it. I'm in this just as deep as you."

He was right. She needed Element 42. She did her best to calm her rage.

Her phone clicked with another incoming call: Anatoly Mokin, one of the few board members outside her control. She said, "Do you know where the vials are?"

"Not exactly." Verratti said. "I am calling because you claimed to know someone close to her. I need to know where she's been. Where she might have taken them."

"I'll call you back."

She clicked over to the incoming call. "Anatoly, what can I do for you?"

"Stalin send my grandfather to Astana. There he establish our family. He teach us old Russian proverbs. My favorite: *bird is known by its flight*. You not tell Chen truth, and he is very angry. Now I discover you not tell me about missing blood vials. You not tell Chen either. We begin to know Violet Windsor by her flight."

"Mukhtar lost a few vials on the Borneo expedition. I didn't think it was worth getting him in trouble."

"Very big trouble." Mokin was silent for a moment. "But not for Mukhtar. Pia Sabel took them and now she is back in USA. Your project manager, Teresa, know this but did not tell Mukhtar."

Violet felt her jawbone tighten. She stared across the city for two beats. "What do you want?"

"I want to know what Violet Windsor think."

"I think Mukhtar should be shot for allowing the operation to be compromised by anyone who walked by. I think you should be ashamed of the way your incompetent security team—"

"Why you steal Element 42?"

"Don't try to change the subject. You need to take responsibility for security. You need to track down those vials and destroy them."

"You not answer question."

"I won't answer a loaded question. If you have any board-specific business relating to the direction of Windsor Pharmaceuticals, then state it. Otherwise, this conversation is over."

"I leave you with other Russian proverb: *Every cricket must know its hearth.*"

She clicked off and tapped her phone against the railing.

She strode back into her penthouse and into her bedroom. She shouted to her maid. "Bring me coffee."

Tossing her robe on the floor, she kicked off her house-leg and considered the closet brimming with clothes. Turning her attention back to her phone, she chose "Prince" from her contacts and dialed. She placed it on speaker and set it on a shelf while she chose a business suit.

"What do you want?" Prince said.

"Hello, how are you? It's been too long. I left you a message and hoped you would—"

"I'm busy. What do you want?"

"Well, I'm trying to get hold of Pia Sabel and she's never home these days. I don't have her mobile number. Do you know where she's been lately?"

"You heard someone shot up her old school?"

"Oh my god. Is she OK? Did she go straight to the police afterward?"

"She doesn't go to the police. They went to her. They met her at NIH."

"Why there?"

"She gave them some kind of grant for research."

"Of course, I should've known. Well, can you tell her I'm thinking about her?"

"Does she know who you are?" Prince clicked off.

Her maid held out her designer-leg and fresh stump sock. Violet grabbed them and put them on herself, then slipped into her skirt and pulled on a blouse. Violet sat at the table, dialed Ed Cummings, and opened her jewelry drawer.

The maid returned with a cup of coffee, premeasured creamer and sweetener, and set it on her dressing table.

When he picked up, she said, "Marco's men are in police custody."

"Jesus! Did they at least get the vials?" Cummings asked.

She chose a Mouawad Lava necklace and slipped it around her neck. "He can't be trusted. We need to replace him."

"I'm sending you the number for the Velox guy, Kasey Earl." Cummings sent her the contact. "But we can't replace Verratti's guys on deployment."

"You said Velox could do it."

"They can supplement on things like logistics, delivery of unmarked boxes, that kind of thing, but not deployment. Only Mafia guys will send up drones over every major city without asking questions."

"We can't use Marco." She picked up a matching bracelet and earrings. The dark yellow diamonds and citrine contrasting perfectly against her black velvet dress.

"I see. Call Kasey at Velox. Keep me out of it."

Chapter 13

Tania tried to intimidate me with her glare, but she blinked too slowly.

I said, "Babe, you're sick."

Addressing her with a term of endearment was a mistake. Like a rattlesnake trying to strike, she took a deep breath and pushed her nose up to mine. "What do you mean, *not a promotion?*"

"She's punishing us for failing to back her up. I think she's going to make us find the killers and take them down."

Tania's eyes darted around the visitor's room. She knew I was right but would never give me the satisfaction of admitting it. She wobbled on her feet.

"Sit down." I grabbed her arms, held her steady, and guided her back to the chairs.

"Shut up." Her eyes closed for a long time. "I'll be taking care of myself."

Ms. Sabel stepped in behind me. "We were in a quarantined area. You're going to the hospital for a full exam."

Tania dropped into a chair. "I'm just a little tired, that's all. Don't mean I'm sick."

Ms. Sabel told the cop on duty to call an ambulance. Then she dialed Doc Günter, the Sabels' doctor, and set him up to meet Tania at the hospital. He walked us through some basic tests for heart rate and fever.

Mercury said, Yo. Told you it was Ebola. Now the only woman you had a shot at is going to die. You should've gotten tests as soon as you got back.

I said, It's not Ebola. Now shut up, I need to think.

Mercury said, Go ahead, think. I know how hard that is for you.

Her eyes had a hint of blue in the sclera. My stomach twisted in knots as I realized just how sick she was and how many opportunities I'd had to do something smart.

The ambulance arrived and whisked her away in minutes. Ms. Sabel and I made some serious eye contact.

"You look good," she said.

"So do you," I said. "I mean your eyes look good. Uh, your eyes aren't blue."

She wrung her hands, a movement I found myself imitating without thinking.

"She's strong and healthy," I said.

Ms. Sabel nodded, unconvinced.

Doc Günter called and assured us he would give us periodic updates from her isolation room, but we were not to visit until they understood her condition.

With our ability to help her ended, we resumed our mission and followed a detention officer to the visitor's room.

The gray-haired thug, now clad in bright orange, sat in a booth behind inch-thick Plexiglas. Shiny silver handcuffs kept his wrists close together.

The booth was narrow, so I motioned for Ms. Sabel to take the seat. Kevin, the attorney, carried himself like a former soldier, so I whispered, "Parade rest."

He and I stepped into the small space slightly behind Ms. Sabel. We clasped our hands, planted our feet shoulder distance apart, squared our shoulders, chests out, and fixed our eyes on a distant horizon.

Zebo Amato—Gray-hair—stared at us, pretending he wasn't impressed. He picked up the handset tethered to the wall.

Ms. Sabel picked up hers. "Mr. Amato, my sources tell me the LaRocca Family has recalled their lawyer. You took a job on the side, off the Family's turf, and word has it they're pissed."

Amato sneered.

"Whoever asked you to do this job should've done it himself. But he didn't. He left you in jail with a public defender. Why did he leave you hanging like that?"

Amato didn't move.

"No doubt you've figured it out by now. Your friend forgot to tell you I employ three thousand veterans of the wars in Afghanistan and Iraq. He set you up to fail."

Amato shifted in his seat.

"You have two options. First, you can do the tough-guy thing where you do a little time instead of talking. The prosecutor will go hard and the jury will be horrified that you shot up a school in Montgomery County. But you'll only get a couple years. The drawback to that option is not the sentence, it's Jacob's friends—the other twenty-nine hundred ninety-nine Sabel Security employees who plan to take turns visiting you back home. Do the math. You'll have a visitor every day for more than eight years."

Amato smirked. Then coughed.

"Before you think you're tougher than them, remember, they were not only trained to kill, but they've had plenty of practice—not scaring strung-out dope dealers and young prostitutes, but going up against insane fundamentalists who think dying for Allah is a good thing. However many people you killed, my veterans have killed ten times that, each. Don't get me wrong, Mr. Amato. I don't condone violence in my organization. I'm just telling you what my people do in their free time when someone attacks a member of *their* family."

Amato's gaze swung up to check me out then back to Ms. Sabel. He squinted while the wheels of logic creaked into action in his head. Anyone watching him could tell he didn't like the odds of a rumble against my team. What could LaRocca put on the field, twenty gangsters? Thirty? We had a hundred veterans show up for a company Frisbee game. I forced back a smirk of my own.

"You have another option." She tossed a thumb over her shoulder at Kevin. "I'm offering you this man as your attorney. Kevin charges a thousand dollars an hour and will get you off as lightly as possible. I pay the bills. You go home sooner rather than later. Jacob's friends will complain, but I'll let them take down Boko Haram for fun, and they'll stand down. Probably."

Amato leaned toward the glass. "What I gotta do?"

"Tell me who called you."

Amato looked like he'd been slapped. He leaned back.

"He set you up to fail. Do you owe him enough to take a fall for him? Don't worry, I'll take care of the guy. He will never know how I found his name." Ms. Sabel paused. "You have five seconds to decide. Then I'm walking to the room down the hall where I'll offer the same deal to Mr. Pecora. I spoke to you first because the guards said you were the smart one."

Amato said nothing.

Ms. Sabel put her phone on the counter and held up a hand with her fingers outstretched. After the first second ticked by, she pulled down her thumb. Then her index finger.

Amato grinned.

She pulled down her little finger.

Amato frowned.

Just as she tucked in her ring finger, leaving only her middle finger fully extended, he leaned forward and nodded at her handset. She picked it up.

"Marco Verratti. And go ahead, tell the fat fuck I squealed. He let me do his niece a few years ago and called this in as payment. Fuck that shit. She was fat and ugly like him." Zebo Amato put the phone down and nodded at the guard.

We played the same game with Mr. Pecora and came up with the same name. Pecora didn't like Verratti either. Since the answers matched, we headed out.

Doc Günter called from the hospital. Tania was very sick but he was stumped about the cause. A battery of tests were underway. She ended the call as I held the detention center's door open.

In the distance, burning leaves brought comfort-scents our way. Autumn surrounded us with a damp chill and slow-moving clouds obscured the moon.

Jaz Jenkins stood on the walkway outside. "Hey Angel! It's a fabulous night for a moon dance beneath October skies. Care to take a spin in a convertible?"

She stopped. I separated to maximize my field of fire. My eyes locked on Jaz. He was hardly a threat so I surveyed the rest of the area. Kevin strode past us, his mind on the billable hours he was about to rake in, and stopped at the Maserati, staring at it the way some men look at strippers. Just beyond him, Otis Blackwell pulled up in his van.

"I'd love to," Ms. Sabel said with a glance into Jaz's eyes. "But I'm busy right now. Something's come up."

She took a step, then stopped. "How did you know where I went?"

"Cousin Elmer," Jaz said with a curious look.

Without another word, she brushed past him.

In that instant, all rivalry fell away and I felt sorry for the overprivileged bastard. Dissed in public after badly misquoting an old love song. That kind of thing could leave a man shriveled for days. I gave him an empathetic shrug.

"Pia, why are you visiting the Detention Center?" Otis Blackwell scrambled from his van, bobbling a large video camera.

"I told you I'd call you later." She never broke stride.

I stepped between them and gave him my soldier stare. Otis had never seen that look before and staggered back.

Ms. Sabel took pity on Kevin's Maserati-lust and let him drive. She took shotgun and I sat behind Kevin.

Falls Road was closed for an accident near the Rockville Fire Station, so Kevin detoured down Glen Road. The route took us past some of the equestrian estates that made Potomac famous. Huge houses sat back from the road overlooking expanses of grass with white rail fences. A pair of graceful horses galloped alongside us. We were deep in the woods a few seconds later.

"Why were you so hard on Jaz?" I asked. "You don't like him?"

"He's handsome," she said.

"But he's a wuss."

She smiled in profile, lit by the orange dashboard. She was too polite to agree. She told me how Jaz's father, Bobby Jenkins, married a young woman every ten years and divorced them after they'd delivered two children. Despite being over sixty, he was on his third wife and had two kids in elementary school.

"So what's Jaz's story?" I asked. "He's everywhere."

"My dad and his dad are best friends. So Jaz ends up invited to the Gardens all the time."

"The dads are trying to hook you two up?"

"Do your parents have someone picked out for you?" She leaned around the headrest to face me.

"Yeah, but I don't want to talk about it."

She faced front. "Same."

Mercury said, Dude, you should quit listening to the babble of beautiful babes and start thinking about your future. This shit's about to get serious.

You might expect an ancient Roman God to have an upper-crust English accent—after all, eloquence is among his holy duties—but he has a screwy theory that rappers will define twenty-first century rhetoric. It wouldn't be a bad theory if he would bother to get it right.

A bang, a jolt, and we were instantly traveling sideways. Air bags exploded and crunching steel groaned. Shattered glass flew everywhere. The driver's side of the car collapsed to the edge of my left knee. Kevin was dead before the bullets raked the car.

Chapter 14

Ms. Sabel burst out her door and rolled into the dark. I untangled my seatbelt and followed.

A man shouted. The language sounded familiar, but I couldn't place it.

One roll from the car, I saw a shadow running into the trees. I fired two rounds but heard nothing fall. Rolling farther, the bullets from an AK-47 followed me by a yard. Four trees separated me from the shooter before I rose to my feet and took a peek around an elm.

Lights from a riding stable silhouetted a man with a gun. I put him down.

Muzzle flashes erupted from three points around me.

Dead center in a crossfire was not a good tactical position, so I ran and tripped on thick weeds. I fell face-first and slid down a slope until I found a tree with my forehead. Listening intently, I heard them begin a systematic search from the hilltop. The language sounded Arabic but not quite.

I listened for Ms. Sabel. Nothing. She'd gone more to the left where I'd gone right. I traversed the slope and picked my way through bramble into an open area. The darkness was nearly total. I had no equipment with me and made a mental note: never go anywhere with Ms. Sabel without body armor, night vision, and an assault rifle at a minimum. Full battle rattle preferred.

Three muzzle flashes in rapid succession blinded me an instant before a body dropped to the forest floor five yards behind me.

I dropped and scrambled in the dark to the fallen body. A man stared at me with glassy eyes, the flaccid paralysis stage of a Sabel dart. He stunk like a wet dog and his breath smelled like crap. I patted him down and found nothing but empty pockets and two magazines. A quick search of the area around him earned me his AK-47 which I slung and crabbed my way back under cover.

No one had fired back at Ms. Sabel when she took down the man stalking me. That meant the last two were the serious pros, probably the squad leader and his top guy. They knew enough not to shoot blindly in the dark. Which meant we were in Darwinian Combat mode: only the smart survive.

Two more muzzle flashes gave away her position. But no more bodies dropped. They would approach her in a v-formation, ten to twenty yards from each other, closing down. I circled around to a position at right angles to their path, hoping to nail one. My ears strained to hear anything.

The only sounds I could hear were the treetops brushing each other in the soft breeze. In the distance a siren wailed. The police station was more than two miles away. We'd have help in five minutes.

But I could wipe out a village in five minutes. No doubt these guys could do the same.

A shadow moved in an unnatural way. As I snuck up on it, it moved again, this time in the right direction for a bad guy. I stepped toward the shadow's right, slightly behind him ten feet away.

A quick snap of a branch and the shadow was gone.

Putting myself in his place, I figured going to ground was the best bet. I squeezed under a fallen log, my fingers clawing through the decayed leaves and mud. In that composted space, the charming scent of autumn smelled more like pond scum.

Mercury said, Aw man. Need a flashlight? He's right in front of you, bro. Feel the vibes he's giving off.

Dark was the only thing in front of me. As I peered forward, something just beyond my weapon's sights looked out of place. My eyes labored to make sense of shapes in the darkness. It was a white triangle smaller than a fingernail, six inches off the ground, five feet ahead.

There were two of them.

Then the triangles blinked.

I pulled the trigger.

He exhaled some seriously bad breath.

Three more shots from Ms. Sabel's Glock shattered the quiet. No thuds. No return fire.

Ms. Sabel had been through the Sabel Security training program several times. She knew to count down her shots fired. She also knew to carry an extra mag, but she carried it in her purse, and I was sure that was still in the wreckage.

She had one dart left.

She fired it.

Nothing fell.

I scrambled to my feet and ran sideways, away from where she'd found cover. An AK-47 flashed half a magazine in my direction. The light was blinding but I caught a glimpse of the guy. He had the same stocky build and wore a cheap shirt.

There was a thump, then another, followed by an 'oof'. I flicked on my phone's flashlight in time to see Ms. Sabel with a fistful of the man's shirt in one hand and a right cross smashing down into his left eye. She followed up with knee to the groin and another to the stomach. She let go of his shirt, let him stagger back a step, and stepped in with a rapid combination. Left, left, right cross, uppercut, and a blur of jabs. She stopped for a second and he swung a weak roundhouse in her general direction. Her knees bent, and her torso swayed back, defying gravity, while his fist passed harmlessly in front of her nose. With his momentum carrying his right shoulder past her core, she put a hand on his shoulder and pushed.

His head smacked an oak. He slid to the ground.

I'd seen soldiers get on each other's nerves and light into each other, but I'd never seen anyone like Pia Sabel. It wasn't her strength that won the fight, it was her quickness. Each blow had come faster than the guy could defend himself.

Ms. Sabel held the light while I went through his pockets. Nothing. His clothes were brand new, still creased from the store. His boots were military. Thick leather with heavy soles meant to last a million marching miles.

"Who are these guys?" Ms. Sabel asked.

"He has the same ethnic look as Chapman's men back on Borneo."

"Can we make him talk?" Ms. Sabel said.

"In what language? I heard them earlier but couldn't place it. Sounded like a Turkic language, but that's a range from Bosnia to Western China."

The sirens grew louder and so did our victim's gasping. He was coming around. We dragged him up the hill as the cops arrived and lit up the scene with spotlights. We staggered out of the woods, dropped our captive, and held our hands up until the cops were satisfied we were the good guys.

We walked around the tangled wreckage while an officer drifted behind us taking notes and asking questions. A truck with a snowplow attachment was parked in the middle of the Maserati.

"They wanted to kill us with that?" Ms. Sabel asked.

"No. The AK-47s were for killing. You often travel in a bulletproof limo, so they used this contraption. It would've cracked anything in half. They did their homework."

"The neighbors reported this truck stolen an hour ago," the officer said.

Ms. Sabel said, "They're not working for Verratti then."

I looked at her, trying to figure out how she came to that conclusion. She stared at me with those gray-green eyes. She knew something but wasn't sharing. Either she didn't trust me or she expected me to have figured it out. I didn't want to look stupid, so I nodded as if I knew.

I turned to the investigating cop. "There was an accident on Falls Road by the fire station. What happened?"

"Car fire, right in the middle of the street."

"You haven't found the driver, right?"

He shook his head and watched us, impatiently waiting for an explanation.

"One of the attackers set the fire," Ms. Sabel said. "That forced the detour. They were waiting for us." She faced me. "How long would it have taken them to set this up?"

"Assuming they'd already located a truck with a snowplow with an eye toward an ambush, all they had to do was steal it and attach the plow, steal another car and torch it, get into position … a couple hours."

"What time did we leave dinner?"

"A couple hours ago."

We continued our inspection of the car. The interior of the Maserati had been rifled. The contents of Ms. Sabel's purse were strewn on the ground. The glove box had been ripped open with a crowbar.

She stared at Kevin's lifeless body while a tear formed in her eye.

The cop asked, "Why kill your attorney?"

"Look at the bullet patterns on the car," I said. "Everyone knows Ms. Sabel likes to drive. All the bullets came from the front left and into the driver's seat."

"They wanted to kill her." The cop nodded slowly and left us to ponder her enemies.

It wasn't the first time someone wanted to kill her, but this attempt was closer than the others. Ms. Sabel's gaze remained fixed on the blood and gore that stained Kevin's shirt and suit.

"They don't need to kill me to get the vials," she said.

Chapter 15

Ms. Sabel stepped into my personal space. "Kaya and twenty-eight others were killed. Tania's sick, gangsters shot up my school, and now Kevin's been murdered. I'm going to press the opportunity immediately. I'm going to follow the vials wherever they lead and bring down whoever's behind this before any more mass graves appear. Hopefully, I'll find a cure for Tania along the way. Are you with me?"

This was how her disasters always started. Her indignation flares up and she takes off on a mission to nowhere with inadequate intelligence and underwhelming resources. Anyone who cared about Ms. Sabel would talk her down, have her think things through, let the authorities follow the leads. Only a fool would join her.

"Damn straight," I said.

Mercury said, Wahoo! That's my homie! Living the hero life. Never fearing death. You da man, Jacob.

When the investigators finished their questions, Cousin Elmer picked us up in a bulletproof stretch Bentley. Agents Miguel and Carmen waited inside with our pre-packed overnight bags. Ms. Sabel's plan was to follow the Verratti lead in Milan, Italy. But first, she had to check on her lab rats.

We pulled into the National Institute of Health's sprawling campus and stopped at the NIH Bio-Defense Institute. Ms. Sabel and I went to see the bugmen while the others waited.

Doc Günter waited for us with two security guards in the lobby, his shiny, bald head giving him away at a distance. One guard waved us forward, swiped his badge across the sensor, and opened a large door. As we walked, Doc gave us a rundown of Tania's condition: high fever, blue sclera, difficulty breathing, and several other factors. They'd given her tests for known diseases such as dengue fever, Ebola, flu, malaria, and everything else they could think of with no results. He'd brought a vial of her blood for the NIH docs to study with the others.

We went up a level and through a maze of empty gray cubicles in a darkened cube farm before coming to another big door. Another swipe and we were in a biohazard lab right out of a horror flick. Tyvek suits hung along the wall leading to a glass-encased room with yellow warnings all over it. Everywhere there were tangles of computers, scanners, sterilizers, shakers, and spectrometers. Our guard-guide pointed down the rows to the back where lights were still on, and then left without a word. A doctor in a lab coat waited in the otherwise deserted lab.

Doc introduced us to Dr. Carlton, who gazed at the floor and scraped a toe across the carpet. "I appreciate the urgency, Ms. Sabel. Doctor Günter told us about your friend. We discovered many things, but, sorry to say, how to cure your friend is not one of them. However, we do have a better idea of the nature of her disease."

"And that is?" Doc Günter said.

'We know it's related to the Ebola virus."

Mercury said, Dude, what'd I tell you, huh? And you've been sniffing her, standing next to her, talking to her. You're a sick bitch. Get away from me.

"She has Ebola?" Ms. Sable asked.

"That's the strange part. It has several Ebola genes—and its protein coat—but then there are significant differences. For one, it appears to have been engineered."

"You mean man-made?" Doc Günter asked. "With gene splicing?"

Dr. Carlton brightened at Günter's question, preferring to talk to another scientist. "This virus is more advanced than even our worst fears. It carries three genes for the viral coat, the chief way the immune system recognizes the virus. This one shape shifts every time it replicates. Completely random. Your body would have a terrible time developing an immune response before it kills you."

Doc Günter tapped his chin and frowned. "That would make it particularly virulent in the young and old."

"Worse, with the gene splicing technology, the company that produced this could easily insert new genes and start a new pandemic all over again. They could adjust the virus to defeat vaccines or attack specific ethnic groups or pre-existing medical conditions."

"What do you mean pre-existing medical conditions?" I asked.

"The virus we've seen attacks a weak immune system, anyone under two or over seventy, or with diabetes, cancer, or medications that weaken the immune system. But it could be re-engineered to specifically attack people with asthma or high cholesterol."

"What was that about ethnic groups?" Ms. Sabel asked.

Dr. Carlton sighed with sadness. "You know how there are ethnic diseases like sickle-cell disease among Africans or celiac disease among Jews? This could be re-engineered to specifically target Arabs or Mayans or Eskimos, any distinct ethnic group."

"Why the blue eyes?" I asked.

"Side effect of one of the coat genes, or an intentional marker. We think all the internal tissues would be blue as well. We need more time to figure it out."

"Sclera is the only visible internal tissue," Doc Günter told us. "The inside of Tania's mouth was blue, also internal tissue."

"Why would someone create a disease? Bio-warfare?" I asked.

"Despite all the sci-fi themes, biological weapons are too slow and too easy to isolate. If someone wanted to commit crimes against humanity, they'd work with more effective agents like nerve gas."

"But, could it be weaponized?" I asked.

"An engineered pathogen is a weapon. How lethal it is depends on how communicable it is and how it's delivered."

"They said it was contagious," Ms. Sabel said.

"Not in our early tests. We know it's not airborne, but we don't know the route of entry yet."

"But Tania caught it on Borneo," I said.

"She might have ingested it, cut her finger, or poked herself with a needle, or maybe it was administered in a way she didn't notice. We don't know."

"Ingested? Like a pill or injection?" I asked.

"All I know is, it doesn't replicate from host to host."

We didn't drink the water and they didn't give us injections. Then I remembered the dying man's last word at the death camp: "bad cloth."

Mercury said, Did you feel that, dude? Air currents are moving.

I said, We're in a secure facility.

Mercury said, So was Julius Caesar.

"What about the rag?" I asked Carlton.

He shook his head. "What rag?"

Ms. Sabel said, "We found an old rag with the vials, but I didn't send it."

"It could hold the key to the transmission," he said. "Have it sent right away."

Ms. Sabel turned her back on them to whisper in my ear. "I didn't want to play all my cards in one lab."

I remembered the extra vial and managed to keep my mouth shut. The docs kept talking and Ms. Sabel moved behind me.

Mercury said, Bro, you're head of personal security, act like it.

"What's the cure?" Ms. Sabel said loudly from a few yards away.

Without my realizing it, she'd moved five paces down a row of shoulder-high lab equipment and had her weapon drawn.

I drew mine and glanced around the lab. Catching Ms. Sabel's gaze, I silently asked what worried her. She nosed at the next aisle. I went left, she went right.

Our brainiacs kept talking while I focused on whatever was bothering the boss. I moved to the next aisle and took a peek around the corner. Empty. At the far end, she cleared the aisle, her barrel aiming at me briefly, then moved to the next. There was a loud crash, followed by a banging door and an alarm. I ran to the far end in time to see Ms. Sabel disappear through the door into the cube farm.

Running in top gear, I caught a glimpse of her turning down a row of head-high cubicles. I saw nothing out of place as I flew by the aisles. I turned one row ahead of Ms. Sabel and stumbled over a lab coat with a researcher's badge someone had dropped in the aisle. I stopped and listened for any sign of what was going on. Ms. Sabel was running an aisle over but there were no other footsteps. She rounded the end of my aisle and saw me.

A blur crashed into her, throwing her sideways.

I made the distance in five quick bounds, leading with my weapon.

Ms. Sabel was facedown on the floor with a man on top of her, holding a gun to her head. The man said, "Hands where I can see them. NOW!"

She pushed her Glock forward on the carpet.

When he leaned over to pick it up, I stepped quietly behind him and pressed my weapon to his skull. "Same for you, Verges. Hands where I can see them."

Another alarm went off. This time behind me. Grabbing Verges by the shirt collar, I dragged him backward a few steps with me, just in time to see a man disappear down the fire exit at the far end of the aisle. I dropped Verges and ran after the shadow.

"Drop your weapon now!" Verges shouted. "I swear to god, I'll fire, Stearne." He was just green enough to do it without realizing how much paperwork the FBI would make him fill out afterwards. "Get on the ground now."

I dropped to my knees with my hands out and up. On the building's backside, a motorcycle started up and sped away.

Ms. Sabel ran up behind Verges, ready to beat the daylights out of him.

"Don't!" I waved her off. "He's a federal employee."

She stopped and threw me a puzzled look.

"Assaulting a federal employee is a felony," I said.

She shrugged *so what* and took off running down the aisle past both of us. I jumped up and ran after her. Instead of going to the exit, she went to the window on the backside of the building. She screamed "shit!" and pounded her fists on the giant panes so hard the glass shook like a drum head.

She turned around and stormed back to Verges, grabbing the lab coat off the floor. "Goddamn, it! You son—"

"Guns are not allowed in federal facilities, ma'am. I don't care who you are, you're not above the—"

"That was Dr. Chapman!" She yelled so loud it hurt my ears. She held out the badge on the lab coat: Windsor Pharmaceuticals, Consulting Researcher, Chapman, A. "The man responsible for the mass graves on Borneo. The man who put Tania Cooper in the hospital. I would've caught him. But you stopped me. Why?"

Chapter 16

A light fog of toxic dust rolled through Guangzhou's central district with silt so fine that only a few people donned their surgical masks. Violet's driver opened her door and offered a hand.

"Umbrella," she said.

She had no intention of ruining her Akris pantsuit in the pollution. The driver returned a second later with the covering fully extended. She rose, felt her leg shift and limped forward. The designer leg had more style, and gave her the option of wearing her Rupert Sanderson pumps, but it slipped too often. She would have words with the technician who'd fitted her.

Ed Cummings called as she walked to the tower under the canopy.

"What the hell did you do, Violet?" Cummings asked.

"What are you talking about?" She pushed through the revolving door while her driver loped back to the limo.

"I didn't give you the Velox contact for this," Ed said.

"Don't talk to me in riddles. What's going on?"

"Look up the *Post's* website."

Violet clicked off and pulled up the site on her phone. She scanned the short update: Pia Sabel attacked, one dead, four in custody, the sleepy Washington suburb of Potomac, MD shocked.

She called Cummings back.

"How could you possibly think I had anything to do with this?" The elevator doors opened on her floor.

"I gave you Kasey's phone number," Cummings said. "It's being treated like a terrorist attack. This better not come back to me."

"Verratti," she said. "I gave him an earful about failure. He must have overreacted."

"Marcus wouldn't ... would he?"

"I didn't do it. Did you?" She steamed through her executive reception area.

"On another topic, one of Sabel's best friends came down with it. She's in the hospital."

"How do you know—"

"It gets worse," Cummings said. "The Malaysian authorities are—"

Her secretary held up a hand, *stop*, and pointed to the back of the reception area where a slight figure stood alone.

Chen Zhipeng stood with his back to her, examining something on a chest-high table.

"I have to go." Violet's voice sank as she clicked off.

She checked her prosthesis before crossing the marble and came up behind him. "*Shifu*, I had no idea you were in town. I would've sent the limo—"

He turned halfway to her, his fingertips touching a small plant. "This is a bonsai tree."

"Yes. Quite lovely. An amazing art form."

"It is not. Bonsai is a Japanese bastardization of Penjing, the original Chinese art."

Violet turned to her secretary. "How could you let this happen? Have the decorator replace it immediately, then fire him."

Chen reached out for her hand and took it in his. "I did not plan to visit Guangzhou today, but I am quite surprise to find you here."

Violet's eyes darted from side to side. "This is my office. Where would—"

"You failed to tell me about three vial of blood." He squeezed her hand hard.

"The security man, Mukhtar," she said, "reported it to Anatoly Mokin. Anatoly told me about it and I had the impression that he had already discussed—"

"Do not leave it to board member to keep me informed." Chen's face reddened and he leaned toward her as he spoke. "This project is very sensitive. You have my phone number. When trouble happen, you call me. No more mess around."

Violet leaned back, then bowed. "I understand, *Shifu*."

"You do not." He stepped closer. "Wu Fang handled those vial. They must be retrieved immediately." His black, unblinking eyes stared at her. "I need insurance that China will survive if the program become public. You must supervise the search in person."

"Of course, I—"

"Have you found the missing Element 42 and Levoxavir?"

"I've asked Anatoly to conduct a thorough investigation. I don't expect to hear back from him until later today. In light of all the missing items, I'm afraid I must replace Mokin Enterprises immediately."

Chen bounced on his feet and clasped his hands behind his back. He turned back to the bonsai. "Do you have a reliable security company in mind to replace them?"

"I understand Velox Deployment Services is capable of handling a site without losing the most important components."

Chen nodded without looking up, a thin smile stretched across his mouth.

"Have you heard of them?" she asked.

"Mokin Enterprises is based in China, and is an operation I can control if anything leaks to the press. Do not make any changes."

"They allowed Wu Fang and Pia Sabel into the compound, they've lost the very things they were hired to protect. I need to make a— "

"You listen to me. I do not say thing twice. Windsor is based in China and subject to Chinese law. This is most important issue. You get all three vial back from Sabel."

Chen went to the elevators. When the doors sealed him inside, she closed her eyes and took a deep breath. Letting it out, she turned to her secretary. "Get me on the next flight to Washington and put a driver on standby all week."

Violet ran to her office and closed the door. She dialed her Velox contact.

"Who is this?" a gruff voice answered.

"I'm Violet Windsor, I was referred to you—"

"What is this, some kinda joke?"

Violet set her purse on her desk and stared out her window. "No, I'm Violet Windsor and I've been referred—"

"Lemme guess, Shane put you up to this, right?"

"What?"

"C'mon, who are you really?" the gruff voice said.

"I'm Violet Windsor, President and CEO of Windsor Pharmaceuticals and I'm calling because Ed Cummings told me Velox provides better security than Mokin Enterprises. If you think that's a joke, perhaps I should speak to your superiors."

"Holy shit, you really are Windsor. Well, what can I do for you, sugar?"

"For starters, never call me 'sugar' again. After that, I need to recover a package that Marcus Verratti, of Milan, Italy stole from me. Are you capable of a simple operation like that?"

"Where've I heard that name before?"

"I asked a simple question. Are you capable of—"

"Hang on, lemme Google that one. Verratti. Mafia boss, right? Wait a sec, he's involved in the Collettivo, the financial mafia, investments and that shit. Yeah, that's the guy. They call him Milan's Don and you want me to steal from him? Steal from the Mafia—in Italy?"

"Actually, I have reason to believe my stolen property is in Philadelphia, in the hands of a smaller group."

"Sugar, you must have a lot of money."

"Don't call me that again. I was told your organization is qualified for an operation on that scale."

"I have the operations, but you pay in advance. You know what I'm saying, sugar?"

"If you call me 'sugar' one more time, I'm going—"

"What, take your business to Sabel Security?" The man roared with laughter.

~~~

Kasey Earl clicked off from Violet Windsor's call and stared at his phone for a moment. He checked the caller ID, then typed it into his database. The number belonged to Windsor Pharma of Guangzhou. He tapped his finger on the table for a minute then leaned back in his chair and dialed his boss.

When the call connected, Kasey said, "You ain't going to believe who just called me."

Chapter 17

Ms. Sabel's jet has a great couch. It's long enough for a six-foot guy like me to stretch out and get some rest. There's another couch opposite that fits a six-foot woman like Ms. Sabel. Once you're used to the noise of the engines, the ride is sweet and you can close your eyes and wait for the inevitable shriek. After the horrific murder of her parents, Ms. Sabel became an insomniac who wakes up screaming after three hours of shut-eye. When you're resting on the couch across from her, you wait, tense with anticipation, for what you know is coming.

An hour before landing in Milan, it happened. She shrieked.

It embarrassed her when we jumped up and formed a defensive perimeter, so I faked sleeping through it. She went forward and sat with Carmen. The noise of engines drowned most of their conversation but I heard enough.

"He's not exactly a hunk," Ms. Sabel said. "So why do women fall for him?"

"He's dangerous and unstable," Carmen said, "kind of a fixer-upper."

"Bad boys have a certain type of appeal for a short time, but why do they go back?"

"If he's not handsome, rich, or charming, what does that leave you?"

In the stunning silence that followed, I could feel their eyes turn my way.

The jet angled downward for the approach into Milan. I'd not slept a wink. I dove into my kit to grab a Provigil—the alertness

medication and wonder drug of modern armies around the world—
to keep me on my toes.

We were following our only lead, Marco Verratti, to Italy in the
hopes of finding a cure for Tania and discovering who was
responsible for the mass graves on Borneo. It was the slimmest of
leads, but the only one we had.

Milan is a fashion town where the glamor masks the region's
sordid underbelly. To shake down a global mega-corporation the
Mafia had to evolve, and Verratti's international investment fund, the
Collettivo, was the latest evolutionary step. They would short a stock
and knock off the CEO or plant underage girls in his bedroom and
reap a windfall profit when the share price fell.

After landing, we drove into Monte Napoleone, the fashion
district where the buildings sparkled above streets so clean they
seemed to be waiting for a fresh coat of blood. Marchisio, Sabel
Security's Italian agent, met us in Cartier's on Via Gesù. He'd tracked
our target to Brioni, the men's store for millionaires, half a block
down.

We left separately to take up positions. Carmen watched the street
in front. Miguel wound his way into a courtyard in back. Ms. Sabel,
Marchisio, and I moved in to take down Verratti.

We strode down the quiet, narrow lane with planters defining a
sidewalk on one side. Vespa and Lambretta scooters created their
own parking spaces between the planters. Cold, low clouds cruised
overhead smelling of rain. I wore my leather jacket and jeans with a t-
shirt that read, *Helping martyrs reach their goals since 2002.* Ms. Sabel
wore her trademark yoga pants and microfiber shirt covered by a
steampunk jacket.

*Mercury said, I saw that glance, homeslice. Never sneak a peek at the boss—
your words.*

"Shut up," I said.

Marchisio looked up. "What did I say?"

"Nuthin." I shoved my hands in my pockets.

Ms. Sabel barged into the Brioni store with the authority of a rich
woman assault-shopping. With a quick survey, I counted two

employees, Verratti's two goons, and one older, weather-beaten, but well-dressed Eurasian shopper. In the center of the store was a guy who matched the pictures we'd found of Verratti, looking at shirts.

The biggest goon turned his attention my way. I ignored him and nodded to Marchisio. "She needs you to translate."

Marchisio pinched a frown but moved without argument. As the big goon moved his attention to my comrade, I pulled my Glock and put a dart in the big guy's leg.

The other goon had a Beretta aimed at my head before his pal hit the floor. Swinging left, Ms. Sabel dropped my assailant with a single shot. Verratti spun around with a right hook that caught our Napoli agent in the wrong place. He fell.

Ms. Sabel hit Verratti with three rapid punches that didn't faze him in the least. He might have been old and fat, but he had built his career on the streets. Weaving through mannequins to approach from his blindside, I pressed my Glock to his neck.

"We're not here to hurt anyone," I said.

His hands went up cautiously. One eye tried to peer sideways at me while the other met Ms. Sabel's cold stare with equal intensity.

"You must be Pia Sabel," he said.

I slipped plasticuffs around his surprisingly cooperative wrists while she pressed her weapon under his chin. I did another quick check. One store employee stood at the counter with a phone in his hand and his mouth hanging open. The other employee stood in an entryway to the back room, his mouth even wider. The well-dressed customer leaned an elbow on the counter, watching us as if we were children on a playground.

"Put the phone down," I said to the guy behind the counter.

He didn't move.

The well-dressed customer gave the employee an amused nod and the employee fumbled the phone back to the cradle.

"Your man Zebo sends his regards," Ms. Sabel said to Verratti. "But I'm not sure if he wanted me to repeat his remarks about your fat, ugly niece."

Verratti stared back, blank.

From the corner of my eye, I saw the well-dressed customer stifle a laugh.

"Why did you try to kill me last night?"

Verratti smirked. "You are unpopular, everyone wants to kill you."

"What's so important about the vials?" I moved to his side.

"I say nothing to you."

"Why do you want them back?"

He tightened his mouth and lifted his chin.

Mercury said, Whoa, dawg, the bad guys are coming, you should do something useful like—run away.

I have their boss, I'm good.

Mercury said, No, you're not. Get to the roof.

Carmen's voice crackled over the comm link. "Abort. Repeat, abort."

Miguel said, "Confirmed, abort."

The sound of two muffled shots followed. Ms. Sabel and I stared at each other for what felt like an eternity but was half a second.

"Abort now," Carmen repeated with urgency. "Three ski masks converging on the store. Heavily armed."

"Two here," Miguel said. "Darted. Come my way—now."

"I need help with our friend," I said. "And Marchisio."

"Negative," Carmen said. "Leave them. Go now."

Ms. Sabel darted Verratti and I grabbed Marchisio as he regained his senses. We ran for the back room. We left the well-dressed man watching while the two employees followed us. We burst through the door into the courtyard behind the store, setting off an alarm. Miguel stood in a shooter's stance, aiming behind us. I stumbled over a black-clad operator lying on the ground but kept my balance. We ducked around the first stone wall and stopped.

"Who are these guys?" Miguel asked.

The two employees babbled in Italian, pleading and accusing at the same time from the sound of their voices.

"They think we're the bad guys," Marchisio said. "They think someone worse is coming. The customer inside was warning them of a hit on Verratti moments before we came in."

"Why would the Mafia warn them?"

Marchisio shrugged. "To avoid collateral damage. Even the Mafia cares about bad press."

"He didn't look Italian," Ms. Sabel said.

Miguel peered around the corner. The burping noise of automatic weapons erupted inside the store.

Carmen's voice came through the comm link. "Go north. Repeat, north on Via Gesú."

"Roger that." I pushed my way around Miguel. The narrow courtyard we were in led to a small alcove, closed on all sides. Miguel nodded upward to a ladder bolted to the wall that ran up four floors to the roof.

Mercury said, Stay frosty, homie. Watch your back, these mofos will hunt you down.

Holstering my weapon, I scaled the rungs with Ms. Sabel right behind me. Miguel and Marchisio covered us and we returned the favor when we reached the top. The Brioni boys decided to wait it out, flinching and trembling, on the ground level. Treading carefully across slick metal-sheathed roofs, we made our way north along the rooftops looking for a ladder down. We were looking into a restaurant courtyard when we heard rounds ricochet off the roof.

A figure stood at the top of the ladder behind us, an assault rifle in one hand.

Miguel and I drew and fired with more hope than expectation. Sabel darts are the longest range, non-lethal projectile available, but the accuracy squirrels as the distance increases. The lone figure dropped to all fours, his rifle clattering down the sloped roof. He scrambled to catch it before it fell to the ground.

We turned to see a third-floor balcony directly below us and a restaurant courtyard at ground level. With only a second before the killer found his weapon, we leapt to the balcony *en masse*. A loud *crack* had us looking in all directions until Marchisio pointed to the wall. Our perch was separating from the building.

A surprised elderly man in pajamas stared at us through French doors. Ms. Sabel gestured for him to open the door, but he stood immobile. She pouted and gave her best puppy-dog look. Nothing. She blew him a kiss. His face lit up. He shuffled to the doors, unlocked and opened them while Ms. Sabel muttered *men* under her breath. He threw open both doors with a warm smile. Ms. Sabel planted a big kiss square on his lips while Miguel, Marchisio, and I slid past. As the last foot left it, the balcony tore loose and crashed to the courtyard below.

My associates found the front door and cleared the hallway. Ms. Sabel brushed past me and we were out in the hall a second later.

We leap-frogged each other down the wrought-iron staircase to the ground floor and out to Via Gesú. Half a block south of us, two men in black scanned the street. Miguel and I spread out, aiming at them but holding our fire while Marchisio and Ms. Sabel ran to the corner and covered our exit. We reached the cross street to find Carmen holding two cabs. Miguel and Marchisio grabbed one, while I jumped in with the ladies. We sped off down the street.

"What just happened?" Ms. Sabel asked. "They followed us and killed him to keep him quiet?"

"I doubt that," Carmen said. "No one outside the Gardens knew where we were going."

"They were after Verratti before we were," I said. "The guy in the store was the point man."

Ms. Sabel said, "He had the same ethnic look as the guys in the woods last night."

After the attack in the woods, Ms. Sabel had figured something out. Now I understood what it was: we had a traitor in our midst. Someone had tipped off the bad guys to our destination. Carmen came to the same conclusion.

We handed Ms. Sabel our phones. There was a mole in our midst and she deserved to know he wasn't among her personal security detail.

She faltered a beat, then took them. "Sorry, I'll have to suspect everyone, even you, until I can clear you."

"We aren't complaining. It's the only course of action," Carmen said.

Ms. Sabel checked my phone and handed it back. "You were with me and your phone log is clear. But you could have another phone, so I—"

"Understood," I said and pocketed my phone.

She turned to Carmen. "Your call log is blank from when you left the Gardens until the Major called you to return. Where were you?"

Carmen took a deep breath. "I was with someone."

"Um, 'with' as in friends?"

Carmen stared out the window. "No. It was just sex."

Mercury said, Dude, do you know who it was? No, because you don't pay any attention to Carmen. You should know everything about everyone in your cohort.

I said, They haven't been called cohorts for centuries. They're battalions.

Mercury said, Whatever.

Ms. Sabel stammered through a couple syllables without forming a word.

"Face it," Carmen blurted, "I'm not the first girl the guys pull to the dance floor on Saturday night. I'm built like SpongeBob, for Christ's sake. That's why I liked the Army, I could play queen-for-a-year on deployment. Stateside, I have to be more aggressive. But I was involved in something last night that I'd rather not..." She glanced at me then rubbed her face. "I'll explain it privately. You'll understand."

We drove the rest of the way to the airport with an uncomfortable silence draped over us. I kicked myself for not knowing her better. She'd saved my ass too many times to count and never once judged me. Yet I couldn't tell you if she was single or married or what.

When we boarded the jet, Ms. Sabel pulled me aside. "What's queen-for-a-year?"

"Five thousand men and twenty women on an Army base for twelve months. For some women, those odds—"

"Yeah, I get it."

Chapter 18

Shady Grove Adventist was our first stop when we returned to DC. It smelled of the cleaners and chemicals that hospitals rely on to hold back the smell of death and decay. It lacked the comfort of family germs and pet smells and the dirt you ground into the couch yourself. It's not a good place to heal. I wanted to take Tania home, prop her up with pillows, and spoon chicken soup into her.

The first thing I saw when I peeked in the isolation room was Tania's dad, Jorge Ramos sitting in a chair by the window. He was lost in thought and didn't notice me. Tania's older sister was rotting in jail, having chosen the gangster path early in life. Her little brother suffered brain damage from a subway accident when he was eight. Her father's last hope for the family's future was Tania. Her illness hit him hard. I pushed the door open wider and tiptoed in.

He looked up with bloodshot eyes. After an awkward silence, he nodded at me and went back to watching Tania, his expression half angry and half heartbroken. I stuffed my hands in my pockets. The machines beeped and nurses walked by outside.

"Where's mom?" I asked softly.

"Cafeteria." He sighed.

"We'll get the guys who—"

"The Major told me," he said in his gruff Cuban accent. He adjusted his weight in the chair and softened his tone. "She was a Brooklyn Mako, *compay*. Eight years swimming with the club. Anchored the relay team."

I eased my way around the curtain and studied her. Gray skin, faded lips…she looked dead. I said, "She talked me into doing the

Chesapeake Swim one time. By the time I'd made the first pylon, she'd won the women's division."

He chuckled twice before melting into tears.

"Ms. Sabel is here," I said after he wiped his eyes.

She strode in and he jumped to his feet, smoothed his rumpled shirt, and stuck out a hand. She ignored it and gave him a long hug. The tough Cubano melted into her shoulder and cried again. They spoke in hushed tones for a long time. He told her how Tania had always been the smart one in the family. Ms. Sabel told him how Tania had pulled her from the Atlantic after pirates weighed her down and tossed her overboard.

Tania slept, feverish and trembling.

I stroked Tania's cheek. My deepest regret in life was ruining my relationship with her. Ms. Sabel was a captivating woman, but only a fantasy for a guy like me. Out of my league in every dimension. Tania was different. Tania and I were broken souls, broken in the same places. We both served our country longer than we should have. Her reward for her service were long stretches of scar tissue, like badly welded steel, that ran down her thighs to her knees on both legs. Burns suffered on her last mission in hostile territory. In the prime of her youth, her marred beauty left her with endless insecurities beneath her brash exterior. When we were dating, I would hold her in my arms, trace her disfigurement with my finger, and say, "This is your Medal of Honor." Other times, when I would wake up gasping for air, she would wrap her arms around me and tell me, "It's OK. You're home."

As my knuckle ran down her cheek, her eyes fluttered open. We shared a long, wordless look. It was all I could do not to cry at the sight of her blue eyes.

Through parched lips, she whispered, "Is Jaz here?"

Her eyes rolled back in her head and closed.

Mercury said, Bro, you're gonna need a new marriage option. Of course, you could always kill that pipsqueak.

I said, Jaz Jenkins is as good as dead.

Mercury said, Atta boy.

120

"Doctor Günter said she's stable," Mr. Ramos said. "I hope he's…"

We stood still for a long time after his voice trailed off.

I sensed a presence on the other side of the curtain and leaned around it. FBI Special Agent Verges curled a finger at me.

Ms. Sabel followed us out of the room and down the hall.

Verges had shoes so new they squeaked when he walked. His slacks were expensive and his dress shirt still had out-of-the-package creases. He was serious enough about his new role to spend money on it. We made it to a waiting area before he lit into me.

"What the hell were you thinking?" Verges asked. "You don't leave the country after a terrorist cell wipes out your lawyer and rattles the city."

Before I could answer, Ms. Sabel grabbed his arm and spun him to face her. He leaned back. She took advantage of being two inches taller and leaned in until they were nose to nose. "You have a problem with where I go, you talk to me."

"All right then," he choked out, "why the hell are Kazakh terrorists trying to kill you?"

Mercury said, You hear that homeboy? Kazakhs. You know what that means.

"You have information about them and *this* is how you tell me?" Ms. Sabel asked.

"You haven't been straight with me," he said. "I caught a lot of flak for that attack. You need to tell me what this is all about. Did you stiff some terrorists?"

"Since when does Kazakhstan have terrorists?"

"That's not an answer."

"You asked a loaded question."

Verges was leaning so far he was about to fall over. He stepped back. "I have to answer questions from the Attorney General about—"

"A friend of mine was shot to death in my car. You think I give a damn about who tugs your leash?" Ms. Sabel asked.

Verges started to speak, then thought better of it. He ran his fingers through his hair and glanced down the hall. "Look, you need to tell me what's going on. Why did you go to Milan? Why did La Rocca come after you? Why did Kazakhstan invade Potomac?"

She hadn't moved a muscle since she first grabbed him. Her eyes drove into him with brutal ferocity. Twice Verges gazed up at her, then muttered something before looking away. He said, "Are you going to answer my questions?"

"Not until I know who you work for."

He met her gaze. "The Director of the FBI. And he reports to the Attorney General."

I stepped in. "Yesterday, you told me the Director assigned you to help us. A moment ago, you said you had to answer to the Attorney General. Answer her question. Who do you work for?"

He rubbed the back of his neck. "Look, I'm stuck in the middle here. The Director is a friend of your dad and the AG is a friend of President Hunter. What the hell am I supposed to do?"

Ms. Sabel gave him a sympathetic look. "Who do you trust?"

Right before my eyes, the green FBI agent grew a backbone. It was like watching one of those comic book guys transition into a superhero. He stood up straight and squared his shoulders.

"Montgomery County has four Kazakh nationals in custody," he said. "They'll be arraigned shortly on illegal entry, weapons possession, and other preliminary charges. They don't speak a word of English between them. They've asked for a lawyer and we can't talk to them until someone's assigned to their case."

"How many crossed the border?" I asked.

"We're not sure."

"More than the four?"

"It would be wise to assume so."

"Stop by the Gardens and see the Major," Ms. Sabel said. "She'll give you a vial we want checked for fingerprints."

"I'm on it."

Ms. Sabel headed toward Tania's room.

Verges called to her. "Hey, that stuff about the Kazakhs is not public knowledge."

I offered a fist bump to Verges. He turned back to me and bumped my fist. "If I get fired over this…"

"Can you cook?"

When I caught up to Ms. Sabel, she said, "Anatoly Mokin was a Kazakh commando."

"We didn't catch him last time because he disappeared into central Asia."

"Let's keep focused on the vials. I want Tania healthy before we do anything else."

She took a call as we neared a small crowd outside Tania's room. Doc Günter read charts, Alan Sabel rocked on his heels chatting with Jaz, sans cravat. Guess the fashion craze he was hoping for never materialized. Last in line was Otis Blackwell, speaking Chinese on a call.

She held the phone away from her ear and nosed at Otis. "Get rid of him."

I glanced around. "I tried earlier, but he pointed out that it's a public space. I can push him around."

"That would be worse. I'll handle him." She went back to her call.

When she finished, she shoved her phone in her purse, and nodded at Doc.

He said, "We still don't have a clue about causation. We know it's a DNA virus like Ebola so we're trying her on IV Zovirax hoping she'll respond. Her liver is showing stress and her chest x-ray is showing patchy infiltrates, likely a pneumonic source of entry. We think she may have inhaled the virus. Knowing the source is a step in the right direction." Doc waved his hands at the others. "She needs rest, so I've asked everyone to leave. That includes you."

On his last syllable, Jaz stepped in.

"How can I help?" Jaz asked. He searched her eyes like a beefy hunk on the cover of a romance novel.

"You're here," Ms. Sabel said. "You're a sensitive guy. That's nice. Thanks, but the best thing you can do is go home."

"But I'm offering my moral support, a quiet shoulder." He smiled. "Just don't call me a sensitive guy. Nobody likes a sensitive guy."

Especially me. I use them for target practice. But I kept my mouth shut and gave him the *back off* look. He backed up.

Otis stepped in. "Pia, Tania has a deadly virus that—"

"Where did you learn Chinese?" she asked.

"The documentary. I was there for months. How did Tania contract—"

"I still owe you a call," Ms. Sabel said. "Excuse me, gentlemen, I have a game."

I gave the guys a shrug as she headed for the exit. Catching up, I asked, "Game? What game?"

"St. Muriel's plays their first game of the season tonight. I promised I'd be there."

"Whoa. You're going to a soccer game? No. You can't go. People were trying to mow us down with machine guns last night. We need to stay indoors, in a safe, controllable environ—"

"When someone tries to ruin your life, the best response is to continue living it. Show them your strength not your weakness."

"But I haven't made arrangements. I didn't know anything about this."

"It's on your calendar," she said and walked out to the waiting limo.

I dialed the only person who could help me.

When she picked up, the Major's first words were, "Forget to check Pia's schedule?"

124

Chapter 19

Night had closed in, leaving a cold bite on my cheek. Autumn leaves shook loose from their moorings and floated across the field, catching around my feet. Lights high above me draped an aluminum glow over the ground.

What I like about working with veterans is how they watch out for me. The Major had already deployed Miguel, Carmen, and a new guy. They had the area secured half an hour before Ms. Sabel and I arrived. I took the fourth corner of the field and patrolled casually, chatting with fans and players. Otis Blackwell set up his camera on a tripod up the slope. I waved to him and he waved back. A limo dropped Alan Sabel and Jaz Jenkins near the halfway line.

I heard "Pia Sabel" bubble up like popcorn in a microwave. Several Falcon's players and parents crossed the field carrying soccer balls and markers, making a beeline for the boss. When the refs joined the parade, I stepped into their path and held up a hand. Ms. Sabel grabbed it and gently pulled it down.

"Goes with the territory," she said. "Besides, it's nice that someone still recognizes me."

She took the nearest pen and ball and chatted with a grinning teenager. She engaged each player, parent, ref, and coach until everyone was satisfied.

Ms. Sabel spoke to the St. Muriel's girls, inspiring them with a speech about playing as a team and not for individual glory. She sent them out to the field with a rousing cheer. She joined me as I backed up a gentle slope to survey the park from the high ground.

The whistle blew and the Virginia Falcons kicked off against St. Muriel's Eagles. A St. Muriel's player rushed into the Falcons' midst and stole the first pass. Without looking up, she sent it to another player running up the sidelines. The two of them passed it back and forth three times, advancing quickly up field and distracting the Falcons from a third player who'd run between the two center defenders. The girl who'd stolen the ball back-heeled it to the girl in the middle. She volleyed it straight into the net. The Eagles' side went wild.

Ms. Sabel jumped up and down, clapping her hands and calling out the players by name. When the celebration subsided, she turned to me. "Did you see number two? Betty Weir. Keep your eye on her. She told me it was her goal to break my records before senior year. I love that kind of focus."

"Records?" I immediately regretted asking what I should've known.

"Senior year, I set the state records for one hundred, two hundred, and—"

The crowd on our side of the field broke into another cheer. While we were talking, the Eagles had scored again. Instead of cheering, Ms. Sabel chewed a fingernail.

The Falcons' third kickoff in three minutes went the same way. Betty Weir, center-mid for the Eagles, stole the ball and weaved down field for a goal all by herself.

"Not good," Ms. Sabel said.

"They're winning, right? What's wrong with that?"

"The only thing you get from a blowout is hubris."

I followed as she marched down the slope to the Eagles' bench and pulled three yellow pennies from the coach's bag. Walking onto the field, she ignored the referee's warnings to clear off. He gave her his undivided attention. She handed the pennies to Betty Weir, a defender, and the keeper.

"Bring out your backups," she told the Eagles' coach while the Falcons glared at her. "Betty, you three take up positions to coach the Falcons. Don't play for them, give them pointers. Tell them how to

126

anticipate the play, where to send the pass, how to read the field. Let's turn this game into something worth the time to play it."

"What if they beat us?" Betty Weir asked.

"Then you'll know your backups need more playing time."

Ms. Sabel walked toward the Falcons' bench. The ref looked at the Falcons' coach, who shrugged back. The ref blew the whistle.

Movement in my peripheral vision turned my attention to Otis. Freelance TV reporters have to be the whole crew these days. He was running back and forth from behind his camera to the front. As he stepped before the lens, he tugged down his shirt and sport coat, shook his hair back, and pulled a microphone to his face. He jumped back to his camera and trained it on Ms. Sabel. She was talking to the Falcons' coach. The coach had a pad of paper and pen in hand, scribbling notes as she pointed at players and rattled off instructions.

On the field, Betty Weir looked like a Pia Sabel clone. A few inches shorter but just as long-legged, the girl pointed and talked to Falcons players, giving them instructions. In the goal, the Eagles' keeper stood behind her counterpart. I heard her say, "Talk to your defense, tell them to shift left, assign someone to cover the open wing." The Falcons' keeper repeated the instructions to her teammates.

At one point, Betty Weir called out, "Never tell a teammate, 'yours.' Only say 'mine' when you *can* get the ball, or 'help' when you can't. Take responsibility." Across the field, Ms. Sabel gave the girl a thumbs-up.

The game ended 6-3 Eagles. Instead of the standard high-five line, the field erupted into group hugs.

As we walked off the field, Ms. Sabel said, "Do you play any sports?"

"Baseball in high school and college."

"I didn't know you went to college."

Mercury said, No background check? Dude, you are one lucky soldier.

I said, The Major vouched for me.

Mercury said, And she kept her mouth shut about your mental health?

127

Carmen rode shotgun with Miguel taking a lead car and the new guy following behind.

I slid in next to Ms. Sabel and buckled in with a click.

"I graduated high school young," I said, "and went to Iowa State for a year. First day of classes, sophomore year, was September 11th, 2001. I joined the Army the next day."

"Admirable."

Mercury said, Dude, you've got her ear. Show her you can think about something other than sex and women. You only get a second to impress a Caesar.

"I've been thinking about why someone would engineer a virus if it's not a bio-weapon. The only answer I can think of is because they have the patent on the cure. A company like Jenkins Pharmaceuticals could make zillions of—"

"No," she said. "Bobby Jenkins would never do a thing like that. It would be murder."

"OK, what about someone else in the company? A rogue unit, someone new, or trying too hard?"

Ms. Sabel scowled. "God, I hope not."

We entered Sabel Gardens' main building and were met by the Major. "Do you want to see the bad news first?" she asked.

We filed into the drawing room. Verges rose from a chair. A TV screen dropped from the ceiling. The Major clicked a remote and a newscaster appeared on screen. "…attack on Pia Sabel may have been for publicity. According to our highly placed source in Homeland Security, this might be a mirror of the stunt Miss Sabel pulled last August when she attacked a US military…"

The Major pushed a button and switched to another channel. "…source who prefers to remain anonymous said, and I quote, 'Miss Sabel is a threat to the community, and because that community is our nation's capitol, she's a threat to the nation.' End quote."

The Major said, "Ready for the good news?"

She switched to Channel 4, and played a clip by Otis. "…a different side of Pia Sabel. When she saw a team outclassed by her alma mater, she didn't let her side run up the score. The World

Champion stopped the game and turned what should have been a rout into an educational—"

"Goddamn it!" Ms. Sabel grabbed the remote from the Major's hand and switched off the TV. Red-faced and steaming, she paced the room while she dialed her phone, then clamped it to her ear.

Carmen, the Major, and I exchanged puzzled glances.

Ms. Sabel shook her head and regarded us as if we were dim. "The people who killed Kevin could track down anyone on the team."

"Coach." Ms. Sabel returned her attention to her phone. "I need the cell numbers of all your players. I'm sending Sabel agents to everyone's home."

She clicked off and fiddled with her email. In the corner of the room, a printer whirred to life. She sprinted for it, tore the printed page into sections, and handed them out. "Call these players, get them covered."

"What? Why?" I asked.

"I have bodyguards, but the girls don't." She turned away from me as her next call connected. "Annette, Pia Sabel."

Still puzzled, the rest of us followed her lead. I called three families, all of whom were both concerned by the call but happy to have Sabel agents assigned to them.

Carmen frowned and checked her phone's display. She pulled Ms. Sabel's arm, a puzzled look on her face. "What if there's no answer?"

"Who are you calling?"

"Betty Weir."

Ms. Sabel turned to Verges. "I need to report a kidnapping."

Chapter 20

Situated between the Embassies on Massachusetts Avenue and the White House, the exclusive Jefferson Hotel kept high standards: no blue-collar conspirators allowed. Violet, dressed in an Armani skirt suit, met the bellman's condescending gaze and demanded directions to her meeting. She followed him to the Book Room, an intimate space off the lobby. Ed Cummings wore a gray Zegna suit and sat at a small table by the fireplace in the otherwise empty alcove. They eyed each other as she waved the bellman away and took the chair opposite.

Cummings leaned toward her once they were alone. "What the hell did you do?"

"Me? I thought you did it."

"Why would I kill Verratti? I told you we needed his people for the operation. You're the one who said we needed to replace him."

"Maybe the Collettivo didn't like his investments." Violet glanced around.

Cummings squinted. "How can I trust you now?"

"Oh, for Christ's sake, Ed. I'm meeting your Velox man in a few minutes at the National Geo around the corner. Tag along and ask him."

Cummings leaned back and drummed his fingers on the table. "I'll do that."

"I think it was Sabel. Either for revenge or to send a message."

"No way. I looked her up, she's just a kid, twenty-five. Pretty good looking too, if you like 'em buff."

"Keep your dick in your pants. Inside that amazon beats the heart of a tiger." Violet leaned forward and tapped her index finger on the table. "Verratti made her look bad, killed one of her people, so she went after him and killed him."

"You think Verratti's people opened fire on a suburban road to get the vials? He was too cautious for that. And Pia Sabel going after Marco Verratti? I don't see it. She's a trust-fund brat. She likes the spotlight and plays the executive the same way she played soccer, for the applause."

"Check her flight records. She flew straight there and straight back."

"The FAA doesn't release those records."

"The *Wall Street Journal* keeps a database of corporate jets. She flew to Milan, stayed four hours, and left. Verratti was killed in the third hour."

Cummings whistled softly. He didn't move while he thought through the implications. "Will she come after us?"

"Not if we get her first."

"Hold on a second. I'm not going to be part of a..." Cummings checked around them, then lowered his voice to a whisper. "I'm not going to participate in a murder conspiracy."

"What do you think happened on Borneo, Ed? What do you think will happen in Philadelphia?"

"Nobody cares about a bunch of aborigines in the jungle. And Philly's elderly will go peacefully in their sleep. That's not the same as contracting a hit on—"

"Don't make it sound like some cheap gangster movie. I'm hiring her competitor to ensure we stay alive. I think that's a wise investment, don't you?"

"Why such a drastic approach? Why do you hate her so much?"

"Because she's Bobby Jenkins' special pet." Violet lowered her voice an octave. "And she took my goddamn vials."

"You mean the Jenkins Pharmaceuticals guy? Why do you care about him?"

"He's a competitor," she hissed. "I worked for him early in my career, but he was an asshole."

"I don't get it."

"He has six children who adore him and all he ever talks about is his goddaughter, Pia-fucking-Sabel. She isn't even his." Violet glanced around the Book Room again. "Sooner or later, she'll give up waiting for those fools at NIH to figure it out and she'll call Bobby. He'll come running to her and he'll know right away."

"Wait. How will he know it was you?" Cummings thought for a moment. "Holy shit, you started this project when you worked for him?"

"He didn't have the balls to pull it off."

Cummings' nostrils flared. "Why didn't you tell me this before?"

Violet leaned back and sighed. Finally, she broke the long silence. "Next problem: where did Marco hide our Element 42?"

"Did he have the Levoxavir too?"

"You think I'm dumb enough to give him everything?" Violet snapped.

"I'm a hedge fund manager. This kind of thing isn't in my wheelhouse." Ed pinched his nose and started paging through texts on his phone. "His contact in DC texted Marco and me a code to let us know when it arrived."

"You were responsible for landing the package in the US and all you have is a phone number?"

Cummings shrugged. "What do you have?"

She sighed and shook her head. "Let's go."

They rose and left the hotel, pulling their overcoats tight as they stepped into a frigid autumn morning. They walked around the block and across the street to the National Geographic Museum, Violet limping slightly and tugging on Cummings's arm for support. Inside the almost empty hall, a display of magazine covers through the years formed a dark and empty walkway.

An unappealing man tugged his dark pea coat over his shoulder holster and grinned at Violet. He was missing an ear and had a face like a smashed ham sandwich. He sauntered over and leaned against the display in front of them.

"Well hello, sugar," he said. "Is this pansy supposed to be your bodyguard?"

"See here." Cummings stepped forward.

Violet put a hand across his chest. "Can you do what we discussed?"

Kasey Earl smirked. "This package of yours must be pretty special. Someone killed your pal Verratti for it. You'll pay a double retainer."

"Did you kill Verratti?" Cummings asked.

"Who the fuck are you, pretty boy?" Kasey shoved the hedge fund manager back a step. "Ain't got my retainer yet. I don't work for free."

Violet huffed and pulled her phone. "Do you have the routing and account numbers?"

Kasey held up his phone's screen and she thumbed in a bank transfer of $200,000 from the Windsor account to his.

When the transaction completed, he put his phone away. "Who has the package?"

Violet nodded and Cummings provided the phone number for Verratti's American contact. She said, "You can find him from that?"

"When I request NSA info, they never ask why. Not allowed to. I'll have his real-time GPS coordinates whenever I want them. You'll get a text that says, 'Lincoln Memorial' when I have your package."

"Can you handle another operation for me?" Violet asked.

"Depends." Kasey cocked his head to the side.

"We need protection from whoever killed Verratti."

Kasey laughed. "The Mafia? No problem."

"We think Pia Sabel killed him."

Kasey stopped mid-laugh. He looked back and forth from Violet to Cummings. "You got Sabel Security after you?"

"Can you handle the job?" Violet asked.

"We ain't no babysitting outfit like them. We only work proactive like."

Violet smiled. "We were hoping you'd take that approach."

Cummings said, "Hey, wait a minute, what are you talking about?"

Kasey and Violet stared at him. Cummings shuffled and huffed then turned away.

Kasey faced Violet. "We're talking a whole lot of money, full payment in advance."

She glared into his smile. "We also have a side job."

"Yeah, whatever, but I'm going to bring in some people to take on Sabel. You need to cough up a bigger nut. You feel me?"

Cummings pressed his finger in Kasey's chest. "Can you handle the job? Do you know who you're up against?"

Kasey slapped his hand away. "Jonelle Jackson, Tania Cooper, Jacob Stearne? Fuck yeah, I know who I'm up against." He brushed a hand over his missing ear and stared at Violet with narrowing eyes, then spoke through his teeth. "Two million. Now."

~~~

Kasey Earl left by the side exit and dialed his boss from the alley. "Where did you dig up these suckers?"

"Cummings helped me finance the company after I had a little PR problem in Iraq. Why?"

"They just paid me half a million dollars to kill Pia Sabel. I shit you not."

"A fool and her money are soon parted." The other man laughed. "How much did you get in advance?"

"I done got the whole nut up front. Wired it straight to my Caymans account."

"And this time, there won't be any refunds. Wire it to the Velox account as soon as it clears." The man laughed. "Did they tell you where to find Element 42?"

"They gave me a lead."

"Then quit yakking and get moving. Our buyer is standing by." He clicked off.

Chapter 21

It took me all day to negotiate the exchange. The Kazakhs used random intermediaries and their translations caused a lot of confusion. We finally agreed on the Carderock Recreation Area after hours, an empty public space squeezed between the Naval Surface Warfare Center on one side and the Potomac River on the other. My mistake was thinking I could surround them in the dark. My backup and operations team hid half a mile down the road in the parking area.

I smelled the stench before I saw him, a dark shadow moving between the trees. He stopped five yards out and stood still. After a full minute, I said, "I'm alone, asswipe."

No response. Maybe the Kazakhs really didn't speak English.

I held up the vials. "Show me Betty."

Nothing. I repeated in Pashto and Arabic since I didn't speak Russian or Kazakh. Still nothing.

The shadow approached me and put his barrel in my face. He grunted. His bad breath traveled the distance between us like a cloud of mustard gas. One hand held his weapon, the other reached for my vials. I snapped them back and shoved them in my leather jacket.

"No way," I said. "Show me Betty first."

He kept his hand out.

From the bulk of his shadow, I figured he was wearing an extra vest. Even dim-witted Kazakhs figured out how to armor themselves against darts after a single firefight. I'd have to work on Ms. Sabel's infatuation with Sabel darts.

He spoke in what sounded like Russian. I shrugged.

He produced a phone and talked into it. Then he turned the screen to me. A shiny new Nokia Lumia with a translator app on screen read: *Comrades of you take back on parking station. Girl stand on ground. True.*

Part of me was amazed those things work at all and part of me thought they had a long way to go. I relayed the rough translation into my comm link and ordered Miguel to check it out. Ms. Sabel took off, out-running the big guy with her first stride. I tried to order her back to her assigned position but she wasn't listening. I had Miguel take her place on the right flank and cursed not leaving her back at the Gardens.

"I can see Betty," Ms. Sabel reported. "Oh god, she's so scared. There're two Kazakhs. One holding a pistol at my head, the other ten yards out holding a rifle to Betty's."

"You should've let Miguel handle this part. I had a negotiation planned."

"Bad time to mention it."

All the muscles in my body tightened up.

Across the comm link, Carmen said, "It was in his mission brief, ma'am."

"Oh."

Yeah. Oh.

A blown assignment like that could get us all killed. My anger exploded, but I kept myself in check with a deep breath. It was my own fault. I chose to work for Ms. Sabel instead of finding a sous-chef gig.

I handed the vials to the stocky shadow. He shined a UV light on them, the kind the TSA guys use in airports. I didn't know what he was looking for but I knew he wouldn't find it. He texted someone.

Mercury said, Told you this was a bad idea. What's that phrase? INCOMING!

"Bail," I said into the comm link.

A few awkward seconds ticked by. A reply text came in. The Kazakh started shouting at me, his foul breath forcing me back two steps.

I jumped sideways between two oak trees as bullets raked the air where I'd stood. Carmen and Miguel opened up, blasting Sabel darts in every direction. The Kazakhs fired back. Like me, they were firing blind around tree trunks. Across the Clara Barton Parkway, at the Naval Surface Warfare Center, the guards would interpret the Kazakh's distinct AK-47 fire as a terrorist attack on their facility. We were seconds from becoming friendly-fire casualties. A fate I'd barely managed to evade for over a decade in the wars.

After two full seconds, everyone had to switch magazines at the same time.

Grabbing the opportunity in the eerie silence, I shouted a cease fire and took a peek, looking for a sucker. Instead I heard the Kazakh running away from me.

Ms. Sabel's strained voice came over the comm link. "The guy is taking Betty. The other guy's still holding me."

"Bring 'em down, people." I chased after the nearest noisy feet. A shadow loomed out of the dark. I bent under what turned out to be a branch. While I ducked shadows, my quarry turned right. I slipped on muddy leaves. Reports came in over the comm link from all directions at once.

Our backup agents at the park's entrance reported Navy's security massing across the parkway.

Ms. Sabel's impatient voice demanded someone take out her captor and free Betty.

Carmen reported the darts were ineffective.

Surprise.

After losing my man, I headed for the parking lot and arrived in time to see the Kazakh holding Ms. Sabel. I fired a dart from twenty yards and caught him in the cheek. He dropped.

Ms. Sabel took off running into the trees. I followed as best I could to a wide trail where I saw nothing.

When I stopped to listen for them, Carmen's voice blew out my earbud. "They have a boat. They have a boat!"

I heard noises fifty yards north of me, toward the river. Following the sounds down a steep slope, I came to a granite cliff thirty feet above the banks of the Potomac River. Below me two shadows were launching an inflatable boat into the river. I ripped off three shots but didn't hit flesh. Ms. Sabel had taken the same route and was twenty yards to my right, climbing down the rock wall in a place where the cliff offered more hand and footholds.

"Ms. Sabel, hold your position!" I said. "We have the county cops coming. They'll cover the shore."

She kept climbing and reached the mud as I made it halfway down. The bad guys engaged an electric motor and left the shore at a slow but steady pace. Farther up the bank I saw Carmen and the Major running toward us. I reached the ground in time to see Ms. Sabel shedding her body armor, jacket, Glock, and shoes.

"No," I said. "Do *not* go in the water. Do *NOT* go in the…"

Her splash was the last I saw of her. Everything else I heard.

Carmen and the Major joined me on the beach, breathing hard from their sprints.

"If Pia drowns," the Major said, "I'm going to kill her."

The splashes of Ms. Sabel's strong, athletic strokes beat out the little motor on the raft. She caught up to them and dragged herself into the boat. I heard her beating on both men. Having seen her fight before, I theorized they would surrender shortly. But everything stopped. We heard only the whirring motor.

There was no need to see it; I knew what happened.

One of the Kazakhs put a pistol to Betty's head.

Chapter 22

"Problem," Carmen said as she peered through thermal binoculars. "They're not going upstream or down. They're crossing to Virginia."

"Goddamn, son of a bitch," the Major said. She turned and dialed up the Fairfax County police. Before she connected she tugged my sleeve and asked, "Why didn't your drone see the boat?"

"Downside to thermal imaging," I said. "The boat was cold."

Miguel walked down the river bank carrying a Kazakh by the shirt collar the way a country boy would carry a rabbit by the ears. He tossed the man facedown in front of me. "You clean what you catch, Jacob."

The only method I had of crossing the river was by car. With a snap of my fingers, I marched to the staging area. Carmen and Miguel, dragging my Kazakh, fell in behind me.

"What the hell happened?" Alan Sabel stormed across the staging area in the dark, scattering Sabel agents in his wake.

"Your daughter is an operational nightmare, that's what happened," I shouldered past him and grabbed Verges. "Where are your people?"

Verges put his phone in front of me, displaying the text from his boss: *AG says this is a local matter.*

"Really?" I shouted. "Kidnapping across state lines is local now?"

He tossed up his hands. "I'm trying, Jacob."

Alan Sabel is not a small man. Nor is he the kind of man to let someone shoulder past him. When he spun me around, I thought my arm would come off. "Where is Pia? What are you doing to get her back? I want answers, goddamn it."

"If you leave Jacob alone," the Major said, stepping between us and disengaging his grip, "he might get some answers. Right now, you need to step back and let my people work."

"Naval security team from NSWC crossed the road, sir," one of my agents reported via comm link.

"Verges," I said, "please tell me the AG will let you flash your badge and defuse the situation."

Verges took off for the entrance at a dead run.

On my second deployment in Iraq, I'd sworn off getting to know rookies because they were the first to die in a firefight. But Verges was hard to beat for enthusiasm. I began to hope he'd live through his Sabel Security assignment in spite of the odds against him.

Carmen spun her tablet on the hood of the Jaguar I'd taken for the op. She had a GIS map of the Virginia river bank. There were a few homes on the Virginia side but no obvious landing areas.

"What I'd give for air support right now," Miguel said as he leaned over my shoulder.

"What about the county sheriff? Can he—"

"That's what I'm talking about. Sheriff says the river's the flight path for commercial jets. And Fairfax County's a bit slow to respond. They requested a long debrief from the Major."

Carmen, Miguel, and I looked at each other and jumped in the XJR. The Major would handle the Maryland side with the other agents. As soon as I heard all four doors slam, I stomped on the gas.

"Could I have an earbud?" Emily's voice floated from the back seat as we slid around the Carderock picnic area, heading for the exit.

I twisted in my seat as we reached eighty miles an hour, then turned my eyes back to the road in time to evade a police cruiser rushing the other way. My swerve took us off the pavement, around a tree, and across an open grassy area. I eased my way back to the lane. Once I had the car under control, I snapped a glance at Miguel in the passenger seat.

"What're you looking at me for?" he said. "You brought her on ops when you were banging her."

I slammed on the brakes. The screech of tires and the smell of melting rubber broke the car's serene acceleration in an instant. I jumped out and ripped Emily's door open. "I apologize for my associates' callous description of meaningful, consensual relationships, ma'am. Nonetheless, you'll have to get out."

"No way!" Emily said.

"I've read your work. Now get out."

Emily crossed her arms and uttered an obscene challenge. Or invitation, depending on your mood. I wasn't in the mood. Carmen unbuckled Emily's seatbelt and I dragged her to the street. I gave her a shove and kicked her door shut.

"Where is she?" Emily snarled. "Where's your precious boss? You lost her, didn't you? Is that the story you want me to print? Sabel agents lose CEO? That's all you're leaving me, Jacob. I'll print it."

I ignored her, jumped back in and kicked the five hundred supercharged horses into gear.

As we sped up the Clara Barton to I-495, I broke the awkward silence. "For the record, the one time I took Emily Lunger on an operation, I was not *'banging her.'* And also for the record, I do not approve of insensitive phrases for thoughtful, engaging relationships. 'Banging' makes it sound like nothing more than sex."

"You got something against sex?" Carmen asked.

"Did either of you see what she wrote about Sabel Security?" I asked.

"She didn't make the company look bad," Miguel said. "She made you look bad. I'm OK with that."

Gotta love veterans. They'll take a bullet for you in a war zone, but land on the front page of the Style section in your boxers…

"It was all true," Carmen said from the back. "The problem is, you just left a major reporter with the wrong story."

"Major reporter? She was a travel writer until yesterday." I shot her a look in the mirror. "Get Otis Blackwell on the phone, will you?"

"Do I have to bang him?"

"Up to you. I only want him for the rescue story."

"You'll make an enemy at the *Post*."

"True that," Miguel said.

"Otis was Ms. Sabel's date for Senior Prom." I frowned at Miguel. "You've had a relationship with Emily for one night. Which one is our go-to reporter?" I waited a moment but neither of them said anything. "You two have a lot to learn about brownnosing."

"I got something," Carmen said. "Pia's GPS flickered."

"Where is she?"

"Just south of the Madeira School, on the river, heading northwest."

We came to the Georgetown Pike exit and flew at three times the 25 mph suggested speed limit and kept going. Traffic was light but still a serious problem on the two-lane road. I got by two cars early on and had only one more. Passing him on the double yellow at the hillcrest spooked me but it had to be done. We caught some air on the next hill and banged down hard.

"They've landed at a spot called Black Pond," Carmen said. "I think we can get there from the Madeira School's property."

We drove up the tree-lined drive and flew past the private school's main buildings and sports fields.

Mercury said, Wrong side of the river, dude.

I said, They doubled back to Maryland?

Mercury said, Fool, wrong side of the tributary. You took the wrong road.

Who do you trust, a long forgotten god—or satellite GPS?

The drive ended at a circle where we piled out. A hundred yards away, a lone security guard started to jog our way. Carmen pointed our direction, into the woods, and we were off at a dead run. We exited the trees at a large expanse of rock that stretched fifty yards to the river.

Miguel scanned with thermal binoculars.

Nothing.

"They're two hundred yards southwest," she said.

We covered the distance quickly and found the inflatable, its electric motor still warm. Lying on top of the center seat was the boss's phone. Everything around us was dead quiet.

Mercury said, Oh no, don't listen to a god when you can listen to a mortal with a machine in her hand. I should toss you back where I found you—scared and shivering in a Baghdad ditch, praying to Jesus. You never listened to him either. Dawg.

Chapter 23

The same cold breeze slid through the trees, forcing an involuntary shiver across Pia Sabel's skin and wet clothes. Hooded, she relied on her senses to assess their situation. Betty was a step behind her, being shoved into Pia every fourth step. From the bumps, she could feel that Betty's hands were bound on the girl's front, a good sign. Pia's were tied behind her back.

They hiked up a slope a hundred yards where the Kazakhs pushed them against a tree and forced them to sit. Then she heard the Kazakhs walk away a short distance.

"Your agents are coming, right?" Betty Weir asked in a quaking voice.

"Shh," Pia said.

A man's feet strode toward them, crunching through leaves and bramble.

Betty said, "I'm sorry to cause you so much trouble. I should've—"

A rifle butt slammed into Betty. The girl screamed and sobbed, earning a slap.

Pia twisted her hands against the rough rope, but she was powerless. "Stop it! She's just a—"

A rifle butt pounded her belly, knocking the wind out of her.

Pia remained quiet. The Kazakhs said nothing until the women understood them, then the sound of their boots receded some distance away. Pia moved close enough to Betty's ear for a whisper.

"Your hands tied in front. I'm going to put my head in your lap. Get my hood off. Then we'll work on our hands."

"Are we going to fight our way out?"

"Shh."

Pia slid into a prone position and felt Betty's leg with her head. The young girl's fingers wandered for a moment but quickly found the drawstring and freed her.

Clouds obscured the moon but reflected enough city light to see shapes. A slipknot held Betty's hands. Pia picked at it with her teeth until her protégé's wriggling did the rest. A second later, Betty had her own hood off and worked on freeing Pia's hands. A second before they finished, footsteps approached.

Betty froze.

Pia willed her to keep working. She needed her hands for defense. But Betty remained frozen, her eyes as big as saucers.

The footsteps kept coming from deep in the trees. The two Kazakhs appeared out of the shadows, glaring at Pia. One grabbed Betty while the other unbuckled his belt, unzipped his pants, and laughed.

Pia jumped over her hands, landing her feet on the ground in time to smash her bound hands into the man's chin. His pants fell to his knees as he staggered backward into his pal. Twisting her core, she gave him a backhand that sent him to the ground and left her facing the other Kazakh.

He swung his rifle up, his icy stare locked on Pia.

He never saw Betty.

The girl took two steps and smashed her foot into his groin from behind. As he doubled over, Pia brought her hands around his head and pounded his face into her rapidly rising knee.

Betty took the opportunity to kick the fallen man in the ribs. Repeatedly. But the man grabbed her ankle and yanked. She fell on her butt.

Pia finished off the first man with a serious kick to the head as he lay on the ground.

The second Kazakh straightened up and pulled his rifle to his shoulder. Betty rolled away. Pia planted her left foot in the man's hip hard enough to send him over. Betty, back on her feet, jumped up and landed her heels on the man's face. The uneven surface of his skull provided a rough landing. Pia caught her in midair.

Suspended for a moment between heaven and earth, Betty's eyes blew wide open.

"We did it!" The young girl stood up and threw her arms around Pia. "I can't believe it! We won!"

"Could you finish untying my hands now?" Pia asked. "We're not done until we have them in jail."

Once her hands were free, Pia took a deep breath, put two fingers in her mouth, and let out a loud, shrill whistle. Betty did the same. The racket they made stirred one of the Kazakhs. They kicked him at the same time. Then they waited and listened. Pia shivered, her teeth chattering like a machine.

In the distance, an answering whistle and distant shouts came through the trees.

Pia held a rifle on both Kazakhs while Betty went through their pockets, tossing everything into a pile. Knives, flashlights, pistols, cord, tape, ammo, and a phone piled up. Betty tried a few random numbers to unlock the phone but gave up quickly. There was a rucksack where Betty stuffed the pile of weapons. Pia picked at the bindings and cords, tying the ends together until she had a six foot length. With a slipknot at each end, she put it around the Kazakh's necks and drew it tight. If either man were to run, he'd strangle them both.

Taking turns whistling for help and trying to revive the Kazakhs, they eventually got the men on their feet.

"Let's hike out of here," Pia said. "If we head west, we'll find cops."

Yanking the cord three times, the Kazakhs quickly understood their fate and obediently walked between the women. Betty led and Pia brought up the rear. They found a wide, well-travelled trail that led uphill and west. Half a mile later, their whistles were answered by shouts.

A Fairfax County police officer ran to their assistance. Within minutes police officers swarmed the trail. Pia was given a blanket and led to a warm squad car. Betty's parents set out to join her as soon as they were informed.

Several vehicles raced into the park. Alan Sabel arrived first with Jaz and the Major. Agent Verges followed immediately behind them. Otis Blackwell and Emily Lunger fought for third.

"Where's Jacob?" Pia asked a uniformed cop.

He said, "Jacob Stearne and his team were detained by officers responding to an armed invasion of a local private school."

"They were trying to rescue me."

He shrugged. "We know that now."

Verges brought the Major and Alan through the police lines. While Alan wrapped her in a warm hug, the Major filled her in on the AG's order to ignore the kidnapping.

"Pia," Otis called from behind a line of cops. "Are you ready for that interview now?"

The officer nearest her shrugged when she glanced at him for permission. She waved the newsman over.

Otis pointed his camera with a strong light into her eyes. "How did Kazakh nationals kidnap a teenager?"

"They saw your report. You named the school, the place, and several players by name."

"Don't blame me," Otis said. "It's not my fault."

"I'd appreciate it if you checked your story with me next time."

"I tried."

"I thought we were friends, Otis."

"Friends communicate. Work with me."

Pia huffed. "All right. Ask your questions."

"Why didn't the FBI handle this?"

"You'd have to ask the Attorney General."

"Why are Kazakh nationals trying to kill you?"

"Let's hope the police find out."

"Would it be in retaliation for killing Marco Verratti?"

"If that's the case, someone has me confused with Mr. Verratti's killers."

"Do you deny assaulting Verratti's bodyguards moments before he was gunned down in Milan?"

"His associates tried to kill one of my agents. We went there to discuss—"

"Do you deny that Sabel agents used tranquilizers on Verratti's men moments before they were shot to death?"

"Those are not connected—"

"Did Marco Verratti connect you to the mass graves on Borneo?"

"Where are these questions coming from, Otis?"

"Are the Kazakhs marauding around Montgomery County connected in any way to Jacob Stearne's assault on a tribal leader in Malaysia, Borneo?"

Pia slapped the camera off Otis's shoulder. "What is this? Who are your sources?"

The camera crashed to the ground. "Not you."

"Your questions surprised me. I'm … I'm sorry."

"You promised to call. I did a nice report on you. Mine was the only positive spin on the air. You never even said thank you."

Pia stayed quiet.

He stooped to retrieve his camera. "News is a tough business. Why does Emily Lunger get all the inside scoops?"

Pia checked the lens. A visible crack crossed the center. She bent down next to him. "I'm sorry, Otis. I didn't mean to break it."

"This doesn't belong to the station."

"I'll get you a new one." Pia paused a moment. "Tell me who's been contacting you."

He looked up with fire in his eyes. "A newsman never reveals his sources."

Chapter 24

Few things in life are as embarrassing as having sheriff's deputies arrest you while you're sneaking around a girl's school in the dark. One thing that's worse: seeing Emily Lunger waiting to pounce from behind the police tape.

I sent Miguel to cut her off while Carmen and I finished some work. We were twenty yards away when we heard her slap the big guy.

Jaz Jenkins stepped away from Alan Sabel's side and angled to cut me off. "How could you let this happen?"

I paid him no attention. Jaz didn't like my attitude and pushed me with all the power his inexperienced, untrained muscles could muster. I didn't break stride.

"I'm talking to you." He trotted in front of me, his expensive sport coat flapping open, his eyes blazing with anger. "Are you in charge of keeping Angel safe or not?"

I stopped and gave him my soldier stare. He cringed for a split second, then straightened up and lifted his chin. As pathetic as he was, Ms. Sabel had dissed him more than once. He deserved a little sympathy.

"While you were smoking dope," I said, "partying with your frat brothers, and playing *Grand Theft Auto* between classes, I was in the 'Stan fighting for your right to get trashed. Now, get out of my way or I'll snap your arm in half."

It wasn't as sympathetic as I'd planned.

Jaz *born-into-the-one-percent* Jenkins backed up a step. I nodded a quick good evening to him and marched to my next admirer, Alan Sabel.

"If you have something to say—say it to the Major." I pointed behind him.

Carmen kept pace with me as we passed his gaping mouth. Not one single employee in his battalions of butt-kissers had ever spoken to him like that before.

He'd get over it.

We found Ms. Sabel doing a TV interview. No wonder Emily was pissed. Miguel's problem. Carmen and I passed them and marched straight to the deputy sheriff guarding the evidence.

"I need the perp's phone." I held out my hand. Confidence works better than bullshit.

Without thinking, the rookie leaned over the open trunk and picked up a plastic bag. "This one?"

I grabbed it and hauled it to where they held the two Kazakhs at the back of a squad car. The rookie trotted behind me, asking who I was. Too late. Possession is nine-tenths of the law. I grabbed the cuffed hands of the older-looking Kazakh before one of the officers stopped me.

"What are you doing?"

"Getting a look at his vacation photos."

"You can't do that. It would be self-incriminating. The detectives are getting a warrant."

"Those rules apply to law enforcement officers. I'm a civilian. This guy was begging me to have a look at his camera roll. Right, Sergei? Alex? Dmitri? Whatever your name is?" Like most people in his situation, he nodded when I nodded because he had no idea what I was saying, but he knew I was smiling nicely. The cop shrugged. The evidence would never hold up in court, but I looked forward to his funeral, not his trial.

I forcibly swiped the Kazakh's finger across the fingerprint reader and his phone blinked to life.

His camera roll had plenty of incriminating photos: the area where we were attacked on Glen Road; the fire station where they blocked the road; Sabel Gardens from a long distance; Sabel Gardens from the river banks; the soccer field where the fateful game was played; Betty Weir arriving at the soccer field in daylight; a coffee house where Sabel agents often congregate; and several others.

Their body odor told me more of a story. To confirm my suspicion, I spun the roll back to the beginning. There he was, wearing a black uniform and smiling in a jungle standing next to a man with a scarred eyebrow.

"Why take pictures?" Carmen asked. "He could've staked out this op without them."

I checked the text messages and found a stream of foreign language texts along with the pictures. Carmen tried retyping the messages into her phone's translator but the Cyrillic characters were impossible for us to get right. I ended up copying and pasting the texts into the same translator he'd used with me. It worked well enough to determine the strategy.

His name was Yuri and he was sending pictures to a person identified only as *Menedzher*, Russian for manager. It was a running stream of operational plans and approvals. Yuri led a squad of seven. They'd entered the US illegally by crossing Lake Erie and then drove to NYC. Their original mission was not spelled out. But the day I took the Pak Uban's money, the *Menedzher* changed their orders to "get the vials and terminate Pia Sabel." They'd arrived shortly thereafter and camped in the woods of Potomac while hatching their plans.

Carmen looked up. "Gotta be your buddy Mokin, right?"

I nodded and kept thinking. At the Maserati attack, Yuri stationed one up the road, another down the road, while he stayed across the road for containment. The four we'd caught attacked our car. They hadn't counted on us rolling down the wooded slope. Yuri and two others ran off when it went sour. The texts turned toward a plan to ransom someone, anyone, close to Ms. Sabel in exchange for the vials of blood. They settled on Betty. Scattered throughout the texts were references to 'the fountain'.

Carmen was looking over my shoulder. "Which fountain are they talking about?"

"The one that spouts information. Our leak is worse than we thought."

"Why did they go to New York first?"

"They were after someone else. It had to be someone important to send seven guys."

"There were seven guys in Milan for the Verratti hit."

"Interesting connection." I thought for a moment. "Why would Mokin kill Verratti?"

Carmen shrugged and stared at me with more questions than answers.

I typed in the number to Sabel Security's tech team and uploaded the bug that copied everything on the phone back to headquarters. Then I handed it back to the evidence cop while his detective was verbally assaulting him. They stopped arguing to glare at me.

I shrugged.

Ms. Sabel made her way to us clutching a blanket around her. When she was still a few yards out, I couldn't hold back any longer.

I fully extended my arm, pointing my finger in her face. "You abandoned your post, soldier. When you did that, you endangered the operation, your team, and the victim. You gave Betty and the girls a great speech about teamwork over personal glory. You need to practice what you preach. I don't care who the hell you are, or what company you own, I'm not going to work for someone who's so selfish she's willing to get me or my team killed. Am I clear?"

Ms. Sabel stopped, her eyes opened wide, her face drained. "Wha… But I—"

"I ordered Miguel to recon the hostage. You left your post to do it for him. That left our flank exposed. If they'd had one more Kazakh, we'd all be dead right now. This operation, like any other operation, is not about you, it's about working as a team."

"But, I—"

"There is no excuse. Your only remediation is to apologize to every member of the team for compromising their safety. AM I CLEAR?"

Mercury said, Oh, pure genius, dude. Berate her like a schoolgirl. Are you planning to retire on unemployment checks? Cause, that's just not going to work for my lifestyle.

She straightened up, angry and proud. Before she could let loose the tirade she was building up, the Major came up to us. "He's right, Pia. You owe them an apology."

No one argued with the Major. Her voice and iron gaze didn't allow room for it. Ms. Sabel's defiant glare softened. I could see her thinking through the cloud of humiliation and realizing I was right. She set her boss persona aside and remembered her soccer persona, the athlete who thrived on teamwork.

"You're right. I apologize."

She turned to Carmen and repeated her apology with sincere contrition in her voice.

"Apology accepted," Carmen said.

Ms. Sabel continued with the Major before she turned to look for Miguel. She took her medicine better than I expected. If I were her, I would've fired me.

I watched over Carmen's shoulder as the detective introduced an interpreter to the Kazakhs.

"It was nice working with you," Carmen said.

Absently, I said, "Not the first time she apologized to a team. She hogged the ball during the Women's World Cup. The coach made her apologize."

Carmen looked at Ms. Sabel, rapidly disappearing into the dark. "Tania survived calling her a 'rich bitch', maybe you'll survive too." Carmen regarded me. "But then, she likes Tania."

The interpreter fell into an animated discussion with Yuri-the-Kazakh. Both of them gesticulated and shouted. Something about their conversation struck me as familiar and somehow important.

"She knows I'm right. If she doesn't, I'll…" I lost my train of thought.

Mercury said, Finally using your brain for something other than lying to women. Your mother would be so proud.

I said, *What is it? Why is the interpreter making me think?*

Mercury said, We don't hand you shit on a platter, man. You have to put some effort into it.

"Thanks, asshole."

Carmen smacked my arm. "Did you just call me an asshole?"

"Sorry. Thinking about something…"

I trotted over to the detective leaning against a car ten yards from the interpreter and Yuri.

"Hey, detective," I said, "is he getting anything out of this guy?"

"Different culture," he said without taking his eyes off Yuri. "They're negotiating a price for the interpreter to lie to me."

"You speak the language?"

"No," he laughed. "I know criminal behavior. Check it out. My interpreter is trying to sell this clown on his ability to mislead us. He's going to look over his shoulder at me in five seconds."

The detective pulled a bored-dumb face. I waited. Six and a half seconds later, both Kazakhs glanced our way. Then Yuri agreed on the price with a nod and the conversation dropped to normal tones.

"What that dumbass doesn't realize is, I'm recording every word they say and I'll get a transcript in the morning."

The scenario made my skin crawl.

I looked up the mass grave reports on my phone and tried to understand what was bothering me. All the dead were from the Melanau tribe, same as Kaya. I called Bujang, my old translator, and asked him why the Kazakhs had killed only Melanau. He said he was a Dayak and didn't know much about them. I clicked off.

Carmen tapped my shoulder. "What is it?"

"I blew it back on Borneo."

Mercury said, No shit, brotha. I told you to cut that guy's fingers off if you wanted answers. But no. Candy-assed, limp-dicked, sheltered little punks like you don't have the stomach for it. I don't know why I waste my time on you. You're not man enough to clean my sandals.

Miguel came running. "Jacob, the lab at NIH's been destroyed. Dr. Carlton's in intensive care."

Chapter 25

The Jefferson Hotel's wine steward decanted the wine and set the glasses on the cherry coffee table in front of Violet Windsor and Ed Cummings. The two sat opposite each other on facing sofas. Violet dismissed the steward and waited until the suite's door closed before she spoke.

"Have you come up with a deployment plan?"

Cummings swirled the wine in his glass before answering. "I'm a fund manager, not an operations guy. Have Velox do it."

"I'm not going to spend another minute speaking to that filthy cur. It's time you got off your ass and did something." She rose and crossed to the window. "You think he'll actually kill Sabel?"

"I'm not comfortable with that plan. It's a terrible idea and you should pull the plug—"

"How are you going to get Cummings Capital back on track with her breathing down our necks? Are you going to wait for the last investor to pull out of your funds before you wake up?" She leaned her back to the wall. "You need astronomical returns more than I."

"Cummings Capital isn't that bad."

"Then why didn't you buy out the Chinese when I asked you to?" Violet swirled the wine in her glass and took a sip. "I hate having to suck up to Chen."

"Then don't."

"He owns more than half my shares, Ed. If he dumps them on the market, I'm finished."

"What else does he have on you?"

Violet glowered. "Why do you care about Pia Sabel all of a sudden?"

"I just don't condone…" He shrugged.

"Oh my god, you want Alan Sabel to invest in your fund." She leaned forward and glared while he stared at his wine. "Is that what this is all about?"

"Think of the possibilities, Violet. Get him to invest and ten of his billionaire buddies will follow him—"

"His little golden girl will see through you in a second. She'll trace the evidence back to you and you'll be finished." Violet sighed and finished her wine in a gulp. "Do you think Kasey can handle her?"

"He seemed anxious to get started. But it'll bring a lot more scrutiny, especially if they still have the vials."

"I'll worry about the vials. You worry about deployment. The minute Velox recovers Element 42, I want it deployed. I need you to handle that part tonight. Do you hear me?"

"What do you expect me to do, hire day laborers from Home Depot?"

"I don't give a damn. Just get it done."

Her phone rang. She held a hand to Cummings and answered. "Prince, thank you for returning my call. It's good to hear—"

"Why are you so interested in Pia all of a sudden?" Prince asked.

"I care about her, the same as anyone. Since she wouldn't remember me, as you pointed out, I thought I'd ask you."

Reflected in the window, she saw Cummings waving to get her attention and ignored him.

"Luckily, she's safe and so is the girl."

"Oh, Tania is healthy again?" Violet asked.

"Who?"

"The girl who was sick. Tania Cooper."

"Oh, her. No, she's still sick. They sent a vial of her blood to NIH. They think she has the same thing as the people on Borneo. I was talking about the other girl—" Prince muted his phone for a few seconds. "Look, I have to go."

When she clicked off, Cummings turned up the TV.

"That fucking bitch!" Violet screamed. "Now there are four vials. Goddamn it!"

Cummings craned over his shoulder to scowl at her. "Keep it down."

"Did you hear me?" she said. Cummings stared at the TV. "Turn that thing off! I can't think."

"It's about Pia Sabel," he said.

"Did someone finally kill her?"

"She rescued a kidnapped teenager."

"Oh, for god's sake, what is she trying to do, get canonized while she's still alive?" Violet rounded the sofas and sat to watch the newscast.

A newscaster stood in the dark with blue and red police lights sparkling behind her. "...teenager is safe and unharmed. The two Kazakh nationals are in police custody..."

Cummings muted the screen. "Did she say—"

Violet stared at him as she dialed. The call connected. "What the hell have you done, Anatoly?"

"You told me not to call unless for board-specific business," Anatoly Mokin said. "I expect same from you. What board business this is?"

Violet put it on speakerphone and set it on the coffee table. "I'm here with Ed Cummings. I couldn't reach Wu Fang on short notice, but that doesn't matter. We have a quorum. We demand to know why two Kazakhs are kidnapping Americans in Maryland."

"What do they say when you ask them?" Mokin answered.

"The police have them."

"Then this is good thing, *da?*"

"Don't get cute with me." Violet shook with anger and her voice rattled the windows. "If there are Kazakhs going after Pia Sabel, you sent them. I want to know why."

"Seventeen million peoples in Kazakhstan. I know only few."

"I saw your man Yuri on TV. I could go to the police and tell them who he is, and who he works for. But I'll ask you this one last time: why is he in Washington?"

163

"To you, all Kazakhs look same. Your racism does not insult me. Your accusation that I have some doing with this—this insults me. Do not call unless for board-specific business." Mokin clicked off.

Violet paced the room, wringing her hands. "What is he trying to do? He's up to something, I can tell. He knows something. Maybe he put it together. Maybe he knows about Philadelphia. But why would he go after Pia Sabel? Why kidnap someone? For extortion? Money? He could do that in China. No, he's after something. Do you think he's after the vials? Why would he be after the vials?"

"Doesn't matter," Cummings said. "For whatever reason, he's trying to kill her. So, my plan is the best way forward. We go to the Sabels and turn him in. We can pin Borneo on him and forget the whole Element 42 thing."

"Don't you dare walk out on me now. The last man to walk out on me was my father." Violet dropped on the sofa and pulled off her prosthesis and sock. She rubbed her throbbing skin.

"Who's walking out? Think about it. It's a win-win. Sabel's pal Tania gets the drug, we look like heroes, we pin Borneo on Mukhtar and Mokin, and Sabel rewards us with investment capital."

Violet lowered her chin, her face red. She scowled with flinty eyes. "He'll invest in Cummings Capital, but he won't invest in Windsor. So—genius—where does that leave me?"

Chapter 26

Police lights flashed in the park's trees, making it look like some giant Christmas display. Twenty news hounds tried to catch officers and Sabel agents for statements. With Carmen still on my heels, I found Ms. Sabel.

"I need to borrow your jet for a couple days," I said. I didn't realize how odd that sounded until she craned over her shoulder to look at me. "Uh. If that's OK."

Ms. Sabel faced me, pulling her blanket tighter around her. "Where to?"

"I'd rather not say."

"Tell me it's not about Pramashworisasmita."

"Who?"

"The hotel owner."

I felt myself turn red. "Oh. I pronounce it ... never mind. I'm asking you to trust me on this one, ma'am."

She leaned back and considered me. After yelling at her about teamwork, asking to borrow a jet that costs twenty grand an hour was bold even for me. She kept those gray-green eyes locked on mine and waited.

After a few long seconds, I exhaled. "We have more than a leak; we have a traitor."

She crossed her arms and continued with that cold, impatient stare.

"Obviously someone sent the Kazakhs after Verratti several days before we came along," I said. "Yuri and his crew were in the US before then. As you noticed, the attack that killed Kevin required inside information. But they had photos of Betty Weir hours before Otis' story aired. And they just attacked NIH."

"Where are you going, then?"

"Can't tell you." I gauged her reaction. It would take a world of trust to say yes, and she didn't know me that well. When she opened her mouth to say no, I cut her off. "What I'm going to do requires an element of surprise. If you know about the mission, our traitor might pick it up from any scrap of conversation. Whoever he is, he's close to us. If you leave town, everyone will know it. No one cares where I go. Put out the word you sent my team for more training because we blew the rescue. I'll be back in a couple days with a whole lot of answers."

"But we need to find out what's killing Tania."

"I'm no doctor, but what we saw on Borneo killed people fast. Tania's not dead because she's young and strong. She'll make it. She has to."

"You're offering me as bait to the killers."

"Worse," I said. "I want you to bait him, uncover him, but don't tell anyone because he can't be working alone. Someone called *Menedzher* is out there between our mole and the Kazakhs. That guy could be right here or the other side of the world."

She nodded with a slow rhythm. "At times like this, I want to toss feminism aside and return to chivalry. But you're right, it's the only way."

I offered my fist and she bumped it. "Be careful and keep the Major close."

"Take Emily with you," she said. "I want an embedded reporter in case this thing is political."

"Understood, but how about Otis instead?"

"Emily." Her stare left no room for discussion. "I have my reasons. You'll have to patch things up with her."

It was a good choice. As angry as I was at the reporter, her paper had something no one else could offer.

Carmen and I headed back to the Jaguar and found Verges and Miguel leaning against a Kia.

"Guess who won't let me share the NIH security video?" Verges said.

"No surprise there."

"But," he added, "I told the team at NIH that Agent Stearne was coming directly from an undercover op without his ID. They're expecting you."

Miguel punched Verges playfully.

"Anything on those fingerprints?"

"Not in any American or Euro database. We're working on Asia now. That's a manual process."

I fist-bumped Verges as a thank-you and kept walking.

Emily exuded enough tension to feel her approach twenty yards out. I cut her off. "If you want a scoop, pack a bag for hiking in warm weather, and meet us at the Executive Terminal in twenty."

Her gaze darted to Miguel.

He said, "Told you I'd have something for you."

"Do I have to 'bang' him to get it?" Emily sneered.

"I have no desire for an intimate relationship with you ever again, Emily. From now on, our relationship is strictly professional."

She stood stock still, her mouth hanging open.

I said, "If you're not interested, maybe Otis Blackwell—"

"Warm weather hiking, executive terminal, I'll be there." Emily ran to her car and spewed gravel down the road.

"What happened to brownnosing the boss?" Miguel said.

I shrugged. "Turns out, prom was a long time ago."

"You!" Jaz Jenkins approached before I could get in the car. "I want your word that you will step up your game and protect Angel to the best of your ability."

I stuck out my hand to shake and gave him a humble smile. "My apologies, Mr. Jenkins. I will endeavor to do my best in the future."

He pulled up his chin and took my hand.

I spun his hand in mine, turned him around, twisted his arm behind his back, slammed my knee into his coccyx, and cranked his neck in a vicious headlock. My mouth ended up next to his ear. "If you want my respect, earn it."

He landed facedown in a mud puddle.

Miguel watched from a couple yards away. "Harsh, dude. He just wants to be relevant."

I glanced back. Jaz was on one elbow, surveying the damage to his wardrobe. I felt a twinge of guilt. He was making awkward moves on a woman I would never have. He didn't need my jealousy, he needed my guidance. Besides, how can you not feel sorry for a guy who tries to revive the cravat?

Miguel nodded to the car. "Jacob, let's move."

Jaz flinched when I approached, so I left a small distance between us and bent down. "You're hitting on a world-champion athlete who owns a global company. She's not the schoolgirl who had a crush on you ten years ago, so don't call her Angel. In case you didn't notice, she's not comfortable with your familiarity. Show some respect. Take interest in what she's doing and forget about what you want. When she's ready for you to make a move, don't do it. Make her come to you."

He looked indignant but underneath, he was taking notes. Now all he had to deal with was that Ms. Sabel didn't like him. And that he was from Omaha.

~~~

NIH was lit up like a mall opening. Unmarked Fed cars were scattered like Hot Wheels at the end of a broken track.

An FBI man waved us down and ran up to my door. "Agent Stearne? This way, sir."

He led us into the building where we'd met Dr. Carlton and walked us into the shoebox of a security office. He pointed to the desk and left. Miguel took the console seat and played with the controls until he had date- and time-stamped video rolling on the quad-screen.

The intruders had wrecked all the video servers except for the outdated black and white, grainy stuff kept separately on an old machine. When he found the right spot, we watched it. Four hooded

168

men in black rushed into the lobby. They pepper-sprayed the security guards, beat them with nightsticks, and bound them in seconds, then sprinted for the elevator. No footage survived for the lab floor. We re-ran the lobby video.

"Four of them," Carmen said.

"Tall," Miguel said.

Before I could add my observation, the office door burst open and a lean, older guy, his gray buzz cut glistening in the fluorescents, glared at us. "Who the hell are you?"

"Who the hell are you?" I shouted back.

"Special Agent in Charge David Watson. Answer my goddam question or I'll call your unit chief and have you busted out to the nearest reservation."

I didn't know much about the FBI, but I knew a SAC was like a colonel in the Army, always pissed off that he hadn't made general yet. And they wielded about as much power. They reported to unit chiefs, so he thought I was a peer invading his turf.

"SAC where, WMDs?"

"Counterintelligence. Now tell me who the fuck you are."

We were imposters in the enemy camp. I was staring at the same guy who had buried Ms. Sabel's last attempt to expose President Hunter. The urge to sucker punch him was hard to keep under control.

"Agent Jacob Stearne."

He squinted.

"I've seen what I needed to see," I said. I held my hands out, palms up and fingers splayed wide. "Now I'm going to leave. You're going to wave goodbye. Otherwise, you have to file a report explaining why Sabel Security was welcomed into your investigation with open arms."

When something lands on a report in the government, there's no way to keep it from your chain of command. You can make excuses and blame others, but there's no way to make it disappear. Sooner or later, the Attorney General would learn of the egregious mistake that happened on Watson's watch and he would be the guy manning a desk in Tuba City. Personally, I'd consider it a nice place to work. Just an hour's drive outside of Monument Valley, and all you have to do is keep pot hunters from stealing more ancient artifacts. Easy work, but not the right direction for a SAC.

I stuck out my hand to shake on it.

His face turned red and swelled. He squeezed my hand hard, trying to intimidate me. His mistake. Every Midwestern farm boy has spent hours milking cows by the time he's in high school. We have machines for that, but the older generation sees it as a rite of passage. You squeezed udders and pulled teats for hours before school so you didn't go soft. The resulting hand strength lasts a lifetime.

I crushed his hand just short of breaking bones. Pain shot through his face.

As the pain bent him forward, I leaned to his ear. "Only one of your people saw me, and he doesn't have a clue who I am. Now's your chance to make the problem go away, Mr. Watson. Just forget I was here."

I let go. He grabbed his wrist but was man enough not to cry. He nodded.

Outside, I stopped in front of our helpful FBI guide. "Where are the guards now?"

"Across the street. Walter Reed."

"Did they mention anything about smell?"

"No, sir, they weren't conscious."

We left with a smart salute to the poor bastard. He didn't know it yet, but he was about to get the biggest ass-chewing of his life.

Carmen had something eating her up on the drive to the airport. When we pulled into the Executive Terminal and saw Emily standing next to her car, Carmen let it out.

"What are you thinking bringing Emily along?" she asked. "She should be at home, we could call her with updates, send her phone videos. She's no soldier, she's a nice, pretty civilian. Why in god's name are you bringing her to a big, ugly firefight?"

"She can get us something we're going to need."

Chapter 27

The indoor pool house echoed with Pia's lone rhythmic strokes, the chlorine-drenched air dense with trapped humidity. Her fingers sliced into the water on the downsweep, pulled to her chest and pushed to the recovery point. A perfect s-curve. Four kicks per cycle were synchronized to the beat playing on her waterproof headphones. Swimming remained her favorite meditative exercise. After her turn, she noticed the Major—dressed in slacks and turtleneck under her Sabel Security pullover—standing poolside. She coasted to the side and rested her elbows on the pool deck.

"Did you get everyone cleared?" Pia asked.

The Major paused for a moment before answering. "As we expected, our people are clear. There are still three unexplained calls that I'm sure the investigators will finish shortly." The Major tilted her head. "You should investigate me. I should undergo the same scrutiny."

Pia moved to the ladder and rose from the pool. She took a towel from the stack and rubbed down. "If I can't trust you, nothing else matters. What about Dad? Can he account for all his calls?"

"Talk to him. You can't keep suspecting him every time—"

"What should I do, Major?" Pia's voice echoed in the cavernous building. She lowered it. "Do you think I should just come out and ask him, 'Were you hoping President Hunter would have me killed, or did you just sell me out for the fun of it?' Do you know how awkward that makes dinner?"

"He loves you. You know that. He did what he thought best. And you were never arrested for treason."

"Forget about it. Water under the bridge."

"I have him on the cleared list," the Major said.

"Fine." Pia batted the issue away like a mosquito and padded barefoot into the locker room. "What about the guest list?"

"Impossible. There were two admirals, a former ambassador, some congressmen, family friends, and a small army of corporate VIPs. We can't ask for their records without our investigation getting to the press—and they would have a field day."

Pia peeled off her suit and stepped into the shower. She shouted above the steaming jet. "Then how do we figure this out? Can we look at who knew about the game's location?"

"The league scheduled the game. Anyone with Internet access could look it up."

"But they keyed in on Betty Weir."

"Her teammates tweeted it, Instagrammed it, Snapchatted it, they even made a podcast for the school. Four hundred girls at St. Muriel's told all their friends and family about how Betty managed to get you involved with the team. Everyone knew she was your point of vulnerability."

Pia shut off the water, stepped out, and shrugged into a robe. "He had to be in the dining room before I left for the detention center. I told no one, not even you. It has to be someone who saw me leave." She thought for a moment. "Jaz was there."

"Or someone in the kitchen. Or they could've had an observer outside."

"Otis was outside." Pia sat in a chair in front of a mirror. A woman appeared with a blow dryer and a brush and began drying her hair.

The Major raised her voice over the dryer. "I can check him out, but asking too many questions will feed his next story."

"So how do we figure it out?"

"Why do I have a feeling you and Jacob already have a plan?"

"You don't trust Jacob?"

"I'd trust him with my life." The Major looked away, then back at Pia. "But I wouldn't trust him with yours."

Pia waved away the blow dryer and pulled her hair into a ponytail. She leaned closer to the mirror and examined the array of makeup baskets. Tossing her way through several, she found black eyeliner and applied it. She checked out several lipsticks and passed them over. "Do you have any lipstick?"

"Uh," the Major said. "I don't think we use the same shades."

Pia pulled a muted red. "So what's your advice for our next step?"

"Don't go to the ball game with Jaz."

~~~

Pia watched Jaz Jenkins approach the limo, his unzipped Redskins jacket flapping open. Agent Dhanpal opened the door in time for him to slide into the seat next to her.

"Hi Angel, uh, Pia. Sorry. I guess that nickname's a little dated."

"Do they consider it flattery in the Midwest?"

Jaz glanced up as he buckled his seatbelt. "Well. Some. Might." He chuckled. She didn't.

His phone vibrated in his pocket. "Saved by the bell?"

Jaz pulled his phone and answered it in Chinese.

Pia stared ahead. Cousin Elmer drove with Dhanpal in the passenger seat. After the first mile, she drummed her fingertips on her knee. Jaz turned to the window and continued his call in hushed tones. By the second mile, she moved to the seat facing him, leaned her elbows on her knees, and stared at him until his gaze wandered to her.

"Did you invite me to a game?" she asked.

Jaz stopped his call mid-syllable. He wrapped it up and dropped his phone in a pocket. "Sorry. With the time difference, it's hard to—"

"Do you know anyone in Guangzhou?"

"No, Beijing. Dad's trying to slow the flow of counterfeit pills coming out of China and India. Why?"

"When did you learn Chinese?"

173

"Mandarin, technically, but I can fake a little Hakka when I'm in Hong Kong." He smiled and flashed his blue eyes. When her expression didn't change, he cleared his throat. "In high school, then more in college. At least Dad made sure we had a good education. Not like what he did to my sisters."

Pia frowned. "Sisters?"

Jaz waved a hand and looked out the window. "Yeah, from his first wife. They had a nasty divorce. He turned his back on them, gave them nothing. But he took care of my brother and me."

"First-born son."

"Not politically correct of him to favor the male offspring, but I'm not complaining."

"Why the interest in Chinese?"

"Seemed like a good idea. Nebraska sells soybeans and rice all over Asia. And Dad told me it's the language of the future. Back in high school, I lived to impress Dad."

Pia smiled. "Do you still?"

"I've grown up some. Now he just pisses me off. But you know how it is." He rubbed his palms on his knees. "Don't you like to impress your dad?"

"Why work for Jenkins Pharma?"

Jaz leaned back with a satisfied grin. "I aim to change the whole pharmaceutical business."

"Is there something wrong with it?"

"They aren't looking to cure diseases." He threw his hands up. "The big money's in maintenance. No one's looking for a cure to AIDS. No one's trying to cure asthma. They want to sell treatments. Diabetes, Parkinson's, Alzheimer's, everything they make is a maintenance drug. It's all recurring revenue. They've paid $11 billion in fines over the last four years. GlaxoSmithKline paid a $3 billion fine and still made a twenty percent profit. They figure huge fines are a cost of business."

Pia squinted at him. "Did your dad know how you felt when he hired you?"

"He's been out of the country since I arrived. He's trying to settle a huge fine set by the European Union for his statin drugs. There's another maintenance drug, cholesterol inhibitors instead of watching your diet." Jaz shook his head and turned to the window.

The limo slowed and turned into the flow of traffic heading into the stadium. Outside, an endless river of people flowed along the sidewalks.

"Sorry," Jaz said. "I get a little passionate about the subject."

Cousin Elmer slowed the limo and flashed a special card. A parking attendant moved a barricade. They drove down a narrow lane to a ramp that disappeared beneath the stadium.

"Where're we going?" Jaz asked.

"Dad has a suite, so Cousin Elmer will drop us at the VIP entrance."

"You guys have a suite? And I'm taking you to our seats in the stands? Sorry, guess we're slumming here. I should've known."

"Don't worry, the suite's too high up to see much of—"

A sudden movement in the crowd of people hoping to glimpse a player caught her attention. She pressed her face to the dark window, scanning for whatever it was that had caught her eye. A short man stood at the edge of the ramp. A security guard pushed him back with both hands. The short man staggered like a drunk.

"STOP!" Pia pounded on the glass separating her from the front seat.

Cousin Elmer slammed on the brakes, lurching the heavy car to a stop.

Grabbing her Glock, she pushed her empty purse into Jaz's chest. "Wait here."

She threw open the door, hit the ground running. "Stop that man!"

The crowd turned in unison like a dance troupe and watched her for a second. Some, frightened by her aggressive charge, backed up. Others moved in to help. She lost sight of her quarry in the resulting mess. Looking around, searching everyone, she found the short man again.

A security guard stepped in front of her, ten yards out, holding a can of mace. "Stop right there, ma'am."

Pia's focus moved from the man she wanted to the officer. "Get that guy."

Thirty yards beyond the guard, the short man craned over his shoulder. Their eyes met. Even at that distance, she recognized Chapman, the doctor from Borneo.

Sprinting around the security man, she turned uphill in full pursuit.

Chapman's eyes widened in terror. He turned and staggered.

She tackled him and rode him to the ground.

"Don't move, you son-of-a-bitch, or I'll rip your head off." She grabbed his arms. He offered no resistance.

"Help me!" His voice was weak and strained.

Behind her, the security man had his Taser out and aimed. Agent Dhanpal ran to help. The officer pointed his Taser at Pia, then Dhanpal, then back, and shouted, "Nobody move."

Dhanpal panted. "Help her, officer. She's apprehending a killer."

Pia pulled Chapman's arm behind him, planted her knee in his back, slipped an arm around his throat. "Don't try anything."

"My eyes," he whispered.

He coughed and lay still. And hot.

Chapman's body heat radiated into her skin through her thin jacket. She relaxed her grip and watched for any tricks he might be playing. Satisfied, she leaned back and rolled him over to look at him.

Blue sclera.

Chapman's eyes rolled back in his head.

Pia looked up to see fifty camera phones pointed at her. Among them was a shoulder-mounted type used by TV stations. This scene would viral in minutes. Dhanpal watched her eyes and took the initiative. He pushed the news crew back, asking for a little space.

"What were you doing?" she asked Chapman. "Bio-weapons?"

"Didn't do it." Chapman's crusty eyes fluttered and opened. "Not me."

She pulled him up by his collar. "I saw you."

"I got there, Borneo, minutes before you." Chapman coughed and sagged.

Pia squinted. Events came rushing back to her. She'd analyzed the scene the way the Kazakhs had presented it. "You were surprised when I showed you the boy's eyes."

He took a moment to breathe. "It's a marker we used in the lab. We worked with several strains … each with a different color marker so we knew which virus affected you if it got loose."

"Why didn't you say anything?"

"They were going to kill me. I … got away when they chased you."

"I don't believe you."

"I'm dying." Chapman's eyes closed.

"Why did you run at NIH?"

"You were going to kill me. I saw it in your eyes. I came here because … you won't shoot in a crowd."

Pia looked at Dhanpal.

He shrugged. "True that."

Jaz came up but kept a distance.

"You have to…" Chapman took a deep breath. "Stop them. Poisoning Philadelphia in a couple days." He coughed. "Element 42 … kills infants and old people."

Chapter 28

Borneo's silver moon slid behind clouds like it was auditioning for a horror flick. Dark shadows crossed the valleys like evil spirits. We hiked to a hill near the Pak Uban's village and set up an observation blind on an overlooking ridge.

Mercury said, Did I mention what a terrible idea this is?

I said, What's wrong?

Mercury said, All the things you yell at Ms. Sabel for, homie: no intel, no recon, no plan.

I didn't feel like arguing with an immortal reject. I examined the terrain with my thermal binoculars. On the first pass, the scene felt wrong.

"Hey, Diego," I whispered. The *Post's* Singapore-based station chief slid next to me. I handed him my binoculars. "I don't see the Pak Uban or anyone else in the village. Where would they have gone?"

He studied the scene for a long time, then adjusted his position. He looked far to the right, then back. "Where you showed me is not where he lives. That is a Melanau village. He's a Kayan, one of the Dayak tribes. He lives over that ridge, in the longhouse."

"But I saw him in that village. His injured son was there."

"The Kayans were headhunters a generation ago," Diego said. "This Pak Uban is a known racist who enslaves the Melanau. He's been disavowed by the other Kayan tribes but some young men follow him. The village you went to is deserted."

"And my last translator belonged to one of the Dayak tribes," I said. "That explains it."

Emily's paper had the connections to get us a guy with some ethics. Newspaper ethics, thin as they may be, are more reliable than tribal alliances. This time, I could count on more reliable answers without cutting someone's fingers off.

Miguel smacked my shoulder. "Explains what?"

"Bujang belonged to a cousin tribe of the Pak Uban. He sided with his tribal buddy and sold me out."

We moved our position to a new hill to get a better look at the Kayan village. Definitely a better place than the Melanau ghost town. Several small homes lined a walkway paved with stone that led to the longhouse. Smoke wafted from a hole in the roof. Plain and unadorned, it sat on stilts, four feet above the ground, and had the traditional veranda for meetings. There were other shacks and buildings scattered around it. People milled about the village, talking, kicking dogs, yelling at children, carrying chickens. Every male was young, tough, and carried a rifle.

Emily twisted around, looking over her back. "Does this body armor make my butt look big?"

I glanced at Miguel.

"It makes you look perky," Carmen said. She gave the reporter a playful spank.

"Tough fight ahead, bro," Miguel said.

"Did you bring darts or bullets?" Carmen asked.

"Two magazines of darts per person, the rest are bullets."

Carmen felt her pack and counted the twelve magazines I'd allotted her.

I'd planned for the same scenario I saw last time: a wide separation between hostiles and civilians. Most of the people I could see were children. I could be a mean son-of-a-bitch in a war zone, but I wouldn't traumatize kids by killing their parents in front of them.

"Well, then," Miguel said, "it's time for Operation Movie Star."

I nodded and turned to Diego. "Ever been in a firefight before?"

"Before wha—?" His voice stopped working. He shook his head. Miguel headed down the hill and disappeared into the brush.

"A lesser man would probably pee his pants doing what we're going to do, but you're a stud, Diego. I can see it in your eyes." I slapped him on the back.

He smiled as if he were about to puke.

"Hold on," Emily said. "You never said anything about a firefight. I got you a translator, where's my scoop?" She searched my eyes. "What are you … do you mean … I'm not going—"

"You're going to stay right here with Carmen. Actually, you're going to move ten yards away from Carmen, in case they have an RPG."

"You're going to take on the Kazakhs?" Emily asked.

"The Kazakhs wouldn't be dumb enough to stick around after the grave was uncovered. But the Pak Uban can lead me to them."

"That's it? That's my scoop?"

"It's a good scoop. Embedded with Sabel Security, you'll have war correspondent credentials. Investigative journalism at its finest."

Emily shook her head, her eyes bugged out. "What good is all that if I get killed?"

Carmen put an arm around her. "Don't worry, we've been through nastier shit than these guys can dish out. We got this."

Emily nodded and sniffled.

Carmen gave her an extra squeeze, then leaned against a tree and closed her eyes.

I pushed Emily back to a hardwood tree. "Get some rest. Shooting won't start until 0300."

Emily turned white and stood motionless. I tugged Diego's sleeve and led him down the hill.

The road to victory requires careful timing. March in when everyone's fed and awake, and you die. Sneak in when everyone's drunk and bored and asleep, and you win. We had a few hours to kill to get the timing right. I found a nice place about three hundred yards downwind from the village. Diego sat and stared at me while I stretched out and closed my eyes. A Kayan patrol came near us a few times, scaring the bejeezus out of Diego, but they never saw us. A dog sniffed his way to the Milk Bones in my pocket. He went away quietly after I gave him one. His doggy pals heard about it and came for a treat of their own. I went through half my stash before shooing them away.

I was drifting off into a nice dream about walking into a Starbucks where a hundred hajjis waited in ambush when a text came in from Ms. Sabel. "Bio-attack planned on Philadelphia. Find those Kazakhs fast."

I thumbed out a reply. "Stepping it up, ma'am."

At 0300, my phone alarm vibrated and I opened my eyes. I checked in with Carmen and Miguel on the comm link to find them both sleepy but waking fast. Diego and Emily hadn't slept at all.

The Malaysian police in Kuching didn't answer the phone, so I left a message with our coordinates.

My translator followed me toward the village like a condemned man and almost ran into me when I stopped to give out more doggy treats.

On the outskirts of the village, a lone guard manned his post with heavy eyes. They opened plenty wide when I touched my assault rifle to his face. He surrendered in silence, and I shouldered his AK-47 for a spare.

Pushing my hostage in front, I strolled into town on the central path while Diego flinched at every leaf flapping in the warm breeze.

Mercury said, Look at you, marching like a boss down the middle of the street.

I said, Movie star. You could help me out by telling me how many are in there.

Mercury said, Dude, always with the jokes. You got this.

Praying to gods can be more confusing that it's worth. I was within an inch of firing the pagan jerk.

Our reluctant tour guide assured us the Pak Uban slept in the longhouse. I pushed him ahead of me with my rifle in his ribs. Diego clung to my back. A sleepy kid near the entrance jumped to attention and bobbled his weapon. I popped a dart into him with my Glock.

The main room was half the building. On each side were smaller rooms separated with curtains. The silencer was effective, but a loud pop in a small space is alarming. Five guys jumped off their mats and shook themselves awake.

When the old man showed himself, his boys started spreading wide. I popped two of them and traded my hostage for the old man before they knew what happened. That left Diego in the center of the room, shaking like a leaf. The four remaining men eyeballed him like fresh meat.

Miguel coughed behind them, having slithered in the back while I held their attention. He had Diego order them to get on the floor, facedown, hands stretched out in front. They didn't move fast enough so he shot one in the leg. The others dropped quickly.

Then it was my turn. "Pak-man, how ya been, buddy?"

Diego translated but our captive didn't speak. He wasn't that old, maybe late fifties, but his eyes crossed with confusion as he contemplated how he'd been overpowered so quickly.

I pulled an 8x10 picture of Kaya's corpse out of my pack and held it in front of him. I dropped it on the floor. I pulled out another picture, a wide shot of the grave with several bodies on the top layer. I spun it and let it twirl to the floor. I pulled another picture. And another. Ten in all. "Ever heard of Nuremburg? World Court? Crimes against humanity?"

He said nothing.

"Do you know what the USA does to terrorists who plan a bio-attack on Philadelphia?"

His eyes flickered wide open when he processed my accusation, then he slipped his poker-face back on and said nothing.

"How about murder?" I walked around him. "Malaysian authorities are on their way here from Kuching. They'll question you about the Kazakhs and the mass grave full of your Melanau neighbors. Do you want them to find you alive?"

The old man turned to look at me when Diego translated.

Bullets whizzed outside: Carmen's sniper rifle. We heard a body drop on the veranda. He moaned loudly.

I raised my voice. "Your choice. Tell me what I want to know and you'll be alive when they get here to arrest you. Clam up and I finish the job Ms. Sabel started."

Diego translated and the old man replied. Diego said, "He wants to know what you mean, 'the job Ms. Sabel started'?"

Outside, the dying man moaned and called for help.

"She cut your son's dick off. That was before we found out you were selling the Melanau to the Kazakhs. I don't like that kind of thing. I'll make sure none of you can reproduce ever again. After I fix your boys, I'm going to fix you. Problem is, I don't work with a knife."

When Diego finished translating, but before the old man could speak, I had one of his young bucks stand up. I drilled a dart in his groin. My victim fell hard on the wooden floor. The shock value was exceptional.

Even Diego gasped.

The old man spoke fast.

Diego said, "He would like to answer your questions now."

On the veranda, the dying man gasped again. Three more bullets whizzed outside and another body fell on the veranda. Her aim had improved—this time there was no moaning.

"How were you going to pay off my first translator?"

Diego translated. "He knows the boy's village. He was going to deliver payment to his mother."

"I took all your money. How were you planning to pay him? With money from the Kazakhs?"

"Yes."

"How will you get in touch with them?"

"They will come here whenever it suits them."

"You expect me to believe the Kazakhs will come back to Borneo?"

Miguel dragged another young buck to his feet and I put a dart in his groin.

Diego said, "He wishes to revise his answer. He has a phone number to call, but the nearest phone is two villages away."

I tossed him the phone I'd brought for this special occasion. When his call connected, it would upload the Sabel tracking virus to the other end and we'd have the location of our Kazakh mercenaries.

The old man dialed.

Carmen took out a third man attempting to sneak in.

She reported on the comm link. "Headlights in the trees, half an hour out. Gotta be the Malaysians. Fifteen hostiles out front, ready to charge. I can't get them all. Make a snappy exit."

Diego listened in to the Pak Uban's call and confirmed the old man's sincere attempt at extorting more money from his Kazakh masters. They would send a courier to the Melanau village in two days. We darted the Pak Uban and the remaining Kayan and slipped out the back way.

With two of their own dead and one wounded on the front veranda, and what appeared to be a bloodbath inside, the men massing for a frontal assault were slow to chase us. Carmen gave us updates while we put half a kilometer between our pursuers and us. Diego was no athlete yet he rose to the occasion, staying ahead by ten yards.

Miguel was too big to run fast in the jungle, so he brought up the rear.

Mercury said, Save yourself first, brotha.

"Problem," Carmen said in a whisper. "Three tangos in the trees. Rendezvous at Charlie."

Three tangos, wartime slang for targets, would not be a problem for Carmen if I'd left her alone. We could hear her through the comm link, trying to move Emily out of the sniper nest and down the hill. Emily had succumbed to fear and wouldn't move. Carmen coaxed her gently for a moment before raising her voice a notch. The comm link picked up bullets whizzing by.

Emily shrieked.

Making loud noises while enemies try to shoot you is counterproductive. From the sounds coming over the comm link, Carmen gave Emily a swift kick in the ass that landed our reporter five yards down the slope.

The worst feeling in the world is knowing your friends are in deep trouble. Miguel's face rippled with fear and anger.

"We're coming," I said.

"Negative. Meet at Charlie," Carmen said.

Mercury said, Did you hear me? I said, save yourself. Dead guys can't save the team.

I said, Shut up, I can't concentrate.

Mercury said, Listen to me! Remember that teamwork speech you gave the boss? Run now so you can save the team later!

Miguel and I already passed our Bravo rendezvous point and could either turn east for our last-resort meeting point Charlie, or north to help Carmen.

I stopped and sniffed the air. I smelled a wet dog.

Miguel tugged my shirt. "I'll get the women. Meet you at Charlie."

"No. We're in this together."

Mercury said, You fucking idiot. Run! Now!

Movement behind him caught my eye. Shadows passed through a sliver of moonlight. At the same time, Miguel's eyes widened and focused a short distance behind me. On my left, Diego raised his hands in surrender.

Two Kazakhs stood behind Miguel, rifles aimed at his head.

Chapter 29

Dishes clattered and voices echoed in the tiny Greenhouse restaurant off the hotel's lobby. Having memorized their order, the waiter bowed and left them. Violet's phone vibrated. She checked the caller ID and looked around. She nodded to Cummings. "Guangzhou. I have to take this. I'll be right back."

In the lobby, she clicked to answer. "What is it?"

"The government has seized the plant, ma'am," her secretary said. "Soldiers came and sent everyone home."

"What for?"

"Improper working conditions, ma'am."

"Who was it?" Violet asked.

"Public Security Bureau."

"Where is Teresa? Didn't she—"

"Teresa was arrested, ma'am."

"On what charges? Where are they holding her?"

"I don't know, ma'am. The attorneys told me not to ask."

"That's ridiculous," Violet said. "Someone has to know. Who's still in the office?"

"We were all sent home, ma'am. I'm calling you from my personal phone."

Violet checked again: it was not a Windsor number. "Do you know if Teresa sent the last shipment to me? The one headed for Washington?"

"It went this morning, ma'am."

Violet clicked off and slipped her phone in her purse. Pressure built in her head to the boiling point. Her stump throbbed and she crunched her fingers into her hair. She wanted to scream, but there was work to be done.

She called. Chen's cell phone went straight to voicemail. She didn't leave a message and returned to her table. Her croissant and coffee waited for her. Cummings forked his omelet and looked up.

"Have you seen a ghost?" Cummings asked.

"We have to accelerate the program."

"I think it's time to stop throwing money at a bad—"

"Let me think through the timeline. We have them start deployment today. Have you called that Velox animal yet?"

"To call them off?" Cummings asked. "I can do that now if—"

"It'll take five to seven days for incubation. We can keep this thing quiet for a couple weeks. When can he start?"

"Who?"

"The Velox guy, Kasey."

"Start deployment? Never. Call it off."

"Accelerating the time line was your idea," she said. "You were right, but we need it now—today."

"What happened?"

"They seized the production facility."

"That's it, then. We're done. We call off the hit on Sabel, we close the Philadelphia project, we turn in Mokin for murder and kidnapping, and we walk away clean."

"Great plan—for you. What happens to me?"

Cummings shrugged and tossed his napkin on his plate. He looked left, then right. "We'll work it out."

"You're on record for Borneo."

"I never understood all that science gobbledy-gook. I trusted you and Verratti and Wu Fang."

Violet's eyes narrowed and her mouth drew taught. "You think you can sell me out?"

"Nothing like that, Violet. I would never let you take the heat. We'll think of something." Cummings waved his hands. "Get some good lawyers, stay out of Asia for a while, and let the legal eagles do their thing. It'll work."

"And in the meantime, you're cozy with Alan Sabel."

"The man has to invest his money somewhere. Why not at Cummings Capital?"

Violet tossed her napkin on her untouched pastry. "We're going forward. Are you going to call that asshole at Velox?"

"If I call him, it's to get your $2 million back and cancel the hit on Sabel."

"I'll call him then." She leaned back, gripping the arms of her chair until her knuckles turned white. "And I'll send a copy of your real financial statements to the SEC."

"What are you talking about?" Cummings leaned back, his eyes wide, hands and fingers spread out on the table. "I file reports with the government every quarter, right on time."

"China has the best hackers in the world. Chen sent me your real financials, Ed. You have two sets of books, one for yourself and a second for the Feds."

Cummings reached for his coffee and held it in a shaking hand. "I have nothing to hide."

Violet huffed and crossed her arms, watching him as he sipped then clattered his cup back into the saucer.

"You're not as bad as Bernie Madoff," she said, "but you'll still get life without parole."

"Fine," Cummings said, "we'll do it your way. Where is the package?"

"Your Velox man was supposed to have it by now."

"I never saw the message from Kasey confirming it."

"A second package will arrive tomorrow. Enough for Philly and New Jersey."

Cummings nodded. "I'll set it up."

"Who do you know inside the Sabel camp?" she asked. "How would you contact Alan Sabel?"

"His family doctor was my college roommate."

"That's where you've been getting your inside information?"

"What're you implying?" Cummings frowned.

"Mokin must have an insider. Are you providing his information on Pia's whereabouts?" Her eyes narrowed. "Wait. You knew Tania Cooper was sick before anyone else. That had to come from your doctor friend. Are you feeding this information to Mokin too?"

"I'm shocked you'd even suggest—"

"Why're they using the family quack anyway? I thought Bobby Jenkins was Alan Sabel's best friend. Why didn't they call the biggest asshole in pharmaceuticals?"

"He's tied up in Brussels. His son is trying to fill the gap."

"How interesting. Do they think the boy's as smart as his father?"

"I don't know. I don't care." Cummings tapped his fingers on the table. "This whole thing is getting out of control, Violet. We have to consider—"

She leaned forward and whispered. "If you walk out on me, I swear to God, I'll kill you myself."

"I told you, we'll do it your way." Ed Cummings folded his napkin, placed it carefully on the table. "I disagree, but I'll do as you wish, Violet."

"Don't you dare call Alan Sabel or his pet doctor."

Cummings rose and bowed vaguely in Violet's direction.

She looked away.

He waited a moment, then crossed the lobby and went outside.

A text from Chen Zhipeng tugged Violet's attention to her phone. "Chapman is talking to Pia Sabel right now. It's all over the news."

Tears welled up in her eyes; a lump formed in her throat. The world seemed to fade from her vision. She texted Chen. "Who seized my company? Why is Teresa in custody? Who is doing this to me?"

The waiter brought the bill and left it for her. She ignored it. For ten minutes she stared at her phone, waiting for Chen's reply. The busboy came and took away the dishes. Still she waited. No reply.

She signed the check and limped out into the cold morning air. After some thought, she dialed Kasey Earl.

"Hey, sugar," Kasey answered. "What's up this morning?"

Her jaw clenched. "Ed Cummings is going to the authorities."

"Why tell *me* this?"

"I need you to kill Ed Cummings."

"Two hundred grand. All upfront. Where do you want the body?"

Violet Windsor felt sick at the thought. "I don't know. However you dispose of it, make sure it's not traced back to me."

~~~

Kasey Earl called his boss. "Dunno if it's scary or funny, but she done paid me fifty large to kill Ed Cummings."

"Fifty? You could get more, she's desperate."

"That's all she'd pony up, boss."

His boss said nothing for thirty seconds. "Are you forwarding all the money to the Velox account?"

"Oh, absolutely sir."

"You're not skimming anything off this deal?"

"No sir. I'd never do that to you. I value working for—"

"Get it in cash. She doesn't have any credit."

"Should I do the job? I thought he was a friend of yours."

"Hell no. He's a Wall Street guy, they don't have friends." He paused. "Jobs are piling up. We have real customers waiting. I'll call you back with a priority list."

Chapter 30

Pia stroked Tania's face and thought it felt cooler. She glanced at the machines. They blinked and whirred and displayed numbers that meant nothing to her. Mr. Ramos kept his gaze fixed on his daughter while his ex-wife dozed in a big chair. Pia reached across the bed to squeeze his hand. When Ramos's eyes met hers, she whispered, "Tania survived Afghanistan and dating Jacob. I'm sure she'll survive this."

Tania opened one eye. "Jacob was worse."

Mr. Ramos smiled. "Your fever's gone down, *mi pequeña*"

Tania breathed hard from the exertion of sitting up. "They found a cure?"

"No," Pia sighed, "but I found Chapman. Actually, he found me."

"Did you kill him?"

Pia thought Tania's sclera were a lighter shade of blue and moved closer to be sure. "He's in a room down the hall, dying."

Tania swung her feet over the edge and pushed against Pia. "Show me, I'll finish him off."

Pia grabbed her agent by the shoulders, but Tania lost her balance and fell backward. Pia scooped up her legs and placed her gently back in bed. Tania closed her eyes.

"He's going to help us," Pia said.

"Yeah," Tania said. Her voice slowed. "You think the lying son-of-a-bitch will tell us the truth this time?"

"I was just going to check on him. Rest now." Pia slipped out.

Down the hall, she found Chapman asleep. She put her hand on his forehead. His fever was much higher than Tania's.

Chapman twitched awake at her touch and turned his head in her direction, his eyes still closed.

"I had no idea," he said in a voice so weak she had to lean in. "It was an experiment ...an exercise. We had Levoxavir."

"What's that?"

"Antibiotic ... cure." He coughed.

Pia spelled it aloud as she typed it into her phone. He nodded and she texted the name to Doc Günter for more information.

"I swear I didn't know," he said. "The project was supposed to be an academic experiment. I found out by accident. I couldn't believe ... they'd turn it loose on people. That's why I went ... but they didn't have Levoxavir."

Chapman coughed and struggled to wipe his eyes. "Turn your camera on, selfie. I want to see..."

"Your eyes?" she asked.

He nodded and forced his crusty eyelids open.

She turned it on and aimed it for him. His eyes rolled around before finally finding a focal point. He let out a breath and pushed the phone away. "Too late."

Pia leaned close. "Too late for what?"

He sipped water from a cup on the table then shook his head. "Record this. I'll make a statement."

Pia turned on the video recorder.

"I am a research doctor." Chapman coughed. "Windsor Pharmaceuticals. I was responsible for clinical trials of Levoxavir, an experimental drug intended for use against bio-warfare agents. To test it, we developed 'Elements' by splicing genes from viruses like Ebola and Hepatitis C. We made sure it doesn't transmit between humans. Then I found out about an unauthorized field trial on Borneo. I made a surprise inspection. I arrived twenty minutes before you. No Levoxavir. They gave a gray powdered compound to unsuspecting village elders. It killed them. When you saw the grave, they scrambled to chase you down. After that, they gave me a dose by holding a cloth to my face until I gasped for air. They started blaming each other and got in a big fight. I stole Teresa's phone and drove the other way. I crossed into Indonesia."

Chapman's eyes rolled back in his head and closed. His breathing came wet and slow.

Pia asked, "Teresa was the lady with you?"

"Project manager." He took a breath. "She ran the ... field trial."

Chapman stopped talking. The machines whirred and beeped. The air was still. After a long time, one of his eyes opened.

"The gray stuff. Element 42. They plan to dust Philadelphia, then the eastern seaboard in the next few days. People will die. Levoxavir is the only cure. The sick will pay anything for it. You have to stop them."

"Where is her phone?"

Chapman nodded at a small bag in the corner. She rifled through it, found the phone, dialed her techs, and had them download the contents.

"Levoxavir will save everyone?" Pia asked. "Where do I get it?"

"My lab at NIH." He wheezed a couple breaths. "Two buildings over ... from where I saw you."

"Hang in there, we'll get some for you."

"I'm too far gone." Chapman coughed and closed his eyes for a long time. "I was born with immune deficiencies."

"Will it help Tania?"

"If she's young and healthy, it will help. But Element 42 was designed for a short illness, like the twenty-four hour flu. Victims will improve or die in few days."

Pia texted Doc Günter to track down the cure. As she thumbed out her message, Chapman's machines beeped loud and long.

"What I ... don't understand," Chapman said, "Is why Wu Fang..."

She waited a moment. "Wu Fang? Why Wu Fang ... what?"

His eyes closed. His mouth slackened, his body relaxed.

A nurse rushed in. Then another.

"Can you revive him?" Pia asked.

The first nurse scowled and checked his pulse.

A doctor rushed in.

"He was about to tell me something important that could save hundreds of lives. You have to—"

"Are you family?" the first nurse asked.

When she shook her head, the second nurse pushed Pia out into the hall. She came back to the doorway and watched them work on Chapman for a long time.

"Is he going to make it?" Pia asked.

"Ma'am, let us do our jobs."

"You don't understand, lives are at—"

The nurse closed the door.

Pia leaned her ear to it and listened to them working. The doctor spoke and the nurse answered. And machines that should beep didn't.

Finally, their efforts ceased. A doctor said, "Call it!"

Pia drifted down the hallway feeling no pity for Chapman, only anger at the lack of actionable information from his statement. Teresa was a weak lead. A "Wu Fang" search on her phone produced thousands of hits with nothing conclusive. The last clue was gone. She leaned against the wall.

Otis Blackwell emerged from Tania's room. Pia gave him a withering glance.

"I'm here as a friend, not a reporter." He pointed inside the room. "I brought dinner for her mom and dad."

Pia's stare drilled through him.

"I got to know her when I did the report on the Romanian thing." Otis dropped his eyes. "I asked her out a couple times, but it never went anywhere."

Doc Günter walked up and waited for acknowledgement. At the same time, Jaz approached from the elevators. Pia faced Günter. "Did it work?"

"Medicine takes time," Günter said. "Listen, I have to apologize. I've made a terrible—"

"No apologies until Tania is healthy," she said. "But that gray rag Jacob found might be more important than we thought. And we have one more vial."

"I thought all three vials were destroyed," Otis said.

At the same time, Jaz said, "You have another vial?"

Pia and Doc Günter turned to them.

Realizing he was speaking out of turn, Jaz flushed. "Sorry, it's just that the news—never mind."

"I'm asking as a reporter," Otis said, "but let me guess: you don't have a comment."

"No, but I'll call you. Really."

Otis scowled and spoke over his shoulder. "I'll hold my breath."

Pia faced Günter and squeezed his arm. "Keep focused on Tania."

He bowed slightly and disappeared into Tania's room.

Pia turned to Jaz. "What brings you here?"

He smiled. "You."

She kept her face blank and focused her electric gray-green eyes on his blues.

He stammered. "I was hoping to help in some way. I mean, I'm not much of a fighter, but there must be something I can do. How can I help?"

"Tell your dad to answer his phone. I have one last chance to figure this out and I can't trust anyone else."

"He goes off-electronics when he's concentrating on a project like the Brussels thing. I'll call his admin, she'll know a way to reach him."

Pia spun away from him and dialed the Major.

Jaz took the hint and backed up two steps. She ignored him while he waited for a wave or a smile. After a few awkward seconds, she heard his footsteps trudging away.

The Major said, "We tracked a phone call that we think will lead us to our spy—"

"I know who the traitor is, and he's not using a phone we can trace." Pia looked up and down the hallway. "We'll talk when I get back."

"OK." The Major was silent for a moment. "Are you in danger?"

"I can handle it."

The Major patched them into a call with her tech staff, who gave Pia a rundown on the contents of Teresa's phone. It held records of calls, texts, and emails to several employees of Windsor Pharmaceuticals in Guangzhou. Encrypted reports showed death rates, exposure times, among other data for Element 42. Cold and analytical, the reports identified stages of illness and recovery, the length of time for each stage, and the likelihood of recovery with and without treatment.

"Nothing about Levoxavir?" Pia asked.

"No, ma'am," her tech reported. "The only pills dispensed were placebos."

"Hard evidence," the Major said. "We have Windsor cold."

"Have Verges run this up to Homeland Security and have them keep an eye on Philadelphia."

"I will, and they'll take it seriously, but it won't do any good until we know what to look for. Windsor isn't going to drape a rag over the city. They'll have a system to reach farther and faster."

"Get the Chinese to arrest the Windsor people in Guangzhou."

"That has to go through the State Department."

"We can't contact China directly?"

"Contact who? The Chinese invented bureaucracy three thousand years ago. I tried putting in calls to the Public Security Bureau, their version of Homeland Security."

Pia sighed. "Then we can go through the investors. Who owns Windsor?"

"Excuse me, ma'am," a new tentative voice said on the call. "Agent Carter here. I found the executives and the board members. One of them stood out. Marco Verratti."

"Interesting. Why kill a board member?"

"Maybe someone worried he would talk?" the Major said.

"Who else is involved in Windsor?" Pia asked.

"They have four board members," Agent Carter said. "The other three are: Anatoly Mokin from Kazakhstan, Dr. Wu Fang from Beijing, and Ed Cummings from New York City."

"Mokin," the Major said. "He should be our—"

"I'm working on Mokin," Pia said.

"You have a project under way and never told—"

"Chapman mentioned Wu Fang," Pia said. "Do we have his contact info?"

"Yes, ma'am," Agent Carter said.

"Send it to me. I'll call him—"

"No," the Major said. "You might spook him. We need a face-to-face to see if he's lying."

"Right." Pia said. "Agent Carter, track down Wu Fang for me. What can you tell me about Cummings?"

"He's a hedge fund manager," Agent Carter said, "nice website, solid—"

"Hold on a sec," Pia said. "I have a call coming in."

She flipped the call over.

"Ms. Sabel, I'm Ed Cummings, and I can help—"

"What is your role in the mass graves on Borneo?"

His gasp overwhelmed his phone. "You already traced that to…" The line was silent for a moment. Then he cleared his throat and took a breath. "We need to meet."

Chapter 31

Kazakhs must have strong stomachs, because their campsite smelled like a year-old porta potty. I guessed they were short on handcuffs because three of the Kazakhs held Miguel and two more held me. Another man busied himself by smashing our phones, presumably to foil GPS tracking. I saw no need to tell them Sabel agents carry spares.

Mercury said, Some people listen when the gods speak to them, bro. Some people would consider it an honor to have a God tell him to save himself. But not—

I said, And some Gods are above pettiness.

Mercury said, Yeah? Well, He doesn't return your calls.

I focused on Diego.

"He says they have been waiting for you all week." Diego's voice wavered as he spoke, which was understandable since the rifle barrel under his chin pushed his whole head back. "He wants to know where the tall woman is."

"What language is that? Kazakh?" I asked.

"Kazakh's a Turkic language. I speak a little Uzbek, also Turkic. We're making do."

I turned my head as much as I could with four hands and a rifle muzzle holding me in place. Straining at the corner of my eye socket, I caught the gaze of the head guy and spoke in Pashto. "Let Diego go. He's just a translator."

Afghanistan and Kazakhstan are only a thousand miles apart. I hoped he understood me. In a mad attempt to avoid one more combat deployment, I'd learned Pashto and Arabic and put in for a desk job at the Pentagon. Instead, the language skills made me popular with battalions heading for the nastiest deployments. It took two Purple Hearts and a Silver Star to get me transferred to the Defense Intelligence Agency, where the babes-to-guys ratio was more agreeable than the war zone.

He nodded and grunted.

Not a definitive statement, so I tried a different tactic in Arabic. "Your pal Yuri is helping us back in the states. He told me where to find you, but not your name."

His head came up fast. He shouted in Kazakh.

Something as thick as a baseball bat hit the back of my leg. I fell to the ground. Three Kazakhs jumped on me. They held my face in the dirt. I could see nothing, but I heard a thud and Carmen screamed. Emily wailed in sympathy but another thud cut her off. She continued crying through what sounded like a gag.

Another bat whooshed through the air followed by the sound of it striking meat. Whooshes came from all around me. Many of the blows landed on me but I could hear plenty more landing on my team. The pain in my back and legs mounted.

Silver and black dots winked from the edges of my vision, filling in more and more until I could see nothing. Just when I thought I'd pass out, someone grabbed my body armor and yanked me upright.

My legs crumpled beneath me.

"Mukhtar," the head guy introduced himself. "*As-salaam 'alaykum.*" *Peace be upon you.* A formal Arabic greeting. His men laughed.

I responded in Arabic. He welcomed me and waved an arm around his encampment as if he were showing off a palace. In the dawn's first light, I saw several tents lining an acre clearing, a small fire smoldering in a shallow pit, a stack of supply crates leaning to the tipping point. Next to one tent was a stack of mosquito foggers, insecticide sprayers with five-foot aluminum barrels and small motors that belonged in a sci-fi movie. Two of the three trucks that had been parked at the death camp were parked down a jungle trail.

Mukhtar's hand grabbed my chin, twisted my head to the right. It took a moment for my eyes to focus but I saw what he wanted me to see: two freshly cut posts, anchored in the dirt with an iron ring bolted to the top of each. Whipping posts or firing squad poles.

I swallowed a dry lump in my throat and cursed myself for *pressing the opportunity immediately*. The Army was big, bureaucratic, and slow, but no Army officer would've let me run off as poorly prepared as I had been for this mission. Guessing the Kazakhs had fled Borneo was a horrifying miscalculation on my part. Which begged the questions: why hadn't they?

I strained over my shoulder to check on my teammates. Our hosts had effectively destroyed my ability to fight or flee. Miguel suffered similar blows. Two Kazakhs stood under his arms to hold him up. Carmen and Emily were farther to my left. As I turned my head to assess their fate, a Kazakh swung a big stick into Carmen's breasts.

"You stole from me," Mukhtar said in Arabic.

"I gave the vials to Yuri."

He laughed and snapped his fingers. The man with the big stick slammed it against Emily's breasts.

Carmen screamed at them, Miguel yelled death threats. Emily shrieked in pain.

"Stop this," I said, "and I won't kill you."

He laughed. "And how will you kill me?" He scowled and yelled. "Tell me where are the vials?"

"Your men destroyed them at NIH."

"You gave Yuri fakes." Mukhtar looked a question at me. "What is NIH?"

Memory is a funny thing. Men in black on the NIH video were automatically Kazakhs in my mind. Mukhtar's reaction had me revisiting that video and I remembered Miguel calling them tall. The guys at NIH were Americans, six inches taller than the average Kazakh.

Mukhtar's thinking moved at the same pace as mine. Our eyes met when we figured it out. But he was free and I was tethered to his sadistic henchmen. He stepped away and pulled out a standard satellite phone with the big, cigar-like antenna. When he connected, he spoke in Kazakh. I glanced at my translator.

Two men tied Diego's hands to the iron ring on the whipping post. His bloody face rose for a fleeting moment. Our gaze connected.

"Anatoly Mokin," Diego said.

Mukhtar cut his conversation mid-sentence and whipped his gaze to Diego.

In my state, I didn't understand what Diego was telling me until Mukhtar reacted. Mokin had tried to steal crude oil with mercenaries posing as Islamic fundamentalists. He'd planned to blame al Qeada, Boko Haram, or ISIS for the raids. British Petroleum had hired us to defend their sites and we stopped him cold. In the mercenary business, reputation is everything and Sabel Security ruined his.

Mukhtar shouted in Kazakh at the men restraining Diego. A tense moment passed before he looked at me. In Arabic, he said, "Who destroyed the vials?"

I didn't speak.

A Kazakh knelt next to Diego, grabbed his foot, and pulled it over his knee like a farrier shoeing a horse. With a dramatic flair, the man brandished a long dagger, holding it high above his head before slashing it through the sole of Diego's foot.

My translator screamed.

Another slash across his foot, followed by another gut-wrenching scream.

"Stop!" I shouted first in English then Arabic.

"Who has my vials?" Mukhtar asked.

"No one. They were destroyed."

Mukhtar returned to his call, his back to Diego and me. His farrier slashed Diego's foot a third time then dropped the foot. My man howled in pain. The Kazakh picked up Diego's other foot, forcing him to stand on his injuries. My toes curled with sympathetic pains.

"Mukhtar, c'mon man. I could make something up, but they're gone. Stop this."

Mukhtar faced me. "How were they destroyed?"

"I wasn't allowed into the crime scene, I only saw video of the entrance. I thought they were your men."

He waved his hand and two men dragged Carmen to the second post.

The stick whooshed again and my legs buckled before I felt the strike. Landing on my knees, I heard another whoosh. It slashed across my back.

"I still don't know." Another blow cracked my back. "But Pia Sabel will pay you more than Anatoly Mokin has paid you in the last five years."

Mukhtar raised a hand. His men pulled the rope binding Carmen's wrists through the iron ring, tugged it tight, and tied it off.

Mukhtar asked, "Who is Anatoly Mokin?"

"Yuri told me he's your boss."

"Who is Pia Sabel?"

"The tall woman who took your vials to NIH. She's very rich and—"

"How do you know her?"

I shot a glance at Emily to convince her to keep her mouth shut, then remembered we were talking in Arabic. "She's a big deal in Washington. Everyone knows her."

"Do you work for her?" Mukhtar strolled toward me, stopping a few feet away. "She will pay for your safe return?"

I stood up, regretting my big mouth. "We can always ask her. It's worth a try."

"Will she return the vials in exchange for your life?"

"Mukhtar, listen when I speak. The vials have been destroyed."

Mukhtar's first punch landed on my chin, his second and third in my belly. "I want the pieces."

He spoke in Kazakh again. Nothing good happened when he spoke in Kazakh.

One of his men raised a rifle and aimed at Carmen's head.

Chapter 32

Washington's ubiquitous gray stone buildings met the gray sky high above Violet's gaze. A frosty drizzle fell on her shoulders as she dashed for the cab with her phone to her ear.

"I am shocked," Chen Zhipeng said, "to hear about it from someone else instead of you."

Violet Windsor stared straight ahead, holding her phone to her ear. When the cabbie glanced at her in the mirror, she turned to the side and leaned her head against the glass. "I'm sorry, *Shifu*. Teresa never said anything about a missing cloth."

"It is not for her to tell you. It is for you to inquire." He paused to control the rising volume of his voice. "Your employee must be honest with you."

"I will try harder."

"Have you been honest with me, Violet?"

"Yes, *Shifu*."

"Borneo cannot be connected to Windsor in anyway," Chen said. "You must be certain the cloth is incinerated."

"I understand." Violet watched the Hay-Adams Hotel fade behind her as they turned onto H Street and circled Lafayette Park.

"You do *not* understand," Chen snapped. "You must be certain of every detail. I have taken precaution to distance myself from your operation but this is a disaster. When you ruin Chen, you ruin the Party and China."

"I will take care of it right away, *Shifu*." Violet took a deep breath. "I need my company back. I need my resources. I need Teresa."

"That is something I cannot control. The authorities have seized the plant until the chemical agents have been recovered and the Levoxavir found. When they find those thing they will release everything to you. Do you know where to find Levoxavir, Violet?"

"No," she said. Which was true. Chapman's office in Washington was empty, and the researchers there said Chapman had moved everything to his satellite office in the NIH complex just before he left for Borneo. And NIH was crawling with FBI.

"I fear someone think it a good idea to deploy Element 42 and sell Levoxavir."

"No one would do a thing like that, *Shifu*. I'm sure we'll find it as soon as Anatoly and his men are questioned by the authorities in Guangzhou. Are they in custody now?"

"Do not concern yourself with Mokin. Keep your focus on the cloth."

"But Anatoly's men are here in Washington. Are they here on your orders?"

"No."

Violet's heart stopped beating, her stomach flipped. "You've not spoken to him about this?"

"I do not associate with men like Anatoly Mokin."

Violet wanted to scream. Instead, she took a deep breath. "You insisted I choose him for the board, along with—"

"Find the cloth." Chen clicked off.

Violet kept her nose to the window as 15th Street bent around the Washington Monument and hurried by the Holocaust Museum. Even from thousands of miles away Chen Zhipeng knew everything, yet he'd never mentioned Chapman's death.

Her cab slowed to a stop.

"Jefferson Memorial," the cabbie said.

Violet stared out the window at the tree-lined walkway as if it were a picture at an exhibition.

Chen had to know the cloth would be impossible to find. How do you find a rag? Had it been at NIH? Did they send it to the CDC or throw it away? How did Chen even know about the cloth?

"Ma'am," the cabbie said, "you wanted the Jefferson Memorial, right?"

Startled from her thoughts, she paid the fare, buttoned her long coat, and stepped out. The nippy air swept her hair into her face, and the swamp-scent of the Tidal Basin tinged her nose. Deep in thought, she negotiated her way through a throng of hyperactive schoolchildren. She walked to the east side of the memorial's broad apron overlooking the water. She leaned against the massive stone barrier and assessed the crowd, looking for Kasey Earl.

He stood with his back to her and held a phone up for a photo of the memorial's rotunda, then turned toward Violet. He grinned at her and sauntered over, leaned on the high balustrade.

After a moment of silence, he said, "You owe me fifty thousand extra for NIH."

"Absolutely not."

"My business at NIH drew the attention of the FBI's Counterintelligence unit." Kasey leaned closer to her. "Using my black ops get-out-of-jail-free card costs money. There are documents that have to be forged, bureaucrats who have to look the other way. Send the money now, while we're talking, or I call a cab and go visit a man named David Watson at the FBI. Me and David go way back."

She pulled her phone from her purse and, with another glance at Kasey, entered the requisite passwords and numbers. She showed him the screen. "There, satisfied?"

He nodded.

"Where is the package?" she asked.

"Not here."

"You sent me the code word, Lincoln Memorial, and told me to meet you here."

"There's been a wrinkle, sugar."

"Do you have it or not?"

"I do." He grinned, his breath bad enough to wilt a salad. "But there's another bidder."

"Bidder? What? You told someone about this? How dare—"

"Someone knows about whatever's in the box. He contacted me."

"I've already paid you. Give me what belongs to me."

"Or what? You going to the police?"

Violet stepped back and gripped her coat around her.

"I want another million."

"That's outrageous," Violet shouted. "I'm not paying you another—"

Kasey turned on his heel and began walking away. Violet ran in front of him and pushed his solid body with both hands.

"Where is it? How soon can you deploy it? That million covers deployment, right?"

"Do you even have a million more?" he asked. "Word is, your accounts are empty."

Violet backed off and checked her phone. The last transaction had failed—insufficient funds. "Goddammit! The fucking Chinese froze my accounts."

"Not my problem." He paced away.

Violet ran in front of him again. "Just a minute. I'll get this all cleared up and pay you a million, but I need that package and I need it deployed."

Brushing her aside, he kept walking. "Not happening."

"Cummings!" She ran in front of him again. "I paid in advance. Same with Sabel. Have you finished the job on either of those?"

He stopped and grabbed her wrists. His face lowered into hers. She bent backward at the neck as far as she could without popping out of her leg.

"I reckon you're right about that. I still owe you two dead bodies. Let's start with Quattro."

"Who?"

"Cummings the fourth. Quattro."

His grip bruised her arms. She tried to wrench herself free but gave up.

He shoved her away and turned his back. "Do you know where Quattro is?"

"He's staying in the Jefferson Hotel, the Martha Suite."

Kasey turned around. "He ain't at the Jefferson, sugar. He's on his way to meet Pia Sabel."

Chapter 33

Pia knocked on the door and pushed it open in one continuous move. Tania stood by the window in street clothes, staring out, lost in thought. A duffle bag sat on the bed, zipped closed.

"Should you be up?" Pia asked.

"I'm good."

"You were out of it for—"

"My fever went down before I took the medicine. I'm good now. The doctors cleared me. I'm going after these guys."

"I need you to work with the Major. We have a traitor in our midst and—"

"You were right, we should've acted when we found them." Tania pressed her head to the glass. "I'm going to Borneo."

"Jacob's already there. He's hunting for Anatoly Mokin."

"That's why I'm going. He'll screw it up."

"Tania, you were on death's door yesterday. The Major and I need your investigative skills here. We have a serious problem."

Tania crossed her arms and kept her gaze on the parking garage three floors down.

"I'm the one who'll meet the team on Borneo," Pia said.

Tania took a slow breath. "When my sister was a teenager, she'd rave about the hyper-clarity and alertness that crystal meth gave her. Watching her fall into that chaos made me sick. I joined the Army to keep away from the life that swallowed her." Tania paused. "But the Army isn't a perfect place either. For some people, combat's just as addictive as meth. It's the adrenaline rush. Fighting for truth and justice, facing death and winning, is a high like nothing else. After a while, you get kind of immune and need more."

"I've been in a few dangerous situations," Pia said. "I know what you—"

"No you don't. You've been in tight a couple times. You've never been in a war zone. Death can come from any direction: IEDs, artillery, suicide bombers, mortars, grenades tossed over a wall. A battlefield stretches for miles over mountains and valleys and somewhere up the slope there's a sniper taking shots at you. Across the valley, there's another. The rounds come in from any and every direction, you have nowhere to hide and damn few targets. Every day you're on patrol you're constantly analyzing every distant object: is that a hajji with a rifle—or a boy with a stick? You make life-and-death decisions in a split second. You live in danger every minute, picking them out: this guy lives, that guy dies. You get hyper-alert, hyper-clear real fast—or you don't make it. Think about what living with that tension does to your head. Most people can't deal with it for very long before they go crazy. Two, maybe three tours and bang, permanent PTSD."

Tania grew quiet. The hospital buzzed outside the room.

"Jacob signed up for combat," Tania said. "He went back for more. Not once or twice but over and over again. He'll tell you different, but he wanted to go back. He transferred from one battalion to another, jumping in to any company that was shipping out. He learned languages so every combat commander would want him. He was the best. They called him X-Ray because he could see through walls. But they knew something was wrong. He was too lucky. They had him evaluated after one incident." Tania faced her boss and grabbed her arms. "Pia, Jacob hears voices. They moved him to the DIA so he could get treatment but he blew it off. He didn't quit the Army to become a cook. A two-star general cut a deal to keep him out of an institution."

They were silent for a moment before Tania looked at her hands and let go of Pia. She turned back to the window.

"Jacob's an addict. Addicted to death and danger like a hopeless junkie—like my sister. Next thing you know, he'll be letting people shoot at him for the thrill of it." Tania sniffled back some tears. "So far, he's won all his battles, but it's like playing Russian…"

Tania pressed her cheek to the window.

Pia wanted to hug her and say something soothing and affirmative. Instead she stood still.

"You're catching the high," Tania said quietly. "You're becoming an addict. Don't do it. Stay home. Marry your rich boyfriend and have rich kids. Jaz is your future."

"I can't marry him." Pia sighed. "His real name is Jasper Bernard Jenkins."

Tania took a moment. "For real? Jasper? Look, that's not what matters. What matters is: I'm going to Borneo, you're staying here."

"What about you? Aren't you becoming an addict?"

"It's too late for me. Miguel, Carmen, Dhanpal, people like us, we stay safe too long and we start drinking. Getting into fights. Falling in love. Blowing up relationships. I can't stay here. I can't shop at the mall. Sit in a cubicle. Meet for coffee. I'd end up like my sister. The only way I can stay on the right side of sanity is when somebody's trying to kill me."

Tania stepped around Pia, grabbed her duffel and strode out of the room.

Pia touched her earbud and the Major came online. "You were right. She's gone."

"You do realize that the two people you put in charge of your personal security have left the country and we're not sure how many assassins are still out there."

Pia took a minute before answering. "Yes, that's a problem. Got any ideas?"

"It's your company," the Major said, "you can order her back."

"Tania and Jacob are a team. They work better together than on their own."

"Keep Agent Marty on the job for another week. He's smarter'n those two put together anyway."

"OK." Pia sighed. "Were you going to tell me about Jacob's mental health?"

"No."

"Is he dangerous?"

"Not if you keep him busy. Right now he's busy. In other news, pretty boy Jaz came through. He managed to get Bobby Jenkins on a plane this morning. They're waiting for you at the Gardens."

~~~

On the third floor of her wing at Sabel Gardens, Pia's staff had set up a temporary lab. Spartan and low-key, her contemporary décor offered the perfect space.

When she walked in, Bobby Jenkins jumped from his chair with a megawatt smile and embraced her like the second father he'd always been. Doc Günter and Jaz watched from the corner of the room.

Günter crossed anxiously to Pia. "I must speak to you … privately, if you don't mind."

"I'd rather not keep a CEO waiting."

"But I must apologize for—" Günter began.

"Apologies can wait." Pia turned back to Bobby. "Were you here long?"

"I spent the time wisely," Bobby said. "After I checked out your new electron microscope and left Jaz to admire your trophy room, I caught up with your dad for a while."

She turned to Jaz with a small smile. "Sorry, the trophy room was Dad's idea. Terribly boring."

"So many National Championships," Jaz said. "I had no idea."

"We got lucky a few times."

"Why don't you play anymore? Word is the National Team's begging you to come back."

She faced Bobby. "Has Jaz told you his ideas about the pharmaceutical industry?"

Bobby patted his son on the back. "Idealism is a good thing. Once he has to answer to investors for profits, he'll realize nothing beats a patented maintenance drug. Right, boy?"

Pia frowned. "How far would a company go to maintain a patent?"

Bobby laughed. "Hell, some of my competitors would bring back the Spanish Influenza if they could patent a cure for it!" Bobby noticed her concern and coughed. "What do you have for me?"

Pia showed him the vial and the rag. "Jacob said the Kazakh guy used an ultraviolet light. We tried that but only saw a set of numbers. We tried code-breaking but we have nothing."

Günter stared nervously at Pia and tried to get her attention. She ignored him. He gave up and turned to Bobby to add a few observations of his own.

Bobby leaned over a desk and shined a UV flashlight on the vial. "Batch numbers. For the kind of field trial you described, this would be a project number and patient number. But it doesn't tell us who ordered the test and sacrificed the subjects."

"We have a video confession from Dr. Chapman. He named Windsor Pharmaceuticals."

Still a few feet away, Jaz said, "Wasn't he delusional? Tania was delusional."

At the same time, Bobby stood up, his face drained. "Windsor? Violet Windsor? If you know she did this, why do you need me?"

"We missed something. Günter did what he could, but we don't know why they would kill to get these back. There has to be something in there. And then we have the rag that Chapman described as the delivery vehicle. We need to figure out how they plan to distribute it. Water supply? Aerosol? Food?"

Bobby and Jaz exchanged a glance.

"You think she plans to distribute this virus?" Bobby asked.

"Her project manager had a schedule for Philadelphia on her phone."

Bobby trembled and looked around the room. Slowly, he sat at the microscope with its multiple hi-resolution displays. Günter showed him the images he'd saved to his cloud drive before the lab was destroyed. The two of them began talking in scientific terms.

Jaz looked at her expectantly. "Why not let the government handle it?"

"We did." She kept focused on the two scientists at work.

"Not NIH—I mean Homeland Security or the CDC."

Pia turned just a few degrees to look at him out of the corner of her eye. She said nothing.

Bobby looked up from the desk. "How have you been handling the vials?"

"Not carefully until after the first attack. There's only one legible fingerprint other than mine or Jacob's. I gave it to Verges, they're working on it."

Bobby nodded and put his eyes on the microscope lenses. "Give me a few minutes to concentrate."

Günter rose from his seat and glanced at Jaz. "Pia, could I have that word with you now?"

Pia nosed toward the next room and led the way. Behind her, Jaz crossed to his father and began a tense, whispered conversation.

Günter began talking before she closed the door. "I am terribly sorry. I hope you will forgive me. I am the one who leaked information."

Pia spun to pull the pocket doors closed behind them before facing the bowed doctor. "What happened?"

"We were grasping at straws, calling everyone with bio-tech experience. I ran out of names to call so I called my college roommate, Ed Cummings. He's backed several pharmaceutical ventures and knows all the brightest minds. He promised to make some inquiries but he asked me a lot of questions. He called back, very concerned, but with even more questions. When he called this morning and asked if I could arrange a meeting I realized what I'd done. I'm so sorry. Of course, I will resign immediately."

"When I called you from the Detention Center and asked you to take care of Tania, were you at home?"

Günter thought for a moment. "Yes."

"Where were you the first time you spoke to Cummings?"

"In Tania's hospital room."

"Don't talk to anyone about this except the Major and me."

"What about Alan?"

"Especially not Dad." Pia opened the pocket doors and rejoined Bobby and Jaz.

Bobby tapped a pencil on the desk and stared out the window.

Verges came in from the hallway. Pia held a finger across her lips: *shh*.

After a moment, Bobby stirred. "Lyophilized."

Pia raised her brows and waited for an explanation.

"We'll have to hydrate it and run a culture to be sure, but the gray stuff on the rag is a virus that's been lyophilized, freeze-dried." He frowned and checked one of the displays. "Pure speculation, but I'll bet the rehydrated version is this nasty little bug right here."

"How does that work?"

"Viruses need a system of transmission from human to human. Something to carry them from host to host. Water, food, anything can help the bug get from one place to another." Bobby's gaze floated to the ceiling while he thought. "But a lyophilized bug looks like dust until it finds its way into your warm, moist lungs. There it reanimates and ravages the host. The powder on this rag could be sprayed into the air and no one would find the source."

"Can you prove the powder carries the disease?" Verges asked.

"I think I can," Bobby said. "But I'm going to need some petri dishes, pipettes, centrifuge maybe, and—"

"I can get that," Günter said. "Let's make a list."

"Not to be rude," Bobby said, "but I need to concentrate on a project like this." He glanced at each of the non-scientists.

Pia led Jaz and Verges down the hallway.

"Do you have enough to round up the Windsor people?" Pia asked Verges. She led them into a room with a billiard table.

"Deathbed confessions are strong," Verges said with a wary glance at Jaz, "but you can't prove chain of custody for the evidence and the phone info is inadmissable, so we don't have enough to make an arrest."

Pia faced Jaz. "Could you give us a moment?"

Jaz dropped his gaze to the floor and wandered down the hallway.

"Being a 'special liaison to the Director' gives me privileges that I'm just now learning how to abuse." Verges watched Jaz disappear around a corner. "I wandered around the Counterintelligence division this morning. Every division is trying to get ahead of you guys on this but I think Counterintelligence is in the lead."

"I'm glad to hear they care," Pia said.

"Maybe. Maybe not. They confiscated a shipment of Element 42 from associates of Verratti and shipped it to China's Public Security Bureau. They think they've minimized the threat to Philly. But they're scrambling to find a second shipment that left Guangzhou yesterday. Before I could get details, they got territorial and closed ranks. I'm not sure what to do next."

"Bluff Violet Windsor. Use your badge to scare her into making a mistake. I think she's in the city."

"Why do you think that?"

"Ed Cummings called and led me to believe they're both downtown. I'm meeting him in an hour. Join me."

Before he could answer, Agent Dhanpal ran toward them. "Pia, a body's been dumped in the driveway. We think it's Ed Cummings."

Chapter 34

Borneo's jungle shadows pulsed with darkness in my pain-addled mind. Nothing could help us. Not even the dawn could break through the overcast sky.

"No. No. No!" I shouted in English and repeated myself in Arabic.

The damn stick whooshed and smashed into my legs again. I fell facedown in the dirt. Miguel bellowed at them while I rose to my knees and pleaded for Carmen's life. "Mukhtar, you can't do this. Don't listen to Mokin. Please. Killing an innocent woman is wrong, not just for a soldier but for a Muslim. The Prophet said, 'whoever is not merciful toward people, will not be treated mercifully by Allah.'"

Mukhtar regarded me then waved a hand and the stick whooshed, landing hard on my back.

Diego cried out for help. He tried to rest his weight on the sides of his feet but it wasn't working. Every movement tore at his slashed tendons. Even the Kazakh soldiers winced.

In Arabic I said, "We treated your people well in the US. We would never murder them in cold—"

"Yuri tried to kill you," he said, "but you were not man enough to kill him when you had the chance."

Carmen stared at Mukhtar, her face defiant. Emily sobbed, half in pain and half in desperation.

"Take me," I said. "If you need to kill someone. I planned the raid on the Pak Uban."

"I don't care about that scum." Mukhtar faced me. "Can you bring me all the vial pieces?"

"Yes."

"Then you lied to me earlier."

"No, I tried to discourage you. You would've done the same."

Mukhtar smiled and said something over his shoulder in Kazakh.

His man tilted the barrel and fired a warning shot over Carmen's head.

"Which answer should I believe?" Mukhtar asked.

"I'll do my best … and I'm good. I can make some calls. Please. Give me a few minutes. I can probably have all the glass delivered here. Mukhtar, I'm begging you, let me use your phone for a second. Just don't shoot a prisoner."

Mukhtar frowned and spoke in Kazakh again.

His triggerman fired a three-round burst into Carmen's head.

Her blood and brains spattered over the post. Her body spasmed for a full second, then she sank, her weight hanging by her bound hands.

The world stopped. Nothing moved or made a sound for a full minute.

Then the world began to spin again. Emily threw up. Diego passed out. Miguel and I stared in disbelief. After another minute, Emily started screaming at the top of her lungs.

Rage can triple a man's strength. Like a wild rhino, Miguel bucked and kicked and threw men off his back. One of the men holding me went to help. I struggled against the men holding me. My roped hands chafed. I hit them with my elbows and kicked them. Mukhtar watched as if it were a sport. One of the men punched me in the gut. I head-butted him and he staggered away. Then he came back, blood covering half his face, and took a swing. I ducked and he hit his pal.

I managed to move the scrum closer to their leader, my eyes found his. "You're a dead man, Mukhtar."

He laughed. "Who is the dead man?"

Emily kept screaming.

Mukhtar raised his Beretta and aimed at Miguel's head.

A Kazakh jumped on Miguel's back. Miguel bent at the waist, tossing his assailant like a rag doll just as Mukhtar fired. The man rolled three times, stopping at his leader's feet, bleeding.

Mukhtar stepped over his dying soldier and raised his pistol, his arm extended in front of me. I leaned forward, pulling two Kazakhs with me, and sank my teeth into his forearm. Mukhtar screamed and dropped his weapon. I sensed one of the men holding me relax his grip as he reacted to my vicious bite. With a twist of my neck, I pulled a chunk of muscle out of Mukhtar's arm and spat it at his horrified soldier.

Mukhtar shrieked and stared at his arm.

Both soldiers holding me went slack, appalled by my violence. I head-butted one and kneed the other in the groin. As soon as he bent over in pain, I slammed my knee into his face. The first guy shook his head for a second before realizing he was about to die. He pulled out a revolver and jammed it in my face. His eyes swirled in their sockets, still woozy from the head-butt. Bending my knees, I dropped my head into his belly and burst forward with my legs. We both went down in a tangle, my hands still tied.

Only two Kazakhs left.

Miguel stepped up, beast-mode, and roared like an angry lion. He twisted, tossing one man on top of me, pressing me against the man with the revolver. I heard the blast and waited for the pain to register. Instead, the man on top of me groaned. I pushed him off and struggled to my feet. I stomped on the revolver, breaking some of the groggy-guy's fingers in the process.

Emily's scream reached a crescendo and continued louder and higher.

The hardness of a gun barrel is a distinct feeling. I recognized it immediately when Mukhtar pressed it to my shoulder.

Miguel borrowed my method and powered into his last man. He smashed the guy against a tree and kneed him in the balls. When his man bent over, Miguel jumped over his tied hands and slammed a double-fisted punch into the guy's face.

The odds whittled down, Miguel eyed Mukhtar carefully and moved toward us.

"Come around to my right," I said in English.

In Arabic, Mukhtar said, "Tell him to stop or I'll kill you."

I spun to my left, forcing the muzzle and his wounded arm behind me. He fired, and I head-butted him. He crumpled.

The third head-butt made me dizzy and my back burned where the muzzle flash seared my skin. I staggered back a step and tried to assess the situation.

The man with the revolver sat up, tried to aim, but Miguel kicked him in the head and repeated the kick several more times for good measure.

Miguel came to me and untied my hands. I returned the favor. I went straight to Emily and untied her. She stopped screaming only long enough to gasp for air. Her eyes fixed on something behind me.

I turned to see Miguel cutting Carmen's body from the post. He cradled her limp body in his arms and dropped to his knees. A slow moan came from deep inside him. His face wrinkled into a pained grimace that quickly dissolved into a lonesome sob. It was a side of Miguel I'd never seen in the decade of war we spent together.

"Find a knife," I shouted at Emily, "and cut Diego down."

Mukhtar stirred, rising to his hands and knees. I picked up a rifle and aimed it at him. I kept the barrel aimed at his head as I stepped up and kicked him in the face as hard as I could. He collapsed and I pounded him with the rifle butt.

Emily picked up a pistol and aimed at one of the Kazakhs.

"No!" I grabbed her arm. "You'll relive that shot every night for the rest of your life."

"Yeah, happily." She took aim a second time.

The man had a concussion but knew he was in danger. Survival instincts took over. He grabbed a grenade from his belt and put his finger through the pin. I stepped between them and took the grenade before he armed it.

Emily turned and raised her pistol at Mukhtar.

"No more," I said. I pried the weapon from her fingers with some difficulty.

Her face was as blank as if she'd watched hours of television.

"Help Miguel," I said.

Zombie-like, she walked slowly to where Miguel sobbed over Carmen.

I cut down Diego and laid him out with his feet elevated.

Behind me another man got to his feet. I whacked him with the rifle then ran around picking up all the weapons. I made a pile next to Diego. I bound the living Kazakhs and moved them into a circle, facing outward, hands tied together. If any of them moved the whole circle had to move.

With that done, I found first aid for Diego. I irrigated his wounds, taking care that Diego couldn't see his tendons and muscle hanging out of his skin. We had to find a hospital quickly if he was ever going to walk again. Once I had him stabilized, I walked over to Miguel and Emily.

Carmen's dead eyes stared at me from her broken head.

The big man's face, streaked with tears, looked up at me, helpless and inconsolable. Emily sat by his side, stroking Carmen's leg.

Mukhtar moaned and sat up.

"Will Allah be merciful to you?" I asked him in Arabic.

"He already has been. He sent you. You're not man enough to kill me."

Mercury said, He has a point, homeslice. A Roman soldier would've crucified Mukhtar's crew by now. Don't just sit there throwing guilt around—kill the mofo.

Some gods preach love and mercy. I have the kind you have to worry about.

Walking slowly, I gave him my soldier stare. I untied him from the rest, pulled him to his feet, and kicked him in the balls because I don't play fair. He staggered back, bent in pain. I tossed him a loaded Berretta, turned my back on him, and walked twenty steps. He squinted into the sun. I raised my Glock and aimed at his head.

Mercury said, Shoot him. C'mon, do it.

I asked, Where's the thrill in that?

Mukhtar held his pistol halfway up, hesitant. Still racked with head and groin pain, he took his time raising the weapon with a shaky hand. I waited until he had it leveled at me. He pulled the trigger.

The round whizzed past my head on the left. His second shot went even wider. I felt the first cold shiver of adrenaline driving into the crevices of my extremities. His third round warmed my right ear as it flew by. I smiled at him.

The cold drug of danger felt good.

Mukhtar closed his swollen eye and steadied his aim.

Mercury said, You are one sick puppy, Jacob.

Mukhtar lined his barrel square with my eye. In a moment of crystal clarity, I could see deep down inside it, all the way to the rounded lump of lead waiting to be released. My body shivered into my newest burst of adrenaline like a great orgasm. This was a decisive moment. It was heaven descending on me in the midst of a life in hell: the bad guy was going to die.

My first round hit the target and blew a hole through his shoulder. Mukhtar's Berretta flew out of his hand. His arm dropped to his side, exposed bone stuck out of his sleeve. He glared at me as he gasped in pain.

"What's the matter, Mukhtar? Can't shoot left-handed?" I said in Arabic.

He looked around for his pistol, located it, then glanced back at me.

"Go ahead," I said. "I don't have all day."

Mukhtar stumbled in agony and picked up his weapon. He rose to his full height, put on his meanest face, and took another shot.

Emily screamed. "What the hell is wrong with you?"

Miguel didn't look up. Tears dripped from his cheeks to Carmen's.

Mukhtar looked at her, then back at me. He steadied his aim.

Emily jumped to her feet and ran to the stacked weapons, drawing Mukhtar's attention. Picking quickly, she chose a Silver Eagle .45 revolver.

"Put it down," I said.

"My dad used to take me hunting," she said. "I know how to use it."

"This ain't a hunting trip and that's a bad choice of weapons."

She raised it and found out why. It was heavy and hard to aim even for an experienced soldier. Using both hands, she eventually found Mukhtar in the sights.

Mukhtar watched her, shook his head and raised his Berretta quickly.

I put him down with a round through his temple.

Emily screeched, high and long, then settled into incoherent screaming.

"Wish you hadn't done that," I said. "He didn't deserve a quick death."

She screamed, "You're fucking insane."

Mercury said, Whoa, dude, the nymph knows what's going down. Whatever you do, don't tell her about me, OK? I was never here.

I held out my hands, palms up. "I gave him the sporting chance he didn't give Carmen."

Gasping as if she'd climbed a mountain, Emily bent over and retched. After she'd gotten it all out, she wiped her mouth with the back of her hand and eyed me like a feral animal. "Which one of them pulled the trigger?"

I pointed at the circle of captives.

The guilty party hung his head. He didn't need to speak English to know why I was pointing at him.

Emily staggered toward him and hefted the revolver with both hands.

"You shouldn't do that," I said.

"You gonna stop me?"

"You're going to see his head explode every night for the rest of your life—in hi-def. It'll be like a demon coming to visit." I eased toward her, one step at a time.

"I can live with that."

"That's not the only demon that'll haunt you."

She dragged her eyes off her victim and blinked at me.

"It's the fact that he's tied up, defenseless. That's the nastiest demon 'cause it's just plain murder."

She repositioned her feet and looked at the man, then back at me, then at the man.

"Go ahead," I said. "Untie him."

I held my hand out for the .45. She glanced back and forth one more time, then handed it to me. She cut him loose from the others, then freed his hands.

Thinking I was his savior, the man fell to his knees and kissed the back of my hand like a dog.

Emily held her hand out, waiting for her weapon. After a moment's hesitation I handed it to her, grip first. She stepped back and aimed. The barrel rolled around enough to put me in the danger zone if she pulled the trigger at the wrong time. She bit her lip, aimed, turned her face away, and squeezed on the trigger. Except, she didn't squeeze enough. She relaxed, repositioned her feet, took another look, and tried again. And failed again.

"You sure you want this, Emily?"

She blurted, "He killed Carmen."

"His commander ordered him to."

"That's no excuse. He knew it was wrong."

"So is killing him without a trial."

"Yes it is," Emily said. She held the gun steady and aimed with one eye. "It's very wrong."

The sexy, charming Emily was gone forever.

I'd seen men bend their morals in a war zone, but seeing a travel reporter turn into a cold-blooded vigilante was making my skin crawl. There was only one way to save her last shred of humanity.

I pulled my pistol, grabbed the man's hair, twisted his head, and shot him through the top of the skull. My aim was diagonal, the round went through every critical part of his brain. He never felt a thing.

"You write the story, Emily. I'll fight the demons."

Mercury said, Holy Minerva. You'll get the Congressional Medal of Horror for that one.

She stared at the gore for a long time without making a sound. She nodded and said, "Got what he deserved."

I said, "Emily, go help Diego."

Her hollow, darkened eyes showed a glimmer of light when she asked Diego if she could change the blood-soaked gauze on his feet. Rendering aid soothes the sinner's soul.

I explained to Diego and Emily that our statements to the authorities would need a chronological alteration: the two Kazakhs died between the death of Carmen and the cessation of hostilities. They readily agreed.

Sabel Security HQ kept tabs on us via the comm link. They summoned the Malaysian authorities to our GPS location and reported Carmen's death to the Major. It would take hours for anyone to arrive. Would they charge us with murder or call us heroes? I didn't care.

I walked over to Miguel and sat in the dirt next to him. Carmen's body was cooling fast, but he wasn't ready to put her down. I leaned against the big guy's shoulder, put my arm around him and let my tears flow.

Chapter 35

Two men in suits stood in the Jefferson Hotel's colonial yellow hallway when Violet opened the door.

"Special Agent Verges, ma'am." He held up his FBI ID. "This is Dhanpal Singh, technical consultant."

She shook hands with both men and ushered them into her suite. She pointed to a silk-covered divan nestled between corner windows. Looking down her nose, she checked the handsome, compact Dhanpal.

"You look military," she said.

"Navy Seal," he said. "Retired."

"What do you do now? Are you one of those infamous Sabel agents?"

"I'm assisting Special Agent Verges, ma'am."

"Coffee?" Violet asked. "Decaf would be appropriate for this hour of the evening, I suppose."

"Decaf would be nice, thank you."

She pressed the room service button and ordered coffee and tea, then took a seat facing them. "Now, gentlemen, what can I do for you?"

Verges pulled out his phone and pulled up a picture of the last vial. "We believe this is one of yours. What can you tell us about it?"

She took his phone and stared at it for a long time. "Those appear to be Windsor's project numbers, but who knows? Number sequences are not unique. I can look into it for you. When was this taken?"

"This morning, ma'am."

The last vial. Violet swallowed her gasp in a small cough. "That recently? Where did it come from?"

She glanced at Dhanpal, who sat erect, feet planted on the floor, hands on knees, his eyes watching hers as if he were trying to see through them into her brain.

"What project is this from?" Verges asked.

She shrugged. "I have no idea. In Asia, we sell used equipment. That's why we use glass instead of plastic. That vial could've been ours at one point, but now, who knows?"

"Why were the project numbers stamped in UV ink?"

"I'd have to ask the project manager."

"OK, that would be great." Verges leaned back on the couch and spread his arms across the back.

Violet watched him and frowned. "You *do* know there is a twelve-hour time difference? She's not in at the moment. I'll call later this evening and let you know what I find out."

"Why was the vial on Borneo?"

"Was it?"

"We did some checking on Windsor Pharmaceutical project numbers and noticed the project codes are all sequential. Your company submitted a project with a code only one digit lower than this one to the FDA recently. Wouldn't that mean this project is new?"

"It could." Violet gazed out the window.

"Were you on Borneo in the last few weeks?" Verges asked.

"Certainly not." She glared at him then looked away. "Why would the FBI want to know?"

"Is the project related to Element 42?"

Violet felt her neck and face tighten, her hands clench into fists. "What do you mean, Element … what was it?"

"Forty-two, ma'am." Verges let the statement hang, waiting for her response.

She forced her fingers open and smoothed her skirt. "Could you give me a hint? Is it something I'm supposed to know from the periodic tables?" She glanced from Verges to Dhanpal. Neither man said anything. "Why is the FBI interested in vials from Borneo?"

"Where is the shipment of Element 42 that's missing from your Guangzhou facility?"

"I have no idea what you're talking about and I certainly don't like your tone of voice."

"When was the last time you saw Ed Cummings?"

"What does Ed have to do with this? Is Element 42 one of his hedge funds?"

"He was found dead last night, ma'am."

Violet felt lightheaded. How did the FBI arrive on her doorstep so quickly? "Oh my god. Is that how you talk to the man's friends? You announce his murder just like that? What is wrong with you?"

"Murder?" Verges asked.

"Well, he was young and healthy," she stammered. Her head sank, she gazed at the floor. "I guess it could've been an accident. But here, in central DC, it's reasonable to assume…"

"Central DC?" Verges waited. "What do you know about his death?"

"I don't know anything about his death. I didn't know he was dead until you told me."

"You were close to him, is that correct?"

Violet snapped her face up and glared at the young man. "Since when does the FBI get involved in a murder investigation? Murder is a police matter. You're outside your jurisdiction. Who do you work for?"

"I'm investigating potential terrorist threats, ma'am." Verges leaned forward. "You haven't answered my questions."

Violet stood up. "I know when I'm being set up. No more questions until I have an attorney present."

"Why, do you have something to hide?"

"Not another word until my attorney arrives."

Verges and Dhanpal stood up. Verges said, "Here's my card. When your attorney is ready, call me. Tonight would be good. If you take too long, we'll have to bring you in."

"How dare you! I..." Violet stood and gestured them out. She opened the door to a uniformed butler holding a coffee tray. The three of them stepped aside to let the butler through, then Violet waved them out.

Dhanpal stopped in the hall as Verges continued walking away. He caught Violet's eye. "Not going to offer us a cup to go?"

She glared at him for a second then lightened. "What kind of consultant are you? What's your specialty?"

"Liars."

She slammed the door.

The butler set the tray down on the table and began setting out cups.

"Get that crap out of here," Violet said.

She staggered into the bedroom and slammed the door. Leaning against it, her eyes swept the room in an anxious arc. She wrung her hands. How dare they accuse me? Element 42—where did they hear that? Maybe Chapman? No. Ed. Had to be Ed. And he's dead. Good. Why do they think I did it?

Pacing to the edge of the bathroom door, she stopped and stared for a moment, then stepped inside. She placed her hands on the sink's cold marble, hung her head, and stared down. She turned on the water, grabbed the bar of soap and rolled it around between her hands. Over and over, she scrubbed and scrubbed until the bar popped out and landed on the floor. She ripped her house-leg off and smashed it against the sink, beating it until exhaustion made her take a breath. She dropped the prosthesis.

After rinsing, she grabbed the marble again and considered herself in the mirror. "Get a grip, girl. You can fix this. You have to."

Violet picked up her phone and dialed while hopping through the suite on her good leg. It was answered on the third ring. "Prince, what can you tell me about—"

"Violet, they know about you." He breathed hard. "This is not a good time. I'll call you later."

"I need the last vial and a cloth, there's a cloth."

"Later." The line went dead.

She shouted at her window. "Worthless son-of-a-bitch."

Below her, commuters struggled through the crowded streets. Wiggling and writhing, they hurried past each other with a strange sense of desperation.

Violet dialed Kasey Earl. "Since you've failed miserably to kill Pia Sabel, apply that fee to deploying my package. I want it done immediately."

"Too late for that, sugar."

"What do you mean?"

"I've already delivered it to the interested party. I'm on my way out of the country on another job."

"What happened to my $2 million?"

"Oh now, sugar, don't worry about that. I'll get you a refund. My associate will bring it by later."

"Can I get it in cash?"

Chapter 36

Halogen backlighting streaked through the stained glass window illuminating the family chapel at Sabel Gardens as if it were still daytime. Pia was amazed at how fast her HR department had provided grief counsellors and, at the request of Carmen's brother, a pastoral service.

The agents and staff rose slowly and filed out, remembering Carmen to each other in hushed tones and quiet tears. Pia remained on her knees, her forearms resting on the rail in front of her, her head bowed.

She thought about life and death and love. Her love for her parents hadn't saved them. Then she took the reins at Sabel Security and immediately lost Ezra and Alphonse, and later Tony and Safwan the Arab. In the last week, Kaya and Kevin had been murdered. Now Carmen was gone. She dared not love anyone for fear it would hasten their death. Jacob's concerns about her lack of planning and preparation were proving horribly accurate. The weight of leadership pressed hard on her shoulders and tore at her heart.

She sensed someone standing next to her and looked up to see the Episcopal priest who'd just given the homily. Pia tried to remember the woman's name as she sat in the pew and laid a hand on Pia's shoulder blade. It was an oddly comforting gesture, neither too familiar nor too awkward.

"Carmen," Pia said, her voice cracking. "The mass grave on Borneo. The horror in this world is overwhelming. How could a loving God allow so much tragedy? How many innocents will He let die?"

Pia's carefully managed emotions flooded out in tears.

The priest didn't speak for a long time. Keeping her hand on Pia's shoulder, she spoke softly. "Would you prefer a God who does our work for us? A creator who gives us a Disneyland-world full of fun and exciting rides with no responsibilities?" The woman dug her fingers in and squeezed hard. "Every time we sit back, satisfied that we've done enough, the result shocks us. The Holocaust, Rwanda, suicide bombers, famine, disease—could we have prevented them if we tried harder?"

Pia gazed at her face, searching her eyes for any sign of hesitation.

The woman gave Pia's shoulder a goodbye-squeeze and smiled. "These are mankind's problems. Why should we expect God to solve them? Quit sniveling. There's work to be done."

As Pia watched the priest leave, she found the Major kneeling on the other side of the aisle. The Major wiped her cheeks, crossed herself, and rose. Pia met her in the aisle.

"Stay," the Major said. "Take tonight and tomorrow off and let yourself mourn."

Pia shook her head. "We can't slow down. We have to speed up."

Her long legs outpaced the Major, taking her to the narthex where her father chatted with Bobby and Jaz Jenkins. She strode straight to Bobby, her aggressive approach separating him from the others. She said, "What did you hold back about Windsor last night?"

Bobby said, "I'm sorry?"

She watched him look left and right before he met her gaze.

"Remember the Chinese milk scandal in 2008?" he asked. "Her company convinced baby formula makers to pump up the protein numbers with melamine she sold them. Nearly half a million victims suffered in that atrocious crime."

"That company is still in business?" Pia asked.

"Instead of putting her in jail, China invested in her company. She went on to win NIH research grants."

Jaz opened his mouth to speak but thought better of it and lowered his head.

Pia left them and followed the stone path through the woods to the main house under the last glow of an orange sunset. The Major struggled to keep up with her.

A police detective approached and put a hand out to stop her. "I've finished with the staff, but I still have a few questions for you regarding the death of Ed Cummings."

"Walk with me then." She gave him a cold stare as she stepped off the walkway and around him.

He turned and followed her. "I don't understand why you wouldn't want to see the body. I mean, somebody dumps a carcass in your front yard and you aren't the least bit curious. Can you explain that?"

"Correction: Mr. Cummings' body was left at the front gate, two hundred yards from my front door. I explained this in my statement."

"I'd like to hear it again."

"You recorded it."

"People remember things differently sometimes—"

"My agents cautioned me that the killer's intent could be to lure me into the open. How hard is that to understand?"

"But after they secured the area, before the police removed the—"

"The news crews were there. Eight minutes after Mr. Cummings' corpse was dumped." She scowled at him. "Did you hear Otis Blackwell? He reported, 'Asking for a meeting with Pia Sabel were the last words Cummings spoke.' How did Otis know anything about Cummings's conversation with me? Are you his source?"

"And you're sure you never met Mr. Cummings—"

"I told you once already, neither his name nor his photograph are familiar to me." Pia gave him another scowl. "If you don't have any new questions, or new information you'd like to share, then you're done here."

"One last thing," the detective said. "What was the last thing you said to him?"

"I gave you the recording of the call."

"Humor me."

"I told him to turn himself in at FBI headquarters."

"Did you tell him to walk or take a cab?"

"Neither. Why?"

"He walked. It's well over a mile. Don't you find that odd?"

"Exercise clears the mind. I encourage it."

"Then you encouraged him to walk?"

"One more pointed question like that and I'll refer you to my attorneys."

"Your evasive answer leads me to believe you know what happened to him."

"From your line of questioning, a five-year-old could figure out he was abducted on the street." She stopped walking and faced him, pointing to a fork in the path. "The exit is that way."

The detective glared at her. "Everyone at the FOP Lodge 35 is grateful for your annual contributions, Ms. Sabel. But it won't influence an investigation."

"Good to know." She turned on her heel and strode on to the house.

He sneered and took the exit path.

Pia watched him leave, then pointed toward the main house where Otis was chatting with two Sabel agents. "Who let him in?"

The Major checked with Marty on her earbud to order the reporter escorted off the grounds. She said, "Otis is a guest of Carmen's brother. They arrived together."

"No one kicked him out?"

The Major shrugged. "A guest of the bereaved? Pia, you're angry. We all are. But let's not overreact."

Verges jogged over to join them. "Dhanpal and I rattled Ms. Windsor's cage, but have nothing to show for it. However, Counterintelligence thinks they've found the last shipment of Element 42 and they identified a partial print from the last vial."

Pia entered the main house with Verges a step behind her.

"It belongs to a guy high up in China's Communist Party," Verges said. "But my Feeb brothers closed ranks and cut me out of the loop."

"Did you get a name?"

"Wu Fang, but in China that's like saying Jim Smith."

Pia glanced at the Major, who nodded back.

Verges watched them. "What, you know the guy?"

"We've heard that name," Pia said. "What do you know about him?"

"He's the Party's top bio-med scientist. He's involved in charities, anti-pollution campaigns, birth control, and all kinds of stuff."

"And mass graves on Borneo."

The Major interrupted. "Verges is pointing out that a fingerprint does not prove Mr. Fang's involvement or collusion. It only places him at the scene."

Verges raised a finger at the Major and nodded. "Yeah, what she said. So, where have you heard of him?"

"He's a member of Windsor's board." Pia grabbed her tablet off a reading stand. "But, typical for China, every scrap of news about him is carefully curated."

Alan Sabel came in the room. Pia pointed toward the door and walked through it. Alan dropped in beside her.

She said, "What's Bobby holding back about Windsor?"

"What makes you think I would know?"

"Friends for twenty years, neighbors for ten, a thousand discussions about life."

Alan patted his thighs. "All I know is, it's personal. He competes with lots of pharmas, but Windsor is different."

"Don't hold out on me, Dad."

"Violet Windsor is Bobby's daughter from his first marriage. Jaz is her half-brother."

Pia stopped in her tracks and turned to the Major. "Have the Jenkins family escorted off the property immediately. Tell them I'll call later to explain."

The Major relayed the order into her earbud.

Pia moved forward again and glanced at her father. "Are they close?"

"She calls him 'Prince'. I don't know if that's because she likes him or she's jealous. Bobby treated Jaz better than—"

"Counterintelligence is keeping Verges out of the loop."

"You're not suggesting they're helping Windsor."

"Would they be the first government agency to create a terrorist threat just to reap the benefits of cleaning it up?"

"That's pretty farfetched," Alan said, "even for one of your conspiracy theories."

"They had Element 42 in their possession. But they sent it to China. Why didn't they destroy it?"

Dhanpal rushed to intercept them. "Sorry to interrupt. Bobby Jenkins went back to your library—the vial and rag are missing."

Chapter 37

Several captains and colonels wanted me to finish college so they could put me in Officer Candidate School. I always turned it down. Making the decision about when to pull the trigger was a decision I could handle. What kept me up at night were the decisions that ended in a friend's death. Any psych worth his hourly rate would tell me, *Mukhtar gave the order, his man executed it. Carmen's death was not your fault.*

But it was.

Sometimes, reflecting on things only makes it worse.

I wandered through the camp. It was a training ground for a lot more men than Mukhtar had on hand. Most everything was packed in crates and ready to ship. We'd arrived before the last of them pulled out. When I fed some Chinese characters I found on crates into a translator, the answer read, "People's Pest Control, Flying Insect Specialist". They had everything they needed to make people experts with mosquito foggers. It didn't take a genius to figure out that Element 42 must work in the foggers. But the equipment is easy to operate—I did it for the local parks in high school. Which meant they were training for a covert method of dispersal.

I turned on one of the foggers for a second. Instead of a chainsaw-noise, it was almost silent. They were planning to infect neighborhoods in the dead of night and leave without a trace. Walking around with a fogger, even a quiet one, meant a high probability of getting caught. Especially in a city like Philly. It would only make sense if they were planning to infect powerless minorities, like the Melanau. But powerless minorities are usually short on healthcare and cash. They wouldn't be buying the Levoxavir Ms. Sabel told me about. So what was Mukhtar's game?

I had no idea, so I quit thinking about it. Then I was bored. When I'm bored, I act out. I picked up Mukhtar's satellite phone and called the Sabel tech center. They uploaded the requisite software for snooping. I redialed Mukhtar's last call. When a voice came on, jabbering in Kazakh, I stopped him. "Anatoly, my name is Jacob Stearne. Oh, you remember me then. Good. You ordered the murder of my friend. That made it personal. I'm going to find you and kill you."

"You want personal? Bring me the *pizda*," he said.

"The what?"

"*Pizda*, whore. Bring me your boss, the fucking whore who ruined my business. I let you live, Jacob Stearne."

"OK, where and when?"

"My office in Guangzhou, as soon as you can get here. Now let me speak to Mukhtar."

"Sorry, he can't make it to the phone—ever again. He's busy explaining himself to Allah."

"Impossible! You could never take down Mukhtar."

"Hang on a sec." I snapped a photo of his man's corpse and sent it to him. "I killed him the same way I'm going to kill you, Anatoly. Look for me later this afternoon."

He was ranting in some language I didn't know when I clicked off.

Emily looked at me. "You're going to kill someone?"

"Anatoly Mokin, the guy who gave the order."

"And you know where to find him?" She stroked her .45 as if it were a mink stole.

I didn't answer.

She looked up. "I want to be the one."

"You're a reporter. You're going home."

"I'm going with you." She stood and stuck out her chin, thumbing her chest. "I get to pull the trigger this time."

"Mokin didn't live this much of his miserable life by letting strangers get close enough to kill him. We'll be lucky to live through the assault. If we fail, we need you to tell the story."

She turned away, stuck her silver revolver into her belt. Diego stared at her as if she were an alien.

HQ piped in the healing service from Sabel Gardens via our earbuds. Miguel and Emily mumbled along with the prayers. I left it alone. God forgives everyone, but experience taught me that it's best to give Him some cool-down time before seeking absolution. Besides, I had Mercury. He wasn't much of a god, but he was handy.

I patrolled the perimeter until a squad of four Malaysian policemen arrived. They followed me to the crime scene, where their medic worked on Diego.

The captain took my statement with a mix of skepticism and sarcasm. Finally, he bought into it and time began to move forward again.

We brought their jeeps in for the dead and wounded. Miguel never put Carmen down. He stepped into the open back seat and carried her all the way to civilization.

The rest of the day swirled around me. We put Diego in a hospital, answered police questions, signed statements, arranged to ship Carmen's body home. At some point, I tried to talk Miguel into going with her, but he'd heard me threaten Mokin and was anxious to get moving. Emily became equally difficult, even threatening to tell the Chinese government about our plans for murder and mayhem. In an effort to dissuade her, I made her write the soldier's letter home in case of death. Hers was eloquent, but it didn't change her mind.

Tania met us in the car rental office just after the police turned us loose. HQ had updated her on losing Carmen, and she had repositioned the Sabel jet to the Malaysian side of the island for us. After she chewed my ear off for losing Carmen, we left the island.

I watched the coast disappear from view. I'd thought my plan was clever, giving the Malaysian officials everything they needed to catch the Pak Uban *after* I'd come and gone. I never thought the Kazakhs would hang around Borneo after stuffing twenty-nine bodies in a grave. That miscalculation cost Carmen her life. You would think a god who cared about me would find a way to warn me.

Mercury said, There are limits, you know, bro. Not even Jupiter knows what's going down in Kazakhstan.

I said, You never spread your screwy religion that far east?

Mercury said, Hey now. You got no call to be mean. Nobody has 100% coverage, not Jesus, not Buddha. Well, the Beatles maybe, but nobody else.

Chapter 38

"Where the hell is my shipment?" Violet shouted so hard she nearly dropped her phone. "Did you find the tracking?"

"Yes, ma'am," the shipping operator said. "I mean no. Well, I found the tracking. But Hong Kong customs held it up, ma'am. Sorry."

"You're useless." Violet clicked off.

Her Washington attorney called. She asked, "Are you here?"

"I'm stepping into the elevator with them now."

"It's after ten o'clock, can't you postpone this until morning?"

"Only if you want an arrest on your record."

"Fine." She clicked off.

Pacing the room, she dialed another number. "What's the latest news from Sabel Gardens, Prince?"

"I can't talk. Bad time. The last vial and rag were stolen."

"Are you OK?" Violet asked. "No one blames you?"

"Can you get back to China? You should go as soon as possible."

"I've always cared about you."

"Dad sends his regards. I have to go." He sighed. "Sis, be careful."

Violet closed her eyes and rested her head on the window until the knock on her door roused her. She ushered three men in and introduced herself with as much politeness as she could muster.

"Ms. Windsor," Special Agent Verges said, "has your attorney explained to you Title 18, United States Code, Section 1001, which makes it a felony offense to lie to a government official?"

"Knowingly or willfully," the attorney added.

"Sorry, I don't know the code by heart," Violet said.

"It's the fed's favorite trap," her attorney told her. "The same trap that put Martha Stewart behind bars when they couldn't prove insider trading. And they used it against Ali Saleh Kahlah Al-Marri when they couldn't prove he was an enemy combatant. They ask you if the moon is shining, and you say no and they claim it is somewhere, therefore you're lying."

Verges said, "Earlier today, I told you about the death of Mr. Cummings and you acted surprised. Do you recall referring to his death as a murder before I told you what happened to him?"

"Yes, but that was just a guess, it could've been—"

"What did you say when I asked what you knew about his death?"

"I asked to have my attorney present."

"Just before you requested an attorney, did you deny having any knowledge of his death or the circumstances of his death?"

"I don't remember. What is this? How dare you accuse me of lying. If you have any evidence that I've done something wrong, let's hear it. Otherwise, you're just wasting my time."

Her attorney waved his hand. "If you have a transcript of the conversation, pull it out. Otherwise, she can't recall."

Verges nodded at the local detective. "She's all yours."

The short man leaned forward with a digital recorder. "Ma'am, I'm going to play a recorded conversation for you. I'd appreciate it if you could identify the two people talking." He pressed play.

Man: "Why tell me this?"

Woman: "I need you to kill Ed Cummings."

Man: "Two hundred grand. All upfront. Where do you want the body?"

Woman: "I don't know. However you dispose of it, make sure it's not traced back to me."

Violet repeatedly gasped as the room spun around her. "Where…"

The attorney slashed his hand between the detective and Violet. "My client is not answering any more questions. We're done here."

"Have it your way," the detective said. He faced Verges. "Shall we flip a coin, heads you get her for terrorism, tails I get her for murder?"

Verges pulled a quarter out of his pocket and flashed it with some flair. He glanced at Violet. "If you want to answer a few more questions, we might work out a deal."

Verges flipped the coin and watched it rise to the ceiling. So did the detective and Violet. The attorney stuck out his hand and caught it on the way down.

"What kind of a deal?" the attorney asked.

"Maybe a plea."

"What do you have?" the attorney asked.

"I have the man who made the recording," the detective said. "He says she hired him to murder Ed Cummings."

"If that's the case, why didn't you arrest her already?"

"Because Special Agent Verges here is tracking a shipment of something called Element 42."

"I don't know where it is," Violet said. "I made a call minutes ago, and they—"

"Don't say another word," the attorney said.

"Are you saying Element 42 is in transit to the US?" Verges asked. Violet tried not to cry.

"Can you provide tracking numbers?" Verges asked.

"I... I'll need some time."

"We can wait."

"I mean morning. It's tomorrow in China. I'll need a few hours. Can you give me til morning?"

"My client is cooperating here. She's an upstanding member of the business community. It's her word against whatever unsavory character you've managed to scrape up. I think—"

"He's a CIA contractor," the detective said.

"Oh, like that makes him *so* much more reliable than a rapist or drug dealer. No wonder you didn't arrest her right away." The attorney opened his arms. "C'mon guys. Giving her a few hours to contact people on the other side of the planet is reasonable."

After a short, whispered discussion with the detective, Verges turned back to the attorney. "She's a flight risk and a terrorist threat.

If she turns over her passport, and you take responsibility for bringing her to the Hoover Building at 9AM sharp, we'll allow it."

"How did you know there was a second shipment of Element 42?" Violet asked.

"The contractor told the Counterintelligence Division."

"Counterintelligence tracks spies," her attorney said. "Why are they involved?"

"That's a good question," Verges said.

"Don't you work in that division?"

"I am a special liaison," Verges said. "Do you accept my terms for tomorrow?"

They shook hands on it. Violet turned over her passport and the men left.

Her attorney hovered in the doorway, waiting until the elevator swallowed the police, then faced Violet. "They have a weak case, nothing to worry about. But it's strong enough to tap your phones. Be careful what you say to anyone about anything. No jokes, no sarcasm, no unnecessary calls. I'll be here at 8AM. We'll have breakfast and go see the FBI."

Violet nodded and tried to smile. He backed into the hallway and left.

She let the door close and leaned her back against it. Her knees sank. She put her hands on them to keep herself upright. Her head swayed from side to side and tears of self-pity swelled in her lids until they dripped down her cheeks and fell to her skirt. Sobbing started in her gut and traveled up her lungs and into her face. The tears overflowed in streams and washed out her mascara. Wiping her face with the back of her hands, she turned them over to use her palm before running to the bathroom.

Someone knocked on the door.

She took a deep breath and glanced in the mirror. Black streaks carved their way down her face like spilled paint. Screw it. She opened the door, and drew a breath that she planned to spend saying *what now?* to her attorney. Instead, she inhaled a second larger breath.

Before her, a man in a black raincoat raised an accusing arm with a dangerous shadow extended from it.

Before she realized it was a pistol, the muzzle flashed. She felt the bullet enter her forehead. A painless sensation. She was still conscious when the second round entered her left eyeball. Still feeling nothing, she fell limp against the wall behind the door and her vision blurred into darkness. She wondered if she was going to die. Nothing in her body responded to movement requests, not her hands or legs, not even her lungs and heart. But oddly, she thought, she could still hear a little. Then that faded.

Violet Windsor's last earthly sensation was that of her assassin picking up the spent shell casings from the hotel hallway.

Chapter 39

Agent Marty leaned on his cane, dwarfed by the marble foyer around him. His furrowed brow and pale face turned to Pia. "We've been over the house and grounds and found nothing. I'm terribly sorry, Pia. I thought I had everything covered. This is on me, not the agents on duty. It's completely—"

She leaned close to his ear and whispered. "I know exactly where the vial is and who took it. But I need you to keep it quiet. Push the agents to find it." She paused. "Go."

"Right away, ma'am," Marty said. He turned to the agent leaping up the left staircase and yelled. "Dhanpal, reassign quadrants for the search. We're starting over. MacKenzie, no one leaves without a thorough going-over, understood?"

Both agents answered and Marty shouted more instructions.

Pia went down the hall to the drawing room.

Verges ran to catch up with her. "Ma'am, Violet Windsor claims the second shipment never arrived. She's going to have tracking in the morning."

"Was she telling the truth?"

"Well, those methods you and Dhanpal taught me...I'm not sure if I have it down right, but she gave me full eye contact, no pupil dilation, when she said it was missing. Everything else was a lie."

"How do we keep ahead of the Counterintelligence guys on this?"

"We can't," Verges said. "If they swoop in, we're done."

"I have to know who's in this with Windsor. Can you arrest her to keep her out of their hands until we get the tracking?"

"It wouldn't do any good. They can pull rank on any bust in the country."

"This isn't their jurisdiction. Why are they working so hard on this?"

Verges shrugged. "They're working with China. Maybe it's a spy swap or favor."

Pia looked up and down the hallway. "Can you help me with a quick ploy? I don't want to take my people off the project."

"Sure," the young man said.

"Give me a lift down the road in your car. I have to get past the TV crews, incognito."

She stepped into the kitchen and spoke to Cousin Elmer, then slid into the footwell of Verges's Kia Soul, in all its alien-green glory. They passed her agents at the gate with whispered instructions to keep up the ruse. She stayed down as Verges drove past rows of TV crews. They overheard one reporter say, "…unconfirmed reports that this gathering was to mourn a death of a Sabel Security veteran. Whatever war Pia Sabel is waging has taken yet another life from a local…" by then they were out of range.

"None of my business, ma'am, but I could set them straight. What you're doing is—"

"The first time I tried to set the press straight, I'd been given a red card, ejected from an international game. I was sixteen and thought the press would understand if I just explained it." She crawled out of her cramped hiding space and sat upright. "It only made matters worse. Don't waste time with what other people think, just do the right thing."

She gave him directions to a drugstore parking lot on the edge of the village of Potomac, Maryland. In the back corner, a glowering burgundy Ferrari waited with the convertible open to the autumn chill. Cousin Elmer waved to them and Verges piloted his car nose-to-nose with it.

Verges sat perfectly still, admiring the car in his headlights. "Uh. Do you need any help driving, ma'am?"

Cousin Elmer took the Kia back to Sabel Gardens while Verges, like a kid in a candy store, drove. He stopped where she asked, in a modest residential neighborhood.

"Wait here," she said. "I'll be back in a few minutes."

"OK." Verges got out, ran his hand along the hip of the fuselage, around the engine compartment, never taking his eyes off the surface.

A harvest moon glowed high above her as she walked around a hedge and crossed a lawn to an alley that led out to a quiet residential street. She stood under a tree and assessed the house. A colonial split-level with a garage and darkened bedrooms on a half-acre lot. Light glowed in the kick-out middle level. She crossed to peek in a window. A simple study filled with electronics.

A dog shuffled inside, sniffing. Slinking silently into the dark, she made her way to the back yard and tossed a doggy treat onto the patio. An old Lab stuck his nose out the doggy door and sniffed. He went for the treat.

Pia gave a low whistle. The dog eyed her. She showed a treat in her hand before tossing it to him. He gobbled it in a single bite. She approached slowly, dropping a treat with each step, until she reached him, hand-fed him a treat, and scratched his ear. "Good boy. Easy now."

She pushed her head through the doggy door into a small, dark great room. She heard a muffled voice. Stretching her way through the tiny door, she pulled her Glock, and threaded her way between furniture to the hall.

The voice came from two rooms down the hall on the left. The speech pattern was filled with lengthy pauses: a phone call. Looking carefully both ways, she snuck a peek into the dark kitchen. Satisfied it was clear, she slid toward the study.

The voice stopped.

Pia stopped. Her ears strained for clues to who was in the study. One person? More?

A zipper zipped. A rustle of fabric followed. Her target was leaving. It was now or never.

Pia ran up the short staircase and burst into the study, leading with her pistol, aimed straight ahead.

"Going somewhere, Otis?" she asked.

Blood drained from his face. His eyes bulged out. A daypack fell from his hand. He stood behind a large desk wearing dark pants and a dark shirt under a black leather jacket. A motorcycle helmet rocked back and forth on the desk.

"The vial is a fake," she said. "And the rag. You have nothing."

"I don't know what you're talking about."

"Who are you working for?"

"Try to make sense, Pia. Why are you holding a gun on me?"

"I've been on to you from the beginning. You used the fact that we dated in high school to worm information out of my people. But I figured it out. Several people knew I was going to the Detention Center, but only two knew exactly when I left. And the other guy can't tie his own shoes. You were the one who called the Kazakhs."

Otis glanced at his helmet and tightened his lips.

Pia moved two steps closer. "You didn't see Kevin get in the driver's side because you were so proud of yourself for fooling me."

He nodded slowly and sighed. "You are one tough bitch."

A car pulled in the driveway and the motor stopped running.

His eyes narrowed. "How did you get in here, anyway?"

"What happened to the crusading reporter?"

"Google happened. There is no such thing as professional journalism anymore. There's only Buzzfeed and Facebook. Post a bunch of opinions as fact, add a lot of unfounded hyperbole, and anything viral becomes fact."

Pia lowered her voice. "What happened to you, Otis? What happened to the documentary?"

"No one cares. Without cute cat GIFs all over it, I can't get anyone to distribute it."

"You used to be driven by causes. You reported on a corrupt governor until he went to jail. You reported on drone kickbacks until three congressmen resigned. What are you working on now? What cause has you so worked up you're ready to kill me, Otis?"

He sneered. "Some things are bigger than you."

Car doors slammed outside.

"Go ahead," he said. "Pull the trigger. Kill me now." He moved from behind the desk and picked up his daypack. "You might dominate a bunch of washed-up veterans, but you're no killer."

A superior grin spread across his face. He reached back, grabbed the helmet, and threw it at her.

She squeezed the trigger an instant too late. The helmet hit her outstretched hands and knocked the pistol from her grip. Otis dove for the hallway a few yards behind her. She stretched a foot, snagging his leading ankle.

He face-planted into the door jam. "You fuck!"

They scrambled to their feet. Pia searched for her Glock.

Otis felt his nose, wiped the blood, then ran.

Pia spotted her handgun under a leather wingback, dropped to her knees, reached and pulled back just as a boot smashed the back of her head. Her face banged into the armrest, her arm and shoulder drove deep into the side. The weapon skittered across the hardwood floor to the corner.

She heard the garage door clatter as it rolled up.

The boot landed in her ribs. And again in her hip.

Rolling back, she scissor kicked her assailant, forcing his gunshot into the wall. Her would-be killer staggered backward into the bookshelf.

A motorcycle roared to life in the garage.

Pushing off her back, Pia leapt to her feet and landed a swift kick to the shin followed by a second aimed at his groin. The man twisted in time to offer only a thigh. She kicked it anyway. Stepping close to negate his firearm advantage, she slammed her elbow to his jaw and followed with a shovel punch. The heel of her hand connected with his chin just as her powerful legs accelerated her punch. His head snapped back into the oak bookcase. His eyes fluttered.

Pia disarmed him, retrieved her Glock, and darted him. She flew down the hall and out the kitchen door.

Three Kazakhs leaned against a white Mustang smoking cigarettes. They looked surprised when Pia burst into the night. She bolted across the lawn, zigging around trees, heading for the hedge.

Three shots echoed through the neighborhood.

She jumped through the bushes, somersaulted on landing, and kept rolling. She popped back to her feet, ran down the alley, and flew to the Ferrari as fast as she'd ever run.

She yelled to Verges, "You ride shotgun, start it up."

Startled but not stupid, Verges did what she asked.

She vaulted the door, landed in the driver's seat, threw the car in gear, and stomped on the gas.

"What happened back—"

A squeal of tires shrieked behind them.

"Did you see the motorcycle leave?" she asked.

"Yes."

"Which way did he turn when he hit the main road?"

"Uh, left. I think."

Pia gunned the engine, broke the back end loose, and slid into a four-wheel drift that took them left on the main road.

"Is there a white Mustang behind us?"

Verges strained around the headrest. "Yes, ma'am."

"Then duck."

Chapter 40

As far as I was concerned, it was just another day in an industrial town. Guangzhou's pollution rolled across the city like fog in San Francisco. A darted Kazakh lay next to me, snoring like a contented grandfather after lunch.

I said, "You can hit him from here, that's why."

"No way, Jacob." Tania squatted next to me and took another look over the edge. She sighed, dropped her butt on the rooftop, and leaned her back against the wall. "Too many problems."

"I'll fix them. Tell me what you need."

"Jacob, this rifle's been floating around the luggage compartment for the last two days. I'd have to find a range and dial it in. Then there's the glass. We're not straight on with the window. The round will break it, no problem, but who knows where it'll go from there? You can't send a piece of lead at 2,500 feet per second and expect it to fly straight after it hits glass at an angle. For all I know it could deflect and hit the building next door."

"Fifteen degrees. Not that big an angle. And the scope was dialed in a couple days ago. It's good for a thousand meters, this is under three hundred. You could eyeball it."

"What about the escape route? You think your girlfriend can handle her part?"

"Not my girlfriend. She's with Miguel now."

Tania looked me up and down. "So. Emily's smart after all."

My eyes rolled. "It's Anatoly Mokin, right there in that office. Set up your scope and check it out."

"Then why not kill him and be done with it?"

"Because we need to find Element 42 first. And I want to look him in the eye when I pull the trigger."

"You're fucked up. Have you been talking to that Greek god again?"

"Roman. And no."

"This is a distraction, Jacob. We should find this Fang-guy and save Philly."

"This is for Carmen." I said. "Verges said Philly's out of danger for now. Besides, Ms. Sabel's following the clues in DC. We have Mokin right in front of us, overlord of the mass grave on Borneo, mastermind of the Algeria attack, a member of the Windsor board, and the man who ordered Carmen's murder."

Tania turned back to look over the wall again.

I said, "He would've whacked the rest of us too."

"And you want to give him a second chance?"

"Give me that thing," I said. "I could make a decent shot from here."

"You'd kill him." She pulled the rifle out of the case, checked out the action, attached the suppressor, dropped the bipod legs, and chambered a round. She knelt behind the wall and rested the bipod on top. She eased her shoulder into the stock and aligned her eye to the sight. "I hate this position. This is no sniper blind."

"Want a chair? I can get you a chair."

"No. Hang on a second. He's with someone, walking around with a suitcase, fresh off a flight … dang it."

"What?"

"Remember Kasey Earl back in Kabul? You cut his ear off when he bragged about raping a local woman?"

"What about him?"

"He's… Damn. It'd be better if they had picture windows. There's a mullion…"

We stayed silent for three minutes. I'd never been a spotter, but I knew that sniper-mojo revolves around long stretches of stillness.

Mercury said, I've been thinking about your future, brotha.

I said, Not now.

Mercury said, It ain't good. You'll want to hear—

I tuned him out.

Tania said, "You ready to make that call?"

I dialed and Mokin picked up. "Hey Anatoly-meister, Jacob Stearne, Sabel Security here. I told you I'd see you this afternoon. Nice of you to wear a tie, but plaid? Way last year. Here's a bit of advice: If you're going to hang out with slime like Kasey Earl, you should wear a biohazard suit."

"Where are—" he began.

I clicked off.

Tania fired.

Miguel threw the door open for us. We jumped three rickety stairs at a time, winding down six flights to the ground floor where Emily waited. She had her nose in the cracked door and her palm facing us. Stop.

We fell in behind her hand.

She was trembling when she pulled her nose back in. "Three Kazakhs talking to our driver."

Tania grabbed the bag hanging on Emily's shoulder and tossed brightly colored, cheap windbreakers to each of us. We wadded them up and shoved them in the nearest pocket. Changing your color scheme while making a getaway has been known to work sometimes.

Miguel pushed us all aside and stuck his nose into the door's thin gap. He glanced back at me and whispered. "I take the two on the right. You take one on the left."

We slipped past Emily.

Miguel grabbed the closest Kazakh by the back of the neck and smashed his head into the head of the second man. It sounded like coconuts banging together. I punched the third guy in the face while Tania kicked his ass hard. Miguel's guys reeled back, hands to heads, confused and disoriented. He took advantage of the situation and banged them together a second time. I put my guy in a head lock and let Tania kick him in the balls. Emily joined in; she didn't have any skills but kicked for all she was worth. We dropped our unconscious foes on the pavement. Twelve seconds start to finish.

Our driver was running away from us like an antelope fleeing a cheetah. A block away, three Kazakhs were running straight at us, passing our ex-getaway driver. I pressed my face to the Buick's window. No keys.

Miguel tagged me and nosed at two more Kazakhs coming through an alley on the left. Both groups were still a hundred yards out. On the far side of the building, wailing sirens echoed and screeched their way into the neighborhood.

"Plan B," I said. "Rendezvous in an hour."

Miguel grabbed Emily's hand and yanked her down the alley on the right. Tania gave me a dirty look and hustled across the street, into a shop. I pulled out my tourist map and pretended to look at it then strode up the big boulevard. As soon as I was a block away, I unfurled my windbreaker and donned it. Somehow I'd ended up with pale lavender.

Ducking through a couple shops and alleys, I made my way to the wedding dress street. It looked like Rodeo Drive in Beverly Hills, only it was all wedding dresses. Traditional Chinese use bright colors for weddings and reserve white for funerals. Modern Chinese go with the Western concept. The shops weren't taking any chances and had the whole rainbow.

I heard Kazakhs yelling at locals behind me, ordering them to point out the Imperialist Yankee. I rudely pushed past a mother and daughter and ducked into the alley between shops. Mannequins dressed in bright reds and pale greens and deep blues took up most of the walking space. There was little more than a tight pathway between the lesser shops that couldn't afford street-facing real estate. I slowed to an anonymous stroll, looking like any other groom shopping for bargains. I thought about Tania in a wedding dress. Would she wear white? She had a Chinese grandmother somewhere in Brooklyn. Or was it Japanese? Shouting echoed through the alley behind me, and I continued looking for dresses while sneaking a peek at the harried Kazakhs searching for me. Ten minutes of ambling brought me back to the main boulevard, Jiangnan North Road. Everything was relatively quiet.

I leaned against a building and checked out the pedestrians as cars and motorcycles and bikes streamed by. Guangzhou's a lesson in city planning. There isn't any. Every block had a gleaming skyscraper pointing into the heavens surrounded by dirty sidewalks and beaten-up stores and shabby apartments ready to fall over. Alternating blocks of the boulevard were ghetto and Madison Avenue. The storefront in front of me was painted in garish new colors while the shop on its left hadn't been touched since Chiang Kai-shek ran the country.

I watched the eyes of passersby. No one was interested in me. I'd made it.

Mercury said, You're not done. There's more.

I said, Please. I beat those clowns two blocks ago.

Mercury said, Whatever, man. You never listen to me anyway. You haven't even made a single votum to me, much less—

One Kazakh, fifty yards diagonal, scanned down the street while I scanned up. Our gazes met and our recognition kicked in at the same moment.

He raised a big, nasty revolver.

I smiled.

Every third car flying between us on the four-lane road was a delivery van. The vans were small enough to fit inside a UPS truck back home, but they were big enough to derail his aim. Taking a shot at that distance would end up causing an accident and a panic that would bring a herd of cops. There was no way in hell my Kazakh was that stupid.

He pulled the trigger.

Chapter 41

Drivers slammed on their brakes. Ten cars transformed into a sheet-metal accordion on the compression stroke. Glass flew and metal crunched and people screamed—and I fled like an antelope, jumping vendor buckets on the sidewalk and crashing through racks of clothes, spinning past families and parting the tide of pedestrians.

After dodging ten thousand rounds fired by *jihadi* warriors—who at least wanted to kill me on behalf of their god—the last thing I wanted was to be gunned down by the dumbest mercenary in Asia.

A greasy alley gave me a place to dump my windbreaker. Around the corner, the world's tiniest tourist shop afforded me a place to catch my breath. I pulled a tractor cap off a rack and checked the price: 90 RMB. I slapped a twenty, American, on the counter with the tag and nodded to the lady behind the counter. Her gaze slipped past me to the street. I slapped another twenty on the counter and pointed to her back room. She looked at me, the twenty, and back out at the street. She shook her head and pushed me into the corner and rolled a rack of t-shirts in front of me. I peered around. There was no back room. No back door, no window, no way out.

Between the hangers I saw my nemesis looking left and right and left again. His eyes aimed straight at me but kept moving. He moved up the alley and made a phone call. No doubt telling his crew he'd spotted me and leaving out the part about the havoc he'd left behind.

The lady stepped to the front of the store and called out to another shopkeeper across the way. Several back-and-forths led to a man rolling down the steel cover to his shop and trotting out to meet her. Together they stood in her entry and watched my personal

Kazakh until he was a safe distance away. They pulled me out from behind the t-shirts.

"You give twenty dollar." The man held out his hand. I tried to look him in the eye, but he kept his gaze fixed on my hands.

"You speak English?"

"Duh. You too."

"I need a ride."

"I know. She know. You give twenty dollar."

I fished into my wallet without pulling it out and extracted what I hoped was a twenty. It wasn't. I saw only a flicker of President Grant's portrait before it disappeared from my fingers. "Hey. That's a fifty—"

The greenback went straight from his fingers to hers. "She save life. Now give me twenty dollar."

For a moment, I considered taking my chances with the Kazakh. Instead, I pulled my wallet and carefully shielded its contents from prying eyes. I pulled my second-to-last twenty and it too vanished instantly. With his skills, he could've joined Cirque du Soleil.

He put his palm to my face. "Stay. No move."

He went to a storage space across the street and came out pushing an electric green Znen Roar, the Chinese version of a Vespa with a racier look. I joined him and he handed me his helmet. I tucked it under my arm and straddled a sliver of seat.

"Where go?" he asked.

"People's Park."

"No good for you. No foreigners. You go Yuexiu Park."

"I'm meeting someone in People's Park, at the warrior statue of a guy named Zhang Zhixin."

He turned all the way around to stare at me like I was stupid. "No picture in guidebook? Zhixin a woman." He shrugged and began to push off, then stopped.

He pointed at the Kazakh, disappearing out of sight in the narrow alley. "You take swipe?"

"Love to."

"Twenty dollar."

I should've seen that one coming. I dug out my last twenty and he made it vanish. He spun up the bike quickly, dodging the myriad of wares that narrowed the alley to a footpath. He gained enough speed then cut the engine and glided silently behind the world's dumbest Kazakh. I put the helmet on the end of my fist and whumped the mercenary in the back of his head as we glided by.

We watched him face-plant into a bookrack. I hopped off, grabbed the Kazakh's phone and jumped back on. My personal courier snapped the engine back to life and slipped into traffic over the Haizhu Bridge and into downtown Guangzhou. He dropped me at the yellow gates of the park and gave me an idea of how to find the statue.

"My friends and I might need another ride," I said.

"I give phone number. Twenty dollar."

I shook my head. "No thanks. I'm done with the twenty-dollar thing."

He reached in his pocket and pulled out a card. He pointed below the chicken scratches of glyphs that make up their written language. "OK. No twenty dollar, this time only. You need help, you call Tang. You find money first. ATM. How many friend."

"Four."

Tang looked over his shoulder. "No problem. You call Tang."

He sped away.

A moped went by with two guys crouching behind the driver, an inch of toe-hold each. Another bike passed going the other way with two kids on the handlebars and a woman holding two buckets behind the driver.

Tang's bike stood out in a crowd. Ducking behind the park gate, I waited and watched. Mokin's men weren't all stupid. Thirty seconds later a bike stopped, parked on the sidewalk, and a Kazakh dismounted. The man pulled out a phone and made a call as he walked. He strode past me, looking forward. I stepped in behind, pressing my Glock to his head. He froze.

I pried the phone out of his fingers before I darted him and eased his body into a large hedge.

"Anatoly," I said. "I wanted to meet at your office but your men keep trying to kill me before I could get there. That's not how we welcome guests where I come from. So we'll just have to meet somewhere else. I'll find a nice bistro and call you back."

He was yelling in his language when I clicked off. I tossed the phone into a bag hanging from a passing bike and watched it disappear down the block.

I strolled into the park. Right away someone pointed at me and made a joke to his family. They laughed. Tang was right—I was the only Westerner in the park, and six inches taller than the tallest local guy. Pulling my tourist map out, I held it up and slouched, doing my best not to look American. I followed directions and still couldn't find the right statue. Instead, I ended up in front of a gorgeous, naked woman-warrior riding a rearing stallion, aiming her bow behind her. One statue is as good as the other in my book.

Common sense told me I had a good deal of time to wait, since my team would be on foot for at least the first mile. I played the tourist until I tired of looking at historical markers in a language that meant nothing to me. A park bench opposite the naked woman-warrior offered a little shade and seclusion, not to mention a beautiful view.

I called the Major and she filled me in on the latest news from Sabel Gardens. A few minutes later, Tania's voice floated to me. "Hey dumbass, the statue of Zhang Zhixin is over there."

With a quick glance at her, I followed her pointed finger to a stone statue across the grass.

"This is Zhang Zhixin," I said, "says so right on the plaque."

She pulled her sunglasses down her nose, stepped to the naked woman-warrior, and bent down to read the plaque. No translations. She straightened up and frowned at me. "You can't read Chinese."

"That guy told me." I waved a hand in the direction of some people who'd been there a minute earlier but must've left. "Where are Miguel and Emily?"

"They aren't coming," said an English accent behind me.

268

An invisible short man with a buzzcut stepped out of the shadows. Invisible because he was looking away from us as if he wasn't there or we weren't there, or someone wasn't somewhere. Looking at him gave you the impression his words were meant for someone else, and you were too embarrassed to ask. He moved as if he were nothing, an unimportant stranger, and looking at him embarrassed you even more. He appeared and disappeared at will. I'd seen men like him before: Special Air Service, or SAS. They were the British model from which all other countries fashioned their special ops regiments. This guy was the archetype—compact, lean, and muscular like a gymnast. I'd bet a paycheck the guy had a tattoo: a dagger with wings and a scroll reading, "Who Dares Wins".

He sat on the bench, looking at me in his peripheral vision, his nose pointing ahead and slightly away. "The police allowed Miguel a call to the American Embassy. He called me instead."

Chapter 42

Pia's Ferrari outpaced the Mustang until they hit traffic. Downshifting while keeping the engine revved to nearly the 9,000 rpm redline, she passed a sedan full of startled faces. The Mustang made the same pass on a blind curve, clipping the sedan. In the distance, the motorcycle's single taillight crested the next hill.

A catering van pulled out of an estate and onto the road. Pia swerved to the shoulder, snapped a mailbox off at ground level and sent it cartwheeling into the air behind them. The open space shrank faster than she could pass the van. The caterer slammed on his brakes, sending smoke and noise into her open cockpit as she sideswiped a retaining wall and left some paint and bodywork behind. Her angle of re-entry forced her to fishtail before she corrected and got back on track. The adventure scrubbed time off their lead over the Mustang.

Verges clung to the dash with one hand; his other wrapped in his seatbelt, his head leaned out his lowered window. She couldn't tell if he was looking back or puking.

The Mustang passed the caterer over the double yellow, and opened fire. In the mirror, she saw their ricochets like sparklers on the pavement. They started too low then swung wildly up as the bumps in the road, exaggerated by speed, tossed their barrels like toothpicks in a tornado.

Over the hillcrest, she saw Otis turn onto Falls Road, heading into Potomac. His rate of speed indicated a route through town, not into the warren of suburban streets nearby. He didn't expect her to live long enough to catch him. She glanced at her dashboard clock. Two in the morning. Very little traffic. She stomped on the gas pedal.

She took the turn at seventy, using all the lanes to widen her radius, and ended up trimming someone's hedge with her side mirror. Nothing lay ahead but the glow of the village center above the trees. She raised her speed in a car built for that kind of road, taking the sweeping turns and gentle hills like Sebastian Vettel. Coming over the rise before the town's only stoplight, she saw Otis, less than half a mile ahead.

His small bike shuddered through the red light.

It turned green three seconds before she blew through it.

Behind her, the Mustang struggled to match her speed. Another string of muzzle flashes sparked in her mirror.

She yelled over the wind to Verges. "Can you shoot those guys?"

"I can't get a clear shot."

"Just brush them back."

"No ma'am. Not with my service weapon. If the bullet hit a civilian—"

"I get it." She dug her pistol out. "Use mine, the darts won't penetrate anything thicker than a barn jacket. But it might scare them off."

At the next rise, the Mustang appeared and he squeezed off three shots.

The Ferrari's headlights illuminated a cop, standing beside his car with a cup of coffee in his hand. At her high rate of speed, it had the effect of looking like a flash picture. Pia calculated the required events in her head. The cop would drop the coffee, jump in his car, throw it in gear, turn on the lights, stomp on the gas, and pull onto the road. Nine seconds. Then he would accelerate from stopped to full speed. Another fifteen seconds. Twenty-four seconds altogether. She'd be a mile down the road and a lot closer to Otis.

The Mustang reappeared in her mirror. Though farther back and still losing ground, they hadn't given up.

The cop fired up his lights, flashing red and blue through the village center. He pulled onto the road without seeing the approaching Mustang. The Kazakhs swerved and lost control. They slid sideways, their front bumper smashing the cop's door, and spun out in front of him, crashing into a utility box. The cop stopped.

Two problems solved.

From Potomac's center to the end of Falls Road is two miles, and her 458 Spider could reach twice the speed of Otis's small Honda on the straight, empty street. Pia pushed it as fast as she dared, bringing him inside her high beams as he approached the ninety-degree left turn onto MacArthur Boulevard.

Otis slowed. Pia closed, knowing cars can corner faster than motorcycles. Not in tight maneuvers, but a full left turn where the two narrow roads met, the bike could lean only so far while four wheels could drift.

Otis conceded as little as possible, accelerating out of the turn and into the narrow wooded lane.

Pia accelerated too, taking the first sweeping turn faster than Otis and climbed into his mirrors.

She saw his first mistake. Instead of using his eyes, he turned his head to look at his side mirror. The sudden air turbulence threw his balance off. She slowed. He wobbled and corrected and made his second mistake. He hit the brakes in a split second of panic. His almost-controlled weave became erratic. Pia slammed on her brakes.

Otis continued, fighting his out of control bike with force instead of cool composure.

ABS stuttered all four of her tires, leaving her to watch Otis lose it after he'd scrubbed some, but not enough, of his speed. The bike tipped too far and went over in a shower of sparks. She couldn't make out quite where he went until the smoke and dust cleared two seconds later.

At the edge of her headlight beams, a silhouette limped from where the bike was crushed against an elm tree. He stopped, fired two badly aimed rounds, then fled into the forest.

Pia ground to a stop, inches from the bike.

"Holy shit," Verges said. "Where did you learn to drive like—"

Pia swapped her mag for a full one and leapt out of the car. Leading with her Glock, she slid between trees, pressing her shoulder to one, looking around, then moving to the next. She couldn't see him. For every shred of light the harvest moon reflected to earth, the trees overhead, still adorned with half of their autumn leaves, blocked it out.

She listened for animals, footsteps, insects, anything that would indicate his direction.

A flicker of light drew her attention. Deep in the woods, where her headlights barely reached, something had moved.

She ran laterally, ten trees deeper in, a little closer to the Potomac River and a little farther from her personal FBI agent.

She checked again and listened. A branch snapped fifty yards ahead and a little right. She ran half of it.

Red-and-blue cop lights streaked through the trees far behind her, coming from the opposite direction. The cop in town had called in backup. Verges could explain the situation. She refocused on the fugitive.

Turning her head ninety degrees, she let her voice echo to him. "Where's the shipment of Element 42, Otis?"

She jogged three trees to the left.

He fired a three-round burst from ten yards away, five hardwood trees between them. If she remembered her training right, that would probably be an AK-47 from one of his Kazakhs. Her fingers squeezed around her nine-dart Glock. She was outgunned. In that moment, she understood why her veteran agents continually lobbied for real bullets.

"How would I know?" His answer echoed, making it hard to pinpoint, but his footsteps gave him away.

"Aren't you helping Violet Windsor?"

"That psychopath? Hell no."

She tiptoed two trees closer and pressed her back against an oak. "Is the shipment in Philly?"

He moved in a direction she couldn't track.

"Philadelphia? Why would it be there?"

"Quit playing games. Where is it?"

Three bullets ripped the bark off her tree. She ran to her right, four trees this time, and peered back where she'd seen the muzzle flash. A shadow that looked like a man leaned away from her. She fired.

He spun around, firing two quick bursts.

Twelve in all, she figured. Out of thirty, that left him eighteen.

"You won't get out of these woods." She moved two trees left.

"You mean alive? If I take you hostage, they'll let me go." He fired again, a three-round burst, a hundred twenty degrees away from her.

"First, I'd never let you take me hostage." She pressed her back to the nearest tree. "And second, the cops never let a hostage-taker leave the scene."

"Guess you'll have to die, then."

Calculating the risk, she dashed in his direction. She tripped over a fallen branch, landed on her outstretched arms. The pistol fired and bounced into the air.

Otis peppered the trees a foot over her head, four or five rounds at least. She stayed on the ground until he stopped.

When she heard him trotting toward her, she scrambled for her weapon, feeling through the leaves and muck with her fingers. He approached on the wrong side of a group of saplings. She touched the Glock, but his feet neared the turn where he would see her. She jumped up and stepped behind a tree. He fired at the tree next to her, one round.

Pia tried to control her breathing. He was close enough to hear her. His jacket scraped against bark five yards away.

She dove for her weapon, grabbed it and a fist full of grubby leaves, rolled, and popped up on her feet. She ran twenty yards before taking cover behind another hardwood.

He blasted away at the trees behind her. Three more rounds.

A spotlight from the road stabbed through the woods, searching for them. A voice on a bullhorn barked about coming out with your hands up. Verges must have flashed his badge and won them over. She was not giving up her weapon while Otis still had his.

One more round hit the tree she was leaning against. He knew he was low on ammo. She rolled to the side and fired three darts, not to hit him but to give herself some cover. He ducked away. She sprinted back the way she came and found a tree where she could see him.

"Where's Element 42, Otis?"

"What do you think this is, some dumb movie where the bad guy spills his guts at the end? Hate to break it to you, but—I'm not the bad guy." He paused. "I'll tell you the truth, Pia: I have no idea where it is and I don't care."

She stepped out and fired where she'd seen his shadow. He was gone. "Then where are you going to attack?"

One round hit the tree next to her. She'd lost count but he had to be empty. She stepped out, leading with her pistol, and found him. She fired two darts, but he was gone again.

Metal-on-metal sounds came from his direction. Clicking and snapping.

A shiver ran through her skin when she realized he'd changed magazines. He had another thirty rounds.

She had two.

"I don't know what you're talking about. There's no 'attack' planned."

"Chapman told me you were going to spread it over Philadelphia, kill the old people, and sell them Levoxavir."

"Maybe that's what he and Violet Windsor planned. But they're both dead."

Voices approached from the road. A voice on a bullhorn blared out. "Stop! Drop your weapons! Put your hands where I can see them."

A scraping sound came from her left. She turned, faced him, and looked down her Glock's sight into his muzzle.

She fired a dart as she leapt behind a tree surrounded by thick brush. His bullets came so close she felt them buzz through her hair.

She crouched low and peered between the leaves. The cops were coming in with flashlights. Otis faced them in a shadow, his rifle butted against his shoulder. She took two silent steps, aimed carefully at his broad back, then took two more steps. She had him cold.

Something about her Glock registered in her mind. The slide was back, the barrel exposed—empty. No. There should be one left. Unless she miscounted. In disbelief, she pulled the trigger. Nothing happened. No click, no slide movement, nothing. Empty.

Her free hand slowly and silently slid the Glock back into the normal position. She held the pistol steady in the deadliest bluff of her life. "Drop it, Otis."

He smiled when he turned. "You're not a killer."

He reached out, grabbed her arm, pulled her close to his barrel and stuck it under her chin.

"You're no killer either, Otis. You kill me and they'll kill you."

Flashlights flickered over and past them before returning to them.

"PUT THE WEAPON ON THE GROUND NOW!" Verges's voice had a newfound authority. "DOWN. NOW. DROP YOUR WEAPON. DO IT NOW."

Otis smiled into the light. Pia shoved her right arm into the barrel, forcing it wide and pounded his chin with her open left hand. She twisted her core back to the left, bringing her elbow hard into the bridge of his nose. He staggered back and she backed away.

"Put the gun down," Pia said. "C'mon, Otis."

Otis raised it in a haphazard fashion as blood flowed from his nose. He fired a shot halfway between Pia and Verges.

"PUT THE GUN DOWN. GET ON YOUR KNEES." Verges moved in closer.

Otis fired another round.

Verges put a round through Otis's ear that exited two inches farther back in his skull. Two tidy holes that filled with blood. He fell over and blinked at Pia.

She tossed his AK-47 three feet behind him and knelt next to him. "He's down!" she yelled. "I've secured his weapon."

His eyes wandered around, confused. "Wha ... happened?"

"Where is Element 42?"

"Fuck you. Did … you shoot me in the head?"

"Help is coming. Hang in there, Otis."

The cops and Verges ran up, flashlights shining on Otis. His blood was darker than she expected. It spilled into the grass and leaves slow and thick.

"Otis, thousands of lives are at risk. Tell me about it. I don't believe it's about Levoxavir."

"What's … Levoxavir?" He gasped deep and rolled his head. "I feel funny. I feel…"

Pia grabbed his hand and squeezed it. "C'mon, Otis, give me a clue."

"My head hurts. Did you shoot me in the… aw damn. I'm sorry."

"What are you sorry about, Otis? What's this all about? Why risk everything?"

"It's a good cause, Pia. You'd like it. Chen, Wu, Mokin. Not Violet. She's dead." He took a deep breath as if he were relaxing after a hard day at work. "Too many… too many people."

Pia gazed up at Verges. It took a moment for them to get the hint, but the cops backed up a few steps.

"It's just you and me, Otis. Tell me now. What's this all about?"

"I'm… I don't feel too… What? No. I'm not telling you shit … bitch."

He took another deep breath. He clenched his teeth and his face bunched up in pain. His body spasmed, he exhaled and relaxed. Black bile oozed from his mouth.

Chapter 43

I said, "Nigel—if that really is your name—how did it happen?"

The SAS man sighed. "Miguel flattened three of them, out cold. One Kazakh was still standing when his girl lost it and started screaming. The local police showed up and banged them up."

"Yeah, I got that part the first time. I mean, why did he call you? You look like a major or a colonel."

For the first time, Nigel made eye contact. It was only a flicker, but enough to tell me what I suspected. He glanced away to my favorite statue, the naked woman warrior on a horse. "Lieutenant colonel actually, currently the cultural attaché, British Embassy. Miguel helped me out of a right bugger. I owe him a favor."

"You're the SAS officer he helped back in Qatar."

Miguel made a habit of rescuing officers from embarrassing situations whenever and wherever he found himself on leave. Nigel had attended a brothel-party when the Qatari police raided it. Qatar's finest were upset about the ratio of men to women at the party—fourteen men, no women. Miguel happened along and pulled him out of the scrum. Nigel was one of fifty or so officers around the world forever in Miguel's debt.

"Ah." He looked away. "So he told you about that, did he?"

I said nothing.

"Well." Nigel stood. "There you have it. I'll be off then."

"Hold up. As I recall the Qatar incident, you owe him more than a message delivery."

He looked at me out of the corner of his eye and bit the inside of his cheek. "You can always ask."

"Anatoly Mokin's men are looking for me. I need a head count and any other intel."

"You're taking on Mokin?" He squinted, chewed his cheek some more, and gave Tania the once-over. "The lot of you?"

"Already bagged a dozen of them."

He leaned back and gave me a hint of admiration. "Very well then."

Nigel handed me a card for a hotel gift shop and disappeared between the bushes.

Tania sat as far from me as the bench would allow and crossed her arms.

I caught her glance. "Why'd you change your mind and take the shot at Mokin?"

"I didn't. I shot off Kasey's other ear."

I laughed and put out my hand for a high-five. She left me hanging for a long second but gave in and slapped it.

"What the hell was he doing in Mokin's office?" she asked.

"Velox Deployment Services and Mokin International Enterprises, merger maybe? Hell if I know."

My phone vibrated with a call from Ms. Sabel.

"Jacob, patch Tania in," she said. When we merged the calls, she continued in a desperate voice I'd never heard from her before. "I thought Otis was working with Windsor, but he knew Violet Windsor was dead before the police knew. All our leads are dead— Windsor, Cummings, Otis—and we still don't know what happened to Element 42. And they didn't have Levoxavir at the Borneo site. Why not? At this point, Mokin is our only lead, so don't kill him."

"We're working on Mokin," I said. "We should have him cornered soon."

Tania scowled at me.

I shook her off.

We could have Mokin cornered soon. It was possible.

Ms. Sabel said, "Why kill the board and executives?"

"It gets worse. A guy from Velox Deployment is meeting with Mokin."

"The press is all over this," Ms. Sabel said. "They claimed I'm killing all these people to drive up business. Where is Emily?"

"She's busy right now, but I think she'll have a story filed soon."

Tania muted her line and whispered. "Tell her the truth."

I muted my line. "She doesn't need the truth. She needs to feel better, get her confidence back."

"Are you there?" the boss asked.

I glared at Tania and unmuted. "Sorry, background noise."

"I'll join you as soon as I can get Dad's jet in the air. In the meantime, you have to find Mokin. Otis said it was bigger than Philly. I don't know what that means but it scares the hell out of me."

"Who was Otis working for?" Tania asked.

"We traced his calls, but the number is unidentified."

"Wu Fang?"

"That's why you need to find Mokin. He could lead you to Fang, and that might be the answer. But you have to hurry."

"We're on it, ma'am," I said.

"What was that?" Tania shrieked after we clicked off. "*We're on it—ma'am.* Are you the biggest suck up in Asia? You think I'm going to let you cut me out of this job?"

"She needed to hear something positive," I said. "I didn't hear you helping out."

Tania was so mad I thought she would bite my face off. But she turned and stalked away. I slammed my fists in my jacket pockets and left in the other direction.

Our separate paths converged again at the planned rendezvous with Nigel via the card he'd given me earlier. The Landmark Hotel was a shiny new skyscraper overlooking the river and Haizhu Square. I sauntered into the gift shop and looked at a book co-authored by James Patterson and one of his minions. Tania slid to the makeup rack an arm's length away.

I sensed the invisible SAS officer at the candy rack next to us. I asked, "What're we up against?"

"Anatoly Mokin, for starters," he said. "But you know that   "

"His guys filled the mass grave on Borneo."

"The one on the news? Bloody hell." He snapped a glance at me. "They've some fancy friends in China somewhere high up the food chain. At the moment your odds are fair. You've three soldiers guarding Mokin. They've sprung their lad and moved off somewhere."

"How do I get Miguel and Emily out?" I asked.

"Meet them at the British Consulate in an hour. I've pressed the lass and Miguel into service to the Crown, temporarily."

"An hour?"

"He can't walk out. Mokin left a raft of men there waiting for you to show up."

"One more favor. I need to meet with Mokin. Could I borrow your consulate for neutral ground?"

"Good god, man, are you insane?" He stared at me until I convinced him I was both insane and serious. He shook his head. "The Canadians have an empty warehouse, I could abuse them this once. With any luck, the poor sods will forgive me one day."

He texted me contacts and instructions.

"Thanks," I said, "now I owe you one."

"Let's pray it never comes to that."

An hour later, Tania and I stood in the warehouse. We were searched and disarmed by three Canadian intel officers who warned us they intended to record every word. They also gave us the same rules they gave Mokin: no fighting, no biting, no punches below the belt, and no killing until after we left the premises. They opened a door and gestured us in.

Anatoly Mokin sprawled across a chair in a cramped office. Behind him stood a Kazakh with a permanent scowl etched in his face.

I sat across the table, hands folded in front of me. Tania sat next to me, straight across from Mokin, in the same position.

Mokin leaned forward. "Show me ID of yours."

Tania slapped a hand on the table. "Where the fuck is Element 42?"

"You know we not discuss this thing." He kept staring at me. "What ministry do you work for?"

"We know you targeted Philadelphia," Tania said. "Where is it?"

"You know nothing you talk about. What bureau you work for?" he asked me. "Show me ID."

"Terrorism is not something we take lightly."

"You work for Watson, yes?"

"You were never supposed to ship it to the US."

Mokin leaned back, his hands spread wide with innocence. "I never ship to USA. Windsor steals it. We already tell Watson this, *da?*" He squinted. "Who are you peoples?"

"We're done." Tania pushed back her chair and knocked on the door.

An intel officer opened it and led us out. "Did you get something out of that?"

"Everything," she said.

He hustled us out the secret exit that opened onto the street a block away.

Pulling out my phone, I dialed up Mokin. "Hey, Anatoly, Jacob Stearne here. I wish I could say it was nice meeting you. Tell me something. Who did the Canadians tell you we were?"

He was screaming Kazakh obscenities when I clicked off.

Tania and I bumped fists. We peered around the corner and saw no one suspicious.

"Did you suspect Watson and the FBI?" Tania asked.

"It makes sense now. They weren't investigating the break-in at NIH, they were cleaning it up."

"You think they're a step ahead of us?"

I shrugged. "I trust the FBI implicitly, but David Watson and Counterintelligence has too much power and too little oversight. We can't contact our own embassy without him getting wind of it. *Sua Sponte.*"

"Is that the Ranger motto? What's it mean?"

"Of their own accord. Or, we're on our own."

Tania and I took separate sides of the street, with our comm link open and our earbuds firmly in place. The last thing we wanted to do was disappoint Mokin by not taking down the men he left out front to kill us.

We approached from two blocks back, hoping to pick off a Kazakh or two. Instead, we watched a car full of Kazakhs join the party. My long-lost pal Kasey Earl, with one ear missing and the other ear sporting a ton of gauze and white medical tape, gave out assignments. We circled the Canadian warehouse until we counted eight thugs waiting for us, plus Kasey.

Tania and I retreated to a narrow alley full of bicycles, cardboard boxes, and blankets.

"Does Mokin have a pipeline full of these guys?" Tania asked.

Doing the math in my head, I realized we had faced at least two platoons from the beginning. One led by Yuri and the other by Mukhtar. It was possible that Mokin brought in Kasey to replace his lost lieutenants. If I was right, there were forty to fifty Kazakhs altogether. We'd captured, killed, or incapacitated only a dozen or so between Washington and Borneo. We had to reduce that number, but a large-scale killing spree was not an option.

"We need to get them in trouble with the Chinese."

"Yeah." I snapped my fingers. "They're armed and the Chinese have strict gun control—"

She rolled her eyes. "No, we're not going to make them shoot us."

"These guys couldn't hit the broadside of a—"

"Fine, they miss you. What about the innocent people behind you?"

Mercury said, Dude, that's what happens when you work for a girl. Even a cowardly Centurion would've mowed 'em all down. Just saying.

The mouth of the alley darkened with three men, Kasey in front. "There you are, Jacob. I've been looking all over for you."

Tania and I ducked and fired three times before he finished his sentence.

The alley came alive with moving cardboard as if a biblical swarm of insects was coming to life underneath them. Thirty Chinese homeless people looked at us, looked at Kasey, and started a screaming panic. They fled with their bicycles, leaving behind anything bulky. We tailed the stampede, charging at Kasey.

When we reached the alley's mouth, she fired left and I fired right. They went down hard on the sidewalk.

Sabel darts are quieter than regular firearms but the noise was unmistakable. China has half the police-to-citizen ratio as the USA but a more extensive reporting system for state security. We dragged the darted Kazakhs into the alley. I snapped a picture and sent it to Mokin.

We fled the scene a few steps ahead of the police and ducked into a street market two blocks away. Unadorned boxes of oranges, bananas, apples, and other fruits lined the sidewalks and spilled into the narrow road. One oddball in the crowd was selling chopsticks. It gave me an idea.

Grabbing Tania's arm, I stopped, pulled out Tang's card, and called him.

"Tang, I need two motorcycles, helmets, and a roll of duct tape." I listened to him for a second. "Yes, I'll find an ATM before you get here."

I clicked off and looked at Tania. "How many twenties do you have on you?"

Chapter 44

It took longer to pull the darts out of the brass shell casings than I expected. We had to be careful not to snag the needle on a finger and wind up sleeping it off for the next four hours. We taped them to our newly acquired chopsticks and examined our work.

"We'll need momentum," Tania said. "The plunger in these things is based on stopping from eight hundred miles an hour."

"Dhanpal did it in training once," I said. "Took down Miguel, and all he had was a running start with a hand thrust at the end."

She looked skeptical but didn't have a better idea.

For every five minutes Tang and his pal had to wait, we slapped another twenty in his hand.

When we were ready, Tang and his pal took to their jobs with glee. It was all fun and games to them. We sped through the city toward Mokin's office where a Kazakh stood on the corner. Tang took the corner tight, I leaned over with my dart-on-a-chopstick and stuck Mokin's man in the thigh. His reaction was slower than usual, but no less effective. He couldn't raise a defense of any kind before he flailed to the ground.

Three blocks away, Tania had similar results.

Collectively, we neutralized five guys before Tang and I rolled several blocks without finding another Kazakh. Then Tania and her driver flew past us heading for the bridge.

Tania shouted into the wind. "They stole our Buick."

I glanced behind me in time to see a Kazakh lean out of the Buick's window with a Berretta.

Tang saw the man in his mirror and twisted the Znen's gas, flinging us into the fruit market. Ducking and weaving, we drove under t-shirts hanging from overhangs and mounds of melons and citrus. The Buick plowed straight in, scattering people and fruit in every direction. One lone merchant-vigilante smashed their windshield with a baseball bat. When the vigilante saw the pistol, he whacked the man's arm. I saw it fly into the air. But they had more than one.

Two blocks later, brand new, first-class skyscrapers lined the streets. Tang took us across a pedestrian plaza and around a fountain. I caught a glimpse of the Buick going the long way around with a spider-webbed windshield. The passenger leaned out and fired two shots across the plaza. His driver threw caution to the wind and bounced up the curb and across the plaza heading straight for us.

Tang's eyes were bigger than the grapefruits we'd dodged. He overcorrected and dumped the bike. The polished granite burned my hip and thigh as I slid across it, coming to rest against a vehicle barrier. Tang landed five yards away and his bike five more. I ran to it and pushed it upright as the Buick bore down fast. Tang jumped on in front of me and would've taken off without me if I hadn't wrapped my arm around his waist. As I wrenched myself upright, he drove between the car barriers and into the building lobby.

We zoomed past stunned security guards.

I waved and smiled.

Tang yelled in Chinese and someone on the lobby's far side held the door open for us. We plowed through a gaggle of young men, bounced down a grand staircase and into the street. He crossed four lanes of high-speed traffic with an inch to spare, swerved onto a broad bridge, and sped down the sidewalk.

Once we were across the river, we fled down a side street where Tang brought us to a stop. "You get off. Get off! You crazy person."

I heaved my sore leg off the seat. He gave me a dirty scowl until he saw the fifty I held between us.

"British Consulate, two more riders. One of them is a big guy."

He hesitated, almost reached for the bill, then pulled back and shook his head. "No-no. Guns no good. You in trouble with Triad. No good for Tang."

"Triad?"

"Hong Kong mafia, like movies. Very bad guys."

"No, they're Anatoly Mokin's men, from Kazakhstan." I added another fifty and waved them both.

Tang no longer salivated over my cash. He leaned back, waving his hands between us. "Oh no. No good, no good. Mokin very bad man. Worse than Triad. No good for Tang."

He snatched both fifties, twisted the gas, and sped away into the night.

Several blocks away, Tania had a similar experience. We met in a nearby department store. I tried Miguel's phone for the twentieth time and Nigel answered. Without preamble, he named a restaurant near the British Consulate and clicked off. I entered the name into my mapping software and determined it was within walking distance.

Tania and I both had a Glock with three darts, a magazine of bullets, and four chopstick-darts. Enough to take down the remaining Kazakhs should they show. A quick check of Mokin's GPS showed him on the far side of the city heading out of town. We felt good about our chances.

We made our way on foot into the neighborhood, an international district teeming with nightlife and fancy buildings. We passed nicely kept alleys filled with people who congregated around tables. Streetlights glowed above bustling streets along the main road. International hotels filled every corner with small but perfectly manicured green spaces in their driveways. We were as far from the gritty streets of Mokin's operations as we were going to get.

Tania cleared every store we passed, checking out anyone looking vaguely Euro. She was on full alert, ready to kill Kazakhs first and ask questions later. I relaxed, safe in the knowledge that my long-forgotten god would warn me should trouble rear its ugly head. His unemployment benefits had run out fifteen hundred years ago and he needed the work.

It was hard to keep my eyes off Tania after running down the wedding dress street. She was beautiful. I could picture her in any of those dresses, even the white ones. I thought about a thousand different things I could say that might lower her defenses enough to rekindle our relationship. Nothing sounded good enough. I decided to blurt out my love for her. I'd throw myself at her feet and let her humiliate me or accept me—I was beyond caring which.

Just as I steeled myself for my confession, my phone broke the mood with a beep from the mapping software.

A shoulder-wide alley disappeared into the dark between two storefronts. Our destination was sixty feet into that dark space.

Mercury said, Dark alleys on foreign soil, dawg. Do you even need me for this? Look high and right.

Tania and I gave each other a glance and drew our weapons. I led with Tania's back to mine. I sensed a presence above me, right where Mercury predicted. I stopped and raised my arms in surrender. Tania positioned herself at my shoulder, tense and ready.

Nigel dropped from a second story window a foot in front of me, his Browning HP in my face.

Tania slipped under my upraised arm and shoved her Glock under his chin.

I said, "Dramatic, Nigel. Put it away before Tania gets nervous."

He lowered the weapon and held a finger to his lips, pointed to a door. I led, Nigel followed, Tania kept her Glock pressed against the back of his head.

Through the door was a windowless room. Miguel and Emily stood on the other side of a map table.

Emily's hug was hard and sustained. She was no longer a travel reporter trying to scrape a lurid headline from her connections inside the Sabel empire. She was a veteran who'd lost a friend in combat. There are two crossings in the soldier's life, losing your first friend, and making your first kill. She'd made that first horrible crossing. From now on, everything in her life would be more vivid, each friendship more precious, every moment more valuable. As I let go of her embrace, I prayed she would never come to the second crossing.

"Miguel's sketched the scenario for me," our host said. "I've appealed for official support but the Foreign and Commonwealth Office is slow on a good day. I'm all the resource you'll have from the UK. And officially, I'm not here."

Tania stood behind him, shaking her head slowly. Miguel caught the signal and scowled.

"Thanks," I said. "We'd rather go alone if you don't mind."

"I've an arsenal." He pointed to boxes in the corner. "And transport."

"He's coming with us," Miguel said, staring at Tania. "We need the help."

Nigel pointed to the map. "Have you Mokin's location?"

Tania pushed her way to the map. "Jacob can drive us there. Mokin's location is a need-to-know situation, and you don't need to know."

I glanced at Mokin's updated location and spotted it on the larger map. The man was still on the move, but his heading was easier to predict. He was on a lone road in an empty mountainous area.

Nigel looked down his nose at her. "It would be helpful to know the terrain—"

"You aren't bringing any resources. If you want to come with us, all you need to do is play whack-a-Kazakh."

He studied the others for support, his gaze stopped at Miguel.

"She's got her reasons," Miguel said.

Nigel shrugged. "Very well, then."

Outside, a Jaguar beeped and my new pal handed me the keys. Miguel hefted two crates of hardware into the trunk, took the passenger seat, and buzzed it back.

Tania grabbed Nigel and pulled the phone from his pocket. She tossed it under the car's back tire and gestured to the middle seat.

"Hey, I'm helping you," Nigel said.

"I'd hate to have to kill you because someone accidentally followed your signal."

"Show some respect. I've—"

"This is respect. Miguel vouched for you or you'd be nursing a broken nose on the sidewalk."

He climbed in and we were off. Miles of endless city droned by, followed by a long steady climb into the mountains. The roads grew smaller and less traveled as the night wore on. My traveling companions were bored to sleep. Eventually, even Miguel gave out and tucked his head against the glass for a snooze.

I kept checking Mokin's GPS signal, surprised he was vulnerable to a simple hack like ours. One day my luck would run out and my victim would figure out he was connected to Sabel Satellite's WiFi signal. But Mokin was happy enough to have a signal in the middle of nowhere and afraid that questioning it might make it disappear. On he drove, and on I followed, his coordinates heading north and east.

Three hours later, with everyone still asleep, I rolled to a gentle stop in front of an abandoned restaurant on the rain-slicked one-lane road, several miles short of Mokin's location. The Kazakh King had been stationary for the last half hour. The only road between us followed the jagged coast of a mountain reservoir before spiraling up switchbacks over the ridgeline. Five miles as the crow flies translated into twenty-two miles of mountain roads.

I texted a short, upbeat report to the Major while my imagination spun up hundreds of ambush scenarios. There was only one reason Anatoly Mokin would place himself at the far end of impassable terrain. One way in. One way out. No doubt he had already sealed our exit. The only course of action available was to move forward into an unknown terrain, against an unknown number, armed with unknown weapons, and seize the initiative. *Press the opportunity immediately.*

It was one of those leadership decisions I hated to make. Press on and lead my team to their deaths? Or sit here and wait for death to come to us?

I leaned back in the seat and thought about life and death and love. All anyone wants is to fill that gap between life and death with as much love as possible. Family love, friendly love, romantic love, eternal love are all facets of the same jewel. Cops and criminals, hajjis and soldiers, pacifists and haters are filling their lives with love in the way each thinks best. People on both sides convinced that they are the good guys. I'd made a career of hastening death for those whose love didn't meet my society's standards. And like the bereaved of those I had dispatched, I felt the pang of losing a loved life to the silent void of death.

And just like that, the dark demons from Borneo came to me. I'd murdered a prisoner just to keep Emily from doing it. Worse, I followed Mokin here to kill the Kazakhs for letting them ambush me. And Borneo wasn't the first time. Good guys don't do things like that.

I closed my eyes and felt the tremors coming back. The ones I'd left behind so many years ago.

Chapter 45

Alan Sabel's jet roared through the sky, carrying Pia and her crew to an uncertain future in China. From the corner of her eye, she saw her father pour a glass of water in the galley and carry it to her. He placed it on the table and waited in the aisle. She never looked up from her tablet.

He sat across from her. "I thought I raised a girl who said—"

"Thanks for the water."

"You found Wu Fang's address. What else do you need?"

"Lots of things."

"Any way I can help?"

Pia glanced up. "Sorry, Dad. I couldn't explain it."

She nosed into her tablet again, zooming and turning the screen.

"Try me. Sometimes talking it out—"

"They're boxed in," she said. She leaned back, her eyes still on the tablet. "No way out and an unknown situation on the ground. Jacob estimated Mokin has forty men left, but it could be a hundred for all we know."

"You're not worried about the odds."

She pushed the tablet away and gazed out the window. Somewhere in the predawn dark, fifty thousand feet below, the Pacific Ocean sloshed from Asia to America.

She sighed. "The satellite images, they're crap. Manhattan is clear and crisp, but rural China is a haze."

Alan leaned over the table and pulled the tablet closer to him. He checked out the map and zoomed in.

"No matter how you zoom in," she said, "the smallest identifiable object on the ground is so fuzzy you can't tell if it's a car or a stadium."

Alan nodded and pushed the tablet back to her. "What happened to that old friend of yours? The one you had over for dinner a couple times."

Pia shrugged. "Who?"

"That pretty Latina girl, used to be a soccer rival in high school. I think she was the captain at Bethesda or Rockville?"

"Bianca Dominguez? She's one of Jacob's girlfriends." Pia leaned forward, her eyes intent on the tablet again. "Dad, thanks, but I need to concentrate."

"Didn't she work at the NSA?"

Pia looked up again and nodded. A slow smile tugged at the corners of her mouth. "You got rich by being smart."

Pia checked the time difference—morning in DC—and dialed Bianca's number. Her old friend was thrilled to help out and promised hi-res files would reach her soon.

Five minutes later, instead of the files from Bianca, Pia received a terse call from the NSA's director. In the next minute she received a bitter call from Under Secretary of Defense for Intelligence, which was followed by a nasty call from the Deputy Secretary of Defense. She sent the next incoming call straight to voicemail and drummed her fingernails on the table.

"That went bad quickly," Alan said.

"Bianca's going to jail." She kept drumming her fingernails. "We've known the feds are keeping tabs on us, but that escalated a lot faster than I expected."

"To escalate that quickly means someone is monitoring that patch of China. And that level of attention comes from the Oval Office."

Pia thought through her options. Once she made up her mind about what to do next, she picked up her phone and started to dial.

Alan pulled it from her hands. "A pragmatic approach is always best. Think before you make that call. You'll only get one shot at it."

He placed the phone down between them.

Pia stared at it while she drummed her fingernails on the table some more. She picked it up, put it down, and picked it up again. After a long, hard look at her father, she dialed.

"Madam President, thank you for taking my call."

"You've interrupted my morning schedule, Ms. Sabel. Make it quick."

"We've had our differences, but I have an opportunity for you to do something good. My agents have tracked the people responsible for the mass graves on Borneo to rural China and—"

"Allow me to jump for joy. Now go through proper channels for whatever you need and never call me again."

Pia glanced at her father, who listened on a muted line. He shrugged.

Pia said, "We believe they're connected to someone in the Chinese—"

"You're way out of line here, Pia. Relations with China are strained. It's not like Russia or Italy or Argentina. China owns enough of our national debt to send our credit into a tailspin if they chose. I'm not going to risk an international incident to capture some band of outlaws just so you can get a good press release out of it."

"This is not about Sabel Security. This is about biological disaster and justice for the dead."

"Yes, I've heard about Kaya, the little girl you left behind. I hope you feel guilty. Nonetheless, upsetting the delicate relationship between two superpowers so you can finally sleep at night is not going to happen."

"My people are in position to stop another mass killing," Pia said. "We don't know where they're planning to strike, but I have people positioned outside their base of operations. I can shut them down and the Chinese will never know we were there."

"You're asking me to assist an attack on the second biggest economy in the world? You obviously don't know anything about sovereignty, young lady. The US cannot enter a country illegally and kill people at will because of evidence you claim to have against—"

"For God's sake, get on the right side of history for once." Pia pounded her fist on the table. Her father flinched. "You have the opportunity to save thousands of lives, possibly hundreds of thousands."

Alan Sabel turned white and waved his hands back and forth over the table, begging his daughter to stop.

"The world is bigger than Pia Sabel's problems, you little shit. Get over yourself."

"I have Bill McCarty's deathbed confession."

President Hunter said nothing for a long time, then took a deep breath. "We've been over that operation. Anything he said about Snare Drum is sealed."

"I'm not talking about Snare Drum. I'm talking about the murder of my parents. He made a video hours before committing suicide. He named the person who gave him the order to kill American citizens on American soil."

President Hunter gasped loud enough for Pia to hear. Alan Sabel buried his head in his hands.

"I don't have time for any more of your cheap theatrics, and I will never give into extortion. Do you understand me?" The President took a deep breath. "Now. What do you want?"

"Release Bianca Dominguez and drop the charges against her. Then authorize the release of the satellite maps she tried to send me."

"Fine, but the little bitch won't get her job back."

Pia clicked off, placed the phone on the table in front of her father.

"You shouldn't bluff the leader of the free world," he said.

"It's not a bluff."

"The FBI confiscated all of McCarty's things, including all his blackmail material."

Pia placed her hands flat on the table and stared at her father.

"Anything they missed," he continued, "we need to turn over to them."

"Hours before Jacob tracked him down," Pia said, "McCarty made a video addressed to me. He knew he would die. He felt bad

298

about his involvement in the murders and wanted to get it off his chest."

"But the FBI had a warrant to retrieve—"

"Everything illegally obtained by McCarty. This video was legal. It was addressed to me. It's mine." Pia watched him, her gray-green eyes drilling for truth. "Dad, is there anything you want to tell me about the day my parents died?"

"You and I have been over that a thousand times with the best therapists in the country."

She stared at him.

He leaned back and tugged at his cufflinks. "No, Pia, there's nothing I want to tell you about that day."

She nodded, her lips drawn tight, her eyes narrowed.

Small beads of sweat formed on his upper lip. "Why? What did McCarty say?"

Chapter 46

Visions of long-forgotten battles in Afghanistan and Iraq resurfaced with the moral choices I'd made at the ripe old age of eighteen when weapons filled my hands and easy decisions filled my head. I shook off the past only to confront the dark shadows of my present.

Miguel's steady hand on my shoulder felt good, but I still wanted to throw up. I'd lost a friend on every one of Ms. Sabel's missions. Either she was worse luck than a green lieutenant or I'd lost my killer instinct. Neither option was good for my team or our collective future. Miguel squeezed my shoulder again. My shaking subsided a little.

He said, "There are always risks. I know them. You know them. Carmen knew them. Each of us made a decision. We came."

I glanced at the back seat, where sleepy stirrings were giving way to blinking eyes.

"Why have we stopped?" Tania asked. She bolted upright when she realized she'd snuggled to the Englishman during the ride. "Is Mokin here?"

Emily and Nigel took their first waking breaths and smacked their dry lips.

"How long have we been here?" Tania asked.

"A few minutes."

"They could be here." She scrambled out and listened in the dark.

We joined her and stretched. The night was quiet, a bit of wind in the trees. An owl hooted somewhere in the distance.

"Holy crap, it's cold," Emily said. She hugged herself.

Everyone turned to look at Nigel.

"No, I didn't bring any blankets," he said. "You refused to tell me we were leaving Guangzhou where it's always twenty-six degrees." He looked at each of us. "Twenty-six Celsius, eighty Fahrenheit."

A text from Ms. Sabel flashed on my phone. It directed me to refresh my satellite maps of the area on my tablet. When I did, I found them crisp and clear and extremely detailed. If you knew anything about horticulture, you could identify the genus of every tree in the forest from the new maps. I set it on the trunk and showed the team where we were without giving Nigel coordinates.

Nothing got past the Englishman. "Astonishing detail, that."

Miguel and Tania looked at him, then at me, then at the tablet. In a couple of wordless seconds, we pieced together the Brit's implication. Hi-def satellite imagery takes mega-resources, not to mention a few repeat passes for clouds and light. Spy satellites map every square inch of the planet, but they reserve the gigapixel bandwidth for special points of interest. We were in a rural area, far from anything noteworthy, yet when I zoomed in, I could see a squirrel on a tree branch. Whoever ordered the spy satellite to spend several days mapping out the neighborhood had committed a large amount of time and money and that meant whoever it was had a lot of power. Tania and Miguel and I shuddered in unison.

Mercury said, What are you brothas worried about? You've taken on the government before.

I said, Not two at once.

"We can ponder this later," I said. "Right now, we have to dig Mokin out of his hole and slap him around until he tells us where to find Element 42."

"Then we kill him?" Emily asked.

Everyone's eyes turned to her, except Nigel's. His eyes judged me.

"Babe," Miguel said. "You're creeping us out here. Chill."

We returned to the maps and checked elevations and distances and structures. Our intel was good but lacked critical background info.

I glanced at my watch. "They couldn't be too much farther behind. We should set up."

Nigel opened the boxes in his trunk.

Emily grabbed an MK5. Miguel grabbed it back and held out a Remington 870 pump-action shotgun. I thought it was a good call. We didn't need our untrained Emily firing 700 rounds per minute.

"I want a real gun," Emily said. "I've been to the shooting range."

"With an AR-15?"

She shrugged and yanked the shotgun out of his hands.

Miguel and I went with MP5s, sound suppressors attached.

Tania took an HK417 sniper rifle and faced me. "Let's take these fucktards down."

Tania started for the restaurant roof, but stopped with a thoughtful look. She wheeled around and opened all four doors on the Jaguar. She connected her phone and cranked up the stereo playing an old rock-n-roll tune from the 60s that my grandmother used to listen to— "Can't You Hear Me Knocking" by the Rolling Stones. The music blared through the deserted lakeside. She scampered to the rooftop and propped her rifle on the ridge.

Miguel ran a hundred yards up the road to the first bend. Our Englishman took the most dangerous position across the road. I stepped behind the restaurant wall and pushed Emily behind me.

We checked our comm link and settled in for the wait. Five seconds or five hours, there was no way of knowing.

After a long radio silence in which the song played twice and was near losing its appeal, Miguel reported on the comm link. "Headlights, ten minutes out."

I felt the adrenaline begin to flow. It started in my core and moved outward like a microscopic and unstoppable Mongol horde charging through my veins. It flowed into my arms and legs, past my elbows and knees, and up my neck.

Mercury said, Psyched yet, psycho?

I said, Yes, I am. Bring it.

Emily squeezed up close behind me. She trembled with excitement. I pushed the barrel of her shotgun away from my shoulder.

"Oh, sorry," she said. "I haven't shot a gun since—"

I pressed my finger across her lips.

Headlight beams swung into the mist hovering over the water, then disappeared. One more bend and they'd see the Jag. My heart doubled the music's beat, keeping time. Then it tripled. I lifted the MP5 and lined up the infrared scope to the road where they'd appear.

The headlights broke the corner a couple seconds before the truck trundled into sight. The driver slammed on the brakes and shuddered to a stop halfway between Miguel and me. It was a Chinese knockoff of the Humvee called a Norinco. It had light armor and, lucky for us, no turret gun. For a full second, the guys inside scrutinized the unexpected Jaguar.

We waited in silence. We needed them out of the vehicle.

Mercury said, Act like a Roman. Lead a brave charge. Make it a heroic death. Courageous and bold to the end. If you want to be a real playah, go out valiant. Women love that shit.

Sometimes gods have great ideas—if you're immortal. I like living through my heroic deeds. Handing my gun to Emily, I stepped out from the building, zipping up and looking surprised. I blinked in the light with my mouth open and ran back around the corner.

A spray of lead followed me as the Kazakhs opened fire.

Emily stared at me, mouth open and eyes bulging out, on the verge of panic-screaming. I took my gun back and pressed my finger to her lips again.

Turning back to the wall, I edged to the shredded corner and waited. I heard a door squeak open, then another. Boots dropped from the cab to the ground but were lost in Tania's loud music.

Then the music stopped, mid-refrain.

"Six guys," Miguel whispered on the comm link. "Four out, two in."

"I've got the driver," Tania said.

"Armored windshield?" I said.

"It's thick, but it's still glass. At this range, I can get him right through it."

"On Tania's shot then," I said. "One … two …"

Tania dropped the driver with a head shot. We lit up the night from four directions. The Kazakhs hit the dirt and fired blindly in all directions. I ducked back behind the wall and counted off seconds. The Kazakhs held their triggers down like amateurs. Three seconds later, they were scrambling to swap magazines.

My team stepped into the open while the Kazakhs fumbled with their hardware. Miguel took his guy out with three to the chest. Nigel did the same. My guy rose on his knees, his hands up, but his AK-47 still in his right. I popped four rounds into him, one in each limb. He dropped the rifle and fell to the ground, writhing and crying out.

"Out of practice, then?" the Englishman's calm voice floated on the comm link.

"Hold your position," I said, my weapon aimed at the truck.

Shadows were all we could see of the last two still in the car. They stirred, aiming out the doors, unsure of their best move. One of the shadows had a white bandage on the side of his head.

"It's OK, you can come out and aid your man before he bleeds out."

The wounded man screamed for help in Kazakh. Or maybe he cursed me.

From inside the car came a feeble voice. "Is meaning, medic for safe passage, yes?"

"Yes."

The shadow opposite me pushed his door open and stuck his empty hands out. He stepped out, slow and cautious, and made it a few feet before Nigel knocked him down with his rifle stock and hogtied him with plasticuffs in a split second.

"You say safe passage," he said with dirt in his mouth.

"I lied."

The wounded man kept screaming.

"Hey," came the last voice, still in the truck, "is that you, Jacob?"

"C'mon out, Kasey."

"I'm just the point man. There's another fifty men—"

I said, "Kasey, get out here and let me trim your ears."

He didn't move.

"You remember Tania Cooper?" I asked. "She's on the roof with a scope. She can shoot you where you sit if you'd like."

He kicked his door open, pushed the Chinese version of the M4 out, scooted to the edge, and took a look around. Miguel stepped up behind him. I stepped into the light, my scope trained on his head. Emily followed me and racked a shell for effect.

Kasey showed his hands first, then hopped to the ground and stretched out, facedown.

Miguel disarmed him and bound him with plasticuffs. Nigel dragged the dead and wounded around the front.

"Wounding a man and letting him scream for his mates is a terrorist trick," the Englishman said. "You're a right nasty bugger."

"Effective," I said.

He turned over a couple bodies, examined their faces. "Well, you have five Kazakhs and one American. How'd they get together?"

"Not sure," I said.

Tania came steaming toward us, ready for another female-empowerment session. I pushed my arm out and brushed her back.

"Kasey," I said, "I'm going to ask some questions, you're going to answer. Otherwise, I let Tania rip you to shreds."

"What's her problem?" Kasey asked.

Tania stuck her thumb in his eye and pressed. I waited a second, maybe two, before pulling her off.

"Your boys killed a friend of ours." I grabbed him by the shoulders and checked the damage. One eye was still working. That's all I needed.

"Have you been up the road before?" I asked.

He gave me a blank expression. Dew glistened on his backlit bandage, reminding me we were losing the dark.

"You can be useful or injured," I said. "Your choice. But I need to know, do you know the security arrangements at Mokin's compound?"

Kasey remained the stoic prisoner.

I said, "OK, Miguel, strap him to the hood. Let's find out where the first shots come from."

Chapter 47

Kasey declined the human shield option and pinpointed the lone checkpoint on my map. He claimed there were no radio communications due to the low budget. When I was satisfied he'd given up what he knew, I waved Miguel over. He hoisted Kasey onto the hood, uncuffed the boy, and spread his arms out. Tania tied one wrist to the passenger side while Miguel stretched the other wrist across the driver's side.

"Hey, now," Kasey said. "I done told you the layout."

"You're riding up front, Kasey. If you accidently misjudged the checkpoint's location, and we end up driving into an ambush, you'll be the first to know." I patted his head and walked away.

"Hold on." Kasey's words tumbled out fast. "No need to get hasty. Don't wanna make no mistakes. Lemme see that map again."

I climbed on the hood and knelt next to him. I held the tablet out. "Show me the first checkpoint."

He remembered it had been relocated and pointed it out. We zoomed in. Two men, plainly visible from the air, lounged in a machinegun nest surrounded by camouflage. Tilting and turning the shot in near-3D, I spotted what I expected, a radio on the shelf. I tapped it in front of Kasey and he sighed.

"OK," he said, "you can cut me loose now. Fun's over."

"Liars ride up front." Miguel tapped him on the shoulder. "Enjoy the breeze."

While Kasey begged for relief, I hopped down and worked the map, looking through the local terrain. Miguel and Tania joined me.

Wordlessly, we checked and double-checked. We had one road, one checkpoint, and one big compound. We studied the layout. One building had biohazard symbols on the two visible sides. The Element 42 bunker. The map's metadata showed it was a week old. A lot can change in a week. But it was all we had, and the detail told us enough to form a weak plan. We'd been together a long time and communicated with nothing more than glances.

Ahead lay our uncertain future. Somewhere in that dark, moonless forest, down that narrow, winding road, Anatoly Mokin sat on a biological nightmare with enough men and equipment to kill thousands of innocent people. *Why* didn't matter; Mokin was the last person on Earth who should control such a destructive combination. We looked at each other and nodded with grim determination.

We hid the Jag behind a retaining wall and stashed the dead and wounded inside the old restaurant.

The Norinco was just like a Humvee only worse. It was louder, slower, clunkier, but had plenty of room. Five seats inside and a flatbed in back.

Kasey kept begging and crying through the whole drive.

We stopped well short of the checkpoint. Nigel and I went up the hill on foot through the moonlit woods. We slowed as we neared the checkpoint, going into silent mode. My fear-factor skyrocketed. Sneaking up on people is the work of special ops guys like Nigel. They're small and lithe and sleek. I did plenty of special ops work but I was nobody's first pick for a mission and I was never the point man. I'm a big farm boy who walks like a gorilla. I let Nigel lead and followed him, testing each footfall before putting weight on it.

Twenty minutes later, I gave Miguel the signal, a birdcall via the comm link. He put the Norinco in gear, charged up the hill, and rounded the corner with Kasey screaming in Kazakh. Probably, "Don't shoot me."

One Kazakh grabbed the .50 cal machinegun. The other reached for his radio. Nigel blew the radio out of his hands. I blew the shoulders off the machine gunner and we both opened up on the pair. The MP5's suppressors worked like a charm, the sound was little more than *pphhtt-pphhtt-pphhtt*. I jumped down into the nest and checked the men.

We disabled a couple radio handsets and checked the nest for anything useful. Nothing. We ran out of the nest and into Miguel's path. He slowed enough for us to jump in the Norinco's bed where we crouched behind the armored roof and shivered in the icy wind. Tania climbed out the back window to join us.

Miguel turned out the lights, relying on night vision, mashed the pedal down around the last bend, and plowed through the chain-link gate.

The three of us stood and picked off five stunned Kazakhs before the general alarm sounded. Lights went on in two barracks. Parking the truck where it would block the road, we bailed out and ran in all directions.

From the hood of the truck, Kasey cried out. "Jacob, you can't leave me here. Jacob!"

Nigel rolled concussion grenades at the barracks. The explosions shook their corrugated roofs like paper in the wind. Kazakhs spilled out into the main pathway, armed to the teeth but only half dressed. Without body armor, the first wave fell like reaped wheat. Tania and I dropped back to the office shack and used its flimsy wood construction as a barrier. Not that the planks were thick enough to stop a BB gun, but it was all we had.

The second wave of Kazakhs weren't as willing to die for the cause. They split into pairs and ran between the buildings. Tania picked off two coming straight at us.

Mercury said, Wolves attack from two sides, homie.

I spun around and nailed the man sneaking up our backside. Tania tugged my sleeve and ran for a tent a little deeper in the trees. Being quicker, I passed her up and ran straight inside.

Anatoly Mokin blinked at me, one foot in an unlaced boot, the other boot in his hand, and sleep still in his eyes. He threw the boot at me and tried to dive under the tent's back corner.

I pulled my Glock and darted his butt. I grabbed a coat from his wardrobe and tossed it to Tania. She helped hoist Mokin on my shoulder. I staggered outside where Tania dropped a Kazakh.

We pushed into the woods to a concrete bunker, sturdy and new and sealed with a hurricane-proof door that featured a prominent sticker: biosafety level 4. We tied Mokin to a tree next to it, then ran back to the battle.

The pace of shooting slowed. That's not a good thing. It would be Darwinian combat from then on.

I stepped around a windowless barrack made of plywood and navigated the weedy lane between the two shacks. Tania pressed her back against mine and walked backward. When I reached the front, the only thing I could see was the Norinco and three other empty buildings.

Tania pointed to the barrack's front door. I took the hint and tiptoed to it, nodding when I was ready. She tossed a rock that struck the back corner. Someone inside fired a blast through the wall. Which meant his back was to me.

The door screeched when I threw it open. My victim turned his frightened face to me. I aimed and fired. He dropped, howling in pain. I put him out of his misery with a second shot.

Darwinian combat.

Behind me, Tania stitched a long line of lead into the neighboring building. A scream followed.

As I stepped out, I caught a nod from Nigel. He held up a grenade and motioned for Tania. She opened the door and stepped aside. A blast of gunfire came from inside aimed straight out. The guy had figured out his buddy's fate. Nigel lobbed the grenade in as he ran by. Given the thin walls, we dove for cover.

Grenades have a time-release allowing the thrower to arm the device then heave it a good distance. The little bomb landed near our enemy and sat there for a few terrifying seconds before killing him. I know that's what happened because I heard the guy say, "Oh shit..." in Kazakh. Not that I speak the language, but his tone was unmistakable.

Mercury said, Yo, pay attention, far side of the shed.

I heard boots crunching in dry autumn leaves behind me. I dropped and fired from a prone position but saw only empty space. I rolled sideways and crabbed a circle as round after round pumped through the wall I'd used for cover. I let out a howl and triangulated the shots back to a point on the far side. My first shot was low, hoping for a knee or leg. My second was higher, expecting a body shot. Instead, I heard him run away. I gave chase but never saw him.

Shotguns are noisy beasts. Especially after the fairly quiet MP5s. I froze, listening for an indication of who won the gunfight. Nothing.

I ran through some trees and found a path into the woods. Stopping to listen again, I heard groaning. I switched to thermal and saw two heat signatures deeper in the trees, one on the ground. I moved forward, creeping up behind the heat signatures.

Between two trees, Emily stood with a body at her feet, her shotgun still smoking.

On closer inspection, I found a Kazakh with a missing face. Air wheezed in and out of what remained of his air ducts. His pain was gut-wrenching, yet Emily stared with a blank expression.

"You OK?" I asked.

"Yeh."

I approached her slowly. "Scarier than you thought?"

"Yeh."

"First guy?"

"Yeh."

Her victim made a gurgling sound, then exhaled and died. A strange expression came over her. I couldn't tell if she was going to spit on him or puke.

"Are you hurt?"

"Yeh." She looked up at me for the first time. "Um. No."

Her hair fell away, revealing a snow-white face covered in a light sweat despite the chilly mountain air. Her skin shivered like a horse shaking off a fly.

"No, not hurt?"

"Yeh."

I pulled the deadman's bloody coat off and draped it over Emily's shoulder.

Mercury said, Dude, look at something besides babes for once. Check out the trees on your left.

Twenty yards away, a shadow caught my attention. I raised my rifle and took aim.

Emily's eyes followed where my barrel pointed.

The shadow slipped behind a tree and tried to run. I stepped around Emily and opened up on him. Shooting between trees is tricky. At the last second the hostile decided to charge me instead. He screamed some kind of battle cry and fired as he ran. Battle-tested veterans take time to aim; it's counterintuitive under the stress but much more effective. My attacker was not a veteran. He didn't take time to raise his weapon and sight down the barrel. As a result, his rounds were low and left. I let him have several shots at us to maximize the adrenaline rush.

Emily pumped a new round into the chamber, lifted her Remington to her shoulder, anticipated his speed, and fired.

Her blast stopped our attacker cold, peppering him in the chest and right arm. It was a good shot but not lethal. He raised his rifle to his bleeding shoulder and took the time to aim at Emily. I put a round in his forehead.

Behind us, we heard Miguel's voice calling "clear" answered by similar shouts from Tania and Nigel. I dragged Emily, who had lost any words beyond *yeh* and *no*, into a safety zone and helped the others clear the grounds. We piled the eight wounded in one barrack and the ten dead in another. Nigel rigged a grenade to go off should one of the wounded move around too much.

We met back at the Norinco for a quick debrief.

I took one look at Kasey, still strapped to the hood. "You're alive?"

"Passed out." Miguel slapped the boy's face. "Pee'd his pants, too."

"Let's see what the office holds," I said. "Then we grab Mokin and get the hell out of here."

"Any idea what this compound is for?" Nigel asked.

We ignored him and headed for the office.

Emily stepped into my path and stopped me. "Why don't you trust this guy? He helped us every step of the way, gave us guns, and a car. What does he have to do to earn your respect? Hasn't he killed enough of these bastards to get a simple answer?"

I faced Nigel. "You ready to tell us what you know?"

He shrugged.

Emily yanked my arm, pulling me around to face her. Her eyes searched mine. The concept of trust means one thing to civilians, but it takes on a whole new meaning when you trust someone to keep you alive. She had earned an answer to what the rest of us already knew.

"He's a lieutenant colonel," I said. "Back in the SAS, that meant he had up to a thousand Special Forces in his command. The best of the best. He's an important guy. But her Majesty sent him to Guangzhou as a cultural attaché, a spy. That means he's a damn good spy. And that means his assignment is important enough to drag him away from his command. In other words, an important guy was taken from an important command and sent on an even more important assignment. Then we come to town. Miguel asks him for a favor. All of a sudden, this important guy drops everything, arms us to the teeth, and comes along without complaining or asking too many questions. Does that strike you as unusual?"

"He knew about this long before we did," she said.

I touched the tip of her nose and walked around her, heading to the office.

Behind me, Nigel trotted alongside Emily. "You're quite good. What branch were you in?"

"She's not a Sabel agent," I said over my shoulder. "She's a reporter for the *Post*."

"Bloody hell."

For the first time since I'd met him, Nigel looked scared.

"You can do him a favor, Emily," I said. "When you write the story, refer to him as 'Bubba' and don't mention the British part. He's out here against orders."

"Right then," Nigel said. "Here's what I know. My government discovered the Chinese going after bio-research that could target minorities, like the Uighurs. Genocide is not something you can bandy about, so I've been sent to trace it down. I followed the leads to Mokin yesterday, then you lads showed up. That's what I know."

"Thank you," Tania said. "They have a different plan now. Let's figure it out."

Miguel and Tania searched the office. Nigel stood by to translate anything in Chinese they wanted to share with him. I went to Mokin's tent and found his laptop. I hooked my phone's internet connection to his computer and used a translation site to read his emails.

Mokin was not a nice guy. He was *Menedzher*, and his original instructions to Mukhtar were to kill anyone messing with the test site or the Pak Uban. He'd given us a death sentence before we arrived. More emails detailed sending special squads to New York and Milan to kill Verratti and Cummings days before we reached Borneo. A later email changed Yuri's orders and sent his team to DC to retrieve every shard of glass and kill Pia Sabel.

After that failure, he hired Velox Deployment. Kasey had been engaged to eliminate Windsor's key personnel from Chapman to Violet Windsor herself. In one email, Kasey reported the irony that Windsor and Cummings had both paid him to kill each other long after Mokin had contracted Velox to eliminate them.

There were more emails to a guy named Chen Zhipeng. Chen gave the orders and Mokin made it happen. After Algeria, I thought of Mokin as a mercenary kingpin, but the tone of the emails was the opposite. He was Chen's personal bitch. In one email, Chen reamed Mokin for blowing the attack on Ms. Sabel in the woods. After reading five emails, it was clear that Chen Zhipeng was a double-crossing, ruthless liar who would kill anyone who disappointed him. Mokin was as good as dead.

Then I found a scary email only hours old. Two platoons of Mokin's men had secured several barrels of Element 42 and were returning to the staging area with it. They had twice as many men as I thought. Kasey had told me the truth.

I slapped the laptop closed, tucked it under my arm and ran to the office.

My pals were waiting for me. The first hint of sunrise brightened the sky behind them in shades of blue-gray.

"We found Element 42," Tania said. "It's in that bunker on—"

"A convoy is on the way," I said. "With fifty guys."

Chapter 48

Crickets chirped in the dark on the quiet, tree-lined road where China's highest ranking Party officials kept modest homes on large lots. An owl swooped silently over Pia's head and lighted in a tree behind her.

She checked the house at the end of the lane with her NVGs. A half-finished home, its rebar hanging limp out of gray concrete, stood on one side. A recently completed house sat empty on the other. In front of Wu's house was a brick guardhouse with a wooden gate.

The Major pointed out the mission details. "Dhanpal will cover the front, you cover the rear, I'll enter through the side door."

"No," Pia said. "I'll go inside."

"Dhanpal and I both have experience with house-to-house—"

"Last time I didn't like the assignments, I changed the game plan on the fly. Jacob made me apologize. This time, I'm telling you in advance. It's not a request."

The Major gazed at her for a long time before letting out a breath. "We think there are two bodyguards on the property, but there could be ten. It's too dangerous."

"Understood." Pia rechecked the modest but well-kept home.

"After Windsor, Verratti, and Cummings were killed, this guy will be on high alert." The Major patted her shoulder. "Three thousand Sabel Security employees need you to stay healthy and alive. We don't need you knocking down doors like some common combat infantry."

Pia said, "I'd be honored to make the infantry."

Using hand signals, she ordered Dhanpal down the slope and into the yard. Smooth and silent, he confirmed his readiness with a hand signal. The Major went next, stopping where she had a clear view of two walls.

Pia reminded herself of her training with every step. Don't rush, peripheral vision is crucial, hear the ambient sounds, pick up your feet, consider every movement. Years of soccer gave her exceptional balance and awareness, suiting her well for the job. She stepped out of the thick underbrush, past the Major, and continued her slow advance on the yard. When she reached the construction site, she gave Dhanpal the signal.

Dhanpal's Glock popped. She ran for the gate and scaled the side. Dropping down next to Dhanpal, she followed him around the sweeping driveway. To their right, near the kitchen, the Major dropped the second guard. Pia went the rest of the way alone using the memorized map in her head. Past the garden Buddha to the koi pond, then onto the porch.

Listening to the interior near the kitchen window, she heard nothing. She stood stock-still until a refrigerator motor kicked on inside.

Still nothing human.

She tugged the door. It slid sideways a quarter inch with a metallic scrape. Pia put both hands on the frame's top and pushed it up while sliding it to the right. Once it was open enough to slip inside, she stepped into the dining room, leading with her Glock. To her right, an empty living room; to her left, a dark hall.

Pia crept forward, careful to tread softly. Something stirred. She stopped and listened. Her heartbeat pounded hard enough to drown out everything, but she focused and heard it again. Someone was moving. Movement as careful and silent as her own. She glanced over her shoulder and saw a human-sized shadow. Frozen with her pistol in front and her eyes behind, she tried to figure out what the shadow was, and if it had been there before she turned the corner. For a long moment nothing moved.

Then a sound. The shadow was breathing.

Pia's heart pounded hard enough to hear and feel it, from her ears to her shoes. She pulled her Glock around and aimed at the shadow. A small form, barely five feet high.

A light came on.

For a full second, an older woman in a nightgown, holding a small wok above her head, stared at Pia.

"Sorry," Pia said. She fired a dart.

Her silencer muffled the shot, yet the *pop* sounded like a gong in the silent home. The wok banged to the ground as the woman crumpled to the floor.

Toward the back of the house, someone scrambled around in the dark. Light flooded from under one of the doors. Then a man's voice yelled in Chinese.

Pia pressed her earbud. "Dropped the wife."

"Is the situation under control?"

"Probably."

Pia stepped down the hall toward the voice. She opened the door opposite and looked inside: an empty home office. Turning to the lit room, she heard clicking metal sounds through the thin door. Then a sound she recognized: a magazine sliding into a pistol.

Standing to one side, she reached for the knob, turned it slowly, and threw it open.

Nothing happened.

Spinning into the room, she drew on a short, older man who stood quivering at the foot of the bed. A light on the nightstand behind him cast an eerie light that glowed around his shabby pajamas. Abrasions covered his skin, one eye was black and swollen. He held a standard Type-54 Chinese Army handgun in his shaking hands.

"Put the gun down," she said.

He dropped it on the floor and raised his hands. His lips and sagging jowls vibrated.

"Take it easy," Pia said. "I'm not here to hurt you."

He stared straight ahead, his eyes blank.

"Do you speak English, Dr. Wu?"

"You not take me back to reeducation?" He looked up at her, his eyes pleading for mercy, his hands still held up in surrender.

Pia shook her head and lowered her Glock. "Take a deep breath."

Dr. Wu breathed as prescribed and lowered his hands a little, then glanced at Pia for permission to lower them further.

Pia nodded and bowed slightly without taking her eyes off him.

"I need to know about Element 42," she said.

Dr. Wu's eyes widened. His hands flashed between them as if he were pushing away an imaginary object. "I not connect to Element 42."

"Your fingerprints are on the vials of blood taken from the site on Borneo."

He began shaking his head with a slow rhythm, his eyes on her Glock. "It cannot be. I never visit Borneo."

Pia pushed Dr. Wu's shoulder. His eyes rose to hers. She said, "We know you're on the board of directors at Windsor Pharmaceuticals."

The old man shook his head. "I not understand you."

Pia grabbed both his shoulders and leaned down, nose to nose. "Otis Blackwell told me about you. So did Chapman. Why don't you tell me the truth?"

Wu Fang's eyes rolled back in his head, his eyelids fluttered and closed. He fell backward on the bed with no more self-control than a dropped cloth.

The Major stepped in and helped Pia prop the man up in his bed. Pia grabbed a glass of water and a wet washcloth from the bathroom. After a few minutes of soothing, Dr. Wu opened his eyes and drank the water.

"I not agree to them," he said. His head continued to wander from side to side. "Dr. Chapman ask many questions in email. Chen not answer him. I go to Borneo to see. No good. No good."

"But you're on the board, you had to know about this."

"On board because Chen say so. I am scientist. Advisor to government. I am not business man. I am not important in Party. Chen go to Windsor meetings."

Pia looked at the Major. "Think he's telling the truth?"

The Major shrugged. "The woman out front had a blanket and a book on the couch, probably fell asleep reading. We could drag her in here."

"Threaten her to make him talk?" Pia shook her head. "That's not the Sabel way."

The Major turned away.

Dr. Wu tugged Pia's arm. "You good guys?"

Pia tightened her lips to a sliver and nodded. "We try."

He finished his glass of water.

"Dr. Chapman told me a few things before he died," Pia said. "He was trying to stop them. What were you doing?"

"I not know what go on. No idea. When I find trial on Borneo, I resign and report People's Law Committee. Then I report Public Health Committee, Ministry of Justice, National Health. No one do anything. Chen call me. Very angry. He say reeducation for Fang and wife."

Pia sat on the edge of his bed. "Who is Chen?"

"Powerful man. Chen in charge investment for China Social Security. He plan China twenty, thirty year ahead. Chen worry about aging population. I talk about Chen Zhipeng."

Pia and the Major glanced at each other. The Major pulled her phone and searched the name.

"How was Otis Blackwell involved?"

"Chen like Otis for propaganda. Otis like power, Chen have lots of power. Otis do whatever Chen want."

"Otis was working on a documentary about water conservation. But before he died, he said, 'too many people.' How are they connected?"

Dr. Wu nodded. "China aging. Life span longer and longer, and Chen say, no water for crops. No water, no food. No food, break down government. China break down, then India break down, then domino. Civilization end in chaos."

The Major recoiled a step. "China's deep into the biggest drought in recorded history."

323

Dr. Wu nodded. "So too, India, Middle East, Europe, Africa, Brazil, Guatemala, Western USA. Half of world run out of water very soon. Five year, ten year, maybe twenty—but no longer. Chen worry what happen first crop failure." Dr. Wu grabbed Pia's arm. "Old men like Chen remember 1959, thirty million Chinese die in famine. Next time, much worse."

Pia frowned. "Chen plans to kill off the old and the weak to lessen the burden on farming?"

"Middle ages, black plague nature way to cull population. Resulting in Renaissance and prosperity. Modern science stop many disease. People live long life. Ten year ago, Chinese life expectancy 65. Today, 75. One billion three hundred million Chinese live ten year longer. Feed OK today. But no rain, no food. Element 42 disease with no cure."

"I thought Levoxavir could cure it," Pia said.

"Chen kill Windsor, Violet, board members. Me soon. No one know Levoxavir. Also, Element 42 change to Element 43 and so on. Levoxavir no good. Need something new. Element design to stay ahead of cure."

"What was Mokin planning to do?"

Dr. Wu shrugged. "Only Chen know. You stop him. We make water someway. Maybe seawater, maybe make rain. Scientists, good guys. We hope, we try."

The Major tapped Pia's shoulder. "Update from Jacob. They have a problem."

Chapter 49

"There's an alarm in the office," Kasey said as we ran to jump in the Norinco. "It sounds when someone passes the dam at the turn off. I heard it go off a minute ago."

He had no interest in being the first to meet his pals coming the other way, so I took him at his word.

"How far away in minutes?"

"Twenty. Now get me off this thing. I'll help you."

We laughed in unison.

When everyone cleared off, I leaned over Kasey. "If you manage to live through this, you'll get a thank-you note from the Melanau Survivors' Fund. When I found that banking app on your phone, I just knew you wanted them to have the $2 million you skimmed from Velox." I patted him on the shoulder. "You're a generous guy, Kasey."

I slid off the Norinco.

"Hold up, there." Kasey struggled against his bonds. "Can't we negotiate a deal? Maybe you could use a hundred grand of your own?"

"I'm flattered you think so highly of me, but it's a done deal. I emptied your account."

Miguel turned the Norinco around, planting Kasey and the truck facing the narrowest part of the road. The rest of us ran around collecting weapons, ammunition, and setting traps. Tania took up a sniper position on a rock outcropping above the office. She cleared some lateral space for a defensive position if things went south.

"We'll lose the element of surprise when they reach the first checkpoint," the Englishman said.

"You're thinking of manning the checkpoint and faking it? It'd be a death trap if they catch us in there. And it's already four against fifty."

"I could make it work." He nodded at Kasey. "If your friend will tell me the protocol."

"Risky."

"I'll ask him," Emily said. "People love to tell reporters things." She walked away, spoke to him for a minute, and came back. "Radio contact. If that doesn't work, three blinks from the flashlight."

"How many vehicles do you think they'll bring?" I asked Nigel.

"That's why I'm here. I'd like to find out what kind of resources they've committed to this project."

"Do you want to tell me about 'this project'?"

"I'm afraid you know more than I. But I'll tell you what—if we live through this, I'll give you all my notes."

I shook his hand on that bargain.

"Could you spare an extra comm link?" the Englishman asked.

I handed him one of our spares with an earbud. With a couple quick instructions, he joined in our link. Nigel gave me a quick salute and trotted over the ridge, taking the shortcut trail.

Jagged shards of dawn knifed into the sky behind the mountain.

I never liked daytime battles. I preferred the dark, where my Army training held a significant advantage. But you don't always get what you want.

Miguel and I set up crossfire points and fallback routes. We strategically placed backpacks with ammo in hidden but easy-to-reach spots and hid spare rifles where we could get to them. We dragged a few dead guys out and placed them near building corners with a foot or hand exposed to draw enemy fire.

Emily followed us around like a puppy. Miguel and I exchanged a few glances and shrugs until I sent her up the hill with her shotgun and three boxes of shells.

Tania was not happy. Over the comm link she said, "What is this, you two are done with her and now you want me to babysit her ass? No way I'm letting you pass her off—"

"She saved my life with that Remington once. Consider her your personal bodyguard." I lowered my voice. "Besides, how long do rookies last on their own?"

"She'll last longer than you two morons."

Soldiers don't like to talk about the odds for fear of making them real or jinxing the outcome, yet there was a morbid truth to her joke. We were damn good fighters, but we would have to be perfect to survive.

"First truck," the Englishman said on the comm link. "Looks like a long convoy, eight vehicles visible so far. Could be more around the bend."

We waited for what happened next, hoping it wasn't the sound of Nigel dying.

"Holding up the dead radio," he updated us. "They've blinked a light. I'm blinking back. That does it. Lead vehicle rolling. Twelve Wingles."

"Come again?"

"Wingle, a four-seater pickup made by Great Wall Motors. I see a lot of uniforms. Hold on." He stayed quiet for a moment. "Bloody hell, one of them's got out and he's calling for Kasey." He remained silent for another moment. He yelled back with a fake Kazakh accent. "Kasey take shit in woods."

"Did that work?" I asked.

The answer came back in the form of noise. The .50 cal barked bullets into the dawn. Nigel kept a steady pace, pounding whatever was in front of him until we heard an explosion. A fireball rose over the ridge.

"End of surprise factor," Miguel said.

"Hey, Nigel, are you there?" I asked.

The first truck rounded the corner. They pulled up nose to nose with Kasey's Norinco and bailed out.

Mercury said, Holy shit, you guys are outnumbered worse than I thought. This is way over my pay grade. You're going to need Mars, he's good with the war stuff. I'll see ya later, man. GTG.

You might think the gods are on your side, but when the going gets tough, the gods get going—far away.

I watched a squad jog up the road. The adrenaline rush came fast and heavy. I felt like a junkie about to overdose. I took a deep breath and held back a scream of primeval joy. I was in my element, engaging in the one part of life where I truly excel: killing bad guys.

Our crossfire counted on them making a certain tactical move and they obliged us. We waited until the first two trucks' worth of men were in the funnel. Tania took out the men at the back. With all eyes cautiously forward, she picked off three guys in two seconds. The rest recognized the sound of bodies falling and began to scatter.

Miguel and I opened up, exhausting a magazine each in two seconds. When we reloaded, none of our victims were moving. That was good news. It meant, no body armor.

The next squad saw the carnage after rounding the lead vehicle. They fired to lay cover for the squad behind them. They used professional tactics, leapfrogging each other's positions and working together. Not exactly the ducks-in-a-barrel scenario I'd hoped for.

Hiding among the second wave was an older man in a suit. He looked out of place and scared as he ducked behind soldiers. I pondered his presence for a split second until a bullet buzzed my ear. The suit wasn't giving instructions and had no visible weapons, so I focused on critical targets.

Miguel and I emptied another magazine each into our kill-zone and scrambled for our first fallback position on the rooftops. Tania picked off two more before they figured out her position and sent a squad after her.

I clambered onto the office roof and pulled the rickety ladder up with me. The position on the ridge didn't give me the field of fire I wanted but I was able to reduce the number of men going after Tania by two.

Using the column of trucks as a shield, the Kazakhs formed larger groups of three and four squads each. One guy stood in front of them, pointed at our old position, and yelled a battle cry. Twenty guys stormed our abandoned vantage points. Tania took out the leader, Miguel and I did our best to wipe out the charge. But the raw numbers beat us. They came over the berm in large numbers. We killed some, wounded some others, but several made it through. And more were coming.

Time for the second fallback.

I dropped my ladder between the office and the flat-roofed shed next door. It landed on a Kazakh sneaking between the buildings. The ladder stood straight up, halfway between buildings, its legs stuck in the mud below and pinning the Kazakh underneath. Kazakh rounds whizzed by me. I tried grabbing the wobbly ladder without success. I backed up, took a running start, planted one foot on the ladder's top rung, and fired a three-round burst into the Kazakh below. My momentum carried me across, and I rolled onto the shed's roof. The ladder went back to its strange vertical posture.

Diving to a shooter's position behind the short fascia, I picked off three more Kazakhs.

Behind me on the hillside, I heard the sound of desperation, the booming shotgun. Emily's weapon was short range. Tania would have told her not to shoot unless they were in serious trouble.

I checked on them. Tania shooting left, Emily firing right. From where I sat, the enemy was hard to spot between the trees. I found one in my sights and put him down. Another was more elusive. Tania and Emily ran to their last redoubt.

At my feet, a head popped up. His eyes blew open when he realized I was the enemy, and he ducked back down. I scrambled to the edge as his rifle crested the roof. I kicked his barrel upward a split second before he fired. I pushed my muzzle over the edge and fired blindly. His rifle barrel stopped resisting my foot and fell back to the ground. Peering warily over the rim, I found a man on the ground, his head smashed like a pumpkin. Three Kazakhs ran to him and stared down in disbelief.

I landed on the ground next to them, shocking them further, and emptied my magazine at point-blank range.

We had one last stand, an earthen berm behind the barracks. Tania called in on the comm link that she was taking heavy fire and would lead Emily there. I tried to reach Miguel, but his answer was all grunts and gunfire. I ran for the berm.

Tania and Emily were there when I dove over the short wall. Crouching room only. Emily covered the backside. Tania fired a few rounds to cover me, then sank back against the wall. We leaned against each other, shoulder-to-shoulder.

All noises stopped for a second.

Then we heard the Kazakhs shouting back and forth. They were moving methodically and carefully through the buildings after losing most of their men to our tricks.

Extreme Darwinian combat.

Miguel had teamed up with Nigel on the backside of the bio-bunker. They were both low on ammo.

Tania held up an M4 and a spare magazine. "This is it for me."

I felt my pack. One mag plus what was in the rifle already. "A hundred rounds between us, thirty enemies left."

Rounds thumped into the berm. More zipped overhead.

Emily slipped to the ground and crawled to us. "They're coming."

Chapter 50

"They're testing us," I said. "They don't know where we are and they don't want us to jump out at them, so they're shooting at random targets hoping we'll pop up and shoot back. Next step, they'll send out a guy on foot."

Emily scooted over next to Tania and pressed her back to the wall. "You mean, you plan to just sit here and wait for them to kill us?"

"It's a job."

An eerie silence descended on our battlefield. The Kazakhs were measuring distances, deploying flanking squads, maybe sending a sniper up the hill. We could hear movements now and then, right after a whispered order.

"Where's Miguel?" Emily asked.

"Hopefully setting up a crossfire with Nigel."

"Will we get the guy who killed Carmen, that Mokin guy?"

I shot Tania a glance to keep quiet. The last thing we needed was Emily blasting Mokin to pieces. He could be our collateral out of this mess and he was tied to a tree fifty yards away. She could see him if she risked standing up.

"What's your whole hangup about Carmen, anyway?" Tania asked. "I knew her from the 'Stan. You barely knew her at all."

Emily's gaze drifted to the mountains behind us. "She was nice. You know. Thoughtful, attentive, sensual, caring."

Tania looked at me with raised brows, then back to Emily. She poked the reporter. "You slept with Carmen?"

I choked. "Wha—"

"She was nice," Emily said.

Tania prodded her again. "Carmen was gay?"

"No. She just liked people, that's all."

I said, "Wha—"

"I thought you were dating Miguel." Tania looked as shocked as I felt.

"Everyone sleeps with Miguel," Emily said. "She told me you ran with him for a when you were dating dickhead here."

My mind raced. Emily was down for a three-way with another woman—and I dumped her? Worse, I'm just finding out about it now, moments before I die in a hail of gunfire?

There are no Gods.

"Who told you that?" Tania's voice cranked up a notch too loud.

"They both did. Miguel said you were dating Jacob when—"

Tania jumped on our intrepid reporter and slapped her hand over the woman's mouth. She craned over her shoulder to check my reaction.

Up the hill behind us, a Kazakh wandered in the woods near the bunker. If he checked left, we were dead. I raised my MP5 and drew a bead on him. He slipped between the trees, heading uphill and looking away from me. I lowered my weapon.

Emily's words wormed their way through my thick skull. I looked back at Tania.

Guilty as hell. It was written in her twisted face.

"Holy shit!" I said a little too loudly. "You were sleeping with my best friend while we were still dating? And then you acted so goddamn self-righteous when you caught me—"

"Shut up," Miguel's voice came through the comm link. "They heard you."

The things I wanted to scream at both of them flooded into my brain. I swept it all aside to focus on living an hour longer.

"He's right, mate," the Englishman added. "They're spreading around your position now. We'll give them a minute to set up, then we open up on them from behind. We'll give you the signal when they turn their backs on you."

Tania and I shared a tense glance and nod at each other. Nigel's plan could work with a little luck.

Mercury said, Whoa. You're alive, bro? That's good for me. Turns out the Dii Consentes wants you around cuz we're low on believers these days. But that's a temporary thing, don't worry about it. Right now, you should be looking uphill.

The Kazakh on the slope turned around. Our eyes met. I fired three shots before he raised his rifle. He fell.

"Seventeen," Miguel reported. "A third of them on your left, a third in the middle, and the last group moving into place on your right."

"Bloody hell," the Englishman said before the sound of gunfire filled the comm link.

Emily's eyes filled with fear.

Tania patted her back. "It'll be OK. We'll get out of this."

"Are you sure?"

"We usually do."

Emily took a deep breath and pumped her shotgun. A head popped up on the backside of the berm before dropping back. She screamed, ran to the wall, leaned over, and gave the poor bastard a chest full of buckshot.

Tania tried to grab her before she left us but clutched only air. Tania crawled to Emily, who hung half over the short wall, staring at the body. Tania grabbed the reporter's belt and yanked her back to cover. But it was a second too late. A bullet ripped through her ribcage.

Emily screamed, writhed from the shock, and landed on her back.

"Take it easy," Tania said. She pulled a t-shirt from her pack and pressed it to Emily's wound. "It's a through-and-through. You'll be fine after we get—"

"It burns!" Emily cried. "Oh god. Burns like fire. What do you mean, through? You mean, I'm through?"

"No, the bullet went clean through. That's a good thing. You'll be fine. Well, except it'll hurt like a bitch."

Emily bit her lip and closed her eyes.

Tania grabbed a t-shirt from my pack and wadded up a second bandage. She put one under Emily and pushed her back on it. The other she pressed into Emily's front wound. "Keep pressure on this. We need to stop the bleeding."

Bullets streaked overhead in larger numbers.

Tania gazed up at me. "Look, I'm sorry about Miguel. You know how he is, the strong and silent type, all that. It was a short-term—"

We both cocked our ears at a sound we knew too well. The scurry of a pair of boots that suddenly stopped followed by the same sound a whole second later. One soldier was running forward, finding cover, taking a knee, aiming his rifle. When he was in position, his squad leader sent the second soldier to do the same thing, a little farther forward of the first. Then the third. If we let them continue, they'd overrun our position in a matter of minutes.

Miguel and Nigel fought their battle in groans and gun-chatter on the comm link. He'd had a brilliant plan, but it wasn't going to save us. They were too deep in their own fight.

We didn't stand a chance.

Tania and I shared a long look. I thought about life and death and love. I thought about what a great life I'd had, what an honor it had been to serve my country, to meet Tania Cooper, to date her. And now, against my hopes and dreams of marrying her, it was going to be an honor to die with her.

She said, "Look, you were going to cheat on me eventually anyway and—"

"Jesus, Tania! Later." I pressed my hands against my temples.

If I lived through this battle, I was going to date normal women only, from that day forward.

She shrugged and looked at the dirt. When she glanced up, her voice was low and soft. "You know Jacob, we gotta do this. Emily can tell the world about Element 42. You and I, well, we have to make sure she survives."

"Roger that. She signed up for a scoop, not a death sentence."

Mercury said, Now you're talking. Die like a Roman, bro. I'll be your guide to the underworld.

I said, Can you give me something positive here? Maybe even motivational? Like, 'Jacob, you're gonna make it. You got this.'

Mercury said, Think what you want, homie, but you don't have a chance. Look on the bright side, a glorious death is inspirational. Somewhere, someday, someone might remember you and say, 'He never amounted to much and he died in vain, but boy did that guy know how to party.'

"Ready?" Tania asked.

"Trial peek together, I'm left, you're right. Fire blind, change mags, pop up, and wipe 'em out."

She nodded. Even though we both knew it would never work, we bumped fists.

We popped up for a look at the advancing troops. I counted six heads on the left. She looked right. We dropped back behind the wall as rounds flew above our heads.

"I have five," she said.

"I got six. That's eleven. We're short a whole squad."

"Wait, what are you two planning?" Emily asked, her voice high. "You're going to charge them? No. No way. They'll kill you. There's too many of them. It's seventeen to two. Let's surrender."

"Nah. We like doing that macho thing," I said.

"No! Don't leave me! You can't do this."

Another fusillade of bullets flew over our heads. The precursor to a full frontal assault. The last seconds of our lives ticked by.

I felt great.

Mercury said, Your squad is moving to your right. Start with the lead guy, shoot right-to-left, and you'll get some of them before you die. Probably.

"Nice day," Tania said, looking at the sky. She tossed me a glance, grabbed my armor, pulled me in, and kissed me hard. "Why wait to die old and senile when we can be heroes?"

Chapter 51

Pia leaned over Dhanpal's shoulder. The ground swirled five hundred feet below the Eurocopter's sliding door as her pilot kept the platform from becoming a stationary target. She switched sides, careful that her headphone cord reached the distance without snagging, and looked over the Major's shoulder.

"I can't get the right angle," the Major said. She fired off another burst.

Dhanpal spoke to the pilot and pushed Pia away from the opening. He aimed then pulled back.

The pilot flew them away from the battle, down the valley. Dhanpal searched the interior, tugging seatbelts and pulling on cargo netting.

"Where is he taking us?" Pia said. "We need to help Jacob."

"The canyon's too narrow," the Major said. "We have to stay below the PLAAF, Chinese air force radar. We need some rope so we can lean out to get a good shot at these guys."

The pilot brought his bird back up the next valley and swung suddenly over the ridge. As they approached the compound, he turned the open door toward the battle and flew sideways.

The Major and Dhanpal filled the space, firing as they approached.

Pia saw the problem. She threaded a rope under the jacket and through the body armor of the Major and Dhanpal, then ran it through a loading pulley for leverage. "Lean out and I'll pull you back in."

The Major leaned over inside the cabin to test her weight. Pia held her steady a few inches from the floor then pulled her back upright with one hand. Satisfied, the two shooters leaned out of the doorway. With Pia holding their leveraged weight, they could hang nearly horizontal, enough to shoot straight down.

"Holy … can you hold us?" Dhanpal said.

"I could do this all day," Pia said. "Take out some Kazakhs."

The Major and Dhanpal chose their targets and fired precise rounds.

Thirty-three seconds later, the bird had passed the area. The pilot took them over the next ridge to turn around. Pia pulled her agents in.

"That worked," the Major said. "Can you do that again?"

Pia turned them around and grabbed the ropes. When the bird topped the ridge, she leaned them way out.

Between their shoulders, she saw Tania and Jacob jump the berm and come out shooting. The pair ran forward, cutting down enemies in the open while Pia's team took out more from the sky. The remaining Kazakhs scattered for cover.

On the opposite slope, Miguel and Nigel fired on three advancing enemies in the trees and dispatched them quickly. Four more took cover under the canopy.

There were no more targets to hit from the air.

Pia ordered the pilot to put them on the ground. He took them near the compound entrance, where a string of abandoned vehicles blocked the only open space large enough to land. He hovered as low as he dared. Dhanpal jumped first, landing on the roof of a truck and slithering down the side to cover the others. The Major landed next and covered the other side.

Pia jumped and landed on a man strapped to the hood of a Norinco. She lost her footing on the uneven surface and dropped her knees into his belly. She grabbed his face and turned it to look at the scar, then pushed him the other way to look at the bandage.

"You must be Kasey," she said.

Kasey groaned.

"You lost another ear."

"Hey, cut me loose will you? I'm a sitting duck, there's bullets flying everywhere."

"You're fine." She jumped down and followed her team into the trees behind a shack.

Miguel and Nigel were pinned down and running out of ammo. The Major headed for their area. Dhanpal used hand signals to move forward with Pia. They took opposite sides of the buildings, running toward the sound of gunfire.

For the first time, Pia felt no fear. She drove forward on the need to save her agents.

Around the second building, two Kazakhs knelt, one aiming at her, the other trying to shoot Tania. Bullets spewed from his gun and zipped by her into the building's corner post. Pia ducked back and dropped to a crouch a split second before the shooter sent more lead through the wall. He raked backward, expecting her to retreat. She somersaulted forward, rolling up to a knee, and shot him in the head.

The other gunman sensed her presence and disappeared.

Dhanpal slipped in behind her and saw the skull lying open, the brains hanging out like gray hamburger. He patted her shoulder.

Tania had disappeared in the same direction as the gunman. Pia followed. Dhanpal ran right, covering the opposite side.

At the edge of the building, Pia heard breathing. She stepped away from the building, going wide to the left. A rifle barrel poked around the wall and fired.

Pia shot the hand that held the weapon.

A man screamed, drawing back his weapon, spraying bullets everywhere. Pia dropped to the ground, letting the lead fly over her head...but lost her rifle.

A shoulder was visible, resting against the building, as the owner swore in his language. She snuck up to the edge and tapped the shoulder. The man's curiosity was his mistake. When he craned around the corner, Pia slammed her open hand into his cheekbone. His eye socket fractured on impact. He staggered two steps and tried to raise his weapon. She kicked it from his wounded hand, stepped around the building, and banged her elbow to the side of his head. He went down with a concussion.

Pia found her Glock and darted him.

Behind her, Dhanpal fired round after round. Stepping behind him, she slid sideways away from the building and saw three Kazakhs advancing toward the berm where Emily lay wounded. Dhanpal took out two and she dropped the last.

"Clear on the hill," the Major's voice came over the comm link.

"Clear here," Tania replied, stepping into Pia's view.

"We won?" Miguel asked.

No one answered for a tense moment. Then they all released their tension with shouts of joy and anxious laughter.

Pia found Jacob. "So this is how successful missions are executed? You made plans, analyzed recon, allocated resources?"

He smiled. "No, ma'am. This time, I *pressed the opportunity immediately.*"

Chapter 52

We met at the redoubt to divide up duties for clearing the site.
Dhanpal, who'd done a stint as a medic, worked on stabilizing Emily.
Nigel had taken a bullet in the thigh and another in the hip but buried
his pain under a stiff upper lip. I ordered him to have a seat and wait
for Dhanpal. The rest of us cleared the compound and dragged
Mokin back to our temporary HQ behind the berm.

With the area cleared, the Major ordered the chopper to pick up
Emily and Nigel.

Miguel moved trucks to clear a landing zone while the rest of us
made slings from bedding in the barracks. When Miguel finished, he
took one of the trucks around to the back of the compound.

"Miguel, what're you doing?" I said in the comm link.

"Barrels of biohazard in this truck. I'm putting them in the bio-
bunker."

When the bird landed, we moved Emily and Nigel on board but
quickly realized there wasn't enough room. Ms. Sabel spoke to Emily
and squeezed her hand.

She stepped out and looked at the rest of us. "Two seats short. I'll
stay behind—"

"I'll stay too," I said. Everyone scowled at me for my eagerness.

"Better that I stay," the Major said.

"Send the pilot back for Jacob and me," Ms. Sabel said. "The rest
of you take this flight. That's an order."

They stood in shocked silence for a second before they climbed
onboard. Dhanpal stepped close to Ms. Sabel, shouting as quietly as
he could beneath the rotor's roar.

"I should be the one to stay behind." Dhanpal glanced at me.

I pretended not to hear him.

"Jacob's a little …"

"Nutty?" Ms. Sabel said.

Dhanpal nodded.

"Aren't we all?"

"But word is, he hears—"

"Get moving." She turned away with a glance toward me. "Jacob, let's check on the wounded Kazakhs."

The chopper whirled into the sky and down the valley.

Ms. Sabel checked her Glock while we walked. "I have two darts left. And one magazine of bullets"

"I'm out of darts. But we should be OK." I picked an AK-47 off the pile of confiscated weapons and handed it to her.

We disarmed the booby-trapped front door, taking care to keep Nigel's expertly wired trigger in place for later. A mass of humanity scooted to the back and cowered when we entered. They were a beaten army, lucky to be alive but hurting and bleeding. One of them appeared to have died since we left him there.

"Any medics in the room?" Ms. Sabel asked. A feeble hand went up.

The medic crawled forward and took the med kit we'd found in the office. He spoke softly to the others and found a helper. The two of them crawled around taking inventory of wounds to determine the worst cases. The others stared at us, half-thankful for showing a little mercy, and half-hateful for having lost to us.

Mercury said, Check their eyes, dude. Always watch their eyes.

Most of the eyes feared their imminent death. But in the back were a pair of black, angry eyes hunkered down between two shoulders. The crowd blocked the light, making the intense look glow in the shadows. We turned to leave to check the rest of the compound.

Mercury said, What, you didn't see that guy? He's going to shoot in 3, 2…

Ms. Sabel's foot crossed the threshold. I jumped on her back and rode her to the ground. We landed face-first in the dirt and lay perfectly still for a full, awkward second. Her voice formed the consonant digraph of 'what' as in 'WTF are you doing?' when six rounds from an AK-47 blasted through the wall. We heard him change magazines.

"That's why they used to call you X-ray?" Ms. Sabel asked.

We rolled in different directions and drew.

"I'll cover, you run," I yelled. I fired three rounds from my Glock into the wood, high enough not to hit the wounded. It was a scare tactic, but there was no way I would kill another prisoner.

Ms. Sabel sat up and bobbled her AK-47. She brought it to her shoulder and held her fire.

"Run," I said.

She stayed motionless, her barrel aimed at the door.

More rounds came through the wall and zinged over our heads. Had it not been for the sloping ground in front of the structure, he would have killed us outright. The shooter stopped, no doubt holding his ammo and listening for locating sounds.

I rose as quietly as possible and stepped to the corner post. Ms. Sabel watched me and mimicked my movements on the right. I waved her off.

She flipped me off.

Mercury said, Yo, quite the spirited nymph you have there. No wonder you passed up the job at Denny's. Now think about where your shooter was when you saw his eyes and think about where he's going to be in the near future.

I said, Why don't you just tell me where he's going to be?

Mercury said, Where's the thrill in that?

I reached my gun around the side of the building, as far as I could get it, my finger barely on the trigger, and fired a couple rounds intentionally high. The shooter fired back at the spot where my bullets came from. I traced his shots back and estimated him to be right in the center of the group. I glanced at Ms. Sabel and nodded.

Miguel, Tania, Dhanpal, even the Major would've known what my nod meant.

Ms. Sabel stared, lifted her shoulders.

"You pull the door," I mouthed and mimicked the movement.

343

It took a second, but she got it. With a couple quick steps, she reached the door and yanked it open, standing to one side. The shooter emptied his magazine in a straight line while Ms. Sabel and I watched the rounds fly between us. He stopped to swap mags.

I stepped inside and planted my feet, my pistol tucked in my belt.

Twenty wide, terrified eyes looked to me. One pair was in the head of a man in a suit. He stood in the middle of innocent wounded prisoners, his weapon empty and unloaded. He aimed it at me and pulled the trigger, hoping for one last round in the chamber. It wasn't his lucky day.

I stretched out my arm, pointed my index finger at him, and curled it. *Come here.*

Ms. Sabel stepped in behind me and fired one dart that caught the man in the left cheek.

"Don't pull that macho bullshit when I'm around," she said. "If a guy needs shooting, just shoot him."

We dragged his limp body out, let the medics get back to work, and reset the booby-trap.

"This guy must be Chen Zhipeng," Ms. Sabel said as we dragged him through the compound.

We dropped him in front of the bio-bunker and unlocked the door. A streak of daylight followed behind us, but nothing illuminated the darkness of the room. We turned on our phone lights and inspected the place. Foggers were stacked neatly on shelves in the back. Drums marked with warning labels and stenciled "Element 42" lined the walls.

Ms. Sabel disappeared outside.

I pulled a fogger from the shelf and checked it out. Then I opened a barrel and discovered a neat package on top with a measuring scoop and graphic instructions. I assembled my new toy and set it in the center of the shed.

Ms. Sabel returned dragging Anatoly Mokin behind her. She continued inside and dropped him on the concrete. His head banged like a dropped cantaloupe. I dragged Chen in and laid him out next to

Mokin. She put out a fist, I bumped it. She went to the front door and held it open.

I fired up the fogger and set it down between them, the gray mist flowing over their faces.

Ms. Sabel slammed the door behind me. We checked the seal: airtight. We snapped the padlock in place and slapped a new biosafety label across it.

"They'll have to face their own demons in the dark," I said.

She smiled. "Think they'll suffocate first or die with blue eyes?"

Mercury said, O Brotha! We bad! We kicked their asses right back to China. And I came through for you big time, too. If it weren't for me, you'd be dead a hundred times—

"Fuck you."

Ms. Sabel snapped a look at me. "Excuse me?"

I waved at the bunker behind me and walked down the hill. "Just paying my respects."

Chapter 53

A different helicopter came back half an hour later. It had China's star on the side. When it landed, a young American in a suit jumped out.

"You're not under arrest," he shouted over the noise. "But you're to accompany me to the US Consulate. Your friends are there."

Ms. Sabel told him about the wounded men and warned him to have officials stay away from the bio-bunker for a month. He relayed her instructions to someone on a radio. We boarded and took off.

I sat next to Ms. Sabel and looked out the window.

Mercury said, *We were there for you, right, homie? Jupiter and Mars and Minerva all pitched in on this one. We were thinking a feast in our honor would—*

I said, *No wonder Christianity kicked you guys to the curb. All you do is take credit for random events and my hard work.*

Mercury said, *Harsh, bro. Jesus plays the same game, you know. I mean, c'mon, sons of gods are a dime a dozen. Did you know I was fathered by Jupiter? Just sounds all cozy with the Sermon on the Mount and that beatitudes bullshit. Feel-good marketing, that's all he's got going on.*

"Peace and love is more noble than—"

I felt Ms. Sabel staring at the back of my head. I faced her.

"More noble than—what?" she asked.

We flew straight to Guangzhou and landed on a grassy square next to a building that resembled an architectural loaf of bread. Chinese soldiers escorted us to a side building, where twelve US Marines took over. They marched us down a hall, past some solid blast doors, and ushered us into a state-of-the-art meeting room.

Arranged around a shiny teak table were my friends, minus Emily and Nigel. Ms. Sabel and I were shown to the last open chairs, on opposite sides.

Inside the room, the ambassador waited for us with the local consul general. The head cheese had flown in from Beijing just to meet us. He did not look happy. He stood at the front with several staff, talking in low tones, nodding, and making calls.

One of the minions looked up and asked, "Where is Kasey Earl?"

The last time I saw the poor bastard, he was strapped to the Norinco. And I was the last to see him.

I shrugged. "Who?"

The officials went back to their huddle.

My phone rang, a call from an unnamed Sabel employee. I glanced around. The only person who paid any attention to me was Ms. Sabel. Her gray-green eyes pierced me in that strange way she had about her, she nodded at me, telling me to answer my phone.

I pressed the phone to my ear. "Now's not a good time."

"I'm going into surgery," Emily said. "Tell Pia, I'm good and done. Got it? Use those words. Oh, and Jacob, thanks for that thing you did, running at the bad guys. That was brave. I couldn't believe you were willing to die for me. I owe you one. You know. A big one. Any time you want, I'm ready. Bye."

I dropped my phone on the floor.

Emily, Emily, Emily. She defamed me on the front page, put Louisa through hell, and made Sabel Security look like an escort service. I was done with her. Done. I rolled my chair back and leaned down to retrieve my phone. But an invitation like hers, with the exponential mathematical possibilities, is damn near impossible to— my gaze fell on Tania. She sat between Miguel and Ms. Sabel, across the table. She watched the embassy staff as they whispered about our future.

My heart stopped. She'd kissed me. Had she wanted a kiss from just anyone before she died? Was it guilt? Or did she still feel something for me?

Tania was beautiful and exotic and killed bad guys.

Yeah. I was done with Emily. Completely done.

But was Tania the one I wanted to marry? I'd kicked myself every day for most of a year because I thought I'd been unfaithful. Well. OK. That was true. But she did it first—and with my best friend. I glanced at Miguel. If he ever finds out about the time I slept with his sister, I can always throw Tania back at him, and we'll call it even.

Tania felt my gaze and met it. She smiled a guilty smile.

I couldn't decide if I wanted to blow her a kiss or turn my back. Why is true love so complicated?

Ms. Sabel made a small gesture. She'd been staring at me the whole time I reviewed my dating options. I reported Emily's words. She nodded.

Suddenly, the ambassador's staff scurried out of the room like football players breaking from a huddle. When the door closed, the ambassador pulled out the chair at the head of the table. He sat and adjusted himself until he felt regal.

He lifted his chin and looked at Pia. "Tell me why you were killing Kazakh nationals on Chinese soil."

"Where is David Watson?" I asked. "SAC in the FBI's Counterintelligence Division?"

The ambassador squinted at me.

"Ask Watson why Anatoly Mokin thought we were bringing him vials when we met him in Guangzhou," Tania said.

"That's not the issue here," the ambassador said.

"Element 42 is the issue," Ms. Sabel said. "Your administration knew about it. You answer our questions, we'll answer yours."

His face twisted while he thought. Finally, he agreed to her terms as long as we went first. Ms. Sabel related the story from Borneo to the present. The ambassador listened intently.

When she came to the attack on Mokin's compound, she leaned toward him. "We know Chen Zhipeng was involved. We know he had plans to poison people with biological weapons. Otis was concerned about water, and Wu told us it was about drought. We also know that the British are not interfering with the deployment of Element 42. And from our conversations with President Hunter,

Watson, and Mokin, we think your administration is in on it. Now that I've told you, will you go public and denounce their plan?"

"No."

"That will put you in an awkward position."

"Not at all. You're not going to say anything about what you've learned. This has been sealed as Top Secret and cannot—"

"Top Secret doesn't absolve me of my responsibility to report genocide."

Unnerved, the ambassador cleared his throat and looked down.

A smartly dressed woman stepped into the room. The ambassador barked at her. "I said no interruptions."

The woman shrank but didn't leave.

"She wants you to see Emily's last article on the *Post's* website," Ms. Sabel said, pointing to the woman.

"Sir, I have it loaded on the screen." The woman pointed to the blank wall behind him and fled the room.

He pressed a button under the table. The wall that had been on wood-grain mode displayed the *Post's* home page with a raw picture of Carmen's body hanging on the post, her head a bloody mess. The headline ran beside the picture. "SHE DIED FOR YOU."

Miguel buried his face in his hands and sobbed.

Everyone turned to him for a moment, then turned away embarrassed. Tania rubbed his back. The ambassador clicked the screen off.

"The *Post* has asked me for a statement," Ms. Sabel said. "Explain your position. Give me something, spin it anyway you want."

"You set us up." The ambassador rose from his chair, knocking it over, and stumbling backward. "Goddamn it."

"Blaming the people who caught you, Mr. Ambassador?" She crossed to him. "Stop thinking about yourself and start thinking about the people who're going to die. Tell me why your administration is involved."

The ambassador twisted the watch on his wrist and straightened his tie. He pulled his chair upright and dropped into it. He sank his head in his hands. "Drought."

Ms. Sabel waited a long time. "That's it. Drought?"

"Everyone thinks climate change is the next generation's problem. But it's here. A global drought has been sneaking up on the world for decades. Sao Paulo has three months of drinking water left. Guatemala's corn crop failed for the second year in a row. In China, it hits this province and that region for a couple years, then moves to the next area the next few years. Over the last twenty years the affected regions are stitching together and getting hit more frequently. Rainfall on a global scale has been at historic lows for the last seven years. We're pumping ground water but it's drying up. A year ago, 31% of farming water came from wells. This year, 53%. When will the wells run dry?"

"I don't get it. Why not desalinate sea water?"

"Great idea. According to Scripps Institute estimates, California alone pumped 63 trillion gallons of water from wells in the first half of 2014. Desalinization costs $0.29 per gallon, so California would cost $18 trillion. That's a third of the Gross Domestic Product for the entire country. China doesn't have that kind of cash. But even if we could raise the money, it won't solve the problem in time."

"What problem?" Ms. Sabel asked.

"Crop failure. Mass starvation. Riots. The breakdown of civilization."

"But crops haven't failed."

"We're a few years away from the first failures. In California, new wells have to go 2,100 feet or more to find water. It's worse in China, where dry wells aren't finding water at any depth. The tectonic plates squeezed out their aquifers a hundred million years ago. But long term, nothing will solve the biggest problem: longer average lifespan." He blew out a long breath. "The world supports seven billion people right now. The birth rate is slowing, but lifespans are lengthening. If the drought continues at last year's rate, we have ten years of ground water. If it worsens, predictions are harder to make. How many people can we support? Six billion? Five? The idea behind Element 42 is to hasten the death of the elderly."

"So you're willing to watch the Chinese kill millions of their own?"

"What do you think is better?" the ambassador shouted. "Watching the average lifespan in China drop from seventy-five down to sixty-nine, or watching a hundred million men, women, and children starve to death? Is that too Asian for you? What about when the drought reaches critical conditions in India? Venezuela? France? What do you want to see? A billion people starving across the globe? Or fewer Parkinson's and Alzheimer's patients?"

"You condone their project then?"

"Hell no." The Ambassador's face was red and shaking. "No one wants this option. But someone damn well better have it ready when the first well goes dry."

Pia sank back in her chair. "There has to be a better way."

"China is a sovereign nation, and this is their option. They think they have it dialed in to where only the very weak will die. Behind closed doors, we've lobbied hard against it. But we can't stop them."

"Windsor has a cure." I said because I'm just dumb enough to speak when not spoken to. All eyes turned to me.

"They were an unwitting development team," the ambassador said. "China needed an expendable lab in case something went wrong. Chapman figured it out and told Wu Fang. They blew the whistle and Chen decided to terminate the Windsor part of the program including senior management. They had what they needed."

Silence reigned for a moment.

The ambassador looked around at all of us. "Sucks. I know. But there it is. Mass starvation—what do you want to do about it?"

"Why was the FBI Counterintelligence involved?" I asked. "They foil spies, retrieve stolen intelligence, that kind of thing."

"WMDs are part of their turf," the ambassador said.

"Wait." I let everyone stare at me while I tried to corral my thoughts. "Chapman had a Windsor contractor badge at the Bio-Defense Institute, NIH." I looked at the ambassador. "Holy shit."

"You're definitely treading on national security, Stearne." The ambassador shook his head. "Keep your mouth shut."

Miguel swiveled his gaze back and forth between us. "What'd I miss?"

Ms. Sabel leaned forward. "Chapman developed Element 42 for the USA," Ms. Sabel said. "When Chen bought a controlling interest in Windsor, he was, in effect, stealing it."

"And Violet was trying to cash in on the cure," the ambassador said.

Everyone slumped in their seats.

After a long group sigh, Ms. Sabel headed for the door. "The *Post* has several more articles lined up and ready to print. I told President Hunter to get on the right side of history. Now would be a good time."

Chapter 54

A sharp autumn sun exploded from behind a cloud, dazzling the trees at Sabel Gardens when Miguel and I arrived a few days after Guangzhou. Other Sabel agents and staff were climbing out of their cars at the same time. We beheld the pastoral scene like freed inmates. Ms. Sabel had invited us to watch the president's speech and made a company party out of it.

It was good to see Emily again. Even if she was still gray and weak, and in a wheelchair, at least she was healing. We assembled in the drawing room and chatted among the bookshelves and fireplaces. Standing room only. I barely saw Dhanpal before he bumped into me. Buzzing conversations consumed us both before we could speak and we settled for giving each other nods.

Ms. Sabel started with a few words. She thanked my team for our hard work and sacrifices. She conveyed Nigel's regards. He appreciated Ms. Sabel's job offer should his "Highland Adventure" turn out to be unappreciated by Her Majesty. Wu Fang had successfully fled the country with his wife and would soon take up temporary residence at Sabel Gardens. Chen Zhipeng had not yet surfaced in China's obscure system. Experts were baffled by his disappearance. Through the crowd, she found me and winked. She concluded her remarks with a moment of silence for Carmen.

In that long moment, I put my hand on Miguel's back, as did the Major.

A giant screen dropped from the ceiling, tuned to a reputable network, and a moment later, President Veronica Lodge Hunter stepped to the podium. She gave the same cover-your-ass speech that politicians have been giving since the founding of Mesopotamia. She pronounced the Chinese solution to drought shocking and praised the Sabel team for following the clues to the bitter end. Carmen received a posthumous Medal of Freedom and Ms. Sabel a public "thank you." The president concluded with a promise to increase spending on drought relief and open a public debate on solutions.

A couple pretty little things in short-skirted maid outfits served finger sandwiches. I gave the brunette my best sparkling glance and she returned it with a coquettish blush and turn. She came back with a wink, and right when I was about to ask when her shift ended, the worst happened.

Mercury said, Bro, danger—six o'clock.

Tania leaned in from behind me, her nose aimed straight at my next conquest. "He's married."

The girl spun on a heel and offered her silver tray of radish and fava beans on brioche to Alan Sabel and Governor Somebody with a big smile.

"I can always count on you to rescue me from those pesky maidens," I said.

"Boss wants us," she said, thumbing toward a corner of the room. She paced quickly away.

I followed her into a cozy study off the main room where a fireplace crackled behind Ms. Sabel. Even backlit, she looked like a goddess in a business suit.

I stopped better than an arm's length away. I felt it was a smart distance in case she was planning to punch me. She wasn't given to unwarranted violence, but I'd warranted plenty. Tania stood at right angles to us. I stood at parade rest with my eyes fixed on the distant horizon beyond Ms. Sabel.

"I'm glad I chose you two for my special missions group," Ms. Sabel said. "You work well together."

Tania raised one brow.

Ms. Sabel turned to her. "Tania, thank you for your bravery and commitment."

An awkward silence followed and lasted too long.

Tania said, "But we talked about—"

"I will speak to him." Ms. Sabel said. "Alone."

Looking like she'd just been slapped, Tania reeled back on her heels, took a deep breath, and powered herself out of the room.

Ms. Sabel gestured for me to sit on a small loveseat. Tense as I was, I took the seat, planted my feet on the floor a little more than hip-distance apart, and put my palms on my knees. I knew my body language looked rigid, but I had concerns floating around my brain about where this conversation was headed.

She stepped to the side of the space and tugged three times on a wide cloth hanging in the corner, then sat in the loveseat opposite. Not your typical ladylike woman, she turned a little to one side, stretched an arm over the loveseat's back. If I wanted to flee, I'd have to jump her outstretched legs.

"In our business, mental health is a top concern. Giving people weapons and sending them into the field to make life-and-death decisions requires a crystal-clear mind."

Mercury said, Oh shit, we're busted. Bet it was Tania. The Major would die defending you. But Tania, she's had it in for us ever since you messed around with … who was it? Bianca? Bridgette? Brittany? Started with a B, right?

I said nothing.

"There have been instances of people losing a grip on their sanity under the stress and strain of battle and going off on a rampage. I understand a man in General Thompson's command once ran through an Afghan village killing every man, woman, and child."

Thompson.

There was a name I didn't want to hear come up in this conversation.

I stayed silent.

"Naturally, I have concerns about my employees and their mental health."

Mercury said, C'mon, let's go. Nice while it lasted but this job's dead. The good news is nobody gives a damn about a lunatic chef. It's expected.

My gaze dropped to the floor.

"I'll resign, ma'am. It has been my pleasure to serve you and Sabel—"

"Be courteous enough to finish the conversation." She waited for my eyes to travel back up to hers. "I understand your medical records are the subject of lively debates."

Mercury said, Hold up, homie. Tania never saw your medical records.

I couldn't hide my shock. "What did the Major tell you about—"

"Jonelle refused to tell me anything about your medical history. When I asked her about your ability to lead special missions, she reminded me that you saved my life more than once. So I called people in the Army. They pointed me to General Thompson. I had a long talk with the General this morning." She slowed her pace and lowered her voice. "Tell me why a two-star general would spend so much time and energy defending a lowly master sergeant."

My gaze fell straight to the floor and stayed there. "I saved his life once."

"Tell me how it happened."

"The General was giving a speech at the Afghan officer training grounds. He was droning on about the usual crap when I saw the guy. Plain as day. An Afghan major, mumbling his prayers and sweating profusely—classic signs of a suicide bomber. I glanced around and saw what looked like art made from discarded war matériel behind the General's platform. But inside the artwork the hajji had stacked C4. Enough to kill the General and the first five rows of soldiers. I walked over to the guy and grabbed his hand. Only I picked the wrong hand. He held up the remote detonator in his other hand and started his final death prayer. I shot him in the head."

She didn't flinch.

She'd heard it before.

My gaze met hers.

She said, "And?"

"And … nothing. I killed an Afghan major and pissed off a lot of people. Especially a colonel because I let the guy's brains smear his uniform. But that's how some officers are."

Mercury said, That's it? Are you kidding me? I don't get any credit? You get in with these high-society babes and all of a sudden I'm nobody? Fuck you, man.

"At what distance did you see the Afghan?"

"That seemed to be a point of controversy during the inquiry. I just recall seeing him between a bunch of other guys. Clear as day."

"They reconstructed the angles and distances from the video. Seventy-three feet, diagonally through a crowd of soldiers in formation. The C4 was eighty-four feet in front of you, behind a wall of officers."

"If they say so, ma'am."

"Four psychological examinations concluded you should be mustered out of the Army. But General Thompson kept ordering new ones until he got the answer he wanted. What was that all about?"

My brunette in the short skirt stepped in the cove with a silver tray. On it were two shot glasses filled with a yellow liquid. The whole kit rattled with her nerves. She pulled a small end table from the corner and placed it to my right, halfway between Ms. Sabel and me. Even her skin vibrated with anxiety. Either she was serving the boss for the first time or hopelessly in love with me. I watched her backside as she leaned over and placed the shot glasses on the table with care. Ms. Sabel watched me watch her.

"Suzette, have you met Jacob Stearne?"

I jumped to my feet, bowed slightly, and extended a hand. The girl turned my way with a hesitant but flirtatious smile.

"He once pulled me from a burning Chevy moments before it exploded," Ms. Sabel said. "A few days ago he knocked me out of the line of fire a second before a shooter fired. He's my hero."

Suzette batted her eyelashes, muttered nice-to-meet-you, and fled, hesitating in the doorway for a last glance over her shoulder. I obliged her with a little see-ya-later finger-wave. She turned and ran.

I retook my seat.

"I like to help people," Ms. Sabel said. "But now I need your help."

She waited for me to reply. I didn't.

"I need you to tell me what the other four psych evaluations said."

"They're none of your business, ma'am. I'll resign."

She huffed and bit her lip to cut off an angry outburst. "You're not reading me right, Jacob. I…"

I kept quiet.

With a slow and silent look around the room, she brought her electrifying eyes back to me. "We've been on missions together. What happens after I sleep for three hours?"

"You wake up suddenly."

She rolled her hand, asking for more.

I said, "You wake up screaming."

"Do you know why?"

"No ma'am."

"I'm sure the employees have their theories. Thank you for not tossing one of them out there." She leaned back. "I hear a voice, Jacob. The voice screams at me, wakes me up, tells me to get going, there's work to be done." She leaned forward. "Tell me what the other four psych evaluations said about you."

I couldn't look at her. I turned to the fire. "They said I hear voices. That I'm mentally unstable, unfit for duty, potentially dangerous."

The fire crackled and the party in the next room grew louder. She didn't say anything for a long time.

"Spotting a suicide bomber at seventy-three feet doesn't sound dangerous to me. And it didn't sound dangerous to General Thompson." She leaned over her knees and rubbed her hands together. "If you're hearing voices, they're good ones."

Mercury said, Hey now! Did you hear that? She loves me! This could be the start of something big, you know? We could put the Capitoline Triad back together man. Jupiter, Juno, and Minerva—back for an encore. Oh man, and they do miss the spot light.

"You don't know what it's like," I said.

"Really?" she said. "Do you know what I have?"

All I could think of was a great body, insomnia, and Ferraris falling out of her lap like breadcrumbs after dinner. "No ma'am."

"I have a ghost voice." She dropped her head. "I'm going to tell you something only my dad knows. I've never told anyone else. I don't know if it's my mother or not. I tell the therapists it's her, but I was too young to remember her voice. I could be listening to the voice of an ancient goddess or a modern devil or absolute madness. I have no idea. Whoever she is, she yells at me night and day." Ms. Sabel grabbed my shirt with both hands and yanked me to her. "In Borneo, she was screaming at me, 'Don't leave that girl behind. They're going to kill her.'"

I didn't know what to say.

"After Carmen's service, I talked to the priest." Her voice grew in volume and intensity. "Jacob, I can't tell you if that priest was real or imaginary."

Our eyes were an inch apart when she realized where her hands were. She let go of me and looked away.

"The only thing I know is," she said, "the voice I hear is exactly what your fifth evaluation said about yours: it's a good voice. Hearing a good voice is not insanity, it's normal. When the voices tell you bad things—that's when you go mad." Ms. Sabel stood up.

Mercury said, Wow, am I the luckiest god or what? Rich people love me and my gang. We don't bother them with all that guilt and sin and heaven and hell. No, all you need to do is make a few sacrifices—a dove here, a bull there—and we're good with anything you got going down. Blood sports, slavery, bestiality— have at it, homeslice.

I stood. "Um, I'm not convinced it's a good voice, exactly."

"I need your help, Jacob. I've never had any family. No one I could confide in. No one to tell my nightmares to. No one who could understand the torment. I need a brother. We'll be siblings on the edge of sanity."

In that instant, I thought about life and death and love and admitted that I was in love with Pia Sabel. Not as a romantic lover, but as a sister in the family of damaged souls. We weren't star-crossed lovers. We were fragments of the same shooting star. Maybe we could keep each other burning a little longer.

"It would be an honor, ma'am."

She picked up a shot glass and led my eyes to the other one. I took the hint and picked up an aromatic tequila. She lifted hers between us. "To partners in madness."

THE END

Author's note:

I hope you've enjoyed reading this and will leave a review on your favorite book sites. Please join my email list for exclusive giveaways, content, and prizes. If you found any errors, or just want to chat, please email me at seeley@seeleyjames.com